NIGHT AND FOG

SEBASTIAN RIZZO

WARNING

This book contains strong language and depicts atrocities and brutalities that took place in prisons and Nazis work camps during World War II and may not be appropriate for all audiences.

PREFACE

NIGHT AND FOG is the story of the courageous women and men in the underground who risked their lives and families to save Allied airmen shot down in German occupied countries during World War II. This book is a work of fiction, but only in the sense that I have imagined how those people lived through actual events. While I have striven for historical accuracy, the participants were a little too busy saving airmen and trying to stay alive to keep precise records. Their reports at times conflict and inaccuracies are unavoidable. I sometimes found myself having to choose among varying accounts, but I have portrayed the events as I have envisioned them and tried to capture individual personalities from how they have been described by themselves and others. I'm sure I didn't get every detail right, but I have endeavored to stay true to the facts and I sincerely hope that what I have written is a fair portrayal of what really happened during those difficult years.

CHAPTER ONE
Tuesday, August 19, 1941

A threatening beam of light, fifty yards off and closing, prowled the river towpath like a tiger in the night. Dédée softly whistled and waved to warn her political refugees of the impending danger. Her heart pounded as the group, consisting of one young, plump English society woman and ten Belgian fighters, disappeared into the woods. The light had to be either a German or French police officer on bicycle. No one else was allowed out after curfew without permission.

She found a thick bush on the river side of the path to crouch behind as the light swept back and forth. The silhouette confirmed the rider to be a uniformed German police officer. She drew in a deep breath and let it out slowly to calm her frenetic mind. This was it—the first precipice of danger—the first test to see if she had the guts to go through with her bold plan. It had all seemed so simple, so thrilling. But now with the weeks of planning over and a German officer not twenty yards off, the sober reality of the danger squeezed the air out of her like the tightening of a noose. She was defying a merciless enemy, and if discovered, there could be no explaining her way out of it. She'd be arrested or shot outright.

She hoped the prissy Miss Richards, or whatever her real name was, had had sense enough to hide her enormous suitcase. What the hell was in that girl's brain, she thought, bringing a thing like that along like they were going on a holiday. The tremolo of insects faded into background noise as the jangle of the bicycle on the bumpy path neared. A spear of light probed the weeds just above Dédée's head. She held her breath and stilled her galloping heart.

———

Fifteen months earlier in a hospital in Bruges, Belgium …

1

. . .

"I have to get out of here!" An agitated English soldier struggled to wriggle out of his bed sheets and sit up. Bandages covered his chest, shoulder, and the side of his face.

A short, maternal Belgian nurse quickly attended him, holding her hand in front of his chest to restrain him. "*Vous êtes blessé. Reste tranquille.*"

The Tommy twisted violently back and forth to shake her off. "Don't you bloody understand? Doesn't anybody around here bloody understand me?"

The nurse tried to capture his flailing arms, taking care not to bump into his gauze-wrapped chest and shoulder while leaning back so as not to get socked in the face. Despite her efforts, he wrestled his way nearly upright and had one leg completely over the side of the bed when a young nurse firmly grabbed his forearm.

The soldier paused, startled to find his arm pinned by a fresh-faced young woman not much taller than his Lee-Enfield rifle. The twenty-four-year-old nurse, Dédée, held tight and arrested his squirming with a steely look from her dynamic blue eyes. "What's the trouble, Sergeant?"

His face flashed surprise. "You speak English!"

"Yes."

"I've been trying to tell her I have to get out of here."

"But she is just a nurse. She cannot release you." Dédée eased him back down onto the bed and swept a loose ringlet of blond hair back under her nurse's cap. "You must rest. You must heal."

"You don't understand. I have a wife and kids. I can't go to a German prison camp. I can't."

"*Ssshhh.*" Dédée calmed him with a gentle hand on his heaving chest. "This is a hospital. The Germans will not come here."

"It's bad out there—really bad."

"I know." Dédée held his hand reassuringly as she watched a tear run down the tough sergeant's cheek. She swallowed down the sickness rising up from her stomach, determined to stay strong despite all the blood and pain she had seen. "Germany has made a mistake to attack us. This will be no easy war for Hitler."

"The army is in retreat...." The sergeant's words trailed off as his strength gave out. "I've got to get out of here."

"Do not worry. We will take care of you." She patted his hand. "Rest now."

The soldier's troubled face said he was not sure he believed her, but he lay back and quit struggling.

Neither the sergeant nor Dédée had any idea that she would soon cause so much agitation in the Third Reich that she'd drive hundreds of German agents, and Luftwaffe police crazy chasing her phantom throughout France, Belgium and the Netherlands and trying to vanquish her band of subversives.

———

This is what it must have been like, Dédée thought as she worked her way down the hospital ward with the stench of blood and antiseptic in the air. *This is what Edith Cavell must have faced in the Great War.* Dédée wasn't yet two years old when the war ended in 1918, but seeing these grim-faced soldiers pleading with nurses to help their wounded friends, she could not blame Edith for doing whatever it took to save them. The courageous British nurse had given her life to smuggle Allied soldiers out of the hospital and back to their armies. Dédée could almost see Edith standing straight and tall at Tir National Rifle Range—the German officer commanding, *"Bereit, ziel, feuer!"*—and Edith's bullet-riddled body collapsing to the ground.

Blamp!

"Take Cover!" a soldier screamed. "Incoming!"

Dédée hurried to the bed where the yelling private crouched face down in the sheets with his hands clasping the back of his head. She grasped one trembling hand. "There there. It is all right. You are safe." The boy whimpered and squeezed her hand so tightly she thought she might lose circulation, but she didn't let go. *"Ssshhh."* She stroked his head with her free hand. "Tell me your name."

His frenzied breathing relaxed a bit as he peeked out to see her standing beside him. "M—Marbury, L—Lance Marbury."

"You are safe here, Lance. It was just a dinner tray someone knocked over."

The soldier's grip loosened as he realized where he was.

"Where are you from, Lance?"

"Ox—Oxted, south of London."

"Tell me about your home. Do you have any pets?"

By the time the young private finished telling her about the two story stone house, his dog Rusty, and his mum in her wide-brimmed straw hat humming cheerily while tending her rose garden, he was lying calmly back on his pillow.

"Nurse? Nurse?" a male voice called.

"You are a brave lad, Lance." Dédée smiled and patted the soldier's hand. "I have to go now, but I will be back to see you in a little while."

"Nurse?"

Dédée moved on and took the hand of a patient with a bandage wrapped around his head and eyes. "Yes, Corporal?"

"I fear my family might receive a post telling them that I've been killed or that I'm missing. Is there some way I can get word to them that I'm alive?"

She retrieved a pad of paper and offered to write a letter to them. "Tell me what you want to say and I will write it."

"Forgive my manners," the corporal said when she had finished. "I never even asked your name."

"It is Andrée de Jongh, but you can call me Dédée."

"How is it you've come to learn English so well, Dédée?"

"My father has always encouraged my sister and me in our studies. He is headmaster of a primary school for boys."

"Headmaster," the corporal repeated. "I'd imagine he'd be a rather strict fellow when it comes to learning."

Dédée laughed. "Not with me. But I have always been a good student."

Dédée patted the corporal's hand. "I have to leave now to post your letter. I will look in on you later."

Dunkirk, but she realized that hiding the men was only a temporary solution. She had an idea, but it would require her artistic skills and the lieutenant's willingness to take a risk.

Early the next morning, she bicycled to 162 Avenue Voltaire, to the home of a family that a priest had said would help. After Dédée gave the password, Madame Elsie Bell Maréchal, a soft spoken English woman with a round comforting face welcomed Dédée into her kitchen. Following brief introductions, Dédée got to the point. "I have a French officer who needs shelter. Can you hide him for a day or two?"

"Yes. You can bring him here."

Next, she went to the home of the girl where she met French Lieutenant Charlie Morelle. "I am Dédée de Jongh. You have escaped from the Germans, yes?"

"I do not think the Germans were prepared for so many prisoners," Charlie said. "It gave me the opportunity to slip away."

"You are a brave man, Charlie. You could have been shot."

"It was not so daring. I ran off when the Germans were not looking." Charlie laughed. "A Musketeer, I am not."

Charlie's blond wavy hair, pleasant voice and happy face with its large, slightly comical nose, made him a delightful fellow. Dédée liked him immediately. "Where are you from, Charlie?"

"Valenciennes."

"Ah, not far over the border." That was good. "I have a place for you to stay, but first you and I are going to walk like old friends to the *Bon Marché* where we will have photographs made."

She took charge completely so Charlie wouldn't have that awkward look of someone who is unfamiliar with the city. At the store, she teased him to put him at ease, trying on a ridiculously large wide-brimmed hat. "How do I look?"

"It is you." He chuckled.

She tilted her head in the mirror. "I don't think it is big enough."

"If it was any larger, we could camp under it."

His laughter died as two German officers strolled past. Charlie stared nervously ahead.

Dédée nudged him snickering. "Remember the time we went to the park and that stupid green hat of yours blew off?"

"I loved that hat." He relaxed a bit and played along. "I chased it all the way to the duck pond. It was never the same after that."

The danger passed and Charlie smiled a silent thank you to Dédée.

After the photographs, she led him to the Maréchal home where he stayed while she forged his French identification papers. They weren't perfect, but they should get him through. The next day she rode the train with Charlie to the border and wished him luck.

"Thank you, Dédée," Charlie said with a hug. "If there is ever anything I can do for you, do not hesitate to ask."

———

As British bombing raids increased, it became apparent that more men would need help. So many men could not be hidden for very long. Little things like putting out more trash than usual or bringing in extra groceries could raise suspicions of an alert neighbor, and if found out, the host's entire family would be arrested. She discussed the matter with Arnold De Pée and his cousin, Henri De Bliqui, two trusted comrades who worked with her secretly providing food and clothing for men in hiding. She didn't know if they'd be willing to take greater risk, but she'd concluded that there was only one way to solve this problem. "We need to organize an underground line to smuggle fighting men to Spain."

"Spain?" Henri looked at her like she'd lost her mind. "We should work a deal with a fishing boat to take them across the channel."

"Yes, the coast *is* the shortest route," Dédée said. "The Germans know this. They will be watching carefully and checking every boat. That is why we must go to Spain."

Henri shook his head. "It'll never work. Spain is more than seven hundred miles away."

"It won't be like moving men from house to house in Brussels," Arnold warned. "It will require safe houses from one end of France to the other—train tickets—guides—false papers—permits to cross the French border ... and then there are the Pyrenees Mountains to contend with."

Dédée respected Arnold's opinion. He was in his forties and had worked in the hospital with the legendary Edith Cavell, the woman who had smuggled soldiers out of the hospital in the last war. But her mind was made up. Either they would help or she would do it alone. "It is because of these difficulties that the Germans will not expect it."

Arnold conceded with a dip of his head.

Henri's forehead creased. "Most of these men do not speak French," he said, his voice skeptical. "They will be as inconspicuous as yellow dandelions in a green lawn."

Dédée shrugged as if to say that was obvious. "They do not understand the language. They do not know how to get around. They are like lost little children. That is why we must help them."

"All right," Arnold said. "I worked for a while in the Basque country. I know of a Belgian woman, a Madame de Greef, who moved to the south of France and has offered lodging to her friends in Brussels if they have to flee. I will go down and see if this woman would be willing to help us."

Henri tipped his head, conceding her point. "I know a fellow who might help here in Brussels."

"Good." Dédée reached over to the center of the table. "Then we have a pact?"

The two men covered her hand with theirs and nodded.

Dédée chuckled. "De Pée, de Bliqui, and de Jongh—DDD. I like it."

Through the winter, she continued bringing food and clothing to men in hiding while arranging more homes in Brussels to host men. Arnold gathered train schedules and traveled south to enlist Elvire de Greef. Dédée thought she was being quite secretive and clever about it until one day she telephoned one of her contacts. There was no answer. She tried again. There was still no answer.

"Perhaps they are arrested," her mother said without even looking up from her sewing.

Dédée tried to make light of it. "You are saying funny things."

"But my daughter," her mother replied without breaking from her stitching, "you have to know it always finishes like this."

CHAPTER TWO

Prosper Dezitter gazed with staged admiration at the poster of Adolf Hitler while waiting for the man behind the desk to acknowledge his presence. He'd greased back his dark brown hair as well as his prison cell would allow to make himself appear younger than his forty-seven years, but he wished he could have touched up the broad white streak that ran back from the center of his forehead. It didn't really matter. He knew how to turn on the charm to sell merchandise. This time the product was himself.

Rudolf Kohl, the Abwehr chief behind the desk, closed his file without hurry and sat forward with hands folded on his desk, "*Monsieur* Dezitter, please have a seat," he said in perfect French. "I am told you want to see me."

"Yes *Kommandant,*" Prosper said addressing the man by a title above his rank. "First, let me congratulate you on the great German victory which has resulted in the capture of over two million British, Belgian, French and Dutch soldiers." From his years in used car sales, Prosper had learned you had to flatter a person before you tried to sell him anything. Next, you had to convince him that he could not do without whatever you were selling. "I believe I can be of great service to you."

"You can?" the commander asked with a smirk.

Prosper had expected skepticism. After all, why should the German trust a crook like him? He had only moments to persuade the man he could provide a service that no one else could. "Many of the enemy have been taken prisoner. But some little fishes have slipped through your net. Enemy soldiers are hiding all over Belgium. More are falling from the sky, shot down by the Luftwaffe. If not caught they could cause a great deal of mischief, could they not?"

"And you know where these enemy soldiers are?"

"No, but I can help you find them."

Kohl sat back. A slight smile hinted that he was amused by the prisoner's audacity. "I suppose you are looking for the reward?"

Kohl reacted precisely as Prosper had anticipated. "I'm looking for a position—a partnership, if you will. You provide me the resources I need and I will locate and deliver the enemy soldiers to you."

"And what makes you so sure you can do this?"

"I was a detective before the last war, and unlike your other agents, I do not have to *pretend* to be Belgian." Prosper smiled slyly. "I have served in the Canadian Army and the British RAF..."

Kohl lifted a paper from his desk. "Your file says you are in jail for embezzlement and marriage fraud. Is this not so?"

"Yes ..."

"You have also served time for seizure, swindling, theft, unlawful import of vehicles..."

Prosper tipped his head agreeing with Kohl's assessment as if proud to admit it. "I moved cars back and forth between Antwerp and the Netherlands, but who better to catch evaders than a smuggler who knows all the tricks?"

"You are Belgian. Why would you want to help us?"

Prosper began comfortably and casually as if simply conversing with a fellow at a bar. "I have spent years in other countries ... Canada ... England ... the United States ... France. Before the present hostilities, I worked in the Brussels office for the Bayer Company from Munich. I am resourceful, having started my own businesses in Canada and Belgium." Knowing how Germans respected confidence and authority, he sat up tall and spoke forthrightly. "When Belgium ceases to exist we will all be living in Germany. The National Socialist Party has demonstrated that those who serve the party are well rewarded. As a businessman, I see this as an opportunity to join a growing company with great benefits. As a man, I see this as an opportunity to take part in the greatest renaissance the world has ever known."

Kohl, with a finger contemplatively laid across his chin, studied Prosper's face a moment before speaking. "You say you served in both the Canadian Army and the RAF in the last war. How is that possible?"

"I enlisted in the Canadian Expeditionary Force, but because I was a detective in civilian life, the RAF wanted me to work for them, so I trained as a military observer."

"And you put those skills to use in the war?"

"Oh yes—twenty-two missions—among the most in the observation corps."

"Perhaps we should put *those* skills to use."

A chill ran up Prosper's spine. He hadn't anticipated this in fabricating a heroic past. "I am no longer a young man," he said with an uneasy chuckle. "I can be of more use catching fliers than being one."

"I have a number of very good detectives on my payroll. What makes you think you can do a better job than them?"

"Unlike your agents"—Prosper switched to near perfect English—"I am fluent in English. I can be a jolly good fellow—a chap they can trust. I can get through doors that are closed to your agents. I can uncover secret organizations that your people would never find."

Kohl sat up attentively, removing the finger from his chin. "And the resources you would need?"

"An automobile … gasoline of course … men to make arrests when I call for them. Money to cover my expenses, and for myself and my associates." Prosper leaned in, speaking confidentially. "And the freedom to hunt these fugitives down without interference."

———

Loud, cognac-infused laughter bounced off the walls of the bar at the Hotel Euskalduna near the Spanish border. Into this den of outlaws and hardened mountain smugglers strode a short, middle-aged mother of two. But her grey-green eyes warned that Elvire de Greef was not a woman to be trifled with.

The scarlet glow from wall sconces flickered on her short auburn hair like the scorching core of a log fire. She ordered a drink but wasted no time with pleasantries, speaking forthrightly, but discreetly to the Spanish smuggler she had come to meet. "I have a group of ten Belgian men and one woman to be taken over the mountains."

"If we are caught by the *Carabineros*, it will mean prison, *Señora*. And if caught by the Germans, we will be shot."

Elvire leveled her intense gaze on the man. "Yes, and it is more money than you can make in six months smuggling hams and beef." She broke off a bite of goat cheese and sat back indifferently with her glass of wine while the Spaniard stared at her. But she already knew what his decision would be. He understood that if he turned the job down, she would offer the money to one of her other smugglers and that could mean losing out on future ventures as well.

Elvire de Greef, had worked in the office of a prominent newspaper in Brussels. When the Germans overran the country, she and her husband, Fernand, seventeen-year-old son Freddy, sixteen-year-old daughter Janine, and Fernand's mother, "Bobonne", had fled to France where they hoped to board a ship to England. Hundreds of Allied airmen would be forever grateful that the de Greef family *missed the boat*.

The de Greefs had found an abandoned out-of-the-way villa along the west coast in Anglet. Once settled, Elvire telephoned a friend back home in Brussels with their new address and to tell them that her dog, Gogo, had died. The friend lamented the horrible treatment by their Nazi rulers and Elvire offered that if anyone needed her help, they should say, *Gogo est mort* (Gogo is dead), so she would know they were sent by a trusted friend.

One warm spring day a handsome, brown-haired man in his forties had strolled into the yard where Janine was relaxing in a lawn chair. It was Arnold De Pée. "How is Gogo?" he asked.

Janine was perplexed. She had not been told about the phrase and wondered why this man was inquiring about their dead dog. "Please wait here a moment," she said and went inside.

When she returned with her mother, Arnold had laid out Dédée's plan for an escape line.

Excitement had swept away the cobwebs of boredom as Elvire planned the system she would set up—helpers to collect the men arriving from the north, travel routes, bicycles, food, shelterers. Most importantly Elvire would need to work out new arrangements with her band of black market smugglers, one of whom was now mulling over her proposition.

Conversations in Basque, Spanish and French spirited the border town restaurant. Steaming trays of roast suckling Pyrénéan lamb, and platters of shellfish passed by on their way to waiting tables.

The Spaniard finally spoke. "The travelers must do as I say."

"Yes," Elvire agreed. "In the mountains, you are in charge."

The man nodded.

"And outside of the mountains," she added firmly, "*I* am in charge."

———

Dédée stood before the bathroom mirror tilting her head this way and that, exhilarated by her new look. Her hands worked the brush through her hair while her mind worked through the details of their first run.

"Dédée?" her father, Frédéric, now code-name *Paul*, tapped on the bathroom door.

She opened it and grinned at his wide-eyed surprise. "So how do I look as a brunette?" She turned her head back and forth and with an upturned palm bounced her short black springy curls. Her hair smelled of chemical dye.

"Different," he said uneasily. He stared back through his round metal frame glasses. Concern showed in his drawn face. "Your mother said you have sold all of your jewelry."

"I have no need for it," she said with a shrug. "It can be replaced when the war is over."

"You cannot pay for all of these men."

"I know. But even if we find the money to feed and clothe them and get them train passage, I still have to feed myself and pay for my train tickets. Of what use is jewelry?"

"My Little Cyclone." He smiled and kissed her forehead then held her at arm's length. "You look beautiful," he said.

She gave him a quick kiss on the cheek. "I have to go. I'm meeting Nadine."

"You will like her," he called as she scooped up her bag on the way out. "She reminds me of you."

Paul had learned of Andrée Dumon while distributing copies of the underground newspaper *La Libre Belgique* for which the Dumon girl was also secretly working. Because Andrée Dumon was also called Dédé, Paul decided he would call her *Nadine*.

Dédée arrived at the tram stop and spotted the petite, eighteen-year-old girl with silky light brown hair who her father had described. "Nadine?" she asked.

"Yes."

"Paul sends his greetings."

"The roses are beginning to bloom," Nadine replied.

Nadine was just the kind of girl Dédée was looking for, young and attractive, the type who would look quite natural strolling beside a young man who had to be secretly guided. "I am Dédée," she said with a smile. "Shall we walk a bit?"

Shops had been made to keep up appearances for the sake of Nazi propaganda and so German officers could buy gifts for their girls back home. Leather goods were scarce. Jewelry was in short supply. And gone was the sweet smell of confections that once filled Belgian streets in summer. Dédée paused at a window of a toy shop and sighed wistfully at three stuffed characters—Mickey Mouse, Donald Duck and Goofy. "I wish my nephews were still young so I could buy those for them."

"How old are your nephews?" Nadine asked as they walked on.

"Frederic is fifteen and Martin is eleven."

"My older sister, Michou, is not married yet," Nadine said. "She is away at nursing school. And my little sister, Cicine, is *trisomique* (has Down's syndrome)."

Beside a large sign advertising roller derby a bold-faced poster on the brick building warned that: sheltering, hiding, aiding or assisting English aviators in any manner is done so under penalty of death. Anyone with information leading to the arrest of these fugitives will be compensated. Across the words, someone had painted in large black letters, "Death to Hitler!"

Another broadside warned that: anyone caught listening to British broadcasts will be imprisoned. But it was the cartoon clandestinely tacked up beside the warnings that made the girls giggle. It depicted a line of men with swastikas on their backs marching past two pseudo angels up a stairway into the breech of a cannon. Awaiting them on the other side of the barrel were the fires of hell.

"My father has told me that you help distribute *La Libre Belgique*," Dédée said after leading Nadine to a remote bench in a quiet park. "He said you are brave and intelligent."

Nadine smiled modestly. "Your father says you need guides."

"I am taking a group down to Spain in two days."

"I admire what you are doing," Nadine said. "Most girls would not travel unescorted."

Dédée laughed. "Now it is we girls who escort the men. It is a long journey. I do not expect anyone to take the risks I take, but I need girls who can walk beside a young evader like they are a couple to move the men short distances."

"I haven't much experience with men," Nadine said rather shyly. "My father is very protective."

"To our parents, we will always be little children." Dédée chuckled. "My father still calls me his Little Cyclone. But you do not have to be experienced. We do not wish to draw attention. I have even stopped wearing makeup."

"I will do whatever you need me to do," Nadine said, then stopped to look straight at Dédée. "But I have told your father that I will not carry a gun. And I will not kill anyone."

Dédée nodded her agreement. "We do not carry weapons. Our motto is *Pugna Quin Percutias*—fight without blows." Nadine opened her mouth, but Dédée touched her hand to stop her from speaking. "Before you commit to this, you must understand that anyone who joins us may expect to be shot or captured within six months. And when we are arrested, the Germans will torture us to give them the names of our associates."

Nadine answered without hesitation. "I would sooner be shot or die in a German prison than to stand by and do nothing."

———

... Tuesday, August 19, 1941

. . .

Dédée slipped back into the copse as the sweeping light drew closer, and crouched low, her bare arms and knees resting unpleasantly on the rocks and clumps of grass and earth. The rumble of the rubber tires along the dirt path drew nearer. She commanded her jittery lungs to take shallow breaths.

A dozen heartbeats later, the sound of the bicycle began to diminish. Dédée peered out, watching the grey German uniform fade away.

It had been quite a day—their first adventure. It was just Dédée and Arnold now as Henri had been arrested months ago for underground activities. With the ten Belgian fighters and Miss Richards in tow, they had changed trains at Quiévrain and again at Lille, ending at Corbie to avoid border checks of the identity cards she had hand-forged. Giddy with excitement, Dédée had set out after dinner into the dark woods toward the River Somme which was now the artificial border between Belgium and the northern zone of France.

Spirits were high for this first *liberty* group, but there had been grumblings from the ten Belgian men fleeing the Gestapo that the young English society girl, Miss Richards and her leather suitcase, umbrella and handbag would attract attention. The prissy maiden had turned white when Dédée and Arnold broke the news that they would have to swim across. He had found the row boat, but with campers near it, they had no other choice. "Oh no no no no no," Miss Richards said, shaking her head in panic. "I cannot swim!"

Seven of the men could not swim either. Arnold had set out more than an hour ago to find some rope and supplies they could use to ferry the nonswimmers across.

This was one slip-up she could not afford to repeat. She had put together a band of rebels who were counting on her not to make such simple mistakes as not making sure the boat would be ready. Her father, *Paul*, was working his *Résistance* contacts to locate hidden British servicemen. Her older sister, Suzanne, whose Austrian husband had fled to England to avoid conscription into the German army, loaned her money and helped to collect food and clothing. The Maréchal family,

Georges, his English wife, Elsie Bell, their seventeen-year-old daughter, Elsie, and son Bobby would receive and shelter airmen brought in from the provinces. Dédée, Nadine, Charlie Morelle and his sister Elvire would guide evaders down from Brussels to Paris. She couldn't wait to meet Elvire de Greef, the woman in the south of France who Arnold had described as "delightfully aggressive".

Dédée had convinced people that she could do this. Now she had to prove it.

She crept back to the others.

"Where is Arnold?" Miss Richards babbled anxiously.

She understood the girl's nervousness, but the one thing they did not need tonight was panic. "He'll be along soon," Dédée assured her. As a nurse, she had been taught to be firm and positive. As an underground leader, she would also need to remain calm herself and show no fear. "He cannot simply go to a store at one in the morning and buy rope."

It was two in the morning when Arnold returned with an inner tube, a wooden board, and a spool of wire. He set right to work tying one end of the wire to a tree. But he'd barely gotten it tied when another lamp came bouncing down the path and he had to duck into the bushes. After a few anxious moments, Arnold slipped into the water uncoiling the wire as he swam across. They only had a little more than three hours before sunrise.

Dédée waited until she heard a soft whistle. "Okay," she whispered to the first man, an overweight youth, "sit on the tube and use the wire to pull yourself across. When you reach the other side go to the farmhouse and let Nenette know we are crossing."

The boy eased into the water, but the moment his feet slipped in the mud he panicked—flailing about, yelling and splashing until he finally managed to climb onto the tube. There he locked his arms around the wire, shaking his head, refusing to move.

The petrified non-swimmer would never summon the nerve to pull himself across.

Dédée tossed off her skirt and blouse and jumped in. "*Ssshhh.* Calm down. I've got you. Let go of the wire and hold onto the tube. Do not worry, I will not let you fall."

He gripped the tube like it might run away as she propelled him forward swimming with one hand while pushing the tube with the other. The water felt cool and refreshing on this hot August night, but eighty feet was a long way to go even against a moderate current, especially for people who couldn't swim. And time was running out. Somehow she had to get them all across the river and into Nenette's farmhouse before dawn. He had made such a dreadful noise they would be lucky if the entire German garrison hadn't been alerted. She delivered the boy to Arnold who pulled him out of the water. As she swam back across, she thought how foolish she would look if the Germans caught her now alone in the river in just her underwear.

The non-swimmers made the crossings slow and difficult. Then came Miss Richards' turn. Tired and cold, Dédée had no patience for the spoiled girl's insistence on taking her baggage. "There is no negotiation, Mademoiselle, the valise stays or you stay with it. You may choose a few outfits and you may take your pocketbook. I will float them over on the board. Leave the umbrella. You can buy another when you get to England. Now take off your skirt and blouse."

Miss Richards' eyes widened in shock. Her mouth gaped.

Dédée cut her off with a stern look and a hand on her hip.

The society girl's face contorted in annoyance, but she slowly began to undress.

There was no time for that. Dédée grabbed the skirt and yanked it off. Once the skirt was removed, an even greater problem presented itself— huge white bloomers. Dédée pointed. "Now you must take those off, Mademoiselle."

"What?"

"They will be seen by the Germans on the towpath."

Tittering emanated from the woods.

After getting the girl situated on the tire, Dédée began to swim and push as she had with the others, but her biceps burned from so many trips. She moved behind the tube to use her legs to propel the tube and give her arms a rest. But her first push tipped the woman forward. The Panama hat in Miss Richard's lap fell victim to the current. Her large pink butt bobbed up in front of Dédée who briefly lost herself in silent laughter. It took a few seconds of struggle to right her and begin again.

Then Miss Richards cried, "Oh God, look!"

Another light was traveling down the towpath.

"Quick," Dédée said, "slip into the water and hold onto the tire."

The two women remained motionless, holding onto each other and the inner tube. Dédée listened for the bicycle, but the sound of Miss Richard's ragged breathing bouncing off the rubber was all she could hear. Their eyes apprehensively followed the approaching light. The officer was nearing their launch point.

Death hung on that sweeping light. If cast out over the river it would reveal the tube and the board piled with clothing. The two women would make easy targets for the patrolman's rifle. As the light swung out, Dédée held her breath and sank until her eyes remained just above the water. The light stopped ten feet short of them before sweeping away and disappearing down the path. Dédée boosted Miss Richards back into the tube. When they reached the other side, the girl was trembling, cold and pink. Dédée was exhausted, but it was nearly dawn and there were still four more Belgians to get across.

After more than an hour and a half in the water, the ferrying was complete. Two of the men pulled her out of the water onto the bank. Dédée had crossed the River Somme, fighting its current, an incredible twenty-two times. Nenette draped a towel around her shivering friend and ushered her into the farmhouse.

They caught the morning train to Amiens, transferred to the train for Paris, and then took the overnight train to Bordeaux and reached Anglet on the third day.

Arnold took Dédée to the farm where Elvire de Greef was in a field picking eggplants. "Hello, my aunt," Dédée greeted her, "I am your new niece." Perhaps it was the strength and boldness each sensed in the other, but the two liked each other right off. Elvire, or *Tante Go* as the tenacious red-haired matron would now be known in the underground, had arranged for the smuggler Tomás Anabitarte to lead the Belgians and Miss Richards over the Pyrenees Mountains into neutral Spain.

After a pleasant day spent with the de Greefs, Arnold and Dédée headed back the seven hundred miles to Brussels to collect another group of *children*. Dédée bristled with excitement that she had done it. They had done it. She'd struck her first blow against Hitler.

Word spread quickly in the Résistance of a young Belgian girl who had helped Belgian fighters escape to England. But they weren't the only ones to hear of the daring act of rebellion. It had also been brought to the attention of Hermann Göering, head of the Luftwaffe and Heinrich Himmler, head of the Gestapo. The German Secret Police set about quickly to snuff out this ember before it grew into a flame.

CHAPTER THREE

W here was Arnold? Dédée didn't want to alarm the three children, but her partner should have been there hours earlier. Nonchalantly she sipped her coffee while stealing glances out the café window. The *children*, two Belgians and a Scottish army private, remained trustful of Dédée, though their faces expressed concern, not knowing that this was only her second rescue mission. She could not let them down.

Dédée had taken Scottish private Jim Cromer of the 1st Gordon Highlanders of Aberdeen, in her group because he stood out like bagpipes in an ensemble of French horns. He spoke heavily accented English and possessed not a shred of French mannerisms. She'd led them off the train miles before the French border and hiked in the hot August sun the rest of the way to La Corbie.

Arnold and his group of five Belgians had taken the train from Brussels to Lille and from there it was a direct run, so they should have reached the café first, but three hours later they still hadn't arrived. Dédée had to make a decision. The lives of these men were in her hands.

She gathered up the *children* and led them to the river where they hopped into the waiting skiff and paddled to the far bank. Then Dédée left the men with Nenette, rowed back across and caught the train to Lille.

Drifting inconspicuously on the fringes of the crowd, she saw no sign of Arnold or the children. An abundance of gendarmes milling about prevented her from getting a closer look. She held out hope that Arnold had seen the gendarmes and detoured to a café or bistro, but after searching every nearby restaurant, she feared the worst.

The sun would be setting soon. She had to make it back to Nenette's before curfew, but if she hurried, she might have just enough time to visit a trusted friend. She took a tram to Valenciennes and found the address she was looking for.

Charlie Morelle, the Frenchman she had smuggled out of Belgium with the help of the Maréchal family, was startled to find her on his doorstep.

"Charlie," she said, "I need your help badly. Will you do a favor for me?"

"Of course, Dédée."

Dédée explained how she and Arnold had taken different routes and were to meet in La Corbie. "I fear he is arrested. Please go to my home at 73 Avenue Emile Verhaeren in Schaerbeek. Ask for Paul." She jotted something down and tore the paper from the pad. "Show him this note. See if he can find out what happened to Arnold."

"I will find out all I can. You can stay here until I get back."

Dédée shook her head. "Thank you, but I must continue on to deliver the rest of the parcels to Anglet." She scribbled out another address. "This is where I will be."

"I cannot believe you are still going on after all that has happened," Charlie said. "Most women would not go down to the basement alone."

She kissed his cheek and turned to leave, but stopped before closing the door. "Please tell my father to be careful. He is too old for this business."

When she and her parcels reached Villa Voisin the next day, Tante Go had more bad news. "Miss Richards and the Belgians were arrested by the Spanish *Carabineros* as soon as they crossed the mountains into Spain. Tomás has found out that they have likely been taken to a concentration camp in Miranda."

"*La vache!*" Dédée's hands flew in the air as she spoke. "They ran the gauntlet to get from Belgium to neutral Spain. And for what?" She shook her head angrily as she paced.

"Come," Tante Go said. "I will fix something to eat."

With an exasperated exhale, Dédée followed Tante Go into the kitchen. "Do you have any connections in Spain?"

Tante Go shrugged as she placed bread and meats on the table. "I deal with smugglers. They are no friends to the *Carabineros*."

Dédée sighed. Then it hit her. "I will go there myself! We cannot leave them until they are in the hands of the British Consul."

"Diplomats will not support such activity."

"We will see."

Tante Go chuckled. "If anyone could convince the British Consul, Dédée, you could. But there is another problem. How would you get there? Tomás will never take a girl."

"He will take *me*, Tante. You wait and see!"

As Tante had predicted, Tomás didn't just say no, he said it with a finality that proclaimed he was in charge in the mountains and it was going to be done his way, period.

Dédée understood his worry. Aiding evaders was already much more dangerous than smuggling black market goods across the mountains. One weak person could jeopardize the whole group, and with death or prison on the line it was not worth the risk to take some girl he thought merely wanted to go sight-seeing. The crossing was scheduled for tomorrow evening, so she still had time to convince him.

"What are you doing today?" she asked.

"I am going to the mountains to see my family."

"May I come along?"

"If you wish," he said with a brush-off tone that let her know he would not make accommodations for her to keep up.

Bronzed, sinewy Tomás set off for the hills like a mountain cat on the hunt. He strode through the vast open fields looking straight ahead, but from time to time she caught his sideways glance and could see the superior look in his eyes like a brash athlete taunting an inferior opponent. She smiled to herself. Having spent many days hiking in the Ardennes, she was confident in her own capabilities.

She stayed with him.

He pushed faster and harder, obviously trying to prove once and for all that a petite girl could not stand up to the mountain. She matched his speed, just as determined to prove he underestimated her.

"It is such a nice day," she said as she breezed along. "I bet the children back in Brussels are all in the park playing football. Did you play football when you were a boy?"

"No."

"Oh, that's too bad. I suppose it would be difficult to play up in these mountains. But this would be a wonderful place to come for a holiday if not for the war."

Even when the path narrowed and Dédée was forced to drop back and follow, she kept up the chatter to show she wasn't winded: "This is such a lovely hike. No wonder you love these mountains."

Tomás grunted only an occasional "Yes" or "No". She could hear in his polite but dismissive tone that he still had hopes of losing her.

"How beautiful," she said as they emerged from the woods into a meadow of bright green broom. "Those hills must look spectacular in early summer when it is all yellow. Good thing this place is so far from people or it surely would have been spoiled by now."

After traveling uphill for quite some time, Tomás' pace began to slow.

Dédée continued talking and walking as if they were merely on a footpath in the park. "This would be a great place for an artist." She swept her hand through the air. "I would set my easel right over there so I could look over this whole valley."

Tomás' breathing grew heavier. Despite the cooler air in the higher elevations it was still quite hot. Sweat dripped down the side of his cheek. The smirk had left his face. Dédée had him and he knew it. But just to punctuate her point, she continued chatting as she breezed alongside, showing him that for her this was no more difficult than *sticking one's fingers in one's nose*, as the saying goes. By the time they reached his family home, his gait was slow and ponderous, his feet were dragging the ground, and he was huffing like an old man. Dédée felt light as a feather, buoyed perhaps by the flush of victory.

When Tomás set off with the men the next night for Spain, Dédée went with them.

On the Spanish side two days later, she changed in the woods into a skirt, simple blouse, ankle socks and flat shoes that she had carried over the mountains in her backpack. Tomás had no idea where to find the British Consul, but led them to a town where they could catch a tram to San Sebastian, the nearest city. After two nights of hiking, the men were struggling to keep their eyes open. Dédée decided that wandering aimlessly would be futile. At Calle de Agirre Miramón in San Sebastian she came upon a repair garage with unattended vehicles.

"In here," she said shooing the men inside a parked automobile. No one protested and all were soon asleep.

A tap on the side window woke her.

"*Qué haces ahi?*" a man in mechanics overalls asked.

"*Lo siento,*" Dédée apologized. "*No llame a la policia, por favor.*"

"*Vous êtes Français?*"

"*Belges,*" Dédée replied.

The mechanic continued in fluent French. "What are you doing here?"

Dédée appreciated the man's coolheaded reaction to finding four vagrants asleep in his vehicle. In his dark temperate face she saw nothing but bewildered concern. He hadn't blustered at them. He hadn't threatened to call the police. The kindness in his eyes induced her to take a chance and trust him with the truth. "We have just crossed over the mountains from France. We have to find the British Consulate."

"You are fleeing the Germans?"

"Yes."

"You must be hungry. Come with me."

The Spaniard ushered them to his fifth floor apartment and introduced himself as Bernardo Aracama. By the time he slipped off his coveralls and joined his guests, his wife, Sarasola Antonia, had filled the table with plates of bread, olives, meats and cheeses.

Dédée explained how the first group she had brought down from Belgium were arrested as soon as they crossed over the mountains. These men she had to bring directly to the British Consulate.

"When we have finished eating, I will drive you there," Bernardo said. "It is in Bilbao, about one and one-half hours south of here."

"I do not want to put you to any trouble. You have already done enough."

He shook his head to insist. "I spent the last ten years in France to escape the regime that took over Spain with the help of the Germans. When the Germans invaded France, I returned to Spain. Anyone who fights the Germans is a friend of mine. I will drive you."

.   .   .

When Dédée showed up with the *children* in Bilbao, British vice-consul Vyvyan Pedrick didn't know what to make of this young girl and her claim of crossing the daunting Pyrenees in a skirt, blouse, and saddle oxfords—at night no less.

Although surely briefed by Arthur Dean, assistant to the head of the British section of the American consulate in Marseilles when she was introduced to Pedrick, his eyes momentarily widened as if thinking, *could this young girl really have crossed the mountains as she claimed?* But he was polite and treated her with respect. "Mademoiselle de Jongh, I have been told you have come all the way from Brussels with two Belgians who want to fight for the Allies, and a Scottish soldier."

"Yes, that is correct."

She could read the skepticism in his face. He seemed to be contemplating how to test her story. "How long did your journey take?" He tapped out his pipe dottle into an ashtray.

"We left Brussels about a week ago," she said. She thought it best not to mention Arnold and his group so as not to cast doubt on her ability to bring more men down.

"How did you get over the Pyrenees?"

"A Spanish guide brought us through. It took two nights." Dédée leaned forward and spoke frankly to the vice-consul. "I have already formed an escape line from Brussels to Saint Jean-de-Luz. There are many men hidden in Belgium. Many are survivors of Dunkirk, but there are also Allied airmen. I can bring them through."

"How old are you?" the consul asked in a tone of disbelief.

"Twenty-four."

"But surely you cannot cross the Pyrenees again."

"I am strong. Please, let me prove to you that I can do it."

The vice-consul contemplated her a long few moments, then said, "We are more interested in British airmen of course."

Dédée signaled agreement with a tip of her head. "All we need is money to pay the guides and to feed and house the men. We are not asking for money for ourselves. But we have to receive the money when the airmen are delivered in order to pay for the next ones."

Mr. Pedrick wrote down the costs as Dédée itemized them. He thought a few moments then said, "I will have to discuss this with my superiors. When can you bring another group down?"

"I will deliver them in three or four weeks' time."

The official extended his hand and Dédée shook it. "Well, Mademoiselle Andrée de Jongh, I shall see you in three to four weeks then."

"But I do not think you should refer to me by my full name. It is better if you call me Dédée."

"Perhaps I shall call you *the Postman*, since you will deliver the parcels."

"Yes, of course."

Dédée said goodbye to the Scot, Cromer, and the Belgians, and returned with Tomás to the mountains. His pack was full of liquor bottles. He'd put a few in hers as well. They delivered the bottles to Tante Go, who explained, "The *Kommandantur* is throwing a big party, and there is nothing more impressive at a German social event than to serve your guests fine food and drink that could not be readily obtained in France."

"Oh my," Dédée said as she added her lot to the huge stash of liquor bottles in Tante Go's back room. "Are all of these for one party?"

Tante Go laughed. "No. Whenever a German officer assists us, he is rewarded."

"So you bribe them," Dédée said knowingly.

"I think the word is blackmail." Tante smiled at Dédée's look of surprise. "Think about it. What officer would want *me* to be caught when they know their name is on my list of clients?"

As Dédée relaxed in the yard with Tante Go and Janine, she had no idea what a hullabaloo her visit had caused. Pederick had been captivated by her spirit and self-confidence. Her daring act also captured the imagination of Donald Darling, chief in Gibraltar, code name "Sunday". But back in London, Colonel Claude Dansey, the head of MI6 railed that Pederick and Darling were fools. "How can they be so damn gullible? The girl is obviously a German spy!"

CHAPTER FOUR

Dédée lounged in a lawn chair beside *Tante Go*, who sat knitting in the shade of a large chestnut tree. The stiffness in her shoulders and legs from the hike would go away, but her mind remained unsettled wondering what had happened to Arnold and his group. In the months of gathering train schedules, recruiting guides and organizing safe houses, Arnold's experience of having worked with Edith Cavell, who smuggled Allied airmen of Belgium during in The Great War, helped prepare Dédée for the dangers involved in evacuating men. Arnold also knew his way around the train stations in the south—something she had yet to learn.

Janine set a tray of lemonade and glasses on the garden table and pulled a chair up beside Dédée. "So are the English going to pay for passage of the airmen?"

Dédée laughed. "Pedrick nearly fell off his chair." She raised one eyebrow and exclaimed in a husky British accent. "Fourteen hundred *pesatas* per man?" She switched back to her own voice, shrugged one shoulder and said coolly, "Yes. The guides are nervous smuggling men over the mountains. We will also need money for food and train fare. I reminded him that we are asking nothing for ourselves."

"I wish I had your nerve," Janine said.

Dédée grinned, but hoped that Janine's admiration wasn't misplaced. "I told Pedrick I would bring him more parcels in a couple of weeks ... but without Arnold ... I thought we would have heard something by now."

Tante Go patted her arm. "It is going to happen in this business we're in. Everyone who gets involved will know the risk."

Dédée shrugged. She was not afraid for herself, but there were three of them when they had begun. "I am afraid that if I am captured before we really get established, the line will crumble. I'm afraid that if we do not show the British we can do this, they will not believe anyone else who tries."

Tante sat up and faced Dédée, looking sternly into her young protégé's eyes. "This is only the beginning. *You*, not Arnold, are the leader of this organization. I am proud to stand with you. You will need courage. You will need all of your strength. But you do not have to carry everything on your shoulders. Fernand and I will handle the south. This is going to be a long hard fight. But we will show them, Dédée. Many others are eager to help. All of us together, we will show them."

They talked until the sun sank into the Bay of Saint Jean-de-Luz. But as the light dimmed, footsteps sounded on the long dirt drive. Then came the sound of someone whistling. In the dark shadows they could just make out the figure of a man carrying a suitcase.

Dédée jumped up. "It's Charlie Morelle!" She grasped his hand and made quick introductions, but was bursting to hear what news he brought. "Did you see my father? Were you able to find out anything?"

"Yes." The darkness couldn't hide the trouble in his eyes. "I went to your parents' house, but the news is not good. Arnold was turned in by a friend for the reward. The police have paid a visit to your home. They are looking for you, Dédée. You cannot go back to Brussels."

———

Five foot six inch Prosper Dezitter sat cross-legged at the wooden conference table at Abwehr headquarters in Brussels. Casually smoking a cigarette as if perfectly comfortable sitting between two strapping six foot agents, he maintained a façade of confidence befitting his stature among his German associates.

Rudolf Kohl descended upon the room like a storm cloud and waved his hand for everyone to sit and not waste time on unnecessary protocol. "We've gotten nothing from Arnold De Pée, and all we've gotten from the Belgian soldiers is a name—Andrée de Jongh. An escape line is known to exist in Marseille. We will *not* let another one organize here in Brussels. This must be dealt with swiftly and decisively." The sweat-steeped air around the table grew hotter. "Follow anyone suspected of

conducting enemy pilots. Arrest anyone found to be hiding airmen."
Kohl clenched his fist. "Be brutal. Make them fear us. When people see
what we do to those who do not cooperate, they will talk."

Kohl fixed his gaze on each man one by one. "I want this de Jongh
girl found. When we have her we will persuade the name of her superiors
out of her."

As the men filed out, Kohl held up his hand to halt Dezitter. "Prosper,
I will have a word with you."

"Of course." Prosper watched as the last agent left and Kohl closed
the door.

"You have done well uncovering the whereabouts of pilots."

"Thank you, *Kommandant*."

"What is your progress on infiltrating the lines?"

"My girlfriend Flore Dings has already made contact with an underground band."

"Do you know if this is the same group?"

"No. But there are other ways to gather information."

"Such as?"

"I have put out the word in Brussels of an escape organization in
which a British officer promises that he can get the airmen back to
England."

"And who is this British officer?"

Prosper jumped to attention and saluted. "Captain Jack Kilanine at
your service."

———

Saturday, October 18, 1941

"Did you miss me?" Dédée asked with an impish grin. "I bet you thought
I would not come back."

A slight smile broke across the generally reserved face of Vice-
Consul Vyvyan Pedrick. "It's good to see you, Dédée. I've had a word
with the two chaps you brought us, Conville and Cowen. They'd both

been captured by the Germans and managed to escape. It is good to have them back."

"Yes. They are brave lads."

"They speak very highly of you."

Dédée brushed the flattery aside with a smirk. "That is because they have made it here. They were nearly arrested."

"Yes. I'm told they were caught with English cigarettes in their pockets. Who is Tante Go? Is she a guide?"

Dédée snickered, remembering Tante's brush with disaster. "She's my chief in the south. She was conducting packages down from Brussels when a customs official at the border became suspicious and took them to his office for questioning. He found the cigarettes and left them alone for a moment. Tante Go waved them out and they all ran away."

Dédée stood looking behind her as she pretended to run. "*'Madame!'* The official called. He pedaled quickly up to them on bicycle. 'Wait a moment!' Tante Go thought they were finished. But the official began to laugh. He returned the cigarettes and told Tante, 'Madame, when you take birds such as these out, make sure you check their pockets!'"

Pederick chuckled. "A rather important lesson."

They paused the conversation while a secretary brought in a tray of tea and biscuits. Pedrick thanked and dismissed his assistant then stirred a cube of sugar into his cup. "They also told me an associate of yours was arrested on your last trip."

"Yes, Arnold. I didn't know of his arrest when you and I last met. The Gestapo is looking for me as well. I cannot go back to Brussels."

His face saddened in empathy. "That must be terribly frightening."

Dédée shrugged. "It is sad that I cannot see my family. I have to accept the fact that my life can no longer be as it was. But there is no looking back. This is the choice I made. I knew there would be consequences."

The important thing was to focus on what they were doing. "I have established a new headquarters in the home of my friend Charlie Morelle in Valenciennes. We will be ready to bring more packages down in a couple of weeks."

"British Military Intelligence, MI6, has agreed to provide the money you have requested."

"It is just for the men," Dédée reminded him. "We ask nothing for ourselves."

Pedrick nodded understanding. "The Belgian Government in London has also taken an interest. They would like to be a part of…"

Dédée stopped him with a shake of her outstretched palm. "No. It is our line. No one is going to run it from London—not the British—not the Belgian Government."

Pedrick beamed. It was if he had been duty-bound to ask her, but had already advised his superiors that she would not go for it. "Of course," he said. "It is your line. We will only assist. Though we are a bit more interested in aviators."

Dédée nodded. She and her father had agreed that trained airmen would be their highest priority. She handed the vice-consul a folded piece of paper. "You could help us with this."

He read it aloud, "*La plume de ma tante est noire?*"

"I need the BBC to broadcast that message from London so the people hiding pilots will know we are truly working with the British."

"I will take care of it. When do you go back?"

"Tonight."

———

Monday, October 27, 1941

Andrée Dumon, now *Nadine* to the underground, tied a big yellow bow in the rolls of her light brown hair and turned about, snickering at the little girl in the mirror. With her white ankle socks, black patent leather shoes, green cardigan sweater, and short green skirt, she looked like a young school girl. Hopefully, that was what the Nazis would think.

Before the war, her parents had been so protective she hadn't even been allowed to go on a date. Now she helped her father distribute an underground newspaper and worked secretly passing along information for the Résistance group LUC. Nadine's mother knew she was delivering newspapers and messages, and maybe suspected she was delivering food and clothing as well, but perhaps didn't ask about it because she was afraid to know more. Nadine decided she wouldn't worry her mother by telling her what she was *really* doing.

Last week a massacre in Paris had shaken everyone. In retaliation for an ambush on German soldiers by a French Résistance squad, twenty-seven political prisoners had been randomly taken out of prison and shot. Nadine shivered at the thought. The message was clear: If she was caught the Germans would show no mercy. She imagined herself standing in front of a firing squad waiting for the bullets to fly. But it was not just her own life she was putting on the line. They could shoot her whole family for her brazen defiance.

Her stomach pitched like a boat in a storm. While most German officers acted courteously, dangers were everywhere. She had seen people dragged off trams by German police and citizens arrested for listening to BBC broadcasts on the wireless. A friend had been beaten by Boche thugs just for smirking at them—a young boy had been shot dead for throwing a tomato at a German soldier. Killed because of a stupid tomato! Nadine took a deep breath and adjusted her scarf while focusing her mind on the mission ahead.

Dédée had brilliantly planned the operation from Valenciennes, arranging the parcels to be handed off from guide to guide without them knowing each other. That way if one guide was caught her contacts in the organization would be limited. Once everything was in place, Dédée telephoned her father in Brussels to send her some *children*.

Nadine was determined to prove herself worthy of the responsibility entrusted to her. Since Arnold's arrest and Dédée's hasty relocation to Valenciennes, Dédée's father, *Paul*, had assumed leadership of the Brussels sector with Nadine and Dédée's sister, Suzanne, assisting him.

A knock on the door interrupted Nadine's thoughts. "You are up early," her mother said with surprise.

"I am meeting Michou for lunch."

"Lunch?" Her mother glanced at the clock.

"I have some things to do first."

"Do you want to eat something before you leave?"

"I will get something on the way." Nadine's stomach was too queasy to eat now. She threw on her jacket and hurried out.

Three airmen had been shuffled about within Anne Brusselmans'— *Madame Anne*—assemblage of safe houses in Ixelles. Anne had recently moved them to homes in Etterbeek where Nadine was to collect two of them. She exited the tram and found the address.

"Josephine?" she asked when the door opened.

"Yes?"

"Are the children ready for their outing?"

"The children will need their coats."

"The park should be beautiful today."

Once the short exchange verified their authenticity, Josephine let Nadine in and called the *children* out of a back room. Michal Kowalski and Stefan Tomicki were from the RAF Polish squadron. Their wary glances at each other showed what they were thinking: *Was this little girl really going to be their guide?*

"*Parlez-vous français?*" Nadine asked.

"*Je parle un petit peu français,*" Kowalski said.

She needed to let them know she was the boss. A misstep could get them all arrested. She adjusted their berets, and said sternly in French, "You will come with me on the train. What I say, you do—no hesitation." She nodded for Kowalski to translate her French into Polish for Tomicki. "You will not speak. If someone speaks to you, you pretend to be mute." She pointed to Kowalski "You will follow fifty feet behind. You do not know us." Then to Tomicki, who at twenty-seven was too old to play the boyfriend of the fifteen-year-old girl she pretended to be: "You are my cousin."

Nadine devised a little scheme. She turned Tomicki's hand over, then tapped two fingers against it once and said, "*Oui.*" Then she tapped twice and said, "*Non.*" She did it once again, but this time after one tap she pointed to him.

"*Oui?*" he asked.

She nodded, than tapped twice.

"*Non,*" he said.

She nodded again. Next she spoke a long phrase in French and tapped once.

"*Oui,*" he said with confidence.

She smiled then tested their silent signal one more time with a phrase and two taps.

"*Non,*"

"*Très bien.*" Then she said *non* while demonstrating appropriate facial expressions. Next, she repeated it with a shrug.

He copied her mannerisms and practiced it a few times.

She smiled her approval. There was just one more thing to learn. Nadine tapped his arm three times. "Danger!" she said.

Kowalski translated and Tomicki nodded that he understood.

Nadine made them wait a block away from the Quartier Léopold train station while she bought tickets to the north side of the city where they exited the train and caught a local tram.

A serious looking man in a dark grey suit and black tie entered at the next stop and slowly made his way down the aisle, his gaze shifting back and forth over the passengers as the trolley gained speed.

Nadine focused on picking bits of invisible lint off her skirt, but tapped Tomicki's arm three times. Then she stole a peek. There was no doubt that the man was secret police—and the way his gaze dwelled on Kowalski told her he wasn't buying the pilot's disguise.

The evaders had been warned that if any one of them was singled out they would be on their own. But if Nadine didn't act Kowalski would be finished.

She opened her purse pretending to look for something, then tipped it into the aisle. Coins rolled down the walkway. Nadine jumped up and gave chase as people reached down from their seats to pick the money up for the young girl. The German in the grey suit gallantly assisted. She stepped up the aisle collecting the coins and profusely thanking all her fellow passengers, and as the tram slowed for the next stop, she stood in front of the suited man babbling how embarrassed she was. "My mother would be upset with me if I lost the money!" Still chattering away, she looked left and right, and up and down to see if there were any coins she might have missed. As the man looked with her, Nadine signaled behind her back for the children to exit while she kept the German distracted. Once the evaders had safely gotten off, Nadine thanked the man one last time and hurried out.

They rode another tram to their destination and the men waited down the block while she exchanged pass-phrases at the door. Once the packages had been safely delivered, she strode away checking back to make sure no one was following her then ducked around a building. There she stood trembling with all the fear she'd kept bottled up for the past three hours. Others said how they admired her *sang-froid*—her coolness under pressure. As she stood there shaking and fighting back the urge to vomit, she chuckled silently, thinking, *If they could only see me now!*

By the time Nadine rode the train back down to St. Jean Berchman's College where her sister, Michou, was studying to become a nurse, she had removed the little girl ribbon, shaken her hair down and transformed back into eighteen-year-old Andrée Dumon.

Just walking from the dorm beside her sister eased her queasy stomach. At only five feet tall, Michou looked younger than her twenty years, but her proficiency and quiet self-confidence left no doubt that she was both competent and intrepid. Andrée already felt calmer. The two were so in tune with each other, they often communicated with nothing more than a gesture or facial expression, but this was one time Nadine hoped her sister couldn't guess what she was involved in.

"I like your skirt," Michou said as they walked a few blocks to a small café. "I might have to borrow it some time."

Nadine couldn't tell if her sister was poking fun because she was still wearing her low-heeled shoes and ankle socks. "I like yours, too."

"Thank you," Michou said with mock pretentiousness as she smoothed down her starched grey uniform and straightened the white necktie. "They are very popular around here. Everyone is wearing them."

"Men are attracted to nurses," Nadine said.

"Oh? And where are these men you speak of?" Michou pulled open the café door for her sister to walk through. "All I ever see are little boys and pensioners."

"There are the Germans," Nadine suggested rolling her eyes.

Michou scrunched up her nose. "Please," she said. "I would like to enjoy my lunch."

As if on cue, two tall handsome German officers sauntered through the door and paused at the girls' table. *"Bonjour, Mademoiselles."*

"Bonjour," the girls replied, dutifully courteous.

"Voulez-vous nous rejoindre pour une déjeuner?"

Michou shook her head politely refusing his lunch offer.

As the young officers walked on, the girls shot each other a quick glance before shifting their gaze down to their menus, each knowing that the other was suppressing giggles. Thankfully, the waiter came before laughter broke out. The Germans would not take it well if they thought they were being laughed at.

After the waiter had delivered their lunch, Michou ventured a side-ways glance at the Germans seated a few tables away. She broke a *frite* in half and dipped it in the dish of mayonnaise as she leaned in toward Nadine. "I heard if you stare at a German officer's brass or shoes, he will become very flustered—embarrassed that you are seeing imperfection." She sat back with a smug grin and dipped the other half of her fry. Then she said loudly enough for the officers to hear, "American cinema stars are so handsome. Don't you think? Wouldn't you just love to meet some handsome American men?"

"But of course," Nadine said, playing along. "Jimmy Stewart, Tyrone Power, John Wayne..."

"John Garfield..." Michou sighed with dreamy eyes. "And Jimmy Cagney..."

"I would not like gangsters."

Michou laughed. "He is not a real gangster. He is an actor." She once again leaned in as if to share a secret. "Are you seeing anyone?"

Nadine shrugged. "Who is there to see? Like you said there is no one but old men and little boys left in Belgium."

"And ..." Michou flicked her eyes toward the Germans, and giggled into her sandwich as she brought it to her mouth.

Nadine shook her head. "Even if there were any men, Papa has not yet grasped the idea that I am no longer a little girl." She paused, a fry in hand, and sighed. "Besides what would two people on a date do? Go to the cinema to see a German film?"

"Haven't you read the posters?" Michou said glibly. "The Germans have come here to protect us from the terrible British. We should be thankful that they..."

Nadine cut her off by pinching her thumb and forefinger together.

Michou shut up and glanced sideways.

The Germans who were passing on their way to the exit, paused once again beside the girls' table. One officer gave them a generous smile. "Are you enjoying your lunch?"

"Yes we are," Michou said politely, but with a touch of aloofness.

Nadine sensed that her sister's sentence finished with *up until now.*"

"You are a nurse?"

Michou cast her eyes toward her uniform. "Good guess."

The German chuckled. "Do you know a nice restaurant around here where we could have dinner later?"

"Three blocks down, turn left and you will find several. They are all good."

Nadine had to suppress a smile when Michou dropped her gaze to the officer's brass insignia.

He didn't seem to notice. "Would you ladies like to join us for dinner later?"

"No," Michou said a bit more coldly this time while continuing her eye assault on his uniform. "We are busy."

"Ah, that is too bad. Perhaps another time." The officer followed Michou's gaze down to his uniform and looked a bit unsettled as he turned and walked off.

As the door closed behind the officers, a smile broke across Michou's face. Nadine turned around to make sure the Germans were gone.

Michou grinned. "He will go back to his billet to see what was wrong with his uniform."

The November sun broke through the Valenciennes apartment window as Elvire Morelle, a tall buxom brunette and the sister of Charlie Morelle, set a plate of hot buttery biscuits on the table. "There are two children for us to guide today?"

"Three," Dédée said waving a hand over the fresh ink on the identity card to dry it. "The two Polish sergeants that Nadine moved last week and a Canadian." Her forgeries had greatly improved since Tante Go's husband, Fernand, had stolen blank forms and an official stamp from his employer, the German Kommandant in Anglet. "You and I will leave as soon as I finish these papers for Charlie to deliver."

Dédée and Elvire Morelle watched for the noon train from a café window in Quiévrain. *Paul* soon arrived with two children in tow. A helper, Octave, followed with the third. Dédée strolled out clutching her jacket closed to the cool breeze, chatting with Elvire and showing no interest in the children who were now seated on a bench eating sandwiches. She and Elvire continued their conversation as she sat down beside the Canadian airman. After allowing them enough time to finish their lunch, she gave the airman an inconspicuous nudge and said softly without looking at him, "When we go, you follow." She lifted her hand from the bench a bit to reveal a folded napkin that she left behind when she got up.

The Canadian, Ives, discreetly opened the napkin to find boarding tickets which he passed along to the Polish aviators. She didn't say another word to them until they were all on the train and together in a first class compartment. "*Hallo*, I am Dédée and this is Elvire. I hope your journey so far has not been too unpleasant." She handed each airman his new *carte d'identité* and collected their old ones. "If someone asks you a question, you do not speak."

"*Sourd et muet*," Ives said with a knowing nod.

"Yes," Dédée said, "deaf and dumb. Are there any questions? Good. Rest now. It will be a few more hours before we reach our destination."

After several local trains and trams, they arrived at the Douai station at dusk and waited until the next guide arrived to take over. Dédée gave each airman 250 francs for the ferry and wished them luck. There was nothing else for her and Elvire to do now but go to Nenette's farm and wait.

At ten o'clock, Nenette stole through the dark fields to the vineyard by the river where the *children* were hiding. She led them back to the house and poured glasses of wine, ladled out bowls of soup and set out brown bread and sweet butter. "You all must be starving after your long trip." She raised her glass of wine. "Welcome to France."

"*Viva la France*," Ives toasted back. After a few bites, he said, "Boy, I thought we would never get here. Your trains are so slow."

"We purposely do not take direct routes," Dédée said. "It is slower but less risky."

Ives conceded her point with upturned palm. "I would certainly rather take the route that is less risky, but your trains are really really clunky. Trains in Canada run so much smoother."

"Perhaps we could move the war to Canada," Dédée said. "Then we would all be happy."

At Amiens the next day, the girls slipped the children their new boarding tickets. They arrived at the Gare du Nord in Paris at half-past-six, ate a buffet meal at the station, then proceeded south to the Gare d'Austerlitz and boarded the overnight train.

Tante Go and Janine took over in Bayonne at nine o'clock the next morning, Three hours later, Dédée met up with the *children* again at Saint-Jean-de-Luz and bicycled with them to a farmhouse in the foothills where they waited for nightfall and the arrival of their Spanish guide. They crossed the Bidassoa River into Spain at four o'clock in the morning on Armistice Day, November eleventh, the anniversary of the end of the Great War, completing their first trip after meeting the British vice-consul.

———

Captain Jimmy Langley, the one-armed intelligence officer of MI 9 was astonished by the depth and organization of Dédée's *Postman Line*. The Polish and Canadian airmen he debriefed had been helped along by not less than forty people. Dédée herself had met up with the aviators and passed them off three times. She had conducted them over the mountains and hadn't left them until they were safely in the hands of the British Consulate in Bilbao. The girl with the incredible plan, the one he had been silently rooting for, had done it. She had delivered her first airmen.

Langley hid his glee as his boss, Brigadier Crockatt, delivered the news to Colonel Dansey, a tough old bird who had been forged in the trenches of the last war.

Dansey humphed. "She is going to muck things up just like Edith Cavell."

"She should be given credit, Sir, for accomplishing what had seemed impossible," Crockatt said.

"I don't want these damn amateurs interfering with my intelligence agents. I want proper oversight of this thing."

"Understood." Crockatt let Dansey's blood pressure subside a moment then added, "I will need another officer to assist Captain Langley if we are to give proper oversight of the underground."

Dansey nodded agreement and left.

Frowning, Jimmy turned to Crockatt. "Proper oversight?"

Crockatt smiled. "He can think of it as oversight. For us, it will be assistance. I want you do everything you can to support this girl."

Delight erased Jimmy's frown. "Yes, Sir!"

"And I want word spread throughout the air corps that men have been rescued and returned by the French Underground."

"Dédée is Belgian, Sir."

"Whatever. Start looking for an officer to work with you."

CHAPTER FIVE

One evening, Dédée took the train up to the Schaerbeek neighborhood in Brussels and asked the host as usual, "Are the children ready for their journey?"

"They are very excited," the woman said. "I told them they would have a special visitor tonight—I told them our leader wanted to meet them."

Dédée wasn't sure how she felt about that. She was honored by the respect, but given the increased efforts by the Secret Police to track down underground members, it would be better if no one knew she was anything more than a guide. When she opened the door, it turned out the woman hadn't given anything away.

The three men lounging on the bed jumped up with delightful looks of surprise and confusion. They glanced toward the door as if the *real* leader might be walking in behind her.

"Had'ya do?" a jockey-sized lad hopped off the bed and pumped her hand. "I'm Hilary Birk. But you can call me Larry."

"Yes, you're the Australian," Dédée said, nearly bowled over by the friendliness of the little fellow.

"Yeah, that's right. And you must be the daughter of the missus?"

"No. I am Andrée, but you can call me, Dédée."

There was a moment's hesitation, and then Larry spoke up again. "Are you the special visitor we were told to expect?"

Dédée chuckled. Their apprehensive glances told her all she needed to know. "Yes. I am the leader of the Postman Line." This was nothing new. She was used to having to prove herself to men.

She shook hands with Howard Carroll and Jack Newton marveling at how young the handsome dark-haired fellow seemed—almost too young and innocent to be a gunner on a Vickers bomber. But that was the way of war, young men risking death before they even had a chance to live. Jack had become her first RAF airman when Albert Day, an American pilot flying for the RAF, fell ill and had to be left behind to recover from bronchial pneumonia before hiking the mountains.

"You're the one who is going to get us back to England?" Jack asked poorly veiling his disbelief in a casual voice.

"Yes. I will be the mother and you will be my little children. You will listen and follow my instructions and I will get you safely to Spain."

One black eyebrow rose. "I beg your pardon," Jack said. "Did you say Spain? I'd venture that's a rather long jaunt!" He glanced sideways to see if his companions were thinking the same thing.

Dédée accepted his point with a nod. "The Germans expect evaders to take the short route and have blocked all roads to the coast. There are two prohibited zones, each requiring additional passes, and each with very rigorous checks. It is the quickest way to a German prison camp." She smiled when that revelation left them wide-eyed. "Rest now. I will be back tomorrow and we will begin our journey." She closed the door, imagining them fretting that their lives were in the hands of some little girl instead of some macho guerilla fighter.

The next morning, Dédée dressed in a common blue flowered dress, white ankle socks and dark blue jumper and went to their room to calm their anxiety a bit so their nerves wouldn't give them away. "Tell me a little about yourselves," she said. "How about you, Jack?"

"I'm *Jacques Dumonceau* from the *Arrondisement de Dax...*"

"No, I do not mean your evasion name. Tell me about your family. What will you do when you get back to London?"

"I'm going to spend time with my wife, Mary. We were married in April and I was shot down sixth of August."

"Oh you poor fellow. We will do our best to get you back to your wife before Christmas."

"That would be Splendid." Jack's attentive gaze said she was gaining his trust.

"What about you, Howard?"

"I'd like to get back to England before Christmas, too—so I can deliver special presents to Herr Hitler."

Dédée chuckled then turned her attention to Larry.

"I do a great priest impression," The Australian offered.

From the aviators' smirking, Dédée could tell there was a story. She tipped her head a bit to encourage him to go on. But Larry didn't just go on, he jumped out of his chair and acted it out. "I knew I wouldn't get very far in my flight suit, so I nicked a priest's long robe, hat and crucifix. I looked a fair dinkum…" Larry interrupted himself and said somewhat apologetically, "I hope I am not offending anybody…"

Dédée waved her hand. "I am not religious."

"Yeah, my Dad's a minister, but I'm not much for it," Larry said. "So anyway, I'm in the middle of this town and people are waving and smiling, and I'm giving them the ol' …" He strolled in place cutting the air with a grand sign of the cross. "Piece of piss. No worries. Right? Then outta nowhere come these three big German blokes … of course everyone looks big to me. So I just keep on walking and nodding and blessing the air, and just when it looks like I'm about to get past them, they shout something to me in French. But I don't speak a bloody word." Larry paused, his eyes rolling upward in mock contemplation.

"So what did you do?" Dédée wondered aloud.

"Well when my Dad didn't want to stop and listen to a parishioner yabber, he would just say something in Latin and keep walking. Of course I don't speak Latin either, so I bless them and mumble something like, *Dominous, Domiscibum Delierium,* and I keep on going." Larry, piously nodding back and forth, crossed the room blessing everyone as he went.

Dédée laughed and applauded the performance.

"So tell us, Dédée," Jack said, "what's your story?"

"There is really nothing to tell. I am just one of many people who will help you get home." The boys looked disappointed she didn't have tales of the underground, but it was best not to say more than necessary. "I will refer to you as packages," she said growing more serious. "Jack will be package number one, Larry two and Howard three. You will do things in that order. We will pick up package number four when we cross the River Somme. What I say, you do. No questions. You will follow me, but we will all stay separate pretending not to know each other." The boys listened with sober attention. "If the police take you away, you are on your own. We do not know you. That would simply get others arrested as well. We must preserve the evasion line."

She paused a moment for each to nod understanding, then continued. "Show your papers without emotion, and pretend to be mute if asked a question. You must be silent on the train too, and whenever we are in public. If someone suspects you of being English, they will try to trick you. They might say, *Can you tell me the time*? If you look at your wrist they will know you understood. Someone may ask you for a light. If anyone sneezes, you say nothing."

At breakfast Dédée had the men eating in silence, warning them, "Do not ask to pass anything. Do not say thank you when food is passed. I know this is not easy. You must be aware at all times."

She rewarded them with a smile when they completed their meal without a word.

"Our journey will be dangerous, but if we stay alert and work together, I will get you to Spain." Jack looked particularly nervous. She gently touched his arm to calm his worries. "It will not be easy. But you are tough. You are my brave boys and you will do it."

The *packages* kept their distance and followed their postmistress onto the train. Ninety minutes later, they exited the train at the station in Quiévrain where they were joined by two other guides—Elvire and Charlie Morelle. Each paired with a guide, they walked a couple of miles and rode a tram to Valenciennes, and then caught another train to Corbie.

Dédée was proud of the children as they ate silently in the café and didn't utter a word until they were alone in the woods at dusk. She crouched down in a grove of trees and said in a low voice, "The River Somme is just ahead. It is the border of the German occupation of France. When I signal, package number one will go quickly and silently across. The water level is low but it will be very cold."

By the time it was fully dark, the men were already shivering. She crept up to where she could see the towpath and waited.

"Dédée," Jack whispered. "I have to pee."

"All right. Go find a place to do it, but watch out for Germans."

No sooner had Jack crawled away when they heard someone whistling. Everyone flattened themselves against the ground as the sound drew nearer. A German soldier with his rifle slung over his shoulder pedaled down the river path. After the whistling faded, she signaled for package number one.

Jack tied his laces together, threw the shoes over his shoulder and slipped into the water. His eyes and mouth opened wide with the shock of the cold, but he didn't utter a sound.

As Dédée watched Jack's lower body disappear under the water, she worried that Nenette had misjudged the depth. It had not occurred to her to ask if any of the children knew how to swim. She could hardly see him in the darkness, but he was definitely in over his waist. A cloud passed and he seemed to vanish. Anxious moments later he reappeared in the moonlight, about three-quarters of the way across with the top half of his body still above the water.

She signaled for package number two. She feared poor Larry, the shortest of the group, would have the greatest difficulty, but he bobbed up and down crossing the river in his usual buoyant manner.

Following package number three, she crawled shivering onto the bank on the other side.

Nenette threw a blanket around her friend. "You are smiling."

"I was just thinking about the crossing with Miss Richards and her derriere flying up in my face when her tube tipped."

They both laughed as they walked to the farmhouse where the men were already warming themselves by the fireplace.

The fourth package was already waiting for them. Gerard Waucquez, skilled in explosives and the nephew of the head of the Belgian government in exile, was now in the hands of the Postman for delivery to the British so he could train in covert operations and be dropped back into Belgium.

Four children with just one guide would be difficult, but Dédée had a plan: she and Gerard pretended to be a couple and bought train tickets which she discreetly distributed.

The train trip from Amiens to Paris was uneventful, but when they reached Paris, a train delay spoiled their luck. She would need to somehow keep the children out of sight for three hours.

She and Gerard showed no recognition of the other three evaders they had left on a bench outside the terminal, but as they passed Dédée whispered, "Come along."

She led them down the avenue to the last place anyone would look for people hiding from the Germans—a German cinema. After a two hour dose of a laughably amateurish German propaganda film on the master race, they were ready to make their way back to the train. But first, Dédée stopped along the way and bought a newspaper and two oranges. She enjoyed Jack's confused look when she instructed him on when and how to eat them.

With nothing more than a flick of the eyes, she signaled Jack which compartment to take. He moved in next to the window opposite two elderly ladies. The other airmen came next and Dédée and Gerard took opposing seats next to the door.

Although Jack had no idea what the newspaper said, he did a splendid acting job pretending to be absorbed in it. After milking the newspaper as long as he could, he took out the first orange as Dédée had instructed and slowly began to peel. Dédée peeked over at the two ladies, chuckling to herself at their looks of annoyance. The French considered it rude and rather repulsive to peel an orange and suck the juices in a public place, and this train compartment was certainly too small to be subjected to such an inconsiderate act. Dédée sat back satisfied that these cultured ladies weren't likely to strike up a conversation with such an ill-mannered fellow.

After a fourteen hour trip the *children* flowed out with the crowd at the Bayonne terminal, but instead of joining the lines to present their papers to the German and French officials stationed at each exit, Dédée ushered them to the refreshment room where Tante Go's daughter, Janine, signaled with an inconspicuous nod. Dédée passed coffees to the airmen and whispered, "When you've finished your coffee, packages one and two follow Janine. Three and four go toward the loo."

Janine allowed the boys to finish most of their drinks before slipping away in the direction of the facilities. Dédée took several leisurely sips herself, then set her cup down and headed in the same direction. When her parcels caught up, she unlocked an outside door with a key copied by her associates and led the men to a nearby café where Janine was waiting with her two.

After lunch at Villa Voisin, Tante Go's home in Anglet, the airmen remained in the kitchen while Tante Go and Dédée took their wine glasses into the living room.

"They seem a lively bunch," Tante Go said.

"It's nervous energy," Dédée said. "It has been a tense and dangerous day for them. Now their bellies are full of Bobonne's delicious steaks and this is the first time all day they have been allowed to talk and let it out. Janine and Freddy certainly seem to be enjoying their company."

"Janine makes them all promise to come back and see her after the war." Tante Go jerked her head toward the loud laughter in the kitchen. "That Larry looks to be particularly cheery."

"Yes, he can be very entertaining, but he made me nervous the entire trip. In the cinema, when the crowd stood up shouting Heil Hitler, he jumped up and yelled right along. Thank God only we noticed. Then on the train, he was holding a cigarette torch in his hand. A woman asked him for a light, but of course he did not understand her. So I grabbed the torch and lit her cigarette, saying, 'You must have been daydreaming, darling, the woman is asking for a light."

From now on they would make the children empty their pockets and take away anything questionable—torches, foreign money, loose change, and souvenirs. "We cannot make that mistake again."

Tante nodded and sipped her wine. "I have set the crossing for the day after tomorrow to give the men time to regain their strength." She had found safe house keepers nearer the mountains: Kattalin Aguirre, with a townhome on the bay, and Frantxia Usandizaga with a farm, Bidegain Berri, in Urrugne. Kattalin had sent them a new guide—Florentino Goikoetxea, a Basque with a price on his head on both sides of the border for smuggling. He had fought against Franco's forces in the Spanish Civil War and hated the Germans for putting the fascists in power. The difficulty was that Florentino only spoke Euskara: it would be difficult to communicate with him in the mountains.

Seeing Dédée's look of concern, Tante Go patted her friend's arm. "Don't worry. You are going to like Florentino. He is the best. When he is here, Kattalin or Frantxia can help you work out words and signals to communicate with him on the hike."

Before leaving on the second day, the men wrote their names and addresses in Tante Go's black book where she recorded each person sent over the mountain. Jack said goodbye and hugged Tante Go, but his smile couldn't hide his apprehension about the march. Just before the pilot stepped out into the rain to mount his bicycle, Tante Go squeezed his hand reassuringly. "You will do fine." She flicked her head toward Dédée and smirked with pride. "My little *niece* has hiked over six times with her short legs. And just three months ago, an over-weight, delicate, mademoiselle made the crossing. I am sure you can do it."

Freddy de Greef bicycled off in the grey drizzle about ten minutes before the others. Janine went next with the airmen spaced far enough to just see each other. Dédée waited a few more minutes and then she and Gerard rode side by side. They pedaled against the rain and wind through the town of Saint-Jean-de-Luz steering around fallen limbs and leaves across the bridge to Ciboure and two miles on to Frantxia's farm in Urrugne.

A plain, raven-haired Basque woman widowed by the war and the mother of three young children, Frantxia Usandizaga, had agreed without hesitation to let Tante Go use her remote farmhouse. She knew the risk was great, but the thought of her children growing up in a Nazi ruled world was unimaginable. She welcomed the band of fugitives into her home with dry clothes for each man and a bowl of hearty soup. When dinner was done, the men played with the children in the big living room and Frantxia chatted with Dédée and Janine in the kitchen while they waited for their mountain guide.

Even though Florentino had been described as big and brave, a man that the other smugglers looked up to, Dédée was awed by how small the doorway seemed when he ducked through. Dressed like a farmhand in a long black wool coat, worn grey trousers, and beat-up work shoes, his large bulk filled the opening. His face was as rugged as the Pyrenees themselves, but his infectious smile brightened the room.

A giant hand swallowed Dédée's when they were introduced. Incomprehensible words of greeting wafted out on breath that smelled of strong red wine.

"He is happy that the two of you will be working together," Frantxia translated. "He has heard that you are a woman of action. He likes that."

Florentino firmly gripped each man's hand, pumping heartily. He pointed to their feet and spoke to Frantxia which she translated into French and Dédée explained in English.

"He wants you to take off your shoes and show him your feet."

From his pack, Florentino drew out bandages that he attached to each man's feet in strategic locations to protect against blisters. Next, he produced rope-soled espadrilles which he demonstrated how to tie.

"We call them *alpargatas*," Frantxia explained. "They are quiet and will help your footing on the mountain trails."

When Florentino had finished, Frantxia handed each man a small pack with sandwiches, cheese and a bottle of wine. But Dédée warned them not to drink until they stopped for a break in the cover of the mountains. They would need to remain alert while still in view of the farms and villages.

They stepped outside and Florentino handed each man a rail fashioned from tree saplings to use as a walking stick.

"You use them behind you when you ascend rocky slopes," Dédée said. "Watch Florentino. You see? You push the pole against the ground like a ..." She snapped her fingers ... "What's the word? ... brake ... like a brake to keep from slipping backwards."

Florentino, carrying the largest pack, set a brisk pace through the fields. Dédée marched alongside him with the next largest pack to show the others that a girl could keep up and so could they. In addition to food and drink, her pack contained a skirt, blouse, socks and shoes to change into when they reached Spain. She stole an occasional glance at the powerful fellow beside her. Florentino exuded an inner strength that surpassed that of the other guides. He thrived in the crisp hay-scented air and strode toward the ominous mountain mist like a child heading to the playground.

Florentino pushed hard while the children were still fresh and able to keep up, moving quickly and quietly through small hamlets, and down long winding meadow trails. After about two and a half hours, the grade steepened. The path narrowed and all but disappeared. The sour aroma of wet unshorn sheep hung in the thin mountain air.

Dédée slowed to let men pass her. This was when she would have to start prodding the lads to fight the pain in their bodies and lungs.

"How are you doing, Jack?" she asked.

Breathing heavily, Jack said nothing and simply nodded, too winded to voice a response.

"You're doing great. We will rest in a little while." Dédée understood how difficult this was for the men who had been in hiding for so long, they had no muscle tone, no stamina. But they simply had to get beyond the German patrols and Spanish Guardia before dawn exposed them. She encouraged Howard, Gerard and Larry as they passed. "In a couple of hours we will be in Spain. You can make it."

The mountain fought against them. Steep slopes of tumbled grey rocks tested their resolve, and each man took his share of lumps and bumps. She and Florentino pulled them up the more difficult slopes. They had neared the summit and she was giving Howard a hand when she heard "Ummpf" behind her. She looked down to see that Jack had fallen again. She gave Howard one last push then slid down the slope to Jack.

"Watch out!" he whispered as he pulled her against the rocks and hid his face.

She stayed motionless, listening.

"There!" He buried his head as a light beam swept over them.

Dédée relaxed her taut muscles and let out her breath. "It is just the lighthouse at Irun. It will light the path for a little while. But thank you Jack for trying to protect me."

When Florentino finally called a break, the men collapsed on the cold ground.

"I don't know about you blokes," Larry said as he dug out the cheese, bread and wine from his pack, "but the next time I get shot down, I'm staying in France."

Dédée sat among the children while Florentino disappeared behind a tree.

"Once is enough for me, too," Jack said. He shook his head toward Dédée. "I don't know how you can do this over and over again."

She laughed. "You boys have to stop getting shot down. Then I won't have to climb these mountains."

Florentino returned from the tree with a jug of cognac and a triumphant smile.

The tip of Howard's bottle caught Dédée's eye. She touched his arm. "Do not drink it all now. We still have a long journey ahead."

The descent was even harder than climbing. The sound of rushing water grew until it echoed off the mountain walls. "The Bidassoa," Dédée advised, "the boundary to Spain."

Jack, Howard and Larry swapped grins.

As they got nearer, Dédée held the boys up. "This is a very dangerous area. The *Guardia Civil* will shoot at anything that moves. Wait here. Stay down and remain quiet." She crept through the brush to the edge of the opening.

Florentino returned to Dédée's hiding place and spoke in Euskara tinged with bits of broken Spanish, a word or two of French and hand gestures. Dédée nodded and crawled back to the men, frowning. "We have to go back."

"What do you mean go back?" they asked almost as one.

"The river is too high. The current is too fast."

"Couldn't we just try?" Jack asked.

Dédée shook her head. "Even a good swimmer would be swept away and drown."

"I hate France!" Jack, nearly in tears, spat on the ground. "I hate this rotten place!"

"No!" Dédée shook her finger at him. "This is our land. You do not spit on our land!"

It took a few minutes, but Jack calmed down. "I'm sorry. It was a bad thing to say. Forgive me."

Dédée accepted his apology with a hug. "We will try again in a day or two. Florentino says there is a foot bridge five hours upstream."

Frantxia was shocked by their return, but remained a gracious host. Dédée didn't wish to put the young mother at any greater risk, but she had no other choice. They both breathed a little easier three days later when the party set out again.

This time they had to leave earlier in the day for the farther hike. A heavy mist hung in the air, and when they reached the mountain trails, Dédée warned them to stay close together. "It will be very dark and one can easily get lost."

The extra hours made this trip even more difficult than the last, but having done it once the men felt more prepared and were eager to get on with it. They thought they knew what to expect. Then they reached the guarded bridge.

Dédée sensed their apprehension as they peered from the bushes at the rickety old foot bridge below. The ropes and slats swayed in the beam of flood lights. On the road beyond a small guardhouse, two guards with carbine rifles watched over the passage from an excellent vantage point. Anyone caught on the bridge would be penned in by the ropes like a calf in a slaughterhouse chute—an easy kill.

The prospect made her stomach queasy. But she could not let the men think that she was afraid. She had to trust Florentino and cast her own trepidation aside.

After a while, a car pulled up to the post with two new soldiers to replace the first two. Florentino advised through Dédée that they would wait for the guards to get tired and go inside where only one small window overlooked the bridge.

Finally, in the middle of the night, Florentino decided it was time. Dédée thought about the British Consul's remark that fourteen hundred pesetas was a lot of money for the guides. Florentino was about to risk certain death if his guess about the guards sleeping was wrong. How much was that worth?

With one last nod to the others, Florentino bounded down to the bridge and hurried over the wooden boards, the loud rush of the water muting the sound of his footsteps. On the other side, he ducked beneath the window and slowly lifted his head to peek in. Then he scurried to the bushes on the far side of the road and waved.

Dédée tapped Jack on the shoulder. Her pulse beat wildly as the young airman made his way down to the bridge. She feared for all her children, but Jack had a special place in her heart. Her first British airman was brave, handsome, sweet, kind and clearly attracted to her. He was also devoted to his bride, Mary. She felt an attraction she could not deny—nor could she acknowledge it. There could be nothing more than amorous thoughts. His poor young wife, Mary, was waiting and wondering if she would ever see him again. Dédée couldn't help feeling a bit envious. Soon the young couple would be reunited, but there could be no romance in Dédée's own life, not with the war and with all she must do. In a way, the Jacks and Marys of the world were what she was fighting for.

As she watched Jack negotiate the swaying slats, she wondered if she would live to find her own love. Such thoughts were foolish. She banished them from her mind and sent the next evader. Love would be for the Jacks and Marys and the children who would grow up after the war. For her, there would be no after the war. She wasn't sad about it. That's just the way it was. She'd made her choice. Her goal was to get as many airmen back to England and back into the fight as she could before the Gestapo caught up with her.

Once package number four reached the other side she drew a deep breath and made her dash. Her heart pounded as her feet flew her over the thin slats. Her ears filled with the rush of the water below. She focused on the guard house at the other end, concentrating to detect any movement. She reached the other side and ducked down breathless, but energized. She crept below the window, dashed across the road and scrambled up the slope beyond. "Bravo, my brave boys!" she said softly as she gave Jack's hand a little squeeze.

She crouched down beside Florentino who congratulated her with a huge smile and a slap on the back. They remained still with their eyes on the guardhouse, her chest still heaving. Finally, satisfied that they had not been heard, Florentino grunted something in Euskara and marched off.

Once they'd put some distance between them and the guardhouse they all breathed a little easier. Florentino led them down an old oxcart road and through a long dark tunnel. Finally, they reached a farm road. Even though they were in Spain, they were far from safe.

"I will go on to San Sebastian to make arrangements with the British consul. Jack, you, Larry and Howard will stay in the water tower until I return."

"Water tower!" Larry said.

Dédée delighted at the confused looks on their faces. She snickered impishly at what they must be thinking—no doubt imagining swimming about in a water tank for the next few hours.

They had agreed to follow her instructions without question, but was she really serious? It was Larry who spoke up. "Ah, you're having us on." He looked up at the six foot tall wooden water barrel set atop a tripod of wooden poles. "Aren't you?"

Dédée burst out laughing. "There's a steel tank inside. Between the wood and steel walls it is filled with straw. There is still much danger here. Spain is not really so neutral. If you are caught, you will be taken to a Spanish prison or handed over to the German police. Inside the tank, you will be hidden and comfortable."

Dédée hiked with Florentino and Waucquez two miles to the village of Renteria where she caught the tram to San Sebastian. She returned a few hours later and once more cautiously led the men on the tram back to the British consul. After sharing the dangers of the journey and watching over them for so many days, it truly felt like she was leaving her children. She would miss each of them, especially Jack. She hugged them one by one, but said nothing. She couldn't speak for the lump in her throat.

Dédée turned and walked off thinking about her own family and wondering whether the Gestapo's passion to capture her had cooled a bit after these five long months. Maybe she could chance it.

CHAPTER SIX
December 8, 1941

Evaders knew her only as Madame A.

Anne Brusselmans, a mannerly, plain-spoken Belgian housewife, British as the white cliffs of Dover like her English mother, and fluent in French like her Belgian father, couldn't refuse when Pasteur Schyns came to her sixth floor apartment seeking donations of clothing and ration cards to help British soldiers hiding in Brussels. He also asked her to translate BBC broadcasts into French for the underground.

Anne and her husband, Julien, knew the dangers. Their decision could make their two young children orphans, but what kind of future would it be for any Belgian children living under Nazi tyranny? They could not turn their backs on those who were fighting on their behalf.

Anne had heard of the young Belgian girl who had organized an escape line, but when she agreed to harbor English pilot Jack Hutton for Pasteur Schyns she had no idea it was for the same line. In July she was connected with *Nadine* and began enlisting others to help conceal men and move them about. There was nearly always a "guest" staying in their top floor flat at 127 Rue d'Ixelles.

As autumn drew to a close, the thought of spending another Christmas under German occupation had weighed heavily on her. She'd hidden her sadness each morning as she buttoned her little boy's coat and kissed his rosy cheeks, wishing that her children wouldn't have to suffer with few presents under the tree as she had as a child during the Great War. She shivered remembering the cold winters she had spent with no coal and little food. Now the Germans were foisting those old heartaches on a new generation.

But today brightened with hope. The news was at once terrible yet thrilling. Yesterday, the seventh of December, the Japanese attacked the American naval fleet at Pearl Harbor, and today Germany declared war on the United States. It would be many months before the Yanks could train and equip an army strong enough to take on the Wehrmacht in *Fortress Europe*, but just knowing that they were coming lifted her spirits.

The little German tailor across the street waved vigorously as Anne walked the children to school. He looked near to bursting, no doubt dying to express his joy and excitement over the attack on the United States, but he would have to wait until later. First, she had to get the children to school, and then she had an appointment to—A brief moment of panic struck her. She felt for the chain of her crucifix and relaxed when she found it there around her neck. She dared not go on a mission without it.

After leaving the children at school, Anne rode the tram up to Schaerbeek and walked an indirect route to a private home. Like any woman might, she pulled a compact mirror from her purse and powdered her nose, but used the mirror to look around. Seeing no one following, she drew in a nervous breath and rang the bell. Other helpers had been caught like this—calling on a home and finding the German Secret Police waiting inside.

"Hello," Anne said to the woman who opened the door. "My daughter's dog has gone missing."

"What color is he?"

"He is white with black spots."

As Anne stepped inside, the woman confided with a look of concern, "I am told the airman has been authenticated, but he looks like the fellow with the missing little finger to me." Anne had heard of the Belgian man who was responsible for the arrests of many Allied soldiers and their hosts.

"I will ask him a few questions just to make sure," Anne said.

"Tell me about yourself," Anne said when the English airman was brought out," where you live, what plane were you in and how many others were in the crew."

"I'm Jack Hutton from Done Avenue in Leamington-on-Tyne. There were six of us in a Vickers Wellington."

"Tell me, Jack, if I said someone was on Carey Street, what would that mean?"

"It would mean he was in debt or bankrupt."

Anne smiled, "All right, Jack. Put on your jacket. We are going to go have your picture taken. We will walk down the street like old friends. You do not speak, no matter what."

As they neared the tram stop, two German soldiers strutted out of a café toward them, one holding a newspaper. The other carried an open bottle of red wine. Both were laughing merrily. Anne made a quick decision to continue on without breaking stride, as detouring around them would look suspicious.

The fellow with the newspaper stepped in front of her and stopped. "Where are you going on such a day, Madame?"

"To the store," Anne said rather abruptly. "Shopping is still legal, is it not?"

The German burst out laughing as if she had told a great joke. His breath smelled strongly of wine. While Anne waited for leave to pass, the soldier with the wine greeted all who walked by with a cheery *bonjour*, alternately swigging the bottle. She had never seen such undisciplined behavior from the Germans. What could possess them to be so happily drunk in broad daylight, especially this early in the morning she wondered. They could be in great trouble with their superiors.

She got her answer when three more solders happened by. The one with the newspaper cried out the headlines as he excitedly waved the trio over. From what little German she knew, Anne deduced they were celebrating that they no longer had to worry about the United States because the Americans would be busy fighting the Japanese. Smiling to herself, she nudged Jack and led him around their little celebration.

Loud laughter and voices singing patriotic German songs spilled out of cafés as they passed. *Poor fools!* Anne thought. *We'll see how hard you laugh when you are retreating from the American Army.*

———

The mostly military crowd in the Gibraltar restaurant bar conversed over their pints of beer and newspaper lined baskets of fish and chips. A few enjoyed games of snooker and darts like there was no war at all. Michael Creswell, MI 9's resourceful agent in Spain, regarded the bite of meat poised on his fork. "I feel rather guilty eating a lamb chop. More than one evader has told me that after enjoying a fitting meal they learned that their host only pretended to have already eaten in order to feed them."

"Yes, well, starving ourselves will not help those chaps one bit," Donald Darling said as he dug his fork into his potato. "Jimmy Langley was elated with the delivery of those Christmas parcels. He will make good use of them." Donald Darling, *Sunday,* the MI9 chief in Gibraltar, glanced around before leaning in. "There is a captain, de la Lindi of the Belgian Air Force that I need you to get out as quickly as possible."

"I will contact Dédée."

"She will need money for his passage."

"I'll take care of it," *Monday* said. "Perhaps this will finally stifle the snide remarks from the armchair cavalry back in London."

"Nothing will convince Dansey. It's like giving a donkey strawberries. Instead of appreciating what these people have done, he sees Comet as amateurs who will likely throw a spanner in the works."

They had renamed the Postman line *Comet* due to the speed with which the men were being returned. Airmen were reaching Spain faster than if their passage had been arranged by Cook's Travel Service.

"Well, at least Dansey no longer talks about her being a German spy," Sunday said.

"What changed his mind?"

Sunday chuckled. "Brigadier Crockatt did some investigating. Turns out she was a Belgian nurse. She'd looked after British soldiers, sent Red Cross packages to our boys in German prison camps and wrote letters home for the wounded."

"I would like to have seen his face when the old boy found out he was wrong," Monday said.

"I'd wager it went down like a cup of cold sick." Sunday swished the ice around in his glass and took a satisfied gulp. "I just wish there was more we could do to help her. I wish she would allow us to send her a radio operator. Sending messages back and forth in toothpaste tubes is so bloody slow and unreliable."

"I'm afraid she will never go for it."

"She could authenticate airmen so much quicker. There would be greater protection against German infiltration of the line. Did you tell her it would be a Belgian operator—perhaps one of the fighters she just brought us or de la Lindi after we've trained him?"

"She knows the Germans can track radios. A radio didn't help with the Pat O'Leary line."

Sunday clenched his jaw. Monday had hit a nerve.

"I'd like to get my hands on that scoundrel, Cole," Sunday growled. It turned his stomach to think that an English soldier would sell out his countrymen like that. Fifty odd helpers were arrested—nearly the whole Pat O'Leary evasion network burned. "And MI6 stubbornly refuses to give me authorization to have the bastard liquidated." His words exploded like mortar rounds.

"If you ask me, they're too busy congratulating themselves on the Americans entering the war," Monday said.

Sunday flicked two fingers toward the waiter who came right over. "Two more gin and tonics, easy on the tonic." His tone grew contemplative again. "With the American and British air corps flying about the continent there will be ever more men to evacuate. Now that the O'Leary line is down, that leaves Comet to handle the bulk of the work. It's so damn frustrating that we can't help more. Did you tell her that she would still be in charge?"

"With all due respect, she doesn't need you, me, or MI6 to tell her she is in charge. She has inspired a continent. She is followed by people she has never even met. She's become a legend in the underground. She needs no rank. Quite frankly, I fear for the whole bloody business if she is ever captured."

Sunday sighed and nodded his agreement. "I've spoken with the evaders. To a man they have extolled her daring and fortitude. They can't even talk about her without tearing up. They know they owe their lives to Dédée and cannot bear to think of the tortures the Nazis will put her through when she is caught."

"Nor can I," Monday said softly.

————

Raucous laughter filled the room, most of it emanating from four revelers at the end of the bar. "Your turn, my dear," Prosper Dezitter said with a gold-toothed grin. "But remember if you steal my pot I might just make you walk home."

"Don't worry, Flore," one of Prosper's new recruits said. "There's enough money in the pot to take a taxi."

"*Ssshhh!*" Flore waived her hand in the air as she hunkered down over her coin. "*Fermez votra bouche.*"

Prosper loved the way she rolled her *r*s when she spoke French. Born in Spain, Florentina Leonarda Maria Louisa Giralt, went by Flore Dings, Dings being the name of the husband she'd left but hadn't divorced. She was thirty-seven years old, ten years younger than Prosper, a spirited woman with black shoulder-length hair and laugh lines that framed her mouth. Blood red nails and cherry red lips belied her real intelligence. Besides her penchant for good times and good sex, which Prosper relished, she was also very smart and useful to him. Her fluency in Spanish, Flemish, English and French, and her passable German were talents that came in handy in their line of work.

Flore plinked the coin, sending it sailing right over the cocktail glass. "*Fils de Salope!*" she cursed and dropped a one hundred Belgian franc note on the pile.

"Ah, too bad my love." Prosper raised a gloved hand toward the bar tender and pointed to Flore's glass to signal a refill. He pulled a wad of francs from his pocket, peeled off a bunch and tossed them on the bar. He'd spent too many years trying to make it in business. The Nazis didn't care about his driving violations, his embezzlement charges or his smuggling enterprise—what mattered was capturing enemy airmen and their underground helpers. He was becoming quite good at that.

A raucous "*Ohhhhh*" exploded from his cohorts just after the tinkling on the glass. Prosper watched the *tiddlyed* coin bounce and slide across the bar.

"Thank you for your contribution," he said to Nootens, the portly ginger-haired recruit. "Now step aside and let me show you how it is done."

Prosper stretched his fingers like a maestro limbering up to conduct an orchestra, but the damn gloves were a nuisance. He glanced over his shoulder at the other patrons and saw nothing but Germans. "*Ah* to hell with it," he said and yanked the gloves off. No one would care about his missing little finger—no Belgian would be caught within five blocks of this place. He carefully lined up his coin and pressed down. The metal disc skidded into the front of the glass with a resounding clink.

"At least I got it up in the air," Flore chortled.

"Yes, my love, you always do get it up for me."

She slapped his arm playfully. He often caught her off guard with his innuendo. She was the ideal mistress, tolerant when his eyes chose to wander and silent about his indiscretions with other women. *She is the best piece of tail in the room*, Prosper mused as he looked around. His fantasy broke when an associate crossed into his field of vision.

"Excuse me a moment," he said to his friends. "Flore, take my turns for me, will you dear. If you win, we'll split it."

He followed Abwehr chief, Rudolf Kohl, operating now as *Ralph van der Stein*, outside where the chilly January night would discourage anyone from eavesdropping. Prosper met him at the corner, away from the door.

Ralph drew a cigarette offered from Dezitter's silver case and allowed Prosper to light it for him. He turned the cigarette in his fingers as if contemplating it. "The evasion lines are more organized than we thought. They are becoming a great embarrassment to the Reich. Every little success emboldens them." He lifted his head, fierce resolve lighting his face. "They must be stopped. The Gestapo threatens to take over Abwehr if we cannot handle the matter."

"Have you learned anything from the aviators I have delivered to you?" Prosper asked.

"Some have been very useful. We have made more arrests." Ralph drew a paper from inside his jacket. "These are the names of people we are looking for. See what you can do to find them."

"Charlie ... Elvire ... Paul ..." Prosper raised an eyebrow. "No last names?"

"There is the de Jongh girl. She may be going under the alias Dumon or something like that." Ralph shrugged. "We do not know."

"What about this one? It says it is an English woman—Madame A."

"We are checking every English woman in Brussels. We will find her."

———

The authorities at the Belgian border paid little attention to the girl in the Macintosh and Wellington boots. The kerchief over her head and scarf around her neck and lower face were nothing out of the ordinary for this snowy evening. But Dédée took no chances. She had timed it so she would arrive after dark, but before curfew. She hadn't even told her family she was coming. She would slip in and out like a ghost.

Frédéric de Jongh looked like he'd indeed seen a specter when he answered the door and Dédée pulled off her kerchief and scarf. She hugged him very hard, ending with a kiss on each cheek. He could scarcely contain his delight as he brought her upstairs to surprise her mother.

"Andrée!" her mother exclaimed, smothering her daughter in a great embrace. She pulled back to have a look. "You have lost weight."

"I am healthy. I've been hiking in the mountains."

"Is everything working in the south?" her father asked.

"The British consul says we are making a great difference to the morale of the men. An Englishman, Albert B. Johnson—we call him Bee —is crossing packages while I am here, and we are opening a second route over the mountains with Elvire Morelle as the leader. But let us not talk about war. Where is Suzanne?"

"In the kitchen," her mother said. "Go surprise her."

Dédée went quietly in her stockinged feet. "I'd better keep my boots and coat in here just in case," she said.

Suzanne turned with a start. "Dédée!" She threw her arms around her younger sister. "How long can you stay?"

Dédée shrugged. "A couple of days."

A quiet snow fell outside while the girls sat in front of the fire and talked late into the night.

At lunch the next day, the whole family gathered around the table: Dédée, her maman, papa, Tante Ninie, Suzanne and her fair-haired step-sons, twelve-year-old Martin and sixteen-year-old Frederic, all laughing and teasing like the calendar had been turned back to a holiday before the war. The only thing different was that they all took turns at the front window checking the street below.

"I miss this," Dédée said.

"I miss lemon meringue pie." Martin sighed wistfully.

"I make dessert." Suzanne frowned.

"Yes, peaches and cream," Martin said, "and peaches and cream … or sometimes we have peaches and cream … Please come back soon, Aunt Dédée," he begged with theatrical pathos, "so Mother will make another pie."

Suzanne laughed and playfully shoved her son.

"Tell me, Martin," Dédée said, "do you have a girlfriend yet?"

"No!" The boy blushed.

Dédée laughed to herself as Martin jumped up.

"I'll keep watch," he said, apparently happy for an excuse to avoid further embarrassment.

"And how about you, Frederic?" Dédée asked. "A handsome fellow like you should have at least one."

"Too many to count," the sixteen-year-old said with pretend conceit.

"What are the English saying about the Americans entering the war?" her father asked.

"They are very excited. But they say it will be summer before the American army can be mobilized." She set her wine glass down. "I'm glad we got Albert Day, our first American, through. He'd been so disappointed at becoming ill and having to wait."

"Frédéric, *mon cher.*" Her mother gently patted her husband's hand. "We said we would not talk about the war."

Her father laughed. "You are right. We shall not talk—"

"Quick, the Gestapo!" Martin cried out.

"Very funny, Martin," Dédée said.

"Look for yourself if you do not believe me!"

Dédée peeked out. Two men of the *Geheime Feldpolizei*, the German secret field police, stepped out of a black sedan on the street below. Dédée dashed to the kitchen and pulled on her Wellingtons while her nephew Frederic held her Macintosh for her to slip her arms into. Suzanne scraped the food off Dédée's dish into her own and made her sister's plate disappear.

Dédée ran out the French doors in the back of the house with her open coat flapping in the wind and Frederic close behind. Suzanne closed the doors, drew a deep breath and returned to the table.

Dédée dashed down the garden path to the wall at the end of the yard, and in one quick motion, boosted by Frederic's clasped hands, sprang over the wall and ran down the street on the next block to the home of a friend. Frederic calmly smudged out all footprints in the snow on the path.

The police questioned the de Jonghs and Suzanne, Frederic, and Martin Wittek for more than an hour before they finally left.

———

February 6, 1942,

The cold hard mountain fought their every step. Elvire Morelle struggled to pull herself up the slippery trail and slid down time and again as loose gravel gave way beneath her feet. Banged and bruised on frozen rock, she gritted her teeth and trooped on. "How many times have you done this?" Elvire asked as Dédée reached a hand down to help pull her to the top of yet another nearly vertical rock face.

"I would tell you that it gets easier, but that would be a lie," Dédée said with a chuckle. "Are you sorry that you volunteered?"

"No. You cannot carry the mountain crossings on your shoulders alone. I just thought I was in better shape. But do not worry. Next time I will know what to expect."

Dédée smiled at Elvire's determination. She thought it funny that while others drew inspiration from her, she drew hers from tenacious patriots like Elvire.

Here, though, Elvire's bigger, stronger size was working against her. Then there was the weight of the backpack and the wet winter clothing. And where sure-footed Dédée hopped effortlessly from rock to rock, Elvire teetered back and forth struggling to keep her balance.

Tomás Anabitarte, the lead guide, frowned with impatience, but that was too bad. His fee was more than that of Florentino and with Dédée, Elvire Morelle and *Bee* Johnson all delivering packages, sometimes he was going to have to deal with slower groups. It wasn't all Elvire anyway. They hadn't even reached the river yet when one of the men fell back exhausted and had to be helped by the other guide. Then on the way down the slope, another twisted his ankle. That left only Paul Henry de la Lindi, the Belgian whose passage was paid for in advance by the British, walking unassisted.

Dédée first learned of him when he contacted Baron Jean Greindl and Peggy van Lier, two Comet members assisting her father in Brussels. De la Lindi, a captain in the Belgian air force, was captured in May of 1940 and released two weeks later. The Germans were keeping their eye on him, but not too well it turns out. When MI9 learned of his abilities in flying, aerial observations and radio operations, they asked Dédée to bring him out.

It wasn't until they had crossed the rickety border bridge at the Endarlaza power plant and made it through the old train tunnel at Txikito that Tomás finally began to relax. They reached the farm in Spain just after dawn, cleaned up a bit, and took a tram to San Sebastian to the apartment Bernardo Aracama, who had become a vital friend she could depend on whenever she needed him. The next morning, the men were sent by train to Bilbao and Dédée and Elvire met Florentino at a farm in the mountains for the trek back.

With her skirt and blouse tucked into her rucksack, Dédée wiggled into the straps and bounced the heavy pack into place on her back. "After the trip here I was afraid you'd want to stay in Spain," she teased as she held the pack for Elvire to slip into.

Elvire threw a sardonic look over her shoulder. "When I get back to Valenciennes, I am going to take a very long, very hot bath."

"*Vamos.*" Florentino beckoned with a grin and a wave.

Leaving the balmy breeze of San Sebastian behind, they ascended into the unpredictable climate of the mountain. A heavy, stinging mist swallowed the moon. The temperamental mountain howled and sent its cold, mighty breath to chase away the intruders. Florentino took on the challenge, lowering his head like a bull and taking long determined strides. The girls silently struggled behind him.

The angry mountain hurled snow pellets in their faces. Dédée pulled her scarf tight around her neck, squinting against the tiny stinging crystals. The ground grew slippery. Within minutes, her boots were covered. Dédée fought on, turning her face to the side, away from the blinding wind. Behind her, she could see Elvire doing the same. Ahead, Florentino's long legs propelled him forward.

"*EEEEIIIYYYAHHH!*"

Dédée turned back to the scream of anguish behind her.

The silence shattered as Elvire cradled her leg crying out in pain.

"Florentino!" Dédée called. She rushed back to Elvire. "Florentino! Elvire is hurt!"

It didn't look good. Elvire's leg was pinned under her at an unnatural angle as tears ran down her cheeks. Florentino knelt beside the two girls as Dédée switched on her torch and directed its light over the leg. "It is badly broken," she said. "She cannot put weight on it. We will have to carry her."

"No," Florentino said. He pointed to them, then to the ground, and signed for them to stay. "*Vendo ayuda.*" He tapped his chest and pointed away.

Dédée nodded. It wasn't good Spanish, but she knew what he meant. And she knew he wouldn't let them down.

He and Dédée supported Elvire who hopped to a rock outcropping that might block some of the wind. Then Florentino disappeared into the swirling gusts of white.

Dédée eased Elvire's head back to rest on the lichen growing on the rocks. "I have to find something to splint your leg."

Elvire nodded understanding, her teeth clenched against the pain.

Dédée remembered passing a pasture not far back. She found the fence and wiggled a board until it broke loose, then stepped on it to break it in two. She cut and tore strips of material from the blouse in her pack and tied the boards to immobilize Elvire's leg. As they huddled together against the bitter cold, covered with the skirt from Dédée's pack, both knew without saying that they wouldn't last long lying still in these frigid temperatures. But if anyone could find them again, Florentino could.

CHAPTER SEVEN

A fine rain fell, soaking the girls to the skin. They had no idea how far Florentino would have to go for help. It had taken several hours to hike to this point. The wind had died down, but the rain turned the snow into a heavy slush. Walking would be slow and difficult. If Florentino had to go all the way down the mountain and work his way back, he could take seven or eight hours.

As dawn crept up the mountain, formless blobs became rock faces and hills. They were dangerously close to being exposed in daylight. Dédée closed her eyes to block out her negative thoughts. Florentino would find a way. She had to believe that.

Snumpf eeyaawww

Dédée sat up pulling back her coat collar away her ear.

"What is it?" Elvire asked.

"Listen."

Yaweeeyaw

Elvire lifted her head from the rock. "What is that?"

"It sounds like a donkey," Dédée said.

A ghostly form appeared against the white backdrop. It was Florentino and he had brought a donkey!

Together, they hoisted Elvire onto the beast and Florentino led the donkey in a new direction. Florentino knew the Pyrenees like no other man. Even with the heavy wet snow covering the trails, he managed to find his way to a small hut where they could take shelter. He left and returned fifteen minutes later with ferns for Elvire to rest on until nightfall when they could resume their travel.

Elvire slept awhile and when she awoke, they lunched on cheese, bread and wine from their packs. She ate slowly, her face troubled. "I'm sorry that I have let you down. You saved my brother, and when I try to help you, you end up saving me too."

"Oh my dear friend, you have not let me down. The mountain has dealt us a harsh blow, but you will be all right. You will see."

"With all of the turmoil in Brussels, you didn't need this too," Elvire said referring to the recent arrest of a section chief. It was believed he had been uncovered by an associate of the man with the missing little finger. Elvire scowled at her leg as if it had betrayed her too.

The loss of Mr. Roberts, a group leader in Belgium, was a terrible blow. They had to assume that his entire sector was compromised. "I am sad about our friends," Dédée said. "It is always hard when we lose someone. But we must carry on. Otherwise what was their sacrifice for? It takes many months to train one pilot, gunner, or bomb aimer. Their lives are so much more valuable than our own."

After dark, they worked their way back down to Renteria. Dédée telephoned her friend, Bernardo, who drove out and picked them up. Back in his flat in San Sebastian a doctor friend operated on the two-day-old break. His skill saved Elvire's leg, but she would have to remain in San Sebastian a few weeks. Dédée kissed her cheeks. "I will see you in a fortnight when I return with more parcels."

———

Flore slipped off her gloves and Prosper assisted her out of her full-length mink coat. Handing it to the coat-check-girl, he pointed to the far end of the closet. "Hang it over there, if you please, away from the others." He peeled off a few francs and slid them over the counter, watching for a reaction in the girl's eyes. When she showed no particular interest in his missing little finger, he smiled to himself at how automatically aware he had become. No patriotic Belgian would be seen in a German filled cabaret such as this. He chuckled inwardly and smoothed his greased-back hair while his new associate assisted his lady with her coat.

Flore still cut quite a figure in her sleek, black, rayon, décolleté Elsa Schiaparelli dress with narrow lace straps and bare back. Her raven hair and bright red lips, and the gold necklace with its sparkling diamond lying between her breasts, set his loins on fire. He couldn't wait until the evening was over and they were alone.

"We'd like a table down in front," Prosper announced to the maître d. "That one."

"I am sorry, monsieur, that table is reserved."

Dezitter peeled off another two bills. "Your next best table then."

Prosper walked behind as Flore followed the maître d toward the stage, her ample caboose swinging to its own rhythm, her perfume sexually charging the air as she sashayed. He imagined her slipping out of that dress in their room at the end of the evening in gratitude for the elegant dinner and the necklace, bracelet and earrings he had bought her. As far as Prosper was concerned, whoever said you couldn't mix business with pleasure was wrong.

Before sitting down, Prosper discreetly scanned the aristocrats and German officers at the tables in the audience, imagining that they were all wondering which dignitary had the table up front.

A German colonel and his elegant date were soon seated at the number one table.

A bottle of your best champagne," Prosper announced to the waitress. "And another for the colonel and his lady, if you please."

When the girl delivered the bottle and poured the first drinks for the Germans, the colonel turned to see his benefactor.

Prosper lifted his glass. "*Lang lebe Deutschland,*" he toasted.

"*Auf Großdeutchland! Vive l'Allmagne!*" The colonel lifted his goblet in reply.

Jacques Desoubrie, his exuberant nineteen-year-old Belgian recruit, raised his glass. "*Ein Heil auf Großdeutchland! Vive Adolf!*" He glanced over to see his lady, Thérèse, lifting her glass to his toast.

Not long after the young fellow had volunteered his services to the Germans, Abwehr tasked Prosper with putting Jacques to good use. To Prosper he looked like the American outlaw Billy the Kid. Flore said his face looked like a boa constrictor with blue *tempestuoso* (stormy) eyes and short *atolondrado* (confused) hair. Prosper had liked him right off. Jacques was eager to go undercover. But there were a few things he had to learn first.

"Order whatever you would like," Prosper said to the young couple studying their menus. "We are celebrating tonight."

"Is it your anniversary?" Thérèse asked.

Prosper chuckled. "We are not married."

"I left my husband in Spain," Flore said with a shrug.

Thérèse laughed as she glanced at Jacques. "Mine is in Africa."

"Thérèse is the mother of my son." Jacques threw his arm around his mistress. "My little Jacques is a bastard just like his father," he said proudly.

The young man seemed to be trying to provoke a reaction, but Flore simply smiled at the couple.

"We are celebrating," Prosper boasted, "because my dear Flore has just made us a great deal of money."

"Oh, what do you do?" Thérèse asked.

"Um." Flore glanced to Prosper for help.

Prosper patted her hand lovingly for show, but secretly to reassure her he would handle the question. "We are exporters. She helped locate a number of missing parcels. Just in time, too. They were about to be shipped to Spain. Now they are on their way to Germany."

The ladies set off for the powder room and Prosper got down to business with Jacques. "I am sure you know that the *parcels* Flore uncovered were English soldiers. She infiltrated an escape line which helped the German Secret Police make many arrests."

"I figured that's what was cleverly being said but not said."

"A young Belgian like yourself should have no trouble infiltrating the escape lines. I do not have to tell you that it is dangerous. And it will take a strong stomach." Prosper studied Desoubrie's eyes for signs of trepidation. "It will involve handing your fellow countrymen over to the Gestapo."

"My countrymen?" Desoubrie's chest swelled as to punctuate his commitment and quell Dezitter's doubt. "They are not my countrymen. Belgium is drowning in gentry. Artists and intellectuals gorge themselves like locusts on a wheat field. Aristocracy and Jews ruin a nation. A country cannot be defended by books and poetry, lace and perfume, opera and fashion. Pheasants and peacocks do not fight for their country. They are hunted and devoured. Only brute force can assure the survival of a race. Germany does not allow itself to be pushed around. England will fall next and Germany will become the greatest nation on the face of the Earth."

"Good." With training, Desoubrie would make a great attack dog. Prosper leaned in closer. "You will be given new identity papers and a card to advise the police that you are not to be touched under any circumstances. You should buy a gun and put that swastika pin on your lapel away in a drawer so you do not get caught with it."

Jacques regarded the pin sentimentally. "I could wear it inside my coat."

"Wear it inside your mind," Prosper said. "You are of no use to the Germans dead."

Jacques nodded. "So when do I begin?"

"As soon as you can move to Paris. Visit priests in the suburbs and provinces. Let them know you want to help. They are the ones people go to for guidance when confronted with an English pilot seeking assistance. Do whatever is needed to gain their trust. Show them you are eager and able, and let them lead you to the big fish. That is how Flore did it. Because of her we are about to surprise a few of their chiefs."

The ladies returned and piano music ushered out a dozen scantily clad women kicking their way onto the stage. As Jacques turned his attention to the show, Prosper contemplated the lad's readiness. His zeal would carry him through his missions, the older man thought—as long as Jacques learned to control it.

At Gestapo headquarters in Brussels, six *Geheime Staats Polizei*—Gestapo agents—in long trench coats, pressed bullets into the chambers of their revolvers and clicked the cylinders closed. The February sun had just begun to melt away the morning frost on the three and four story homes in Shaerbeek as their three black sedans surrounded the property. Two men secured the exit to the street behind the house. Two men watched the front. And two men pounded on the door to capture the notorious leader of the Comet escape organization that had been giving them so much trouble.

CHAPTER EIGHT

BAM BAM BAM BAM BAM BAM
Suzanne stopped short.

Hot tea sloshed over the rim of her cup onto her knuckle nearly making her drop the whole lot on the floor. She peeked through the blinds at the two big black sedans lurking below like ghoulish specters in the morning mist.

Her mind went momentarily white. The day she had dreaded for so long had come.

BAM BAM BAM BAM BAM

Suzanne forced in a calming breath and persuaded her reluctant feet down the steps and opened the door.

A trench-coated German with shoulders as broad as the Austrian Alps demanded, "Where is your father, Madame?"

"He is not here," Suzanne said, trying to conceal the tremor in her voice.

He brushed her aside with a sweep of his arm and strode up the steps, followed by three cohorts. "Are you certain, Madame? It will go very badly for you if you lie to us." A flick of his hand dispatched the other agents to the left and right.

As her mind followed the thumping jackboots tramping up the stairs and throughout the house, she visualized each room trying to recall if she'd left anything incriminating lying about. Although she had prepared for this, it was hard to say convincingly what she had rehearsed—to pretend to be completely ignorant of her father and Dédée's, involvement in underground activities.

The agents returned shaking their heads. "Where is he?" The big man barked coldly.

"I—I do not know. He left a week ago. He said he had to go away on business."

"What business?" the agent snapped. "He is headmaster at a school. Is he not?"

"Yes, he is. I—I do not know his business. Sometimes he needs to buy books and supplies for the students."

"You can stop pretending, Madame. We know he is the leader of an underground organization."

"Underground organization? I do not know what you mean."

"Assistance to enemy airmen, Madame."

"I have never seen any enemy airmen."

A heavy thud made her heart jump. Her eyes followed an agent who was systematically flipping through books and discarding them on the floor. The lead officer slowly and deliberately dragged the cushions off the sofa and poked his hands between the seats and arms as he spoke. "Come now, Madame. Do you expect me to believe you had no idea about your father's activities?"

Upstairs, she heard the thump of drawers hitting the floor. The crash of silverware came from the kitchen.

The leader removed picture frames from the mantel and turned the photographs toward Suzanne. "And your sister, Andrée, Madame, where is she?"

"I have not seen her in a year or more."

"But you have talked to her on the telephone, yes?"

"My sister and I are not very close."

The German continued to stroll about, picking up objects and papers and dropping them in his wake without emotion. The questions continued for more than an hour. The big German removed the photos of Frédéric and Andrée, from the frames and tucked them into his jacket. "When you hear from your father and sister, tell them I am prepared to show mercy if they turn themselves in. But if they do not—your entire family will pay dearly." He glowered at her a prolonged moment before slamming the door.

The sedans drove away. Suzanne staggered across the room on wobbly knees and collapsed onto the couch. Then she tucked the chair cushions back into place and closed her eyes trying to reason it out.

"What happened!" her mother exclaimed seeing the books and everything strewn about the floor when she and Tante Ninnie returned from the grocery market.

"The *Geheime Feldpolizei* paid a visit," Suzanne said. "They know about papa and Dédée, but they made no mention of the Maréchals, Morelles, Nemo or any of the others." Her mind cleared as she spoke. "They must not know that I work for Comet or they would have arrested me and asked their questions at Gestapo headquarters." She continued putting books back, but suddenly stopped. "I have to get word to papa. I'm going out for a walk—"

"You cannot go out, dear," her mother said. "They will be watching you."

"I'm counting on it."

She explained her plan and hurried off, rounding corners and turning down streets as might be expected of someone trying to shake a tail. For twelve blocks she stared straight ahead and spoke to no one: Any word, any gesture could be taken as a signal and get an innocent person arrested.

Finally she made for a courtyard that would surely make a good meeting place. Despite the sting of the frigid February wind, she hunkered down on a cold bench in the park and waited. She hadn't seen a single German agent, but she knew they were there—she could feel their eyes watching her.

After more than an hour, with no one showing, she left the square and casually walked back home. Her mom was still straightening up when Suzanne returned and shivered out of her coat to warm herself by the fire. "How did it go?" Suzanne asked Tante Ninnie who was warming herself as well.

"Two men in trench coats followed you. I made sure they were gone before I slipped out." She had gone to the Maréchal's and told Elsie what had happened as Suzanne had planned. "She will get word to Nemo to tell your father to stay put in Valenciennes."

"Very good."

"Here," her mother said pouring brandy into three glasses. She handed one to Suzanne. "I think we could all use a drink."

———

Nothing terrified the civilian population more than a knock at the door by the ruthless Gestapo. Less than two weeks after the *Geheime Feldpolizei's* visit to the de Jongh home, broadsides went up in storefront windows, on poles and in government buildings offering one million Belgian francs for information leading to the capture of Frédéric de Jongh. The close call should have scared Comet into lying low for a while. Instead, Baron Jean Greindl, *Nemo*, who had taken over as chief in Belgium, had already laid out a plan to move more airmen than ever— and young Elsie Maréchal was not about to sit on the sidelines.

She brushed back her long wavy brown hair, tingling with excitement for the coming mission. Her parents, inspired by Dédée whom the Maréchals dubbed "our colonel", had been fully involved since hiding Charlie Morelle. When Suzanne told Elsie she was the kind of young girl Dédée needed as a guide and asked if she was willing to take on more dangerous responsibilities, Elsie didn't hesitate. Studious and quiet, she was taken as being meek. But Elsie was no demure damsel to faint away for fear of the Germans. She was strong and ready to fight for her country. Her parents reluctantly agreed with her decision, knowing they could not change her mind.

Today was to be her first "cold call", and she was excited to go with Nemo's assistant Peggy van Lier, code name *Michelle*, and learn how it was done. But before meeting Peggy at the Swedish Canteen, where her phony work documents said she was employed, Elsie had to pass off identity papers for Suzanne's new *packages*.

She paid no attention to the little grey-haired woman window-shopping the shoe store as she crossed the street to the grocer. With church bells calling people to Sunday mass, the market was empty except for the clerk behind the counter. Elsie paused to make sure no one else had entered, then drew an envelope from her purse and slipped it behind the crate of romaine lettuce.

Moments after Elsie walked out, the grey-haired woman entered and slipped the envelope into a shopping satchel hanging on the crook of her arm. She lingered by the produce, examining an onion looking in no hurry to make her decision. Who would suspect sweet spectacled old Eugénie—Dédée's Tante Ninnie—of being a courier in the underground?

Her errand completed, Elsie hopped on the tram and exited blocks early, She walked the rest of the way to an old run down house on Rue Ducal—the Swedish Canteen. Run by the Swedish Red Cross in Brussels, *Cantine Suedoise*, provided meals and activities for the poor and needy children of Brussels; unbeknownst to its eccentric Swedish benefactor, the Canteen also provided the perfect cover for its manager, Baron Jean Greindl *Nemo*, to hide his underground activities. Besides diverting provisions to feed evaders, Nemo's team also hid clothing for airmen among the apparel stocked for the children. And with so many visitors, who would suspect that not all of the donations were for the children?

The house was old—wood plank floors creaking under well-worn carpets, the smell of aged timbers, dark drapes, dingy plaster walls, and a shabby armchair here and there—Elsie smiled at being among the few knew who its secrets. She descended the masonry steps to a cool, earthy basement, bare except for a sink, stove, small cupboard, and a long table and chairs where the children were fed. Peggy van Lier was already bustling about.

"*Howsit* Elsie." Peggy nodded with a five-pound bag of rice in each arm. "I told *Le Kas* we'd drop these off just now." Peggy's curly bronze red hair bounced carelessly about as she stuffed the rice into two canvas grocery sacks. "Toss me one of those tins of jam and help me fill a couple o' bags with flour, hey? I want to get out of here before the children come to graze."

Once the bags were filled, Peggy slipped on her coat and flipped her hair back over the collar. "Grab a sack, hey? We'll poke our heads in and let Le Kas know we're off."

Seeing the handsome curly-haired Nemo behind his desk sorting through papers, Elsie pictured him under a large-leafed tree in the Congo issuing instructions to the workers who called him *Le Kas* the boss. The stories he and Peggy told about Africa sounded exotic to her. Jean Greindl had run his family's coffee plantation in the Congo and he and his wife and young child had been visiting friends and relatives in Brussels when the German invasion trapped them in Belgium. Peggy had grown up walking barefoot on sandy beaches and exploring vineyards in South Africa. Like Elsie, Peggy spoke French with an English accent, but garnished with flavors of South African dialect.

"Where are you off to?" Nemo asked.

"The Liège district," Peggy said. Nemo had divided the Belgian provinces into four collection centers to route the evaders to Brussels and Peggy and the other helpers had been organizing the provinces to funnel evaders through those centers.

Nemo set his coffee cup on the desk and spoke paternally. "Be careful. That close to the border you're likely to run into a good deal of Germans"

"*Kein problem, Ich hab ja diese,*" Peggy said in German. She pulled from her bag photos of herself with German officers and chuckled at Elsie's questioning look. "Our families met in Africa," she explained. She pointed to one of the officers "I stayed with this boy's family in Germany before the war. The other fellow is his *chommie.*"

Keeping pace with Peggy as she hurried along the busy streets was like chasing a kudu gazelle. Light and energetic like Dédée, she sprang from one task to another without ever slowing down. Elsie laughed when they finally boarded a train where she could plop down. "I'm glad I wore comfortable shoes."

"I'm sorry," Peggy said. "I want to make three towns by dark."

People undoubtedly took the fashionable trim-figured Peggy, with her creamy light skin, carved marble cheeks, and dazzling blue eyes, for an elegant lady or perhaps a fashion model. But Elsie saw a quiet, determined woman of amazing courage—one to emulate. She was excited to learn from her. And she was proud to join Peggy and Nadine on Nemo's team. "Don't worry about me. I'll keep up."

They took a tram south from Liège to a small town, and as soon as they exited Peggy began to size up the people on the street, deciding whom to approach. She chose a little old woman ambling along with burlap sacks nearly dragging the ground.

"May we assist you?" Peggy asked.

"Thank you."

"It is warm for March," Peggy said as she strolled beside the lady. "We are new to the area. Is there a church nearby?"

The woman pointed. "Go down this street and you will see the steeple."

"Thank you very much. Do you know the priest? Is he a nice man?"

"Oh yes. He is very nice. He baptized all of my children and grand-children." The woman stopped walking. "This is my door. Thank you."

"You are welcome," Peggy said. "Have a nice day."

Peggy and Elsie lingered on the steps of the church until the remaining worshippers had left, then approached the priest. "Hello, Father," Peggy said. "May we have a word?"

"Of course. What is it, my child?"

"In private if you please."

The priest led them back to an anteroom and closed the door.

Peggy pulled out a necklace with a tiny religious medal for him to see. "Father, we have come from the underground in Brussels. With the progress of the war, you may encounter an English flier seeking help."

The priest regarded the girls warily, perhaps wondering if this was a Gestapo trap.

"Our organization can help."

The priest said nothing.

"I am sure you have heard of the Germans' tricks. It is difficult to know whom to trust. Give me a name to use as a code. A single uncommon name that only you would know—perhaps someone from your childhood."

Still looking at them skeptically, the priest shrugged. "Xavier."

"Xavier," Peggy repeated. "Very good. Listen to the wireless. In about two weeks the BBC in London will broadcast the phrase, 'Xavier is home' so that you will know that we are working with the British." She handed him a scrap of paper. "Memorize this telephone number and code, then destroy the paper. Someone will contact you, giving the phrase 'How is Xavier?' to which you respond, 'Xavier is home.' Trust no one else."

Peggy called this a cold call and they repeated it at the next town.

When they reached the third small community, Peggy told Elsie, "Your turn."

They had no problem finding the church in the center of town, and Elsie was about to step inside when Peggy grabbed her arm. "Let's talk to someone outside first."

Elsie nodded. They walked down the cobbled street and found a man outside sawing logs while a big black mongrel dog looked on. "Good day, sir," Elsie said. "That must have been a big tree."

The man straightened and nodded. "It has been a hard winter."

She detected a Flemish accent in his French and wondered if he noticed the English in hers. The dog strolled over to have a sniff at the visitors. "We were wondering whether you knew the priest," Elsie said as she scratched the dog's head behind its ears. "We were looking to have a word with him."

The man studied the two and Elsie felt that he was reading between the lines. He thoughtfully looked from Elsie to Peggy and back again. "If that word is not a matter for German ears, I do not think you want to speak with him."

"Thank you very much," Elsie said and flashed him a V for victory with her fingers.

"How did you know?" Elsie asked Peggy when they were on their way back to the tram.

Peggy shrugged. "It was just a feeling."

CHAPTER NINE
April, 1942

B ritish Army Lieutenant Airey Neave had taken just about enough. If it wasn't for the threat of court martial and prison he would tell this young sergeant where he could stuff his bloody questions and walk out of this hotel. But he probably wouldn't make it past the sidewalk. Escaping from the bloody Germans was easier, he thought. Who the devil was MI9 anyway and what the devil did they want with him?

The inquisitor in the clean pressed uniform rolled back the page and tucked it under his pad, which meant the start of another insufferable round of questions. "So, you were with the British Expeditionary Force and wounded in the side by a machine gun bullet as the German advance pushed the B—E—F back toward Calais. You were taken to a French hospital for one day and the next evening, and although very weak managed to push your way past the nurses and escape into the night."

"That's right." They had gotten word that the Germans had entered the town and Airey had wandered through a field until he came to a train station and passed out. He had been awakened by German soldiers who took him prisoner and told him that he'd somehow managed to cross a mine field at night without incident.

The sergeant flipped back to consult a previous page. "From there you were marched with remnants of the British, French and Belgian forces through Belgium and taken to a Stalag in Spangenburg where you once again tried to escape."

"It was at the next Stalag where I first tried to escape."

"Right." The sergeant scratched out a line on his pad and entered new notes.

The musty odor of the frightfully dark solitary cell—the threats of ghastly tortures—the accusations of being a spy without any rights as a soldier came flooding back. Airey once again felt the cold sweat of fear that had awakened him many times since escaping to Switzerland.

"In May 1941, you were transferred to Colditz. Tell me about Colditz."

"It's an old fortress near Leipzig, Poland, where the Germans sent those of us who had tried to escape. It has high stone walls and only one way out—a drawbridge over a dry moat."

"And you managed to walk out."

"I didn't just bloody walk out. Another fellow and I dyed our uniforms to look German…"

The sergeant flipped the page back. "Lieutenant Luteyn."

"Yes. He and I dressed as German officers and hid in the loft of the camp dentist office for a few days. We snuck out with a work detail on the fifth of January and reached Switzerland four days later."

"It must have been a difficult four days."

"Have you ever escaped from the Nazis, Sergeant?" Airey crushed out his cigarette while glaring at the desk warrior. "Have you ever been on the run and had to hide from people who would turn you over in a heartbeat? Have you ever had to worry about the Gestapo torturing the life out of you?" He glared at the stoic sergeant who was probably just doing as he was told. "What the hell is with all the questions? Do they think I'm a bloody spy?"

"No sir."

"Then what-the devil is this all about?"

"I am afraid I am not at liberty to say, sir. That will be for you to discuss with the next fellow."

"The next fellow!"

"Yes, sir. If you will accompany me, I will take you to him."

They took the lift down to a large gaudy room with hideous brown arm chairs. A full-color photograph of the king hung prominently on the wall. London's Grand Central Hotel was like a silent film star still wearing her faded dress and beads from a bygone era. It was anything but grand. Judging from the uniformed men going in and out, Airey surmised it was being used as some sort of military headquarters.

"Ah, Airey, good to have you back." A short man with black bushy eyebrows and matching mustache, dressed in a spotless uniform with the empty left sleeve sewn neatly to his tunic, stood up.

"Jimmy? Jimmy Langley!" Airey said. "I thought you'd been taken prisoner."

"I escaped from hospital before the Germans got their hands on me," Captain Langley said. "Are you ready for a bite of lunch? There's an important fellow I'd like you to meet."

Jimmy took him to Rule's Restaurant on Maiden Lane. The place was filled with officers, but none stood out like Brigadier Norman B. Crockatt. It was immediately clear that the man in Royal Scots uniform was military through and through. He was in his mid-forties, but his intelligent face and quick and easy manner made him seem younger.

Crockatt's firm sure grip said he was no desk officer. Airey found him to be friendly and relaxed, but a no nonsense guy. He liked that.

"So tell me, Neave, have you any stories from the prisoner of war camps?"

"Well sir, there was a story going around that in one camp the boys were tunneling to get out and broke right into the commandant's wine cellar. And after drinking over a hundred bottles, they refilled them with an unmentionable liquid and corked them and put them back."

Crockatt laughed. "I have to tell that one to Winston." Then he grew serious. "You were conducted from Switzerland to Spain by the underground—the Pat O'Leary organization."

"Yes, sir."

"Then you've seen firsthand the difficulties the people working behind enemy lines face. They risk their lives, give up their own food rations to save our boys, and use their personal money for the cause."

"Yes, sir." He could certainly attest to that.

"How would you like to help them? They need money and communications which we can provide. Our business is helping our boys escape and evade the enemy. We work with the various organizations like the one that smuggled you to Spain. We'd like you to join us."

Airey would never forget his gracious host Louis Nouveau and all the people in the O'Leary organization who risked their lives to hide him, feed him and smuggle him through France to get him back safely to England.

"You'd be training agents and looking after communications with the underground in Europe," Crockatt said. "You'd also teach airmen how to conduct themselves if shot down behind enemy lines. It won't be easy. Our resources are quite limited. You'll be working with Langley in room 900."

"I dare say it is not much more than a closet," Langley put in, "but we'll make the most of it."

"So what do you say?" Crockatt asked.

All thoughts of the dreary hotel and his longing to go home melted away. "Yes, sir, I would like very much to help them."

"Splendid!" Crockatt stuck out his hand for a shake. "Go home for a week and report back. I don't have to tell you that what we do is very secret, so you must watch what you say outside of the office. I believe Captain Langley already has something in mind for you to work on."

Jimmy nodded. "I need you to begin building an escape line in Belgium and the Netherlands in case something happens to Dédée."

"Who's Dédée?" Airey asked.

"She's a Belgian girl – twenty-six years old – quite remarkable, but damned frustrating."

"Frustrating?"

"Stubborn might be a better word," Jimmy said with a shrug. "When you talk with returned airmen you'll learn about a courageous young woman they admire and adore. She has organized an astonishing evasion network that covers over seven hundred miles and runs through four countries. They have had problems with Germans infiltrating the line, but she won't let me send her a radio operator to verify airmen quicker, and that frustrates the devil out me."

Spring brought more than just warmer weather. News of the Americans landing in England had everyone buzzing about an Allied offensive. People were more willing to help downed airmen, but the prospect of invasion also meant the Germans increased the number of agents working to eliminate the underground and resistance threat. Anne Brusselmans, Nemo and other chiefs warned their guides and hosts to be ever vigilant.

In March, news of more arrests shook Nadine. One of the victims was Gerard Waucquez, the Belgian explosives operative Dédée had guided to Spain last fall. He had been trained in England and parachuted back into Belgium with radio operators and a British plan to organize another escape line. Then in early May, Charlie Morelle, the lovable stalwart French soldier who had been Dédée's rock since she first began to organize evasions, was arrested as was Henri Michelli who had been a chief in Brussels.

Nadine refused to let that stop her. She accepted the inevitable: one day she would be caught and share the fate of her comrades. It was the price she was ready to pay to save her country. But the arrests made her realize there might be little time to spend with loved ones before her own turn came. So, today she would not be a *passeur* for the Comet underground escape line. Just for one day she would simply be nineteen-year-old Andrée roaming about with her twenty-one-year-old sister, Michou.

But the war had already changed her. Strolling through the crowd on Avenue Louise with Michou, Andrée automatically scanned for men in trench coats and anyone suspicious. She was no longer the naïve school girl she had been.

"*Ooooh*," Michou said drawing closer to a shop window, to admire a pair of Gitane sandals. "Those wooden sabots they were making last year were horrible. You didn't even have to look down. All you had to do was listen to the annoying clicking to know if a woman was wearing them. Let's go inside."

Andrée's eyes widened as she turned the tag over and saw the price. "*Mon Dieu!* They cost the eyes from the head! This is not the shopping district for us."

Michou shrugged. "We might as well look at expensive shoes we are not going to buy as cheap shoes we are not going to buy. Look! Are those handbags real leather?"

Andrée turned over a smart tan bag with silver clasp and trimmings. "They *are* real. I didn't think anyone could get leather anymore. She checked the tag. "But who could afford such things?"

"German officers," Michou said sarcastically. "Or their mistresses," she added with a suggestive flick of an eyebrow.

The bell over the door *ting-a-linged* and a hunched-over, cane-toting pruney-faced old woman, dressed in fine cashmere sweater and gold necklace, tottered past the girls to a rack with even pricier handbags.

"What do you think?" Michou whispered. "Mistress or German officer?"

The girls giggled their way to the next shop where Michou tried on an elegant yellow Caroline Rebeaux hat with a wide rolling flared brim and three feather plumes. The big hat made petite Michou look like a little girl playing dress-up in her mommy's clothing. She turned this way and that in the mirror with fake haughtiness that quickly broke into a cross-eyed, tongue-to-the-side grin.

Andrée had nearly forgotten how good it felt to be silly. She posed in an orange American flapper style hat that seemed left over from the 1920's. The brim ended in crossed tails pinned together with a pewter rose. She turned coquettishly and opened her mouth to crack a comment, but caught herself before blurting out that the German secret police would have no problem following her in a hat like this.

A nearby shop displaying wireless sets, phonographs, and small appliances had a camera exhibit with signed photographs of film stars, a couple of which were American. They could see more photographs inside, but when they entered they were assaulted by a German melody. Andrée grabbed Michou's arm. "I am not shopping in here."

The proprietor stepped in front of them as they turned to leave. "Good day, ladies," he said cheerfully. "Have you seen one of these?" He motioned toward a cabinet with a small green screen. "It is called a television."

"Yes," Michou said. "I have seen one before."

"I can turn it on if you would like—but there are only German programs."

"No thank you," Andrée said curtly. "We are leaving."

The shop owner leaned in toward them. "The music out here is for the Germans. Come. I have some music that you will like." He pulled a cardboard box from behind the counter, opened the lid and lifted each

Bakelite record while reading the labels: "Harry James, Artie Shaw, Glenn Miller, Duke Ellington …all the latest."

It felt naughty leafing through forbidden records like this. Who could have imagined that simply selling records would make you an outlaw? The shop owner was taking a great risk showing American records to strangers, but their interest in movie star photos must have made it clear they were not German sympathizers.

"I would play them for you but …"

"No no." Michou waved her hand. "We do not want you to get into trouble."

"I cannot carry them around today anyway," Andrée said thinking about tonight's mission. "Perhaps another time."

They paused along the way to watch four elderly men playing bowls, but now Andrée's secret life had seeped into her mind. She wondered if Michou thought her younger sister was still immature, dressing in teenage clothing. What would Michou think if she knew she was helping Allied airmen? Andrée sighed to herself wishing she could tell Michou the truth, but it wouldn't do to worry her; the Germans were one thing her older sister couldn't protect her from.

Andrée wished she could spend more time here, but the late afternoon sun reminded her of her other commitment. The wonderful day with Michou ended much too quickly, and Andrée was once again the Comet guide *Nadine*. There was a package she had to deliver to the train station for Elvire Morelle to conduct down to Paris. She hurried back to the Canteen. Peggy was already there.

"I am sorry you had to cut your day short, Nadine," Nemo said, "but there was an arrest of a British agent and Elvire was held in Paris."

Nadine's eyes widened with concern. "Was she arrested?"

"No no. I mean as a precaution they did not send her. We need someone else to conduct him to Paris tomorrow."

"No problem," Nadine said. "I will do it."

"Good. Peggy, you will conduct Flight Sergeant Larry Carr to the Gare du Nord at seven. Nadine, you can take him from there. Good luck."

. . .

For a quiet, organized student like Nadine, these last minute substitutions were unnerving. But there was no time for planning, and there was no use dwelling on her fears. Nadine rendezvoused with Peggy and the RAF pilot just before seven. She slipped Larry a ticket to Paris while hers was for Saint-Quentin so it would not appear that they were traveling together. She carried her usual cover—designs and sketches from a hat maker in Paris for the Queen's milliner in Brussels. Despite the danger, or perhaps because of it, she felt a greater rush of excitement than if she were being chased by bulls in Pamplona. She was living by her wits in the face of danger—brazenly sneaking past the German and French police with a fugitive airman in tow and striking a blow against the *Boches* and their insufferable restrictions.

After three hours of heightened senses and nerves wound like a spring, they arrived at the Gare du Nord in Paris where *Paul* and Elvire Morelle were waiting on the platform. Paul conducted Sergeant Carr away while Elvire greeted Nadine and led her to the fourth floor at 10 rue Oudinot.

Dédée welcomed her friend with a warm hug and delighted smile. "Thank you so much for filling in like this."

"No problem," Nadine said, though still a bit unsettled from the stress of the run.

"The next time you come to Paris, plan on a couple of days," Dédée said. "I'll take you south to Anglet so you can learn the way. We'll surprise Tante Go at Villa Voisin. Bobonne will be delighted."

Her anxiety slipped away as she thought about spending a day or two at the seashore. "I can't wait."

"Is there any word on my brother?" Elvire asked hopefully as she poured out glasses of wine.

Nadine shook her head wishing she had better news for her friend. "Nemo thought he might be able to bribe the guards, but they are too afraid of the Germans."

Dédée sighed. "Poor Charlie."

She set out sandwiches and bowls of soup and they ate in quiet contemplation for a while. Then Dédée's thoughts spilled out with renewed determination. "We have to employ more mountain guides.

We need to move more men out from the north. The longer they stay in one place, the greater the risk. The children become bored and restless. That makes them do stupid things like sneaking out of the house. It is dangerous for everybody." Dédée sat forward and pounded her fist on the table. "We are going to move more men back to England to fight than Hitler's stinking police can count. Are you ready in the north?"

"We are ready," Nadine assured her. "Suzanne has taken over as contact. Nemo has divided Brussels into sectors to route the men through key cities. Elsie and Peggy have been organizing the provinces. We are ready."

"Good." Dédée drew in a deep breath and let it out with fierce resolve. She reached across the table and covered Nadine's hand with one hand and Elvire's with the other. "I am going to tell you what I told my father. The line must go on. No matter what happens to me, you must go on."

Nadine opened her mouth to say that she didn't like that kind of talk, but Dédée continued before Nadine's words came out.

"We are making a difference. My English contacts say that men take to the air now comforted by the fact that if they are shot down there is a good chance they will be rescued." She looked from Nadine to Elvire. "Our job is too important. We cannot let Charlie's sacrifice be in vain. The more trained airman we can send back the sooner our countries will be free."

Nadine left with the disturbing feeling that Dédée was prophesying her own capture. Although she had pledged to continue, Nadine couldn't imagine how the line could survive without Dédée.

———

rrrrrRRRRRRRRRRRrrrrr Sirens wailed.

Without a word, Anne Brusselmans handed two candles to ten-year-old Yvonne and a torch to Jacques, just seven-years-old. They knew the routine.

"Isn't Daddy coming?" Jacques asked.

"Yes, of course, dear," Anne assured him as they followed her to the balcony where their father, Julien, was leaning over the wall.

"Look at them," Julien groused.

Anne, the children and their two Polish pilot house guests joined him at the railing and peered down at the street four stories below. Four German soldiers mocked the frightened people who were scurrying for the shelters, arms full of blankets and pillows.

Bombs rumbled in the distance. The building shook. Dust and bits of debris showered down from the roof above. "We had better get to the basement," Anne said.

Julien nodded. But before he left, he scooped up a handful of the pebbles and rained them down on the soldiers. The soldiers covered their heads and made a mad dash for the protection of the shelter. Anne and the pilots laughed all the way to the basement.

In the flickering light of the candles, the children played cards with pilots John and Edward while Anne recorded the amusing story of the German soldiers in her diary. She had told the children that the visitors were Flemish cousins and since they did not speak French and the children did not speak Flemish they would have to converse in English. As she watched Yvonne playing her cards to gain advantage over the Poles, she wondered whether her daughter still believed that all of the men who stayed with them were really Flemish cousins. The little girl had accompanied Anne when she took John and Edward to the Bon Marché for their identity card photos. But Yvonne seemed to understand that seven-year-old Jacques might innocently let the wrong word slip in school, so she played along with what her parents told her, perhaps knowing what they were really up to.

When the all clear sounded, they returned to the apartment. Anne set right to work broiling steaks and frying potatoes before the gas was shut off for the night. Although Julien worked for the gas company three floors below, they still had to contend with the rationing. Most nights all they had to eat was bread Anne had baked and stew made with vegetables that Julien brought back from working at a farm in the Ardennes on his days off. But their two guests were leaving for Paris with Nadine in the morning and Anne wanted to give them a good meal before they began their journey to Spain. Thanks to the Baroness, a friend who had money to buy goods on the black market, she had meat to feed them.

During dinner, Anne buttered her slice of bread and chuckled, "I wonder if those German soldiers came out of the shelter yet."

"Yes," Waczan 'John' Czekalski, said in his thick Polish accent, "I think maybe they come out to get clean underwear."

Julien laughed. "Those brave men are here to protect us from you fellows."

Anne added, "The little German tailor across the street boasts how Father Hitler saved Germany and is now going to save us."

"He should have been on the farm with me last week when a formation of bombers flew over," Julien said. "What a sight that was, planes as far as I could see heading for Germany."

"Americans," Edward said knowingly. "They raid in day. We bomb when it is the night."

"When the Germans first roared in with their mighty tanks and machines, I thought nothing in the world could stop them," Julien said. "After seeing that display of planes, I know we will win this war."

As they carried their wine glasses into the living room, he recounted an amusing tale he'd heard from one of the farmers. A British plane had crashed in the region, and though the crew got out, the pilot had suffered a broken foot. So the crew carried him to a local farm. They gave the farmer's wife their watches and all the money from their escape kits and asked her to look after him. She took the money, but reported him to the mayor who was a German supporter. He alerted the Germans who came and took the pilot away. Julien's solemn face softened and he began to chuckle. "Well, it seems that the crew learned of this from the Résistance and two of the men borrowed bicycles and gasoline and pedaled back. When the farmer and his wife went to work in the field, they set the farm on fire."

"Well," Anne said, "I guess she got what she deserved."

The Poles turned to each other and burst out laughing.

"You fellows seemed to enjoy that story very much," Anne said.

John laughed even harder. "It is because we are the two who set the fire!"

———

The cool juice of ripe muskmelon sweetened Nadine's morning as she sat at the kitchen table in her grey flowered summer pajamas and fuzzy slippers; then the newspaper headlines soured her day. It annoyed her that the Germans would think the Belgian people were so stupid as to believe their claim of another air victory. Everyone still laughed about the night the sky had filled with British bombers and German civilians poured out of Cologne seeking refuge in Belgium. The next morning, Nazi newspapers reported that German cannons destroyed the bombers with minimal damage to the city and the only casualties were two cows dead in a field.

Nadine's mother, Marie, rushed through the kitchen in her nurse's uniform, scooping ersatz coffee into the strainer basket. She set the pot on the stove to percolate and went off to do her hair.

Nadine pushed away the newspaper as her doctor father, Eugene, sat down to put on his shoes. "I simply cannot read any more trash about the Germans repelling British raids." She stabbed a chunk of pear with her fork. "It is July. When will the Allies begin their offensive?"

"Some say it will not be until next spring," her father said with a heave of his chest.

"Next spring!" The thought was just too depressing. "That means another hungry winter."

Her father nodded sadly. Farms were producing very little in order to starve German troops. Fruit and vegetables were in season, but people were canning everything they could get. He stirred his coffee and glanced back over his shoulder to make sure his wife was not within hearing range before speaking conspiratorially to Nadine. "What are you doing today? I have been contacted by the Felix Line. They have an English airman, Bill Norfolk, they need us to take. He has been authenticated. Madame A can take him this afternoon if we deliver him."

Nadine sighed. "I'm sorry. It's not possible for me. I'm conducting three parcels south today."

"I can do it."

Nadine's mouth dropped open. The doctor's eyes widened in surprise. Neither of them had heard her mother coming.

Marie, crossed the room and pulled an aromatic pan of cinnamon rolls from the oven. "I will collect him as soon as my shift is over."

Eugene regarded her with one raised eyebrow. "Are you sure you want to get involved in this business?"

Nadine did not know what to say. The secret she and her father shared was clearly not so secret, but her mother was too kind and innocent to get mixed up in this. The closest she had ever come to underground work was when she brought home a cartoon of Hitler and had Nadine go around on her bicycle stuffing copies into mail boxes. Her younger sister would be lost if anything happened to their mother.

"I will be there around half past four," Marie said with finality.

Nadine opened her mouth to debate, but thought better of it when her grandfather entered the kitchen with little Francine. He, at least, might still be unaware.

Shortly after Nadine bought four tickets to Louvain at the Brussels station, Georges d'Oultremont, a dashing dark-haired twenty-six year-old former Belgian officer candidate, arrived with three British airmen, John Watson, Bernard Evens, and Joe Pack. At Louvain, Nadine bought three tickets for Saint-Quentin and one for Quiévrain so she could deny they were traveling together. She would upgrade them to Paris en route.

As sometimes happened at the border, a customs official entered their train car. Nadine stole a glance at the airmen hoping they had been taught to recognize key words that an official might use to ask to see their papers. But it was too late to think about that now. All she could do was to act as if this was a routine, a boring papers check, and pray that the children did not betray them all with some nervous gesture.

The official gazed down at the identity papers, then over them at the airman, Watson.

"Vous êtes un travailleur agricole," the official said. *N'y a-t-il pas en Belgique où vous pouvez de travailler?"*

The July day became suddenly hotter. The hairs on the back of Nadine's neck stood up.

"*Monsieur. Vous êtes un travailleur agricole. N'est ce pas?* Watson stared uncomprehending and unresponsive, his forehead glistening.

"*Ils sont sourds et muets.*" Nadine shrugged like it was simply an observation. She held out her papers to the official, though every nerve in her body was popping like soda bubbles. An astute officer might try a trick to test his hearing and speech, like shouting behind the man to see if he jumped. Then they would be exposed.

The official regarded her without expression.

Her mouth was so dry she couldn't swallow.

He grunted, handed back the papers and moved on.

She drew in a deep slow breath and willed her jittery arms to be still.

They reached the Gare du Nord in Paris at half-past nine in the evening. Nadine hurried them along to the Hotel Luxembourg where Paul kept a room for travelers, and slipped out to buy food before curfew. At ten the next morning, Dédée and Paul arrived to take the men away.

Completing a mission always gave Nadine a sense of pride that she had struck one more blow against the enemy, but the incident on the train reminded her how lucky she had been. One day, she knew her luck would run out.

CHAPTER TEN

Nemo approached the door cautiously, scanning up and down the street for black sedans or anyone lurking about. There were no signs of a Gestapo trap, but the mystery of it all bothered him. He was the Brussels chief, the one who usually set these meetings up. Being summoned by Suzanne to this unknown house was unsettling. Certainly, he trusted Suzanne, but who knew if the Germans had gotten to her? There was no limit to the tortures the Gestapo could inflict, the loved ones they would threaten to make people do their bidding. He raised his hand to knock, but hesitated, stealing one more glance up and down the street. Finally drawing a tenuous breath, he let his knuckles go. His pulse raced. He half-expected to hear the clack of jackboots.

The door opened.

"Hello, Jean," a grinning Suzanne said.

"What's this all about?" he asked.

"Wait. I have a surprise for you."

He stepped in to find a captivating, dark-haired young woman standing by the window. She wasn't tall or imposing, yet he was awed by the strength he saw in her compelling blue eyes. With a warm engaging smile, she extended a hand. "Baron Greindl, it is so nice to finally meet you."

"Dédée!" he deduced aloud.

"Yes, that's right. My father speaks highly of you. You have done an admirable job organizing Belgium. We are now moving more men than ever. Thank you."

"That is certainly a high compliment coming from the brilliant person who conceived the whole thing—the girl whose cunning and daring have inspired a nation."

Dédée snuffled at his words of admiration. "I think, Baron, you are confusing me with Joan of Arc. Come sit down. Suzanne has made a fresh pot of coffee."

"Please call me Jean or Nemo. How is your father?"

"He is well."

"I learned a lot working with him. He is very proud of you and Suzanne. He refers to you as the Little Cyclone."

Dédée laughed. "Yes, I know."

Suzanne smiled with sisterly pride as she poured the coffee. "Even as a little girl, she could not sit still."

Dédée conceded with a shrug. "So tell me, Jean, what are we doing to free Charlie Morelle? He is a dear friend and has done much to help us. I hate to imagine the tortures the Germans are putting him through."

Nemo set his cup down. "We thought we had two Belgian guards we could bribe," he said with apology in his voice, "but they backed out. They are afraid of the Germans." Nemo tipped his head. "But there might be another way—a lawyer known as 'Y' says he may be able to help us. He knows a German officer who has influence with the Gestapo. It will cost three thousand francs."

"Three thousand!"

"I have friends who will give us the money," Nemo said.

"How do we know this German officer can be trusted?"

"We cannot be totally sure, but Y is a cautious man and believes the officer is safe. We have to be patient."

"While we are being patient, Charlie is being tortured."

Nemo drew in an exasperated breath. "Reorganizing the north was not my doing alone. Suzanne has been a tremendous help. We have divided Belgium into sectors with the evaders being moved to central collection points and from there to Brussels."

"So, you've really thrown in with us?" Dédée asked. "You realize of course that there are nine chances out of ten that you won't come out of this alive."

Nemo's firm handshake confirmed his decision. This fight was now his as much as it was hers.

———

Dédée opened her eyes to a foggy dawn spilling in through the train window. Elvire Morelle and the men awoke one by one, the last one sitting up as the conductor's voice trailed down the hall outside their cabin calling, "Bordeaux."

Two hours later they reached Bayonne where Dédée introduced two new helpers to the four *children*. "These are my friends *Tante Go* and *Bee*."

"I am Marion Zawodny," the Polish pilot said in his thick accent.

"Bunny Evans here," a British fellow said shaking Tante Go's hand.

"Bunny?" *Bee* Johnson asked.

"*Oui*, Bunny, "*comme un petit lapin.*" Joe Angers spoke with a strong French-Canadian accent.

"Yes," Bee said. "I know what a bunny is."

"You're English!" the fourth airman exclaimed.

Dédée pressed a finger to her lips. "*Ssshhh!*"

"Sorry," the airman said softly. "I'm John—John Watson. Joe and I are from Canada, but I don't speak French."

"Yeah, well," Joe said, "according to the people around here, I don't speak it either."

"Aw, do not feel bad," Elvire teased him, "Bee's accent is worse than yours."

"*Merci beaucoup*," Bee said with pretend hurt as if he didn't already know that besides his limey accent, his tall lanky English frame couldn't be disguised with a French beret.

The station at Saint-Jean-de-Luz was full of Germans unloading supplies so Dédée instructed them to pair up. "When you get through customs, cross the street and take the road to the right until you come to Rue Salagoïty. Go to number seven."

With so much German activity at the station the officials checked the crowds through more quickly than usual, paying little attention to the Comet helpers and their charges. Dédée and the boys stayed two nights at the apartment of safe house keeper Ambrosio San Vicente, and on Sunday, July 19, guides Manuel Iturrioz, Tomás Anabitarte and Donato Errazti arrived to help conduct the men down to the mountains. Dédée sent Donato, the farmhand who worked for Frantxia's neighbor, ahead to scout for German patrols.

The air was damp and heavy. By the time they reached Bidegain Berri, Frantxia's farm, two hours later, the sky had grown ominously dark.

The fact that Frantxia's young children didn't speak English, didn't stop the two littlest ones from making fast friends with the airmen who bounced them on their knees and had them guessing which hand the coin was in. Maiye, the oldest child, helped her mother set the table and serve up soup and warm milk.

At half-past-nine, Dédée, Manuel, Tomás, and the four airmen trudged through the fields in a steady rain that blotted out the moon and stars. From Dédée's position at the end of the line, most of the men were little more than dark blurs through the water dripping from the brim of her fisherman's hat, but it was her job to keep them from falling behind and getting lost. The beginning stretches were among the most dangerous because it was still early enough for people to be awake.

As they neared the first hamlet around ten, Dédée reminded the *children* to walk quietly. The lights were out and the rain made the buildings all but disappear in the darkness.

"A*rrêtez!*"

Two grey figures sprang from the blackness.

"Run!" Dédée yelled. "German police!"

"Ne bougez pas! Je vais tirer!"

Evans dove behind a bush.

Angers followed Dédée toward the woods.

A shot rang out. Dédée glanced backward and saw a figure fall to the ground as she and Angers reached the trees, but she couldn't see who it was. She crossed her forearms in front of her as she ran, shielding her face from branches unseen in the darkness. After a bit, she stopped and crouched on the ground. Angers, breathing hard, caught up and ducked down beside her.

They stayed motionless, listening.

"*Comrade. Comrade,*" someone was pleading in the street.

It sounded like Watson's voice, but there was so much shouting by the German police she couldn't make out what anyone was saying, only that the German's tone was commanding and threatening. The voices hadn't moved from the spot—the police were apparently busy with whomever they had captured. But no one seemed to be coming after her and Angers. She tapped the airman's arm and the two picked their way quietly through the woods, uncertain which way to go in the darkness except away from the voices.

The storm intensified, the rain as heavy as if she was being doused by buckets. All she could hear now was the sound of wind and rain. Disoriented by the darkness, she tried to travel in a straight line, stumbling over logs and rocks and getting slapped by branches. Eventually, they came out in a field. They followed the woods line until they reached the road.

They hadn't gotten very far when they heard a soft whistle. A figure emerged from a ditch alongside the road. The shape of work clothes instead of a uniform told them it must be one of their own.

As the figure rose to full height and drew near, she recognized the Polish airman.

"Hiya, Marion," Angers said softly. "Anyone else with you?"

"Just me."

"Did you see what happened to the others?" Dédée asked.

"I only see guides run away."

"Did you see who was shot?" Angers asked.

"I think they catch Watson, but I don't think they shoot him. Maybe Evans?"

"No," Angers said. "I saw Evans dive into the bushes."

Frantxia was shocked when she was awakened around midnight by the dripping trio knocking on her door. She brought them towels, wrung out their wet clothes in the sink and gave them dry things to put on. Angers assured Frantxia that without Dédée he would never have found his way back, so there was little fear that Watson could lead the Germans to her home.

While Dédée and the two airmen slept, Frantxia contacted Tante Go who bicycled to the Hotel Euskalduna in Saint-Jean-de-Luz. There, she found the guide, Manuel, and arranged another try.

The next evening, Manuel and Tomás brought a surprise—Bunny Evans.

"I hid behind a bush and got away when it started to pour," Bunny explained. "Yesterday, I walked through Urrugne and Hendaye. The Germans were everywhere, but they didn't pay any attention to me. I sought sanctuary in a church. The pastor gave me ten francs and told to take the tram to the Hotel Euskalduna where I found Manuel."

"Did you see what happened to Watson?" Angers asked. "Was he shot?"

"He wasn't shot, but the Germans took him prisoner."

That night, Dédée and the mountain guides completed their trip into Spain and the following night, the exhausted girl crossed back and hiked to Villa Voisin in Anglet.

"I need a bath and a long sleep," Dédée told Tante Go as she dragged herself to a kitchen chair. She slipped off a shoe and rubbed her aching foot. "Have you heard any news on Watson?"

Tante handed Dédée a cup of coffee, knelt down and pulled off her other shoe. "They weren't Germans, they were French Gendarmes. When they learned he was an escaping English airman they sent him on a safe route across the river. Only, he must have taken the wrong path because he was captured by the Spanish Guardia and thrown into Miranda prison camp." Tante set the shoes by the door. She turned back with a sorrowful expression. "But I am afraid I have more bad news."

"What is it, Tante?"

"Your sister Suzanne was arrested two days ago."

CHAPTER ELEVEN

Airey Neave stepped inside the tiny office and chuckled. A ribbon of daylight peeked around the edge of two filing cabinets pushed against the lone window. It was barely wide enough for him to lie down on the floor. A second table had been butted up against Jimmy Langley's to serve as Airey's "desk", he and Jimmy would have to be careful lest they inadvertently play footsy beneath. He'd been told the office was small, but stuffing this brain trust—the entire escape and evasion arm of British military intelligence—into a closet, struck him as tragically amusing. Or perhaps it reflected the little importance MI6 placed on the escape organizations. But Airey wasn't about to let that dissuade him from doing all he could to help them. Men who had never been separated from their regiments or squadrons couldn't understand what it was like to be alone in enemy territory, not knowing whom to trust or even what people were saying. Those desk commanders sitting well behind the lines could scarcely imagine what terror the Gestapo was capable of inflicting on captured airmen and their helpers. Airey vividly remembered the cold dark cell, the wail of men being tortured, and the total disregard of Geneva Convention rules. He had been told that his military discs meant nothing, that being in civilian clothes made him a spy.

Crockatt had given him a free hand at expanding the training sessions teaching not only about escape, but evasion as well. It had been drummed into every man in the armed forces that if taken prisoner they should only give their name, rank and serial number. It was Airey's job to change that thinking.

If he was to give them a chance to survive behind enemy lines, they would have to be taught what to do. He wrote quickly, jotting down his thoughts as smoke ribbons spiraled upward from the cigarette dangling out the side of his mouth: try and stash your parachute immediately and get as far away from the scene as possible; the first twenty-four hours is the most intense search period; hide if possible—look for a hay stack, the loft of a barn, a ditch; A lone farmer might be approached, but if he isn't willing to help, leave immediately without question; a church and a local priest is a good place to seek refuge; if aided by a civilian, do what they say and trust that they will hide you well so as not to put their family in jeopardy; do not seek out the underground as that would arouse distrust —the underground will make contact when they are ready. When questioned by the underground, you must answer truthfully. Underground members are putting their lives on the line. They have to be sure they are not dealing with a German agent who might be using a dead airman's information to infiltrate the line.

Jimmy shuffled in flinging his uniform cap on his desk like it had annoyed him. "I've just gotten intel that Goering has increased the number of field agents and stepped up efforts to crush all escape lines. It seems the Germans have taken a keen interest in the evasion efforts even if our own people think them little more than a trifle."

Airey twisted his cigarette out in the ash tray. "I'll pass it along, but I dare say from my interviews with the returned men that the underground is well aware the Germans are coming at them hard."

"Edith Cavell, Edith Cavell" Jimmy mumbled shaking his head. "You can't have a bloody conversation with Uncle Claude without him bringing up Edith Cavell."

Airey understood Jimmy's anger. Colonel Sir Claude Dansey never passed up an opportunity to grumble about the English nurse executed for helping Allied soldiers escape in WWI, insisting that she blurred the line between intelligence gathering and aiding soldiers. Despite the successes of the lines, the colonel still worried that the Germans would slip one of their agents into England posing as a downed Allied pilot or that the escape organizations would interfere with his intelligence operatives.

"Edith is still saving Allied soldiers," Airey said, "even after all these years. She's inspired so many of the young Belgians. The escape lines have returned nearly seventy airmen—thirty-three from Comet alone. That's an entire squadron of bomber crews."

"Yes, well Dansey has admitted that the numbers are commendable, but we must take care not to tell him more than he needs to know lest we find our operation swirling toward an open drain." Jimmy lit a cigarette as to calm his exasperation. "I'm already dreading his reaction when Brigadier Crockatt tells him about the Pat O'Leary line."

Because of a British traitor and his consorts, the line operating out of Marseille was now known to the Gestapo and wouldn't survive much longer. "I've sent word to Dédée about the infiltration of O'Leary and told her to be on her toes. Comet has grown so large she can no longer recruit everyone herself, and that makes infiltration easier."

A tap on the open door interrupted their discussion. The secretary handed Langley a telegram and left.

It was from Sunday in Gibraltar. "It is believed that what led to Suzanne's arrest was that the Gestapo connected her to the lawyer Y."

Airey stroked his chin. "Maybe Y was really a German plant."

"No," Jimmy said. "The Gestapo is sending us a message—they will not bargain. And anyone attempting to will be arrested."

———

Saturday, August 7, 1942

Nadine and her father met Bill Orndorff in a café in Brussels where he had been delivered from Namur Province. An American from New York City, Bill had joined the Canadian Air Force to fight with England before the U.S. entered the war.

"*Parlez-vous français?*" she asked hopefully.

Bill shook his head.

"Okay. You come *wiss* me," Nadine said in her marginal English. "You may call me Nadine or Dédé,"

She led him by tram to the apartment where Madame Anne was already hosting Australian Ron Pearce. Since neither of the men spoke French, Anne translated for Nadine and did most of the talking. "You're the second fellow named Bill we've had in a fortnight. Do you know RAF pilot Bill Norfolk?"

"No, I'm afraid not."

"Hopefully, he has made it into Spain. Do you have your escape kit?" She removed his Belgian francs and handed them to Nadine. "Nadine will exchange these for French francs and buy train tickets. When she returns you will follow her and do as she says without question. God willing, you will both be in Paris in time for dinner."

The afternoon trip to the Gare du Nord in Paris, the tram ride to the sixth arrondissement and the walk to the Hotel Luxembourg went as planned. Then the trouble began. The clerk behind the desk told her there was no room reserved under the name *Paul*. "What about *Kiki*?" Nadine asked.

The clerk shook his head.

"Dédée?"

Another no.

Seeing her furrowed brow when she came out of the hotel, Bill whispered, "What's wrong, Nadine?"

"Come *wiss* me." She wouldn't worry these men who had put their trust in her, but her gut told her that something was terribly wrong. She led them to a bench in the Luxembourg Gardens and told them to wait." Then she called Paul's number from a phone booth. Elvire Morelle answered. After Nadine explained what had happened, Elvire told her someone would meet her there in half an hour.

Goofs like this were unnerving. She couldn't sit in the hotel lobby with these foreign-looking men, but she couldn't leave them on the bench. She approached near enough for them to see her summon them with a wag of her finger and strolled several blocks before making her way back. She was relieved to see Paul standing outside as she neared the hotel.

"I'm sorry for the mix-up, Nadine. We have stopped using this hotel."

"Does Nemo know that?" she asked.

"No. It is my fault. I should have sent word. I am sorry."

The men were understandably wary when she brought them back to the new room, even as Paul extended a hand in greeting, "Welcome to Paris. I am called *Kiki*."

Bill regarded Kiki warily and glanced over to Ron.

Ron, the Aussie, responded with a raised eyebrow. "How do we know you blokes are for real?"

"Yeah," Bill added. "How do we know you ain't a German agent?"

Paul pondered the question. "Do you know John MacLean? He is RCAF like yourself."

"Yeah. I know John. He went down two months ago in the Netherlands."

"Yes," Paul nodded. "It took a bit of time to smuggle him over the border into Belgium and then down here." He pulled a photo strip from his jacket pocket. "See his tie?" he asked as he lifted his necktie out to show it was the same one as in the photo. "These were taken this morning for his new identity papers."

"Rest here tonight," Paul said. "Tomorrow, Nadine will pass you off to another helper."

In the morning, Nadine led the men north along the edge of the Luxembourg Gardens to a shop near the Odéon Metro stop where she was to rendezvous with a helper, *Jeanne*. Waiting was the worst part, especially in broad daylight with men who stood out like the Empire State Building.

Something didn't feel right—an intuition—like when you think about someone you haven't heard from in years and the telephone rings and it's them. Only this wasn't a good feeling. It was a dark whisper—a foreboding, unexplainable nudge of dread. She backed into the recessed doorway of a shop with her two packages, thinking she might simply be more apprehensive because of yesterday's events.

No one was lurking about. No one was looking their way. Yet she couldn't shake the feeling that they were being watched—or that she should she trust her instincts. The men would become even less trusting if she didn't connect with the next guide, but standing too long in one spot invited trouble. She decided to give it only a minute or two more.

Then she saw him—a man in grey jacket who turned away the moment her eyes fell upon him.

"Come," she said. "We have to go back to *za 'otel*."

"Why?" Bill asked.

"We have a guardian angel."

"A what?"

"I feel *zat* we are being followed."

Bill peeked up and down the street then back at her. "I think you have seen too many detective movies, Mademoiselle."

"Come." This wasn't a debate. She moved down the street a bit and stopped in front of a shop window. When she glanced back, the grey-suited man had moved to a closer intersection and again looked down when she turned his way.

"Come," Nadine said again. She moved quickly, but not so fast as to attract attention. Bill and Ron glanced at each other skeptically, but kept up. When she reached the entrance to the Luxembourg Gardens she yanked Bill's hand. "Run!"

Nadine bolted into the park with the two evaders close behind. She weaved through groups of people strolling by the buildings and statues in the warm sunshine and ran around a fountain and up a tree-lined lane. She didn't stop to see if the guardian angel had followed. Her eyes searched for an escape route while her feet kept moving. Then along a gravel drive she spotted something and slapped Ron's arm. *Zare!*"

They followed her into a gardener's shed and pulled the door behind them, breathing hard. Moments later the undercover agent rushed up the gravel drive at something between a trot and a fast walk. Through the cracks in the door, they watched him huffing and panting as he hurried by in search of his prey.

Bill didn't have to say a word—a soft blow through his lips and his wide open eyes promised Nadine that he would never doubt her again.

She opened the door a crack and peeked out, then opened it more. The man was gone. Nadine changed the blue jacket she was wearing for a red one she kept in her suitcase and stepped out cautiously, sorting the options in her mind. The hotel was out. The contact at the metro stop was out. The only safe way was to take them to a friend in the seventh arrondissement. Even with a glass of wine, falling to sleep that night was slow in coming.

In the morning, Paul relieved her of the men and by late afternoon she was on a train back to Brussels.

But her ordeal was far from over.

Still skittish from her experience in Paris, Nadine used all of her tricks, taking a roundabout way, doubling back on herself and carefully studying the street for signs of danger. It was nearly dark when she reached Madame Anne's, but she had a message that she needed to deliver. "I brought this for you," she said handing Anne a folded piece of paper.

Anne cheerily translated the English note for Nadine. "It is from Bill Norfolk. He has made it into Spain."

"I thought you would like to have it before I went home." Seeing the joy in Anne's eyes, she was glad she had stopped. Nadine was proud to have assisted in more than twenty escapes, but it was always especially buoying when one of the men got word back that they had reached safety. It made their defiance of the Nazis complete.

"Are you just getting back from Paris now?" Anne led her back to the balcony and poured glasses of wine. "You must be hungry. I just baked some bread. I'll make you a sandwich."

"Thank you," Nadine said as the first bite made its way into her empty stomach. She took a sip of wine. "It feels good to relax."

"I thought you left for Paris three days ago."

"It was a harrowing trip."

"What happened?"

"I was followed by a guardian angel in Paris. We had to run for it. I managed to shake him by hiding in a shed in the Luxembourg Gardens."

Anne's cheery face transformed to wide-eyed alarm.

"Don't worry. I was very careful coming here. No one followed me."

"But if you were followed in Paris, it means you are burned. The Gestapo must know who you are."

Nadine shook her head. "I think the Australian's thick black hair drew attention. And I didn't know the Hotel Luxembourg was no longer being used by Comet. I think the hotel was being watched."

"Still," Anne said. "I do not think you should take that chance. Stay here tonight. You might have to stop guiding airmen for a while."

Nadine shook her head again. "I'm sure my family is worried about me. They haven't seen me in three days. And it is already late."

Nadine had just reached the tram stop when a gendarme called out. "You there!"

The anxiety of the past three days zapped her like a charge of electricity.

"What are you doing out this late? It is after curfew."

She breathed a little easier. He had only stopped her because of the time, but she still had to get control of herself or he'd see her trembling. "I am sorry," Nadine pleaded. "I was out with my boyfriend and lost track of time."

"You will not forget again, I think, if you spend a night in jail."

"Oh please, sir. My mother will kill me if I am put in jail. Please, sir, it will not happen again."

The gendarme released her with a stern look. "Go straight home. And do not let me catch you out this late again."

"Yes, sir. Thank you."

Nadine never felt so happy to change into comfortable pajamas and sleep in her own bed. Exhausted from the anxiety and the travel, she drifted off to sleep. Some hours later, she lazily opened her eyes to the sound of long insistent buzzes of the doorbell. Who could be calling at half past six in the morning?

"German police!" her grandfather shouted into their adjoining apartment.

Nadine jumped to her feet, trying to process what was happening.

"German police!" he called again.

Brump! Brump! Brump! Brump! Brump! Brump!

Impatient thuds battered the door of her grandfather's home.

Nadine ran to her parents' bedroom. "What should we do?"

"Try to get out through the kitchen," her father said. "I'll try the roof."

His command sparked her into action. Still in her pale yellow pajamas, she dashed out to the kitchen.

Jack boots tromped up the stairs.

"Hands up!" a German soldier commanded in English.

Her mind raced. This couldn't be happening! She couldn't put her hands up. She looked to the door where two soldiers were pointing handguns at her face. But they were young. She didn't think they would shoot a girl. They would want her alive to make her talk. The door was so close …

More boots clomped on the stairway. Another German appeared pointing his revolver at her. "Hands up!" the first soldier repeated.

She realized that if she ran they could shoot her in the leg to stop her. Her shoulders slumped. Inexplicably, she began to laugh. She didn't know why. It must have been nerves.

"Get dressed," one of the Germans said. "Take your toothbrush and enough clothing for three days."

The young soldier waved his side arm for her to move and followed her down to her bedroom.

"May I please have some privacy?"

The soldier didn't leave the room, but turned his head. When she had finished dressing, she was marched down the stairs and out through the front door. A fierce looking officer shoved her into the rear of a sedan and followed her in. A big burly German got in from the other side. Squeezed firmly between the two she could barely breathe.

Out the window, she watched her father being shoved into another car. In the house next door, a neighbor stood in the doorway observing the commotion. Nadine smiled and bravely gave a thumbs-up sign.

"You'll be laughing on the other side of your face soon," the brusque German said.

There was no doubt in her mind this was true. She tried not to show her fear. She would not give him the satisfaction of knowing she was scared out of her wits.

CHAPTER TWELVE

I have a feeling Andrée has finished her work for Belgium, Anne Brusselmans wrote in her journal. She hadn't slept much while trying to recall if Andrée said she had gotten the feeling as soon as she left the train or whether it came on the next day when she led Bill and Ron to the metro station. Now Anne absent-mindedly flipped slices of egg-dipped bread in the frying pan. It could have been someone who'd spotted her at the hotel. But maybe they had been watching her. The bigger question was had Andrée been the only subject or whether the Secret Police had tracked her through others. She unconsciously plated the toast for the children and delivered the dishes to the table.

"... Can we, Mom?" Jacques begged. "Please."

"Huh?" She hadn't even realized he was speaking to her. "Can you what?"

"Can we go to the park?"

"I have some things to do, but when you are finished, put your dish in the sink and you and Yvonne can go downstairs and play." She gave him a kiss on the forehead and he scampered off. Once they were out of the room she telephoned the Dumon home.

"Hello," a strange male voice said.

"Hello," Anne said. "Who is this? I would like to speak with the lady of the house."

"Why?"

From his guttural accent, she knew immediately the man was Gestapo. "I have the pound of meat she ordered and wanted to know if she will pick it up soon."

"No. Why don't you bring it here?"

Anne mumbled something and slapped the receiver handle down. Fears exploded like fireworks in her mind: How many minutes did it take for the police to trace a call? How long would it be before the Secret

Police knocked on her door? What would happen to the children? Would the Gestapo take them too?

She cracked open the front room curtain and peered out. The street was empty. *Think, Anne*, she told herself. She didn't dare call anyone lest the Gestapo was listening. She wished Julien were there, then felt grateful he wasn't. If she was arrested she could say he had nothing to do with it and he could look after the children. Dread shivered through her at a new realization: if she was arrested, she wouldn't be able to warn him. He'd walk straight into the Gestapo's trap! She wished they had arranged a signal of some kind.

Her only course was to stick to the story about the meat if the Gestapo should call and hope that the Dumons had not said anything. That decision satisfied her mind—but a moment later a new worry hit. What if the Gestapo asked to see the meat? She didn't have any. Anne checked the street again. She had only been on the line few seconds. That wasn't enough time to trace a call. That calmed her for a moment, then her mind fired another worry: the Gestapo would torture poor Andrée and force her to talk. She would have no choice but to tell everything.

Through the open window came the slam of an automobile door— then another—and another and another. Alarm gripped her. She held her breath as she peered down to the street.

It was just a taxi dropping people off.

Anne closed her eyes and exhaled. Sitting here was killing her. She had to do something. First, she checked that her little brown journal was safely hidden behind the loose brick. Then she went through the apartment making sure there were no airman photos or underground newspapers lying about.

She yanked a small suitcase from the closet and opened it on the bed in Jacques' room. The Baroness would surely look after the children and contact their grandparents. *But how much should I pack? she wondered. Enough for several days—a week? If the Gestapo comes, it could be forever*. The thought chilled her.

Anne had sent the children to stay with Baroness before, and the woman had made gifts of food and clothes when Anne told her she knew of people in need of assistance. Then one day, the Baroness had called her while the children were in her care. Anne immediately worried that something had happened to one of them. "No Anne, the children are fine," the Baroness assured her, "but tell me what is going on at your home. Jacques has told me that he had to move from his bed in the middle of the night to make room for Flemish cousins staying at your apartment."

Anne had ridden straight away down to the elegant house in LaHulpe. Although the Baroness was a longtime friend, Anne hesitated to tell her the truth. Even Anne's own family didn't know about her and Julien's decision to help Allied airmen. After a long moment agonizing over it, she finally explained that they'd been aiding downed Allied airmen to escape to Spain. Since then, the Baroness had increased her gifts of food and clothes and assured Anne that she would take the children at a moment's notice.

Anne spent that night burning copies of underground newspapers, identity card blanks and anything incriminating. When dawn came with no early morning raid by the Gestapo, she told the children they were going on a surprise holiday for a few days.

Yvonne, sensing something was wrong, hustled Jacques along and took care of him like a little mother. She may have been too young to fully understand the risks of her mother's involvement, but she knew what her parents were doing was dangerous. Her face showed her concern, but she carried on like a trooper.

Anne kept up the holiday ruse as she left the children with the Baroness. She kissed them both, rubbed her crucifix between thumb and forefinger in a silent prayer and returned to her apartment where she spent another sleepless night.

———

Nadine was marched into a bare interrogation room and ordered down into a hard wooden chair. Her muscles tensed. For the shy, quiet girl who had never so much as been sent to the headmaster's office, sitting across the desk from this stone-faced hook-nosed German frightened her beyond anything she had ever known. She maintained a poker face, consoling herself with her accomplishments: she had directly aided more than twenty men and participated in scores of other underground activities. She had known this day would come and she had prepared herself all along for it. But, she thought now, no one could really prepare for this, could they?

A brutish interrogator sat behind a worn wooden desk with one hand pressed against his cheek as his eyes scanned pages of notes in a manila file. He took a long time on each page. The morgue-like quiet was obviously intended to make her squirm.

She'd had nothing to eat or drink all day, and her empty stomach burned like vinegar. Her mouth was dry as corn starch. She had to take her mind off food, but there was nothing to focus on but a revolting Nazi flag behind the interrogator and a portrait of the vile Fuhrer with his cold dark eyes, and straight black hair that looked as if it had been trimmed by a blind barber. Behind her, a big, broad-shouldered German with holstered luger and a swastika band around his arm, blocked the exit. She glanced casually around the room to show Hooknose she was not intimidated by his tactics.

Then the interrogator removed a long black object from a drawer. No trace of humanity showed in his callous eyes. He slowly and deliberately walked around the desk slapping the implement of torture against his open palm—each unhurried *k-nip k-nip k-nip* of his boot heels jolted her as if touched by a live wire. With no more emotion than a slaughterhouse knacker, he sat one butt cheek on the corner of the desk and set the long black riding crop down beside him right in front of her as a clear warning.

Nadine knew she should be scared to death, but she felt nothing but contempt for his lordly air. She steeled herself for what was to come. No matter what he did to her now, he could never erase the trouble she had caused in his stinking Third Reich. Her own life was inconsequential, just one life sacrificed for twenty-one lives saved. Those men she had helped would fly again and kill many more Germans. If she had to face the firing squad, she'd do so proudly. She sat up straight and expressionless, despite the implement of torture lying on the desk.

"You are mademoiselle Andrée Dumon, correct?" *Hooknose* began in an even voice.

"Yes."

"Tell us everything you know or this will go very badly for you."

"I don't know what you're on about or what you want me to tell you."

The man's voice became curt. "You know what we want. You have committed crimes against the German government. Tell me who helped you. Tell me who you work for, and give me their addresses."

"But I don't know what you are—"

"The game is up, Mademoiselle!" the man snapped. "I do not think you understand the gravity of your situation. You will tell us what we want to know or we will kill you."

Nadine said nothing.

Hooknose drew an annoyed breath and exhaled it impatiently. He paused a moment before beginning again in a controlled unemotional manner as if he were telling a waiter his lunch order "I assure you, you *will* talk. You can tell us what we want to know now or you can wait until we force it out of you. It is your choice. If you make us do it the hard way, it will not go well for you."

When the occupation began, German soldiers had acted courteously and shown respect for women. But soon their horrifying atrocities inflicted on the Belgian people left no doubt what the Nazis were capable of. Nadine knew this was no idle threat, but she had made up her mind. She had thrown in with Dédée knowing the consequences.

"If you do not cooperate, I assure you, you will wish we had killed you instead."

She had no doubt of that. But how could she betray the others in the line and let them suffer in her place? Unlike those who were given guide assignments without knowing the people who delivered the men or the next contact person in the line, Nadine knew too much about the escape organization, from its founders to most of its chiefs. Not even her mother or father knew as much about the line as she did. She was proud to have been entrusted with its innermost secrets, but now her loyalty would be put to the test. Soon she as well as Dédée, Paul, and Nemo would know whether it was wise to allow anyone to know that much. Could she hold out against torture? Somehow, she thought, she must.

The Aryan picked up the horse crop and slapped it against the palm of his hand.

She prepared herself for the pain, telling herself, *I will not let them break me.*

"Andrée, we know you are not the leader. You have been used by the others." The inquisitor slipped into a softer caring persona. "Nothing can come of your resistance. The men you hide will eventually be found and sent to camps where they will sit out the war without fear of ill treatment. Don't you see that helping them remain at large only makes it more difficult for them when they are captured? The sooner they are collected the easier it will be to regard them as prisoners of war. If they are allowed to venture about, we must assume they are gathering military information, and therefore must treat them as spies. Tell me where these men are hiding so I can help them before it is too late."

"I don't know anything," Nadine lied with conviction.

The sweetness vanished. "You recently traveled to Paris. Who did you meet there?"

"No one. I was alone."

"What was your purpose there?"

"I went to shop," she said not mentioning the hat sketches so as not to get the milliner in trouble.

"Do not lie to me, Mademoiselle. Who did you meet?"

"No one."

"It is useless to lie to me—*Didi*. We have been watching you. We know where you go. We have been watching the school. Where is the headmaster? We will learn the truth, Mademoiselle. If you do not cooperate, it will be too late for you. Your death will not save those you have hidden." He snatched a folder from the cabinet and waved it, but returned it without revealing what was actually inside. "We are collecting enemy airmen all over Belgium and France. There is no escape for them. Your assistance in hiding them does nothing but prolong the inevitable. If you persist, Didi, you will die for no purpose."

Hooknose was lying. Men had gotten through—the hand-written message from Bill to Madame Anne confirmed it. Nadine swiped her parched tongue inside her dry mouth as the agent drank a glass of water in front of her.

The man finished half the glass and left the remainder tantalizingly close. "Who are the men who give you assignments? Give me their names."

She refused to look at the glass. She wouldn't ask him for a drink. If he knew how thirsty she was in this hot airless room, it would make him think he was close to breaking her.

"Monsieur de Jongh said he didn't know where his daughter had gone, but now we have you, Didi. Do you think your silence will stop us from finding him?"

Nadine was confused. Was she being mistaken for the other Dédée?

WHAP! The horse crop slammed down on the desk.

Her heart leapt.

"Their names, Mademoiselle! I want their names!"

"I—I have no names to give you, I..."

"Do not treat me as if I am a fool, Andrée! You do not want to anger me. It would be a shame to spoil such a pretty, young face!"

Nadine said nothing.

"Perhaps if we bring your grandparents in ... or your little sister ..."

She remained silent. Pleading innocence would only serve to provoke his anger, but she wasn't going to admit anything either.

It seemed she had been there forever when the inquisitor called the guard closer and said something softly to him in German and the guard left the room. Nadine prepared herself assuming he had told the guard to leave him alone so he could brutalize her without witness and loosen her tongue. She was wrong. The man didn't touch her. Instead, it was a different kind of torture. Two men returned with plates of mouth-watering sausages and potatoes and tall glasses of water which they consumed in front of her.

Hunger panged her empty stomach.

The meal clearly refreshed the inquisitors who questioned her with renewed vigor. It went on all day and into early evening. They didn't beat her. They only threatened. Finally, she was taken away to a musty, urine-smelling cell in St. Gilles Prison. After two days of interrogations with nothing but a couple of cups of water, she was brought a bowl of grey pasta which she shoveled down before the prison guards realized she wasn't supposed to be given any food.

The questioning went on for two more days, at the end of which the fair-haired Nazi said, "Perhaps some time alone will loosen your tongue. You will have much time to think it over. But be assured, mademoiselle, that the next time we question you, if you do not give us a full account, what happens to you will be out of my hands. You will suffer in ways you cannot imagine. You will beg us for mercy, but it will be too late. Take her away."

———

Twelve days after Nadine's arrest, Elsie Maréchal walked twenty paces ahead of Australian evader, Ivan Davies, to the department store for his identity photos. After the capture of the Dumon family and others, she was wary, but not afraid. Mostly, she felt excited and proud—excited to have her first house guest since Charlie Morelle and proud to stand among those who refused to be scared into abandoning the cause. And as soon as she conducted *Melbourne*, as her mother had taken to calling Ivan, back to 172 Avenue Voltaire, she was going to Nemo's office to hold him to his promise.

Elsie slipped the photos into her purse and instructed Melbourne to follow her onto the tram. Staying alert when conducting evaders was essential. Once, a woman Nadine had seen talking to Germans came up to one of her parcels and asked for change for the telephone. Nadine quickly shoved money in the woman's hand to make her go away. Elsie had anticipated having to live by her wits. Today's mission to the department store had gone without incident. She was grateful, of course, but it was a bit of a letdown.

She breezed into *Nemo's* office at the Swedish Canteen and handed the photo strip to *Le Kas*. "I told Melbourne to look serious in the photo. I think he overdid it."

"It's not supposed to look like a mug shot," Peggy van Lier said with a shrug, "This looks like it should be on a wanted poster."

Elsie laughed and handed a letter to Peggy. "This is addressed to you, *Michelle*. Nellie brought it round. It must have come from one of the provinces."

Peggy read the note and passed it to Nemo. "Saint-Antonius—that's in Antwerp province."

"I can go to Antwerp and collect the airman." Elsie said, inching forward, ready to spring into action.

"I thought you were waiting to hear back on your exams," Nemo said.

Elsie grinned. "I *have* heard back. I got high marks. I am applying to nursing school. Until then, I will guide airmen."

Nemo gave a reluctant nod. It was after all what they had agreed upon. She could see that it bothered him to send her into danger, but she was eighteen now and had already assured him this was her decision.

"My sister and her husband live in Antwerp," Peggy offered. "It would be only natural for me to go visit them, hey?"

Nemo nodded. "That makes sense." But seeing Elsie's disappointment, he added, "Elsie, you can guide Melbourne to a rendezvous at the train station once I have readied his identity papers."

Elsie nodded. She understood Nemo's unspoken reasoning: he wanted her to begin with short operations.

Isolated from all human contact except for the guards who brought her meals—no recreation in the yard with other prisoners, no one to talk to, no sunlight—Nadine sat alone in the dark musty cell occupying her mind with musical verses, scenes from films and anything else she could think of to stave off the awful thoughts of what they were going to do to her. She'd seen the bruised and bloodied prisoners carried out of interrogation rooms while she'd waited to go in.

Breakfast each day consisted of dark ersatz coffee—lunch, a piece of bread and bowl of awful-tasting soup. Dinner was more of the same.

There was no hygiene, just a bucket in the corner behind a privacy screen —and not enough water to wash oneself. She feared for her mother and father and what the Germans might be doing to them.

After ten days to "reflect", she was once again taken by car to the interrogation room at Gestapo headquarters.

"Now that you have had some time to remember, I hope for your sake you are ready to talk."

Nadine said nothing.

"Tell us who you work for!" *Hooknose* barked. "Where is Monsieur de Jongh? You may still save yourself if you talk now."

Nadine stubbornly refused to speak.

The inquisitor gave a nod to the brute at the door who left and returned moments later with another man. Nadine had seen him before. She didn't remember his name, but recognized him as a man introduced to her by Monsieur de Jongh as someone in the Résistance.

The Belgian man bowed to the German as he approached the desk.

"Do you know this girl?" the German asked.

"Oh yes," the Belgian said. "She is Andrée Dumon and she helps airmen get from Brussels to Paris." The traitor looked Nadine in the eye. "It is your duty to tell them the truth, Andrée."

Nadine still said nothing, but she knew she was finished. There could be no hope of convincing the Germans that she was innocent.

With a jerk of the German's head, the Belgian traitor exited the room.

Nadine remained silent.

Suddenly, the German's riding crop stung the side of her face. She tumbled to the floor. It surprised her as much as it had hurt. Before she could react, the toe of his jack boot kicked the air out of her stomach. The next kick hammered her ribs, followed by another and another. Gasping for breath, she curled up to protect herself, but before she could recover, she felt herself being dragged upright by her hair. The Nazi flung her back into the chair and got right up in her face.

"Now, stop playing games, Mademoiselle Dumon, and tell us what you know."

Nadine fought back tears and gritted her teeth to suppress the whimpers of pain. She couldn't give the bastard the satisfaction of knowing how much those kicks had hurt.

"Tell me who you contact!" her tormentor demanded.

Nadine pressed her lips together.

A sharp bite on the cheek from the riding crop was his response.

She screamed. Tears trickled down. She cursed her eyes for letting them fall and commanded herself to be brave. She wanted to spit in her tormentor's face. She wanted to shout that he was nothing but a pig who thought himself a big man because he could beat up a defenseless girl. But good sense told her it would be stupid to provoke him further.

After hours of slaps, kicks, punches and worse, she spent a painful night in her stone cell knowing that the torture had only just begun. Her side had bruised to a ripe purple. She tasted blood in her mouth. Although she couldn't see her face, she was sure from the puffy pain beside her eye, that it was ugly-looking.

The last thing her tormentor had said before sending her back to her cell was, "Tomorrow, you will talk, or what you suffered today will seem like a child's game."

Nadine lay awake thinking about how she might appease them without giving anything away. By morning, she had made up what she hoped would be a believable story.

"Tell me what you know," the warthog began.

Nadine hesitated.

"We will get it out of you." He drew back the riding crop high over his head preparing to strike then seemed to think better of it and set the crop down on the desk. "Perhaps your mother will talk if we bring her in to watch…"

"My mother knows nothing. She is not involved."

"So you admit you work for the underground."

"Yes, but my mother knows nothing about my activities. I made excuses to her whenever I was gone away. She has done nothing wrong." Nadine spoke with conviction. Her own fate had been sealed by the traitor, and the guardian angel who had seen her in Paris. But if the secret police didn't know her mother had guided evaders short distances from one safe house in Brussels to another, there might still be a chance to save her.

"Tell us who you work for and who your contacts are."

Nadine spoke as she'd rehearsed. "All I know is a name—Jacques."

"Where does Jacques live?"

"I don't know. I never met him. He gives me my assignments by telephone."

"Who else?"

"That is all I know."

The German drew an impatient breath. "You would not have accepted assignments from anyone unless that contact was established through someone you knew."

Nadine hesitated. She had planned to give the name of someone already arrested so it would be plausible and not jeopardize active Comet members, but now she realized that if she gave a true name, that person would be tortured even more. At least he didn't seem to know about Nemo or Peggy, or he would have said so by now.

"Give me the addresses where you collect the enemy airmen."

"I picked them up wherever I was told to—the park, a church, in front of a café—it was always different."

"You know what I want from you, Mademoiselle." The German slammed his hand down on the desk. "Now tell me something useful!"

Nadine shrugged. "The organization does not tell us anything more than we need to know."

"Where is Monsieur de Jongh?"

"I do not know. I have not seen him in a very long time. I think he has been arrested."

He grabbed up the riding crop and slapped it against his hand. "Where is he?"

"I don't know."

"Liar!"

She suffered the lash of his whip across her upper arm.

"Is he the chief of the operation?"

"I don't know who is chief. I only know I get my assignments from Jacques."

The lie earned her another blow from the crop. She stuck to her story the rest of the day. He continued to beat her, slapping the side of her head, knocking her to the ground and kicking her. It hurt to breathe. Blood dripped from her lip to the floor. After being splashed with water and dragged up to the seat, she was beaten to the floor and kicked once again when she still refused to talk.

That night, in her urine-fouled cell, her body was so sore she could hardly choke down the slop they called food. Sharp pain stabbed at her ribs every time she drew a breath. She couldn't hear out of one ear. She didn't know where she found the bravery to take this kind of punishment up until now, but she knew she couldn't take much more. He had been right, it would have been better if they had just killed her. It was now clear that they weren't going to let her die, and they weren't going to stop beating her.

Lying in her cell, she tried to think of pleasant things to take her mind off the pain—days at the seashore, parties, holiday dinners, her favorite films....

When the cell door swung open in the morning, she marched out without being ordered and walked straight to the waiting car without having to be prodded by her escorts. She knew the routine. She took her seat in the hard wooden chair at Gestapo headquarters and waited for the beatings to begin. Resigned to her fate, she gazed out the window at a tree in the courtyard, and wondered aloud, "What a lovely tree. So full of fruit. Have you tasted any of the pears? You must love having fruit trees in your garden."

The observation caught the German by surprise. He stared at her for a moment and shook his head in disbelief. Then he threw up his hands and turned to the guard. "Take her back to her cell. If she won't talk one of the others will."

Although Nadine was not interrogated again, the Nazis were far from finished with her.

CHAPTER THIRTEEN

On Sunday, after a week of sleepless nights and jumping every time a car door slammed, Anne Brusselmans decided to chance connecting to someone else in the line. Nadine had been her only contact, but when Bill Norfolk had stayed with her, he left a dog collar that he had gotten from a previous host, René Ponty. Bill had given her the name and number in the hopes she could return the collar. Anne rang him up.

"Monsieur P?" she asked.

"Yes?"

"I have news about one of your dogs. He won the race and I would like to talk to you about it."

"Are you the trainer who looked after my dog?"

"I have his collar and want to return it to you."

They agreed to meet at a café in the commercial district. Anne, wearing a yellow chiffon scarf, spotted the fellow with the newspaper sticking out of his left side pocket as arranged. Pulling the silk collar from her purse, she asked, "Does this belong to you?"

René shook his head, wary of a trap,. "It is not mine."

"It was given to me by Bill Norfolk," she said softly.

An impulsive twitch of René's eyelid told her she had the right man.

"Do you recognize Bill's handwriting?" Anne whispered, showing him the note Nadine had brought back on her last trip. "He said a physician looked after his sprained ankle and he stayed with you while it healed. He said there was an occasion when you and he were walking at four in the morning when you saw a German patrol which you evaded by hiding in an attic."

"Yes," René said with a shrug. "I believe the collar is mine."

"You have no doubt heard that some of our friends have been in an accident and are in the hospital. Do not contact anyone that you were connected with before. Here is my number for you to contact me when you come across a puppy in need, but do not call me until I have called you first. I may be a little *chaud* myself."

In bed that night, Anne told Julien, who had just returned from the farm in the Ardennes, of her meeting with Ponty and of another development. "You don't mind that we have taken in a new house guest?" she asked.

Julien kissed his wife on the cheek. "I have already resigned myself to the fact that we are not going to have any time together until this war is over."

Anne wrapped her arms around Julien and laid her head on his chest. "She said it will only be for a month or so until she can find another place. Michou is afraid that the Gestapo will come for her at the nursing school. And who can blame her after what they did to her family. The poor girl had no idea they were involved in the underground."

"She must have suspected something," Julien said. "Even Yvonne at ten years old has figured out what we are doing."

Anne picked her head up to look at him. "Yes, but Michou wasn't living at home."

"And that is what saved her."

In fact, Michou had to bring her birth certificate to the police station to prove she was a member of the family in order to be allowed to see them. Anne sighed and laid her head back down. "I worry about the shock our parents will receive if we are arrested."

"We can stop."

Anne lifted her head off his chest again. "Do you want to stop?"

"Only if you do."

Anne looked into his eyes and shook her head. "I could not bear the thought of our children growing up under Nazi tyranny without feeling that I have done all I can to fight against it. We knew the risk when we signed on."

"Get some sleep." Julien stroked his wife's hair. "Michou can stay as long as she needs to. She will be all right and so will the children."

Anne kissed her husband. "It's good to have you back."

———

Elsie traveled fifteen blocks by tram and walked the remaining two blocks in the bright September sun to the Square Frère Orban in Brussels. Students lay on the plush green carpet with their noses in their books. Elderly couples rested on benches, and young mothers pushed baby prams around. The manicured beds of crimson and gold blossoms surrounded by dark green grass almost let her forget how the Nazi occupation had defiled everything with their crooked black crosses like poisonous tarantulas on a blood red background.

She strolled the perimeter of the square, but it wasn't merely to enjoy the scenery. She was scanning for secret police officers in plain-clothes and anyone else who might look out of place. Stopping beside a tall green sycamore, she stole a glance at the church at the head of the square. That told her all she needed to know.

There, among a handful of young people whiling away the time on the long grey steps of Saint Joseph's Church, sat Albert, a guide in his late teens from the provinces. The man beside him looked to be in his early thirties and quite ordinary, but from his stiff posture she knew he was the one she had come for.

She feigned interest in the trees and flowers as she crossed the cobbled street into the shade of the sanctuary and smoothed the back of her red and black tartan skirt as she sat down on the steps overlooking the square about a yard away from the airman. Albert yawned and walked off. No one paid any attention to the school girl in the black low-heeled shoes and white ankle socks. Without looking up from the textbook she brought, she asked in a sweet young voice "What is the time?"

"Always the same," the airman replied.

Elsie continued softly in English. "Please continue to gaze at the square while I ask you a few questions. What is your name?"

"Ralph Van Den Bok."

"Where are you from, Ralph?"

"East Horsley, in Surrey, England."

"Where is that?"

"South of London—not too far from Guildford."

"What plane did you fly in?"

"A Handley Page Hampden B-M-K-One."

"How many were in your crew?"

"Four."

"Did any others survive?"

"Yes, one, Flight Lieutenant Gordon Fisher. We were together, but we were split up by a helper in Silenrieux."

"Just a couple more questions, Ralph. What is a rhubarb?"

The airman nearly turned back at the surprise question, but caught himself. "It's a low-level fighter sweep."

"What is a circus?"

"A heavily escorted bomber run."

"All right, Ralph. Have a seat inside the church. I will return in about an hour."

She rode down to the Swedish Canteen and reported to Nemo who issued instructions, then she went back to Saint Joseph's Church. "I'm sorry to hear about your other crew members, Ralph," Elsie said when she slid into the pew beside him. "Our journey is less than two miles, but the tram makes many stops, so it will take us about fifteen minutes. We will speak no English until we reach our destination. If anyone speaks to you, I will say you are deaf and dumb, but if someone singles you out for questions, I do not know you and you do not know me. Understand?"

"Yes."

When they reached the Maréchal home on Avenue Voltaire, Elsie sing-songed, "Mummy, I've brought a guest home for dinner."

Elsie Bell welcomed the airman with a warm handshake. "Hello, Ralph. We've been expecting you. Make yourself at home."

"Thank you, Madame. I'm so glad you speak English. That last bloke, Albert, didn't speak a word of it and I'm not any better at French."

Madame Maréchal smiled. "Call me, Elsie. The W.C. is through there if you'd like to freshen up. When you've finished, I'd like to hear how the war is going."

Ralph stayed for two days, and had no sooner left then Elsie went back to the church to question and collect the next airman. She imagined with pride how frustrating it must be for the Secret Police to have arrested more than one hundred and fifty people only to find that they hadn't slowed the underground down. Elsie and the group at the Swedish

Canteen, Nemo, Peggy and an eager new Belgian recruit, Victor Michiels, were busier than ever. In September alone, fifteen airmen were conducted from Belgium to Spain by those connected with the Canteen.

German High Command was indeed furious. At the beginning of the war they were capturing nearly one hundred percent of downed enemy airmen. The numbers had now dropped to fifty percent.

But the Germans were not out of tricks.

———

Peggy van Lier brushed her teeth and ran a comb through her still-wet hair. She applied just a little makeup—no jewelry—nothing that would make her stand out. Her bronze red hair, blue eyes and soft porcelain skin already made her more recognizable than she would like. Being pretty was something to be grateful for, but in this business it could be a liability.

Her stomach was already churning. Every mission put her on edge—rushing about seemed the only way to let out her nervous energy. She slipped into her jacket, swept back her hair over the collar and gave it a shake, and then checked to make sure the pockets were empty. Before heading out, she poked through her pocketbook too. A simple scrap of paper with an address could be deadly if she was stopped and the bag was searched.

"You're up early," her mother said from her bedroom door, tying her robe. "Are you going out?"

"I'm going shopping with my chommies."

"Are the shops even open yet?"

"I'm going to church just now." At least that part was true. She always prayed before and after a mission.

"Will you be here for dinner?"

"No. We'll probably graze while we're out." Guilt washed over her. Being a good practicing Catholic she hated lying to her parents, but she couldn't tell them she was conducting Allied airmen down to Paris. Her mother would be worried sick. She quickly stirred through her bag's contents until she found her insurance—the photographs of herself with the German officers. The photos might not do her any good if she was caught, but it was worth trying if it came to it.

She walked quickly to the center of Halle where the Church of San Martin watched over the town. As she entered, she felt immediate repose. The smell of the old wooden pews, the flickering of a hundred votive candles, and the altar filled with baskets of flowers at the Virgin Mary's feet comforted her. Reverence for the powerful presence of the Madonna filled Peggy with deep spiritual tranquility. Skeptics might scoff, but she could feel the spirit of the Holy Mother in this place and believed she looked after those with a good heart and whose cause was just.

Peggy knelt down in a pew somewhere in the middle of the hallowed building and blessed herself. She gazed up at the Madonna, her golden crown aglow in the sun light and her body black as coal just as it had been turned during the Siege of Halle in 1580 when an overwhelming Protestant army tried to beat the small Catholic community into submission. Their cannon balls flew into the city, but did little damage, for the church was cloaked in the spirit of the Madonna. After the battle, the grateful citizens collected the cannon balls and laid them at her feet where they remain today.

In four days it would be the first Sunday in September, and if it was God's will that she should return from her mission, Peggy would take part in the colorful procession to honor the Madonna. She pulled out the silver chain from around her neck, kissed the tiny medal of the Notre Dame de Halle and asked the Holy Mother to see the men safely through their journey. All was now in the hands of God and Our Lady of Halle.

Tommy Broom and his pilot, Flight Lieutenant Edgar Costello-Bowen, were the fellows that Peggy had collected and taken to her sister's home in Antwerp where her doctor brother-in-law treated Edgar's wounded leg and foot. The next day she had brought them to a safe house in Laeken, a western suburb of Brussels. Today they were at a house on Boulevarde de Waterloo east of the city.

"How's the foot, Ed?" Peggy asked. "We've a bit of a walk to the station. Are you up for it?"

"It's coming along quite nicely, *Michelle*." Ed wiggled it to demonstrate.

"I think he rather enjoys the attention," Tommy said.

Peggy laughed. "I hope we get very little attention on the trip. You can rest your foot when we are on the train. Two more evaders and another guide will meet us at the station. Watch me and do as I do."

Tommy nodded. "You're the boss, Michelle."

"That's right—at least until you get home to your wives or girl-friends," she teased. Both of the men were at least ten years older than Peggy, but they respected her responsibility. "We will travel separately as before. I don't have to remind you that we do not know each other. If you are asked for your papers, act as if it is nothing more than a nuisance."

The Gare du Midi station was still busy with the morning rush and the inspectors were weary from the hundreds of passengers they had already checked through. Peggy gave German-friendly newspapers and magazines to her charges to pretend to read while waiting on the benches. Kazimierz Rowicki, the Polish airman she had taken for his identity photos, was seated on another bench, but other than a moment's eye contact, they showed no recognition of each other. On her way to buy the tickets, she caught sight of Bee Johnson, the English helper who was guiding Rowicki and another fellow, Arthur Fay.

Good God, she thought, *a redheaded girl with an English South African accent, three starched Brits, a Polish airman and the limey chauffeur, Bee Johnson—we're as inconspicuous as giraffes in a herd of zebras.* Bee was the only other one who spoke French and his accent was even worse than hers. It was going to take a great deal of luck and maybe some help from Notre Dame de Halle to make it to Paris with this lot.

But luck was not with them. Just before Lille, France, the door to their car opened and in stepped a pair of inspectors who began methodically working their way down the aisle demanding *certificats de domicil* and *cartes d'identité*. Peggy had taught the phrases to her two and instructed them to point to their mouth and pretend to be dumb if asked a question. Now seated a few rows back she could do nothing but watch as the official examined Ed's papers. When he reached Tommy, the inspector's eyes rose and fell from photograph to man. It felt like little worms squirming up and down her back as she forced her nervous body to sit still.

"Enjoy your trip," the inspector said in English.

Tommy furrowed his brow and turned up a questioning palm to show he didn't understand.

The official handed back his papers and moved on.

"Did you have any difficulties?" Dédée asked when they reached Paris.

Peggy shrugged. "Just a check of papers on the train. The children did fine. The airmen, Ed, has a slight limp from a wound, but he hides it well. How is your father taking the arrests of Suzanne and Nadine?"

Dédée sighed. "All right."

"Not very well, hey?" Peggy said reading the inflection in her voice.

"He tries not to show it, but I know it distresses him. He worries about me more now that Suzanne has been caught." Dédée shook her head resignedly. "I worry about him—he worries about me … It makes it difficult for me to concentrate on my job ... but I guess it is better that we are together in this than him being surprised by the police knocking on his door one day to tell him I have been arrested or shot."

Dédée's words resounded in Peggy's mind as she stared out the train window on the long ride home, imagining the Gestapo's knock on her mother's door. "There are nine chances in ten that you will be arrested or shot within six months," Dédée warned everyone. The arrests of Suzanne and Nadine confirmed it.

When she got home, her mother was standing at the sink drying the dinner dishes while her father sat beside the wireless tuning in the BBC.

"Ah, Margaret," her mother said. "You're back. How was your day? What did you buy?"

"Please come and sit a moment with me in the parlor," Peggy said. "There is something I need to tell you." Her mother's eyes filled with concern, her hands clutching the dishtowel as she braced for bad news. Peggy started right in, not wanting to keep them waiting. "A friend of mine has been arrested by the secret police. She was part of the underground helping British airmen escape from Belgium, the Netherlands and

France." Peggy hesitated a moment and drew a deep breath. "I thought that by not telling you where I was going, I was sparing you from worry. But with the arrest of my friend, I now see it would be a greater shock for you to learn one day that your daughter had been arrested."

The color drained from her mother's face. Her father appeared paralyzed except for his eyes which seemed to be trying to blink away what he was hearing.

Peggy drew a breath and touched her mother's hand. "You have often spoken of the Belgian girl who is rumored to be helping British airmen get back to England. So many times I have wanted to tell you that the stories you heard about her are true. Just hours ago I was with her in Paris. I am part of that escape organization."

She gave them a moment to digest it before continuing on. "You have read the warnings. The Germans will not go easy on us if we are caught. But we are making a difference. We have returned more than fifty airmen to England to fight again—trained men who cannot escape without our help. It is something I must do."

Her mother smoothed the dish towel on her lap. She looked to her husband and spoke for both of them. "Of course as your parents we will worry, but we understand and we support you completely. Everyone who lives in a country occupied by the Germans is in constant danger. Helping the British defeat Hitler is our only hope." Her parents stood up and embraced their daughter.

"Try to be careful," her father said and kissed her forehead.

"I will."

CHAPTER FOURTEEN

édée trimmed down the photograph of a sallow-faced man in a dark suit and held it backward over her shoulder for the others to see. "I'm calling this one Philippe. I need an occupation to give him."

Elvire Morelle leaned in for a closer look as she passed behind Dédée with a stack of dirty dinner plates. "He looks like an undertaker."

Dédée pulled the snapshot back in front of her. "He does!" She laughed. "How would you like to be an undertaker, Philippe?" she said to the photo.

"An undertaker?" her father repeated frowning through his spectacles at her.

"Certainly," Elvire said with pretend seriousness. "If they question him, he can say he is picking up a dead body! What do you think, *Franquito?*"

Dédée snickered every time Elvire called their new recruit Franquito, an affectionate derivative of his name, Jean-François Nothomb. Tall and trim, the twenty-two-year-old was remarkably unpretentious for being the son of a well-known Belgian senator and novelist, and so dark and handsome he could pass for a cinema star. He had been an officer candidate when Hitler invaded and had escaped from a POW camp in Germany before the Germans had time to perfect the containment of the overwhelming number of captured enemy troops.

Dédée loved him for his passion for his country and enthusiasm for the cause, but even more because he was such a courageous good-natured soul. He laughed right along when they shortened Elvire's *Franquito* to *Franco* for his underground name. It was particularly tickling because 'Franco' was the name of the fascist dictator who had overthrown the Spanish government with the help of Hitler's forces.

Now Franco paused with a casserole dish in hand. "That looks like the fellow who buried my uncle!"

"Oh, your uncle died?" Elvire asked sympathetically.

"I hope so. Otherwise, we made a big mistake burying him!" Elvire gave him a playful shove.

Dédée chuckled. "If we had a hearse we could put the men in coffins and drive them into Spain!"

"That is a good idea," Franco said. "That way when the Germans shoot you, the casket will be ready. Very efficient."

"How about a bridge engineer?" Paul suggested.

Franco shook his head. "The Germans would just take him away to repair bombed bridges."

Elvire raised a hand without looking back. "I vote for undertaker. I am dying to meet him."

Franco groaned at her feeble pun.

"Undertaker it is," Dédée said with finality.

"What if the Germans question him?" Paul said. "He cannot pretend to be a mute undertaker."

"Why not?" Elvire snickered. "The corpses will not converse with him."

Dédée giggled. "Corpses are good listeners. They never interrupt." She looked across the table at the sober eyes behind her father's big round glasses and broke out laughing. "*Kiki* thinks we are being too silly," she said putting emphasis on her father's comical underground name.

"We can buy him a pocket bible," Elvire quipped. "Undertakers always carry a bible."

"And a tape measure," Franco added. "If stopped, he can measure the German up for a coffin."

Dédée looked at her father's serious face and had to suppress another laugh.

He shook his head and gave a resigned smile.

"I will let Franco go buy the bible," Dédée said.

"Are you afraid it will burn your fingers because you do not believe?" Franco retorted half-kidding.

"I never said I didn't believe." Dédée shrugged. "I simply think we all should be allowed to follow our own beliefs."

Franco paused his dish drying. "You know what happens when a country does not have Christian values? We call it Germany!"

"Jews are not Christian," Dédée retorted. "Would you have us persecute Jews as the Germans do?"

"We are a Christian country," the young man said. "We should stand up for our Christian beliefs."

"Would you have the government punish Hebrews, gypsies, Muslims and anyone else who isn't Christian? Don't you see? A government that tells its people *what* to believe is no better than a government that tells its people *not* to believe."

"Those who kill others just because of their religion are not true Christians…"

"*Franquito,*" Elvire singsonged, "you are falling behind. The dish drainer is getting full."

Franco took the hint and changed the subject. "You know if the German police paid us a visit right now, they would have quite a catch."

"I hope they do not come tonight," Elvire said. "I am not dressed for company."

"If the Gestapo knocks on that door," Dédée said, "I'm going to tie bed sheets together and drop four floors down into the backyard of the *Gardes Républicaines.*"

Paul set his pen down and wiggled his fingers. Many more identity cards remained to be forged. "With both the Americans and British bombing, there are too many papers to forge now."

Dédée pasted Philippe's photo and set the card aside to begin the next one. "Even with Bee and Franco conducting groups over the mountains, it will be difficult to keep up."

"Don't look at me," Elvire said, "The next time I go over that mountain it is going to be one way—and in warm weather."

Franco paused his drying again. "What about that new British line —Brandy?"

"They only let their agents do six months at a time," Elvire said. "It takes longer than that just to set things up!"

"The British are just being pragmatic," Dédée said. Comet had grown so big, the line had become more vulnerable to infiltration by traitors.

"They know the odds are against us. Anyone could betray us just as someone betrayed the Pat O'Leary Line. It's simply a question of time and luck."

"Comet succeeds because of us," Elvire declared. "The British will never know our countries and our people like we do. Look what happened to Waucquez. He and his radio operator were captured in three weeks."

"It's true," Dédée said, "the British cannot do what we do. That is why Comet must remain Belgian and French until it ceases to exist."

Franco choked his towel in his fist. "We will not cease until our countries are liberated."

––––––

Four days later, Dédée traced two fingers down the fatigued face that stared back at her from the bathroom mirror. Her blond roots were beginning to show, but they would have to wait. There was no time to dye her hair this trip. She and Janine had just returned from the south and were taking more evaders down tonight. She stepped into the tub greedy for the luscious warm water showering down, wishing she could enjoy it longer. But she had to save some of the precious hot water for Janine.

Dressed in a clean skirt and blouse, with a towel wrapped around her wet hair, Dédée followed the scent of onion, hamburger and fried potato to the kitchen. "Can I help with anything?"

"You can sit down and rest," Elvire said as she flipped the patties. "You're going to need your strength. Yesterday, Peggy delivered two parcels from lines broken by the Gestapo. She says there are twenty more hiding in Belgium." She tossed a nod back over her shoulder. "Edgar here will be sitting it out until his leg heals."

"Oh that is too bad, Edgar. Does it hurt much?" Dédée asked with concern.

"It's put a bit of a crimp in my dance moves, but it's coming along."

"And how about you, Arthur?" she asked the second airman. "Where in Canada do you live?"

Arthur chuckled. "I come from a town so small they put *welcome* and *thank you come again* on the same sign post. I couldn't wait to get out. Now, I really miss it. This time of year the whole valley pops with crimson and gold."

"It must be lovely," Dédée said.

"It's spectacular. Come visit me after the war and I'll show you around."

Elvire dished out hamburgers and fried potatoes. "Your father and Franquito left last night with parcels Rowicki, Broom and Price."

Arthur raised an eyebrow as Elvire set a dish of mayonnaise between Janine and Dédée and the two alternated dipping their potato strips. "You got any ketchup? I need ketchup with my French fries and burgers."

"French fries!" Janine exclaimed with mock indignation. "These are not *French* fries."

Elvire laughed at Janine pretending to be insulted.

"They look like French fries," Arthur said taking a bite. "They taste like French fries ..."

"We Belgians invented them," Janine said with a huff. "You *Americans* call them *French* fries because to your fathers who ate them in the last war, we are all French!"

Dédée raised her eyebrows at Arthur to let him know he was on his own. It was fun to tease the men a bit.

"I apologize," Arthur said sheepishly. "So what do you Belgians call them?"

Janine smiled with satisfaction as she dipped a potato in the mayonnaise. "Frites."

"Okay. Frites it is. And just for the record—I'm not *American*, I'm *Canadian*."

Janine covered her mouth and laughed.

"We *French* know they were invented *here*," Elvire declared with a wink to Janine.

"It's no use trying to sort out who invented them, old boy," Edgar said. "Just do as we do. In England we call them chips."

When the meal was done, Elvire hung up her apron and asked the boys to clean up the dishes while she went to buy bread.

"I do not have to remind you, Edgar, to remain quiet and stay away from the windows. Do not answer the door. Our friends all have keys. Paul and Franco will be back tomorrow. Elvire will return the day after that."

The three women left that evening with Melbourne, Arthur and two other fliers, and arrived in Bordeaux the next morning. *Tante Go*, met them in Bayonne with tickets for Saint Jean-de-Luz so it would not appear that the men had come from Paris. Each woman walked with an airman to the flat of Ambrosio San Vicente at 7 Rue Salagoïty.

Tante Go couldn't have found a more enthusiastic host than the dapper Ambrosio, a man in his forties with short dark hair greying at the temples. A well-defined philtrum groove above his lip and a dimpled chin gave him a distinguished look. He delighted in hearing the adventures of the airman as he served up a feast of roasted lamb with mint jelly, savory dinner rolls, potatoes au gratin, Spanish olives and cheeses for dinner—all purchased on the black market through Tante Go.

Ambrosio filled their glasses with rich red wine and lifted his to toast. "To victory!"

Melbourne responded in his thick Australian accent, *"Viva la France!"* then tipped his glass toward Dédée and Janine. *"Viva la Belgique!"*

Jeff Hayden, the other Aussie, leaned over his plate and deeply inhaled. "My God, we haven't had lamb like this since we left Australia."

"So you boys are from the same team?" Ambrosio asked as he passed the bowl of potatoes.

"Yeah—we're all crewmates," Melbourne said. "Halifax Bomber— M for Mother."

"We took a hit on the way to Germany," British airman, Cedric Fox, explained. "The plane went up in flames. Six of us got out. We don't know what happened to the others. Jeff, Al and I met up pretty quickly. We didn't see Ivan again until the train from Brussels."

"I came down in the Netherlands and hid in a ditch," Melbourne said. "A German patrol passed so close I could smell their boot polish."

After their stories, Dédée doled out Spanish money for them to buy food and bus fare in case they were separated when crossing the border. "And this"—she scrawled an address on a piece of paper—"is where to find the British Consulate in Bilbo. Memorize it. Then Ambrosio will burn it."

In the morning, the men signed Ambrosio's book, rode the tram to Urrugne and walked to Frantxia's farm where Bee Johnson awaited them. After dinner they set off across the dark fields in single file with Bee near the front and Dédée in the rear to make sure no one fell behind.

The men marched along in silence hearing only the sound of light footfalls and tree limbs bending in the breeze. Dédée welcomed the invigorating night air, but moisture condensing in the cool higher elevations would make the grass and rocks slippery. With the light from the moon and stars blocked by the thick forests, the trail would become even more treacherous. After the long hike to the summit, she sat among the men as the lights of Irun, Spain twinkled in the distance. "After you have eaten, each of you must massage the calf muscles of the fellow next to you like this." She demonstrated on Melbourne. "Leg cramps can cripple you and we cannot afford to slow down. We must be well past the border before dawn."

Hiking down strained the muscles differently from climbing as tired legs worked to resist gravity's pull. The quicker pace made the men more prone to slipping. Then came the most hazardous part. The tree cover ended about fifty yards before the river. On a moonlit night like this, they dared not dally too long in the open. Crossing the river increased the danger as legs mired in water would slow their getaway if a Spanish patrol happened by on the road above.

"Take off your trousers," Dédée told them softly. "Tie them around your neck like this." Once they were set, she gave the guide a nod and he scrambled low to the river bank where he crouched down and scanned the road on the other side. One at a time she sent the men until they were all in the water holding the trouser leg of the man in front to form a chain. She slipped into the water in the last position. The cold water stung her legs. She gasped and held her breath until the shock subsided.

Once across, they huddled in the brush at the foot of the slope to wiggle their cold wet legs into their trousers while the guide climbed up through the narrow buffer of woods to the road above. With the men lined up behind him, Bee positioned himself half-way up the slope and awaited the guide's signal. The guide waved to Bee, then dashed across the road. Bee whispered down to the others, "Off we go." He sprang up and, keeping low, scampered across.

The men followed in rapid succession. Just as the last man and Dédée hit the pavement, two shadows popped out of the darkness. "Run!" she whisper-shouted.

"*Alto!*" a *Carabinero* raised his rifle.

Dédée flew into the dark woods.

Boots slapped the wet tarmac, their thuds growing frightfully near.

Scrambling up the slope, her foot slipped on a wet branch and she went down hard on sharp rocks. She clenched her teeth against the pain, pulled herself up and hobbled on. Moments later, she was in full trot again.

Shots rang out.

Dédée reflexively ducked, then bounced back up and continued running, struggling against the steep slope, panting for air. Adrenaline kept her going. She ran a little farther, then stopped to listen: nothing but the whoosh of the wind and creak of the trees. Her legs stung as she hiked on. Two shadows appeared ahead of her, but the *Carabineros* couldn't have gotten ahead of her this quickly. It had to be airmen.

"Bee told us to wait here while he looked for the others," they said when she caught up.

Bee and the guide returned moments later with one airman.

"Who is missing?" Dédée asked.

"Davies," Hayden said with worry in his voice.

Bee backhand slapped the guide's coat. "Let's make a sweep and see if we can find him."

"Ten minutes," Dédée whispered.

No one wanted to leave a man behind, but they had to accept that he might be dead. And if they didn't get moving they'd be exposed in the light of dawn.

It was a somber group that reached the top of the mountain on the Spanish side. Dédée caught up with Hayden and Fox when they emerged from the woods into a meadow on the downward side of the mountain as the sun rose. "I was last in line," she told them. "If they missed me, they probably missed him too." The boys nodded their hope as the farmhouse came into sight.

A hearty meal of eggs, potatoes and sausages was served up by the family who spoke no English, but whose warm welcoming smiles could be understood in any language. After breakfast, while the men soaked their feet in tubs of hot water then went to bed, Dédée hiked another five miles to Renteria. From there, she took a tram to San Sebastian and napped at Bernardo Aracama's apartment. Early evening Bernardo drove her back to the farmhouse where he picked up the airmen and she and Bee hiked back into the mountains with their guide. There was still no word on Melbourne.

"You look a little pale," Tante Go said when Dédée arrived back at Villa Voisin. "Why don't you and Bee stay here tonight and go back tomorrow?"

Dédée sighed. Airmen were piling up, and the longer they remained in hiding, the more restless they became and the more likely they were to take risks that could endanger everyone. She have to get back to Paris. Children were waiting.

Dédée slept nearly all the way. When she woke up, her whole body ached. She pulled her jacket closed, but couldn't get warm.

"Are you all right?" Bee asked.

She nodded. "It's a little colder up north."

Bee laid the back of his hand to her forehead. "You have a fever."

Dédée shrugged a shoulder. "I have to meet Peggy in Brussels this afternoon to take three children."

"You're not going anywhere," Bee said firmly. "I'm going to Brussels. You're going to rest."

Elvire saw the cuts and bruises on her friend's legs as she helped her into bed and telephoned a doctor friend.

When Bee returned that evening, Dédée was sitting up in bed eating chicken soup. "Well?" Bee asked. "What did the doctor say?"

"I have an infection from the fall. He gave me an injection and some antibiotics." Dédée chuckled. "He said I was worn down. He told me I should spend some time in the mountains!"

———

Thursday, November 19, 1942

The green envelope sticking out of the letter box had no stamp and no address. Elsie turned it over in her hand. "Mummy," she called carrying the envelope into the kitchen, "what do you make of this?"

"That's odd," her mother said. "I brought the post in hours ago."

"Maybe it is for us to send on to Paris. We've done this before."

"But there's no note," her mother said.

Elsie tucked the envelope into her bag. It might be something Nemo was expecting. But thinking more about it, she realized that Nemo wouldn't have had it sent here without telling them. It hadn't come in the normal post, so someone had delivered it personally. She took the letter back out. "I think we should open it." Her mom dried her hands and looked on as Elsie read aloud: "Deux colis pour jeudi. Two packages for Thursday?" Elsie saw concern in her mother's eyes. "That's today," she said.

Announcements of the arrival of airmen were always on a postcard and sent several days in advance to Nelly, the girl up the street, who would deliver them. Elsie would then go to the church at the appointed time and question the airmen on the steps until she was satisfied they were authentic. There was always this precautionary separation of tasks.

Her mother, shaking her head now with greater alarm, said, "You'd better show it to Nemo when you go back."

The doorbell rang.

It was Albert Marchal, the young guide from the Namur province whose only contact with Elsie had been at the church. With him were two men in khaki clothing. "These men do not speak French," Albert said apologetically to Madame Maréchal, "and I couldn't understand them, but there is something about them that makes me uneasy." He had waited at the church for an hour for Elsie, but it would have become suspicious for him to stay there. Then he had taken the men to Nelly who wasn't home. Her parents had given him the Maréchal address. "I didn't know what to do with them and knew you could question them in English."

Knowing she couldn't leave airmen out in the open, Madame Maréchal beckoned them inside. "Where are you boys from?"

Like others before them, they seemed to be momentarily stunned by her perfect English. "We are American," the taller fellow said.

Elsie was excited. These were her first Americans! "Where in America?" she asked.

"*Joursey* City, New *Joursey*."

Elsie sat at the table and observed the men as they ate. They were both fair-skinned and clean shaven with light eyebrows and firm features. They poked at their food, not as eager to eat as she would have thought after such a long trip. What really surprised her though was how quiet the fellows were. For most evaders, encountering the English-speaking Maréchals was like letting the cork out of a shook up champagne bottle. But these fellows sat at the table without saying a word. Even when Bobby came from school for his lunch break, all they said was hello.

"You're not eating," Madame Maréchal said. "Is there something wrong with your food?"

Looking rather pale, the tall one made a sour face and rubbed his belly. "Our hosts threw us a little going away party last night with much whiskey and our stomachs are not so good today."

They appeared rather anxious to Elsie—not cocky and self-assured like she'd imagined from the way British airmen talked about the Yanks. Her thoughts spilled out. "You do not look like Americans."

"No?" The short one's laughter sounded harsh and rather demeaning. "What do I look like?"

His tone was not friendly either. Elsie had heard that some Americans were rude. The sooner they were rid of these two the better. "What plane do you fly in?" she asked.

"A Halifax."

That was odd. She was sure a Halifax was a British plane. "How many men were in your crew?"

"Four."

"Why are you wearing khaki shirts? Are those your uniforms?"

"Yes."

She wished she knew whether American uniforms were blue like the RAF.

"I need to use the cabinet," the short one said.

Madame Maréchal pointed to the bathroom. "It is right through there."

The taller one excused himself and stepped out into the back yard for some air.

"This is strange," she whispered to Elsie. "Americans call it a bathroom, not a cabinet. And that other fellow didn't even ask permission before going outside."

Bobby left for school and when the airmen returned to the table, Elsie told them, "Let me have the money from your escape kits."

"Why do you need money?"

Usually, airmen gave the money without question. "To have your travel papers made up," she said. His tone was rather curt, not what she would expect from someone being rescued from the Germans. She took out a pad and placed it in front of them. "Please write for me your names, your serial numbers, where you were shot down, what plane you were flying in and your functions in the aircrew."

When they finished their writing, the tall one said, "We are going for a walk to get some air."

"You cannot go out alone," Madame Maréchal said.

"Why not?"

"What if you get lost?"

He laughed sarcastically. "Have you met an American who could not find his way?"

The Maréchals exchanged a glance, but let them leave so Elsie could slip out and consult with Nemo.

At the Swedish Canteen, *Nemo* examined the papers up close then sat back, drawing a crooked finger across his mouth and chin. "I don't like this, Elsie. This script doesn't look English or American to me."

"They said there were four men in their crew," she said, "but I'm pretty sure a Halifax bomber carries six or eight."

He set the papers on the desk. "We need to be careful."

"What should we do?"

"Do not let them leave again. Question them thoroughly. If you have any doubts about their authenticity, any doubts at all, you and your mother get out of there. Contact me when you have established a new address. In the meantime, I'm going to have them checked out."

Elsie returned home and dug her key out of her bag while she planned how to take her mother aside and tell her what Nemo had said. Suddenly, the door flew open and a powerful hand yanked her inside.

"Welcome home," A big fair-skinned man said with a sneer. "We've been expecting you."

A German field police officer on her left and another on her right pointed revolvers at her while the first guy closed the door and blocked it in case she had a notion to leave. Two more plus the so-called Americans were seated in the living room smoking cigars and drinking liquor from the family's heirloom decanter. Plates with food scraps and discarded napkins lay strewn on the coffee table. The 'Americans' had apparently regained their appetites.

The lead officer snatched her bag out of her hands and rifled through it. Elsie held her breath as he pulled out keys, brushes, makeup, wallet … At any moment he would discover her work papers which would lead them to the Swedish Canteen and her friends would be as good as caught.

"Your mother is dead. We shot her," the tall *American* said with no trace of the anxiety he had exhibited earlier. "Her body is lying on the kitchen floor. Tell us what we want to know, Mademoiselle, or your turn is next."

The blood drained from her head and the room started to float away. She somehow managed not to faint.

"Where did you go when you left here?" the German demanded.

She forced herself to think quickly. "I went to La Place de Brouckère to buy goods on the black market."

A swift hard slap stung her face. "Do not play games with me!"

Elsie raised her arm defensively, but a goon grabbed it and twisted it behind her. She felt the bite of another slap. Aggressive blue eyes pierced her as the German's hand closed into a fist. She turned her head away awaiting the next blow. "Please," she cried. "No more. I'll tell you what you want to know." She hoped to buy some time to think. "Just don't hit me again. Please don't hurt me anymore."

They loosened their grip. The man's voice softened. "If you cooperate, you will be treated well."

Elsie hesitated, rubbing her wrist she tried to come up with something. She glanced at her watch—4:30. Imagining her father walking into their trap filled her with worry—would they shoot him too? And Bobby had taken a letter to school to pass to Suzanne's son, Martin. Would he and Martin be arrested? Somehow, she had to lead these Germans away.

"Talk!"

"I—I'm going to meet my boss at five o'clock."

"Where?"

"At the entrance to Bois de la Cambre." The large park on the south side of the city would take a little while to reach.

In a cold dark drizzle, Elsie marched the familiar blocks on Avenue Voltaire to the tram stop, prodded along by the two *Americans* and flanked by two other Germans. When the group boarded the trolley the leader called out, "ATTENTION! Everyone in the front stand up and move to the back." The wide-eyed passengers regarded the prisoner—a school girl in simple skirt, blouse and bobby socks who looked to be no more than fifteen—yet apparently so dangerous, the big Germans had to squeeze her between two of them on the bench, and post one in the seat in front and one behind.

A big black car with two more Germans met them at the St. Michel roundabout. With six burly men, Elsie was made to sit on the lap of the tall *American*. "The car has not moved and Karl is already smiling," the fellow in the front joked in bad French.

"Easy on the bumps, driver, or the girl might get a little surprise," another quipped.

Elsie ignored the pig.

"I say we drive her around a while and she can take turns sitting on all of our laps."

Their bawdy laughter continued all the way to Avenue Louise where they stopped the car before the roundabout. "Out!" the man in charge commanded. The tall *American* and another German each grabbed an arm and marched her up to the statue of the Horseman's Battle Bronze Group where the *American* jerked her to a halt. "Go stand there," he said nodding toward one of the white masonry entrance buildings. She felt a sudden poke in her ribs and saw the *American's* revolver. "Do not try to run, mademoiselle, or I will stop you with this."

The Germans took up positions out of sight at strategic locations. Casually, she looked around as if she was actually expecting someone. She paced in a small circle as one might do while waiting. Behind her, the park stretched for over four hundred acres with vast areas of woods, and beyond that was a huge forest. She ventured a bit farther. The blackout and rain made everything dark. She took a few steps back and forth, and with each stroll wandered a bit farther. Just a few more steps, she decided, and she would make a dash for the woods.

"Mademoiselle!" One of the Germans stepped out of the shadows with his hand on his holster. "That is far enough!"

How long would they let her stand here before they realized she had made the whole rendezvous up?

After an hour, a Belgian gendarme strolled up and asked, "Mademoiselle, what are you doing alone in the dark?"

"Walk away," she advised him softly, "I am surrounded by Gestapo."

The officer heeded her warning and strolled on.

After the second hour, one of the Germans called to another and the two stormed toward her. "You little bitch! There is no one coming is there!"

"Maybe he saw you and left," Elsie stammered.

He grabbed her arm. "*Ta gueule, putain!* We have ways of dealing with bitches like you!" He vise-gripped her bicep and dragged her to the sedan, shouting, "*Chienne! Chatte! Putain!*" as he shoved her in.

He called her every vile vulgar name he could think of all the way to the Gestapo office on Rue Traversière.

Over the next couple of hours she revealed nothing of any value to the breathless pig-faced man who questioned her, admitting only that she was helping two men who said they were Americans.

The next interrogator was a bit cleverer. "Who do you report to?"

"No one. I just receive a note that men are to be moved."

"Who gives you that note?"

"I don't know."

"Who delivers the men?"

"I am told where to collect them."

"Where?"

Elsie shrugged. "Cafés, parks, squares … it is always different."

"Where did you collect the two men who turned you in?"

Her head pounded. "They were led there by someone."

"But you just said you collect the men."

"Those were *your* men. I did not collect them."

He tried for another twenty minutes to catch her contradicting herself before giving her over to another agent.

This man was tall and strong, with eyes of cold steel. "Tell me who you work for!" His words exploded in her throbbing head.

"I already told the last man everything I know."

"I am not toying with you, you little whore! Now tell me who you work for!"

Elsie said nothing.

The man violently shook her. "Talk!"

She remained silent.

Suddenly, a fist stung her face.

"Talk!" He slapped her hard across the cheek. His eyes flared. He grabbed her wrist and twisted it behind her back. "You will tell me what I want to know or I'll break your arm!"

Elsie cried out through gritted teeth.

He twisted harder.

Her eyes welled up.

He gave one last strong twist and shoved her to the floor. The questions stopped and she was led out to the main office.

Across the room stood her father with bruised face in the clutches of another German. Sadly, her diversion hadn't saved him. Together, the two were pushed into a car and driven to Saint Gilles Prison.

Isolated in a cold dark cell, she collapsed onto the mattress. Her head was splitting. But before trying to sleep, she realized they had not taken her bag. In the darkness, her fingers found her work papers for the Swedish Canteen. She tore them into little pieces and swallowed them.

CHAPTER FIFTEEN

At the Swedish Canteen, Peggy stared at the smoke ribbon twisting up from her cigarette. New recruit, Victor Michiels, sat with his newspaper at eye level, but with his leg nervously bobbing, he couldn't possibly read the shaking print. Seated behind his desk, Nemo regarded the clock, unconsciously turning a matchbox over and over between thumb and forefinger. In his long face, Peggy could read that he was second guessing his decision to send Elsie back.

Each person in his little band was under twenty-five and he worried about them like they were his children. Peggy wanted to remind him that Elsie was now eighteen and like Peggy herself, she knew what she was getting into, but that wouldn't ease his mind. It was one of the things they all loved about him.

The afternoon shadows grew long. Each tick of the clock sucked a little more life from their hopes. Victor, elbows on knees, held his head in his hands. As the office light faded, Nemo clicked on his desk lamp and slumped back in his seat with a long, deflated exhale.

"Why don't I go have a look?" Victor suggested.

Nemo shook his head. "It is too risky."

"I'll just walk down the street past the house." Victor was young, athletic and always positive. This sitting and waiting went against his cheerful, energetic nature, and he was growing ever more fidgety.

"If it was a mistake to send Elsie back, I don't want to make another one."

"But how else will we know what has happened?" Victor said. "It is getting dark. I'll stay out of sight and have a look."

Nemo sighed his reluctance. "All right, but don't get too close. Just observe."

.   .   .

An hour passed—long enough for Victor to have a look and come back. Peggy peered through the window blinds. It was fully dark now. Soon it would be curfew. She saw the stress in Nemo's face as he tossed the matchbox on the desk, stretched and began to pace.

Peggy opened a small brass case from her bag. "Cigarette?"

Nemo shook his head. "It's nearly nine o'clock. You had better go home. There is nothing we can do here."

She wished she could walk past Avenue Voltaire on the way, but being on the street at this hour would draw attention. She felt so inadequate.

She lay awake thinking of Elsie. If Victor hadn't returned, there could be only one explanation—he must have been spotted watching the Maréchal home. Her mind was spinning. Was poor Elsie being beaten by the Gestapo? Would she stay silent like Nadine—or would the names of others be tortured out of her? Peggy said a silent prayer, not for herself, but for the Maréchals and Victor and Nemo with his little girl and a baby on the way.

Giving up on trying to read by the light of a small torch, she crushed out her cigarette and said one last prayer, putting it in God's hands. But no sooner had her head hit the pillow than she was struck by another terrible thought. Elvire Morelle was coming on the overnight train to visit her brother in St. Gilles Prison. She would walk right into the Gestapo trap and with the early morning curfew, there was no way to warn her.

In the morning, Peggy packed a large handbag with everything from toothpaste to money to underwear in case she had to go on the run. She grabbed her German photos too. Those certainly could not be forgotten. As soon as the curfew allowed, she dashed over to the Canteen.

"Any word?"

Nemo shook his head. "I've sent messages to my brother Albert and to Georges and Edouard d'Oultremont to stay hidden until I say it is safe."

"You try telephoning Victor's home?"

"If he has been arrested, the Germans will be listening in."

"I will go to his house," Peggy said boldly.

"No. I don't like it, Peggy. Victor would have contacted us by now if something hadn't happened to him. You'll be walking into a trap."

"I will be all right."

"I can't let you go. It's too dangerous."

Of course he couldn't let her take the risk—not after Elsie and Victor —but she had a plan. "Don't worry. I have an alibi." She lit a cigarette and smiled to reassure him. "I will be back soon."

She slipped through the back garden gate out to the avenue beyond, taking a roundabout way in case the Germans were watching. She drew a breath as the house came into view. For her alibi to work, there could be no hesitation. She strode directly to the door and rang the bell.

"Come in, Mademoiselle," said a tall man with deep set eyes said as if he'd been expecting her.

Peggy knew instantly that she was trapped. "Is Josée at home? I've come to see her about a school assignment."

The brute grabbed her arm and dragged her inside. She couldn't believe her stupidity. Nemo had told her not to go, but she was too full of bravado to heed his warning. The German opened the double doors to the sitting room and pushed her in. Two officers stood guard over Victor's sister, Josée, his mother and father, and the maid who would have normally answered the door.

"Sit down!" one officer ordered as he snatched her pocketbook and tossed it to another agent. "How do you know Victor?" he barked.

Peggy forced herself to stay calm and lie as she had rehearsed. "I don't know Victor. I only know Josée." In fact, Peggy didn't know Josée at all, but gambled that the girl would go along with the lie.

"Why did you come here?"

"We had a school assignment that I was having trouble with and I thought Josée could help me."

The fellow rifling through her bag held up the photographs of the German soldiers and their families. "What are these?"

Peggy answered in German. "They are dear friends. I have known them for many years."

He didn't seem impressed with her German connections. Trying not to appear nervous, she sat back with her hands in her coat pockets. Then her fingers touched the long shaft of metal—she still had the key to the gate behind the Swedish Canteen!

For a moment, she stopped breathing altogether. Then she collected herself. The underwear in her bag did the trick. As the agent lifted her panties out chuckling to the others, she dropped her hand to her side and tucked the key under the chair cushion.

After more questions, a young soldier was directed to escort her out to the car. His face bore a troubled look. "You may as well know that we had to shoot Victor Michiels last night."

"Oh, but that is not possible!" she exclaimed. She gasped and covered her mouth, realizing she had sworn inside that she did not know Josée's brother, Victor.

The German seemed too distraught over the shooting to notice. "Say nothing about his death or it will go badly for you."

Taken to a house a few blocks away, she was directed into a waiting room with people she didn't recognize. She'd been afraid that she would see Elsie and that they would be made to identify each other. After an hour of somber silence, she was brought to a room where another woman was being taken out. A chill ran up her spine as she passed the woman whose disheveled hair and clothing looked like she'd been tossed about. It was Elvire Morelle! Neither showed any recognition of the other.

Peggy's bag was handed to yet another inquisitor. A dark cloud of acrid cigar smoke hung in the air, burning the back of her throat as a plump rat-man in a suit and necktie glared at her through beady black eyes.

"Do you know Victor Michiels?" the man asked.

"No. I only know his sister," she answered in German.

He opened her bag and began rifling through as he spoke. "How do you know his sister?"

"I am taking the same course as her at university."

"Why were you at the house of Victor Michiels?" he asked as he lifted out her toothbrush.

"I went to see his sister, Josée."

The inquisitor replaced the toothbrush and drew out a pair of under-wear. "Is this a pocketbook or a suitcase?" he said almost to himself, before continuing his disquieting questions. "Why did you want to see her?"

"I didn't understand the school assignment and I went to ask Josée for help."

"Where did you learn to speak German?"

"I lived with a family in Germany before the war. They are longtime friends."

The rodent let the underwear slip from his fingers back into the bag. He extracted the photos of the German officer and his family. "Who is this?"

"That is the family I told you about, the ones in whose house I lived while studying in Germany." She spoke about them in German, but couldn't read in his blank face whether the photos of her with the Germans had any effect. "They are as close as family. They are both very proud to be officers."

He continued to ask questions, and she continued to reply in German. Finally, around eight o'clock he put everything back into her bag and told her to go.

"I can leave?" she asked with astonishment.

"Naturally," he answered in German.

She walked away on shaky legs, afraid to breathe, afraid that he would change his mind and come after her. She had gone a hundred yards before she was sure it was for real. Then she burst into tears. She went into the first church she came to and knelt down to give thanks.

Elvire Morelle cursed herself for missing the signs that were all too clear —the curious blood on Avenue Voltaire a hundred yards from the Maréchal home and the *garde civile* lingering just down the street—she realized all of this the moment her knock on the Maréchal door was answered by a sneering German with his revolver pointed at her.

"Secret Police," he announced. "So we have yet another visitor." He waved the gun for her to move to the front room. Two German agents joined him and relieved her of suitcase, parcel and handbag. The room reeked of cigar smoke. Glasses of liquor and dirty plates on the usually tidy end tables said the Germans had made themselves at home.

She was asked questions throughout the morning then handcuffed and escorted at gun point into a lorry. With a dispassionate brute guarding her in the back of a truck taking her away to her torture and probable execution, Elvire should have been scared to the marrow inside her bones, but she felt nothing. She had known all along that one day she would be caught and that she would die for her cause. But it was worth it. She had seen the airmen—talked with them—so many young men risking and giving their lives to fight the Germans. She would sacrifice herself gladly for the cause that she believed to her very soul was right and just. No country could long survive if its people were not willing to defend it to the death. She sat up tall and proud, impervious to their intimidation. Her one regret was having been caught in such a stupid manner.

Ordered out at an official-looking building and shoved up a flight of stairs, she was ushered into a large room. The sign over the door read *Secret Police of the Luftwaffe*. Elvire was uncuffed and thrust into a chair before a German rodent in a creased uniform and spit-shined shoes. The disgusting stink of German cigars, like that in the Maréchal home, hung in the air. A large Nazi flag defiled the room, along with ostentatious images of the Führer and Goering. Though still in Brussels, it reeked of Germany.

The officer dragged the suitcase across his desk and opened it, regarding the girl coldly. Aggressive questioning began: "What is your name ... Why were you at the home of the Maréchals ..." He rifled through her clothes. "Why do you have a suitcase? Where were you going?" Pushing the suitcase aside, he started pulling articles out of her handbag ...a comb, hair brush, a small folded slip of paper ... a pen, mirror, prayer book....

Fear shot through her. For the first time today she was truly scared. The flimsy folded paper was the lease agreement for her apartment in Paris. With that information, the Secret Police would pounce upon the entire Paris sector! They would ambush Paul, Dédée, the Aylés, Franquito ... The Secret Police had obviously broken the Brussels sector. If they got the Paris sector too, Comet would be finished.

The officer paid little attention to the paper as he moved on to the curious parcel in brown wrapping. He snipped the strings while watching her face for a reaction.

She revealed none.

"What is this?"

"It is for my brother in St. Gilles Prison."

He poked through the food, toothbrush, and cookies she had packaged. Satisfied there was nothing suspicious inside, he moved the whole lot to the side of his desk. Then he turned around and began thumbing through a file drawer behind him.

Elvire snatched the lease paper from the desk, squeezed it into a small wad and popped it into her mouth. She managed to swallow the whole thing and return to her stony face before the officer turned back around. All that remained of her action was the thumping of her heart.

CHAPTER SIXTEEN

E lsie sat up, awakened by the *clomp clomp clomp* of heavy footfalls in the corridor. The clunk of the cell bolt echoed down the hall. The iron door *eeeeeked* open. "Out!" the guard commanded.

As she stepped into the hallway, the next cell door swung open and the command was repeated. The woman stepped into the light and Elsie's heart leapt. "Mummy!"

"No talking," the guard said.

Elsie whispered as they were ushered into the prison office, "They told me you were dead!"

"They will say anything to get us to talk," her mom whispered back.

After the questions and formalities of being processed in, they were separated again. Elsie was thrown into a solitary cell and figured that her mother must be isolated too. Interrogations would be coming. As she lay under her coat and a thin blanket in the dank darkness, she contemplated stories that might sound like the truth, but wouldn't actually reveal anything. The trouble was, the interrogators would likely ask her mother the same questions and if their answers didn't match, the Germans would know one of them was lying. There simply was no way to coordinate their stories. The only time she was let out of her cell was for a daily walk around the exercise yard. She and her mother would not be let out at the same time, and even if they were, they would not be permitted to talk.

But in the morning, Elsie felt a tiny crumpled up candy wrapper in the pocket of her coat and an idea struck. In tiny words, she wrote abbreviated bits of the story she would tell. Using a bobby pin, she scratched, "Look here" in English into the brick wall in the exercise yard, with an arrow pointing toward the ground. Then as she knelt down to tie a shoe, she slipped the tiny folded paper under a small rock.

The next day, the paper was gone and her lies went unquestioned. Her mum had found the note.

Airey Neave drew a weary breath before entering the conference room. Things were black as Newgate's knocker. Captain Jimmy Langley and Brigadier Crockatt were already seated at the table with the sullen-faced Colonel Sir Claude Dansey, head of MI6. It was going to be a long afternoon.

"The count, as I understand it, is over one hundred Comet underground members arrested," Dansey growled. "Is that correct?"

"Yes, sir," Jimmy said.

"Bloody banana skin," Dansey said. "And you've no idea how many more may be in the offing?"

"They've closed all of the old routes, severed ties and moved their headquarters," Jimmy said defensively. "It appears that the bleeding has stopped."

"That's the damn trouble. We've let them run the show and they don't know what the hell they're doing."

Airey had heard the scuttlebutt—*Uncle Claude* was on the knocker, making his case to people in the war ministry about closing down room 900. To tell the truth, Airey almost felt like giving up and letting him. Some of the blame for the hundred odd civilians in Gestapo custody fell upon his shoulders and those of the British who encouraged their dangerous enterprise. But he couldn't let those courageous people be so defamed without saying something. "They've delivered more than eighty airmen back to us, and there are countless others being sheltered and hidden away from the Germans. They have done this all while being relentlessly hunted by the Secret Police of the Luftwaffe, the Abwehr, the Gestapo, French gendarmes, collaborators, and bounty hunters. They're risking their necks every day while we sit here in the comfort of our arm chairs criticizing them."

Brigadier Crockatt shot Airey a look that said he should shut up now.

Dansey could have blasted the junior officer for his insolence, but perhaps Airey's passion made him take a more elucidative approach. "It is not a question of bravery," he said. "The issue here is whether this business of wholesale arrests can continue. It puts our entire spy network at risk. Every agent from Bordeaux to Amsterdam is in danger of being compromised."

"With all due respect, sir," Jimmy said. "I do not believe it is as bad as all that. The underground has been kept separate from your spies."

Airey maintained a poker face, though he knew this wasn't entirely true. Comet had carried out intelligence information for British agents, and some of Comet's members like Anne Brusselmans in Brussels and Kattalin Aguirre in Saint-Jean-de-Luz regularly gathered information on gun emplacements, troop movements and military targets.

"We just don't know who to trust," Dansey blustered. "This business of little girls and old men was doomed from the start. I told you that. I'm damned sorry I was right. And I'm even sorrier I didn't act on my instincts. It happened with Edith Cavell and I knew it would happen again."

Dansey's voice and blood pressure rose. "We've taken great pains to train agents and drop them behind enemy lines where they can report intel and disrupt the Germans. What we need are more trained operatives. We want to keep the Germans busy repairing bridges and railroads and we don't need amateurs mucking things up."

Heat rose to Airey's face.

Jimmy jumped in first. "One returned pilot is worth as much as a blown bridge."

"One pilot is one pilot," Dansey said. "Any number of pilots who haven't been shot down could blow up a bridge."

"Combined, the escape lines have returned more than one hundred aircrew members," Airey said. "How many bridges might those men blow up?"

"And what bloody good are those lines now?" Dansey's eyebrows stormed with old trench-fighter fervor. "If getting a pilot out is so damned important, why in God's name are we putting all our eggs in civilian baskets? You knew those baskets were bound to break one day. And yet you have no alternate lines in place. What the devil have you been doing up in room 900? Why isn't there another line to shift the evasion traffic to?"

Airey had no answer. Their attempt to start another line with Waucquez had failed miserably and the Brandy line was barely moving. If a Belgian with Waucquez's connections couldn't get a line organized, there was damned little chance an English foreigner could. The better course, it seemed, would be to send in support, which Airey planned to do with Belgian Army Sergeant Henri Decat who was training for such a mission. The recent events showed just how important it was to quickly verify an airman's legitimacy.

But nothing could shake Dansey off his destructive course. "Resources are limited," He said. "We need to focus on what is most important—intelligence information and sabotage."

Steady-tempered Brigadier Crockatt responded in a respectful, but not entirely agreeable tone. "Are we to abandon our fliers? That would most certainly boost morale."

"Our first and foremost duty is to win this war. We never wish to leave men behind, but we cannot save the few at the peril of many."

The meeting went on like this for another hour and Airey returned to his office thoroughly disheartened. He hated to even think about what would happen to those poor souls operating behind enemy lines if the British suddenly abandoned them. They needed more help than provided by room 900's meager resources. Now came the dreadful prospect that they might be cut off altogether.

"Don't worry," Jimmy said as if reading the strain on Airey's face, "Crockatt hasn't given up on us yet."

Airey's face grew longer. "I don't think that's really worth anything."

"I'm told he has some powerful connections."

"I don't mean that," Airey said. "Let's face it. Dansey's right about one thing. We haven't been very effective. Sometimes I sit here feeling the only support we are giving our friends is a pat on the back when they deliver a group of packages, and sympathy when one of their own is arrested."

"Well, that's our lot, isn't it?"

"To be perfectly honest, Jimmy, even if Crockatt can keep room 900 from closing, I'm not sure I am the right person for the job. Perhaps I would be of more use elsewhere."

Jimmy laid a hand on Airey's shoulder. "I understand the frustration, but promise me you won't decide in haste. You have a lot on your mind with your upcoming wedding and all. Maybe getting away for a while will do you good. We'll talk when you get back."

———

Prosper Dezitter eased the black 1939 Graham four-door sedan to the curb and tromped up the stairs ahead of his two cronies. Jean Marcel Nootens, a heavyset Belgian with ginger and grey roots underlying his dyed black hair, sported pince-nez glasses on the bridge of his nose and carried himself like a man of importance—just the type of fellow who could play an official or other character in Prosper's troupe of con artists. Jovial Charles Jenart's broad nose, plump face, and perpetually red hay-feverish eyes made him less refined looking than Nootens, but he spoke perfect English which came in handy portraying a British officer.

Prosper draped his coat on the rack and came away with a women's red hat and a perplexed look. "Flore, dear, who does this hat belong to?"

"It is mine."

"But my dear you don't wear hats," Prosper said.

"I met an old friend who makes them by hand."

"Do I know this friend?"

"No. Her name is Anny—Anny Lall." Flore tipped the brandy decanter over four snifters. "I knew her a long time ago. She was a nurse in Estonia. Now she makes hats and alters clothing to get by. How did it go?"

"We bought a Chevrolet and a Peugeot, and I found a suitable house. It's quite spacious and it has a garage where we can unload the lambs in secret. There is a bedroom for you and me, one for the boy and two more for our guests."

"Serge is my son, not *the boy*. And I hope you do not expect me to keep house and make meals for these men."

"Of course not, my dear. Your job is to convince the airmen to trust us. We'll hire a house keeper to do the cleaning and cooking. So where does this Anny Lall live?"

"She has a small flat on Segers."

"Did you say Segers or Slegers?"

"Segers."

"Oh. For a moment I thought we were going to be neighbors. The place I rented is on Avenue Slegers. You'll have to introduce me when we return from Paris."

"We are going to Paris?" Flore's face brightened as he knew it would.

"Yes. I have a little business and I thought we might visit Jacques and Marie-Thérèse while we are there."

"Desoubrie's gone to Paris?" Nootens asked.

Prosper nodded. "They left soon after the baby was born."

"I need to buy a gift for little Adolf," Flore said.

"Of course," Prosper said with a wink. "We couldn't go to Paris and not do a little shopping."

Jenart raised an eyebrow. "They named the baby Adolf?"

Prosper laughed "Our young friend is a tad over-zealous." He poured another round of brandies, while pondering aloud. "Tell me, my dear, this friend of yours, this Anny—does she live alone?"

"Yes."

"And you say she could use a little extra money?"

"Yes." The questioning inflection in her voice said she suspected he was devising some plan that involved her old friend.

Prosper's smile confirmed it. "Perhaps we could help her out…"

————

It began the same as the last two interrogations—ordered from her cell, marched out to a waiting automobile and driven to Gestapo headquarters. But this time Elsie was taken to a room with blacked out windows and no chair for her to sit in. This interrogation was going to be different.

The room went dark except one intense lamp aimed at her face. She squinted.

"Open your eyes!" one German commanded.

Elsie tried to do as she was told, but the bright light made her eyes burn.

"No more lies, Mademoiselle. Cooperate, or you will wish you had."

"I've told you everything."

"Who is your chief?"

Elsie said nothing.

The questioning continued for twenty minutes before the lights came on again.

"No more games," one said slapping a baton against the palm of his hand. "We know about Baron Greindl. He is your chief."

While the first officer questioned Elsie, the second slowly and deliberately drew a leather belt from the table and folded it in front of her, gripping the ends to let her know his intentions.

"Is Baron Jean Greindl your chief?"

"I've already told you everything."

The fellow with the baton turned the radio volume up very loud. "One more chance," he said. "Who is Baron Greindl?"

She said nothing. Her anxiety rose.

The music grew deafening.

Whaap! The strap bit her back, followed by the baton.

"Then what is his position in the escape line?"

"Baron Greindl only feeds the children at the Canteen. That is all."

Blows came in rapid succession. Burning pain took her breath away.

The music masked her screams.

"Tell me the truth! You little bitch!"

"I've told you everything," she cried.

The strap stung her again and again. The pain was unbearable. The room went black.

A shock of cold water jolted her back to consciousness, the side of her face resting on the floor.

"Get up!"

She pulled herself up on shaky legs. Her head hurt. She must have banged it when she collapsed.

"Tell me who Nemo is!"

Elsie said nothing.

Blows followed her all the way to the floor where she tried to deflect them with her arms. She screamed until kicks to the stomach and ribs made her curl into a ball and left her coughing and gasping for oxygen. She didn't know how much more she could take.

They commanded her to stand. The questions continued. When she still refused to reveal Nemo's identity, they beat her until she no longer had enough strength to push herself up off the floor. Two goons each grabbed an arm and dragged her out of the room and down the hall into a bathroom. Cold wet cloths dabbed at her lacerations. Rivulets of red ran in the wash of water that fell from her body.

Back in her cell at St. Gilles Prison, she lay down on her stomach. Her dress clung to the sticky blood on her back. When the guards had left and she was alone, she broke down into uncontrollable sobs. The cuts and bruises on her back hurt so badly it felt like she would die from the pain. But, that wasn't the reason for the sobbing. She thought of Nemo, and Peggy and Victor—they were all going to be caught because of her stupidity. She should have known something was wrong when there was a breach in the procedure. She should have known the *Americans* were imposters.

The next day new threats accompanied the questions and beatings. "If you do not give us the names of your associates, everyone in your family will be guillotined."

When she still wouldn't talk, they sat her down and a man in a dark grey suit pulled his chair close and stared into her eyes for several long moments.

"What is your name?" he asked without blinking.

"Elsie."

"Look deeply into my eyes, Elsie. Just relax while I ask you some questions."

He stared as if trying to take control of her mind. Several long, unblinking moments passed before he determined that his subject had been adequately primed. "I can see you are tired of all these questions. You want to rest. You are growing weary. Your mind is weary. You want to take a little rest. You are getting sleepy ... sleepy..."

With those big wide staring eyes, he looked like a giant bug. Elsie burst out in giggles.

The trance was broken. The man sat back looking rather shocked and embarrassed. He left without saying another word.

Infuriated, the German inquisitors pounced on her and beat her to the floor, revived her and resumed their questioning. Her refusal to identify Nemo enraged them. They beat her again raising welts on her back. She passed out again and once again they revived her with the water bucket. When evening fell, and she still hadn't given them anything, they dragged her back down to the bathroom, cleaned her up and sent her back to prison.

She collapsed down on the prison cot in such pain that she couldn't tell where it hurt the most. It wasn't just the pain. They had gotten the name of Jean Greindl. It would only be a matter of time before they put it together that Baron Greindl and the elusive Nemo were one and the same. She thought of what they would do to him when he was caught. She thought about his little girl and the recent birth of his second baby and the tears started all over again.

CHAPTER SEVENTEEN
Wednesday December 16, 1942

Dédée opened the bathroom window an inch, letting the crisp cool breeze disperse the acrid odor of the hair dye.

Her father knocked and swung open the door. "Two children and a Belgian aviator are arriving this afternoon."

She held a mirror off to the right, turning her head back and forth, checking the reflection behind her to make sure she hadn't missed a spot. "I should go to Spain like this," she said looking at the syrupy black goop on her head.

Her father didn't laugh. He didn't smile. He didn't even say his usual, *I still can't get used to you with dark hair.*

"Don't worry," she said. "I will be all right."

"I just don't know if we have waited long enough. It has only been a couple of weeks since the arrests."

"Baron Greindl would not send us children if he did not think it safe."

The lines on her father's face remained. "When they warned us about the arrests, they said Brussels was so badly broken that they thought it best not to continue. I am worried Nemo has resumed too quickly because of you."

"Me? I did not tell him what to do."

"No, but my Little Cyclone, people cannot help but follow you."

Dédée shrugged and said matter-of-factly, "He asked if I was going to continue. I told him yes, of course I will continue." She thought back to her discussion with Baron Greindl, Jean Ingels and Eric de Menten. *We have all lost loved ones, but it is for those we care about that we do this,* she had told them. *We are making a difference. It heartens pilots to know that people here will help them. They're fighting the Germans for us, They are the only hope of saving the Belgian and French people. How can we ask them to fight and die for us if we are not willing to do the same? We must go on.*

Now that she replayed the conversation in her mind, she realized that perhaps they *were* drawn back into action by her passion for the cause.

"The Baron is a careful intelligent planner," she said as much to convince herself as to convince her father. "He would not send us children if he was not ready. He has recruited new helpers, Monique … Lily … Albert … Peter…"

"But the Baron himself is not new. How long before the Germans figure out that Baron Greindl is Nemo?"

"He promised to stay away from the Canteen and leave Brussels as soon as he finds someone to take over as chief." Nemo wasn't the only one who needed to escape to England, she thought. Her father now had a large price on his head, but that conversation would have to wait until she returned from Saint-Jean-de-Luz. She changed the subject. "Is the next group ready?"

He nodded. "The American, Forrest Hartin, was authenticated through the BBC broadcast two nights ago. The three Belgians are also ready."

Dédée turned on the faucet and bent down, but paused before sticking her head underneath. "Bee and Franco are crossing them so I can get back to collect the next group."

Her father's nod ended with a chuckle. "You know, I still cannot get used to you with black hair."

Mid-morning, Dédée cautioned Sydney Smith, a Canadian pilot dressed in the three piece suit his host Robert Aylé had loaned him. "We will walk like a couple to the department store for photographs. I may talk while we wait—maybe act playful. If I smile, you smile as if you understand."

"*Je comprehends le français,*" Sydney replied.

"*Très bien,*" Dédée said. "But do not speak."

After photos she left Smith at an apartment in the seventh arrondissement, met guides Eric de Menten Horne—*Peter*—and Henriette Hanotte —*Monique*—at a hotel near the train station. From there she conducted

British airmen William McLean and William "Jock" Brazill and Belgian pilot Didier Scuvie back to her apartment.

"I am sorry it has taken nearly three months to get you out of Belgium, Jock," she said as she poured cups of tea. "We've had some difficulties there."

"I know. A teenage girl *Lily* moved me twice in one day. Nemo told me it was because the line had been infiltrated by Germans posing as American pilots."

"Yes, we lost many of our people," Dédée said.

"Nemo had me question McLean here and he wanted me to stay to authenticate other airmen, but ..." Jock's words trailed off apologetically and he cast his eyes downward as if troubled by his decision to leave. "I-I-I'd had the bells pretty well knocked out of me ... blood running down my face ... my knee swelled up like a bloody balloon ... I'm not a coward, but..."

Dédée patted his hand. "It is all right. You are a very brave man, but you have been through much."

Jock's face relaxed a bit. He reached into his pocket chuckling as he drew out a strip of green polka dot material. "I'd nearly gotten killed because of this."

"A necktie?" Dédée asked.

He nodded. "After a night in a hedgerow wrapped up in my parachute, I limped to a farmhouse and identified myself as an RAF pilot. The farmer turned white and shooed me away, but then took pity on me and cleaned my cut up face and leg. He gave me trousers six inches too short and this bloody tie." Jock chuckled. "Another chap pointed the way on a map and wished me luck. When I reached a small town and went into a shop to buy some apples, a German soldier took a rather keen interest in my tie."

"Oh my goodness." Dédée covered her mouth.

"I was bloody ready to shi—Sorry ... ready to faint."

"What did you do?"

"I said *humpf,* made a face like this..." he demonstrated turning his head sideways and glaring rudely at an imaginary German. "...and I walked away. I spent the night hiding out in the woods." Jock's eyes brightened as he sipped his drink. "My God. Real tea!"

Dédée laughed. "We have connections."

Jock took another sip and set his cup down. "I promised Nemo I'd come back. He gave me a letter to give to his friend in Gibraltar so I can get into the training program."

"Be careful," Dédée said. "If you are caught with a letter, the Germans will say you are a spy."

Jock nodded. "It's sewn into the lining of my coat." He hesitated, then asked if she knew what happened to some of his crewmates. "— Mounts Dalton, Robert Frost, and William Randle?"

Dédée smiled, delighted to tell him. "I don't know about *Monsieur* Dalton, but we got *Messieurs* Frost and Randle through before the arrests. They are very likely flying missions again." The relief on Jock's face was what she imagined it to be like whenever a downed pilot was returned to his base.

Franco and American flier Forrest Hartin joined up with them on the overnight train, arriving at Bordeaux at half past seven and Bayonne at half past ten. Before exiting Dédée softly told them, "Go separately into the building. Do not join the lines exiting through customs. Wait for my instructions."

German soldiers and other travelers crowded the huge Bayonne station on this Saturday before Christmas. As Dédée strode casually through the terminal, *Lulu*, standing near the back wall, acknowledged her with a slight tip of the head and disappeared into the crowd. Dédée signaled with her eyes to Franco who slipped away with Scuvie and Hartin. Once they were gone, she whispered as she passed Jock, "Wait one minute then make your way over to the loo." She moved to McLean and repeated the instruction without looking at him.

When the boys reached the restroom, she unlocked the door with a duplicated key and sent them outside where *Lulu* hooked her arm under Jock's and spirited him away followed by Janine who had taken hold of McLean's hand.

Lulu Lucienne Dassié, daughter of Jean Dassié, a decorated one-armed veteran of the First World War and supervisor at the telephone exchange at Bayonne, led her *boyfriend* to the bridge. Her soft brown hair fell to her shoulders in gentle waves that bounced gracefully as she walked and her face was of such classic beauty that she could have been taken for a magazine model. What young man would not want to accompany her across the Saint Esprit Bridge to the Place Saint-André? She carried herself with such poise and confidence, it was hard to believe that the girl was only sixteen years old.

It took ten anxious minutes to cross the Adour River. The Germans continually monitored the long bridge from the *Citadel* fortress on the east side of the waterway and German vehicles and soldiers crossed back and forth all day. Walking beside a lovely young girl made the evaders less conspicuous. The Belgian guides hurried the children along to the small storefront Restaurant Chez Gachy to beat the lunch crowd from the second large German barracks, *Le Chateau Neuf* just across the square.

"Do not be nervous," Dédée cautioned the *children* before entering. "German soldiers dine here. Just eat your lunch in silence and act like their presence does not bother you."

Although the men looked at her like she was crazy, Dédée, Tante Go and Jean Dassié deemed the Restaurant Chez Gachy to be the perfect spot. Restaurant owners, René Gachy and his wife, Faustina Palenzuela, were Comet allies and the arrogant Germans would find it unthinkable that anyone would be so bold as to dine among them with enemy airmen. It was the ultimate joke on the egotistical master race, a secret jab that gave the underground something to chuckle about.

It was always difficult to say goodbye to these young men whom Dédée had looked after like they were her children, but she had to leave them in Saint-Jean-de-Luz for Bee and Franco to cross them into Spain while she caught the overnight train back north. The memory of their valiant grateful faces melted away as she laid her head against the window and allowed the train to rock her to sleep. At dawn, she awoke in Paris.

Paul greeted his daughter with a kiss and a hug. "Sit down my darling and I'll fix you some breakfast. How are our friends in the south?"

"We have good news. Ivan Davies, Melbourne, found his way from my directions to the British in San Sebastian." Dédée draped her coat over the back of a chair and opened her bag. "I brought you a present from Fernand."

Paul smiled knowingly at the box of cornflakes she handed him. From way down inside the box, he pulled out a stack of papers—stamped *certificates de domicil*—and held one to his face, lifting his big round spectacles. "Even the stamp looks real."

Dédée chuckled. "Fernand liberated it from Kommandantur's office!" She reached into the bag again. "I also have a present from Tante Go."

"*Ummm*, coffee, how wonderful. I have a present for her as well. Lily sent down information on coastal defenses that Madame Anne's group has gathered." Paul whisked milk, cheese, ham and eggs in a bowl and poured them into the pan as he spoke. "The Canadian, Sydney Smith, is staying with Aimable and there's a new English fellow, Herbert Spiller, up there as well."

"And the American?"

Her father slid the omelet from the pan onto her plate. "We have four of them now. We can send them together on the next crossing."

"Good. That will show the Americans that the people of Belgium and France will help them as well." Dédée broke off a bit of bread. Eating breakfast after sleeping sitting up in a train car wasn't very appealing, but the days of waking up in a nice warm bed were long gone. It did no good to think of such things.

"I am going up to meet the English pilot," she said after eating. "When Janine arrives tell her I will go with her to meet the Belgian."

She took the stairs up one flight to Aimable's fifth floor flat and double-knocked three times.

"I told the English pilot our *leader* would see him today," Aimable advised her with an impish wink that said he purposely hadn't mentioned her gender. He delighted in seeing their surprised faces when they discovered that the young girl in the delicate blue skirt and blue blouse was the leader of the escape organization.

"How are you doing, Sydney?" Dédée asked the fellow she had taken for photos four days earlier. "Ready for your trip?"

She caught Aimable's little smile at seeing the realization hit the other airman. "*Hallo*. I am Dédée. I am going to take you to Spain." She extended a hand of greeting. "You are an English pilot?"

"Navigator actually," the airman greeted her warmly, covering any trace of gender prejudice he might have felt. "I'm Herbert Spiller —Bert."

"Okay, Bert. Come sit at table and we will chat. I have booked a compartment on the overnight express to Bordeaux, but we will not be alone. You speak to no one—not even me. Bert, you sit diagonally to Sydney. Sydney, you sit beside me." She held out a hand. "*Carte d'identité s'il vous plaît*."

"*Très bien*. Good," Dédée said when they handed her their identification and work papers. "But your face must not look like you are guessing —or like you are waiting to see if you did it right. Now please stand up and empty your pockets."

She sorted through the contents and took away Bert's Belgian francs. "You do not want to be caught with these. Do you wear a watch?"

He showed her a chronometer watch for navigation.

"Take it off and put it in your pocket. And keep the cigarette lighter in your pocket as well. Do you ride a bicycle?"

Both men nodded.

"Good." She checked the time. "We will use bicycles for part of our trip. Now get some rest. I will return in three hours."

Next, she and Janine went to the flat of Robert Aylé and repeated the instructions to the Belgian, Charles Gueulette who would accompany Janine. The two groups would meet up when they reached Bayonne. "Good luck to us."

While Smith and Spiller changed into their traveling clothes, she buried in her bag a toothpaste tube containing intelligence information gathered by Madame Anne.

When the men came out of the bedroom, she took one look at Spiller and burst out laughing.

"What?" Bert looked perplexed.

"Where did you get that hat?" She asked waving at a small pork pie hat perched like a comedian's prop on Spiller's too large head.

"A farmer gave it to me first night after I was shot down."

She snatched it off his head, chuckling, and tossed it on the chair. "We will leave this behind. You must forget your own name," she added as she passed out folded French francs and train tickets. "The Germans may board the train to check your papers. This is routine. Act like it is nothing but inconvenience—like you do it every day. And do not fall for German tricks. If someone says *bonjour*, only nod. Do not answer—you are mute. If someone says *hallo*, do not show any comprehension. If someone asks you in English for the time, do not glance at your wrist. That will give you away." She regarded their apprehensive faces and eased their trepidation with a smile. "Just do as I have instructed and we will get you through. Good luck to us."

As the train pulled into the station, she said softly, "Go through the barrier separately and enter the same carriage as me." On the train, she silently pointed out which compartment to enter, but held back a few minutes before joining them so it would not look like they were traveling together. Bert slid over to make room for two elderly passengers, then closed his eyes and pretended he was going to sleep. Dédée waited until the train had left the city before closing her own eyes and nodding off.

Hours later a knock on the wall was followed by a German accented voice calling, "*Carte d'identité.*"

Dédée lifted her bag to her lap while sneaking a glance at Spiller who awakened with searching eyes like he was trying to remember where he was. He recovered quickly and passed his papers while frowning at the inconvenience. She commended him with a secret smile.

At Bayonne, she slipped out through the door near the bathrooms with Spiller and Smith and led them to a bench.

"Hello, mates. How are things in Piccadilly?"

The evaders' faces lit with surprise at the sound of a genuine English voice.

"This is Bee." Dédée chuckled. "He will look after you while I go take care of some things."

"Now then, chaps," she heard Bee say as she walked off, "we've got a bit of time to kill so the three of us are going across the bridge like the man on the Clapham omnibus and we'll go have a pint at a little place on the other side of the river."

Janine arrived at the station and Dédée took her aside. "When the eleven o'clock train from Bordeaux arrives, you and Lulu deliver the four parcels to Jean at the restaurant. Then you and Faustina take Bee's parcels to the villa. Good luck."

Dédée left Janine to handle that end while she walked into Bayonne to the back door of a bakery.

"How many bicycles do you need?" the baker asked softly.

"Eleven."

"Eleven!" He looked around quickly to see if anyone had heard him. "Eleven?"

"Can you get that many?"

"Yes, of course."

"What time?"

"They will be there by three," the baker said softly as he handed her two loaves of bread in a paper sack.

By the time Dédée reached Anglet, Janine and the two English airmen were already seated at the table. The nearness of the mountains and the tantalizing aromas of caramelized onions, garlicky green beans and beef steaks sizzling in Bobonne's pans, had the men smiling like schoolboys before a holiday. Bobonne served up joy and love, hovering over them like they were her children and beckoning them to eat up for their long hike.

After lunch, Tante Go passed new identification papers to the men. "These are your permits for travel in this area. We have an arrangement with the local authorities," she said with a wink. She also passed them her black book and a pen. "Before you leave, you must sign my book."

Bert ran his finger down the page. "Gordon Mellor—Lenny Pipkin!" He flipped to an earlier page. "Jack Newton …"

Dédée smiled. "Jack was the first British airman I led to Spain. Say *hallo* for me when you see him."

"Will do." Bert shook his head in disbelief. "I had no idea there were so many."

"You are numbers eighty-one and eighty-two," Tante Go said proudly. "And we have also conducted more than thirty French and Belgian soldiers and airmen over the mountains to fight with England."

After brief hugs and wishes of *bonne chance*, from their hosts, the evaders hoofed it back to the railroad station. The boys played their parts of weary laborers well, bouncing about on the wooden benches of the rickety old local train, but when Dédée sent them ahead to fetch their bicycles at Saint-Jean-de-Luz, they nearly gave the whole business away. Surprised at seeing their former passeurs, André and Marc, and four other Belgians they had met on their journey, they forgot their charade.

"*Ssshhh!*" Dédée admonished them. "Single file now—at intervals—straight down this road."

The boys' mouths snapped shut and they obeyed with puppy dog eyes.

She moved on, outlining the route to the Belgians, when the passeur, André, interrupted her with a tap on her arm and a finger pointed toward the pair who had just left.

Dédée couldn't believe it. She jumped on her bicycle and pedaled madly to catch up. "Hey! Hey!"

Spiller, looked back to see what was wrong.

"Get over to the right side of the road!" She huffed and took the lead. Sometimes, she thought, they were *worse* than children.

When they reached the outskirts of Urrugne, Dédée coasted down a farm lane and around to the back of a barn. They left the bicycles and walked in groups of two and three, keeping a brisk pace up the old cart track and through dangerously open pastures until they came to a white two-story house with red tile roof and shutters. Frantxia greeted the men with a warm smile and gestured them into her large living room.

"I'm sorry there are so many men," Dédée said as she filed in at the end of the long line. "Two of them are English and the other six are Belgian and French who are wanted by the Gestapo."

"There is plenty bread," Frantxia said in her Basque accented French. She drew her long raven black hair to the back of her neck and tied it with a ribbon. "I imagine to myself that every pilot we save to kill ten Germans." She tipped a big can of fresh milk into an enamel pot and lit the burner. "When they take my life, I will know I have traded it for many of theirs."

"From your calculations," Dédée said, "the number of Germans would be well over one thousand."

"Good." Frantxia set a wooden board on the table and cut thick slices of dark brown bread. "Children!" she called into the living room. "Stop bothering those men."

Dédée laughed at the two little ones staring mesmerized at the newcomers. "They are just curious. I think they are trying to figure out why they cannot understand what the men are saying."

Frantxia ladled up bowls of warm milk to go with the bread and Dédée called the men to the table, explaining that they would leave as soon as it was dark. "It will be a long hard walk," she said. "It will take us about twelve hours, but we must be far across the Spanish border before dawn. We must be quiet; no talking, no smoking, no coughing. You must follow orders quickly and without question even if it means lying down in the snow or mud."

The sound of poles clunking on the ground outside got Frantxia's little boy bouncing out of his chair and scurrying to the door. "Florentino is here!"

The mountain man tousled the boy's hair as he stepped through the doorway. Slung over the big man's shoulders were a dozen pairs of rope-soled espadrilles and goat-skin botas. He spoke in the Basque language to Frantxia who translated into French for Dédée. She relayed the message to the men in English: "The river is high and swift, but Florentino has brought a rope so we can cross."

She described the landmarks as Florentino pointed them out on a map —the direction inland—where they would cross the river—the light-house at Irun—the peaks known as the Three Crowns. Then she exchanged their French francs for Spanish pesetas so they could pay for food and bus tickets if they became separated from the party.

While Florentino applied bandages to each man's bare feet where they might be prone to blister and showed them how to securely tie the rope-soled *alpargatas*, Dédée drilled more warnings into them. "Your legs will become sore and tired. Your lungs will burn. But you must push yourselves this one night and tomorrow you will be free." She didn't tell them how close she had come to getting shot or how she and Elvire had nearly frozen to death when Elvire broke her leg. Their apprehensive looks showed they were already worried enough. "It will be difficult and dangerous. But you are my brave boys. Do as we instruct and you will make it."

"Now, before we go, Florentino will demonstrate how to use a walking pole so you do not slip." She added with a playful smile, "If you fall and break your leg, Florentino will have to carry you, and that will not make him happy."

Florentino set a brisk pace across chilly, misty fields, his huge pack bouncing rhythmically in time with his long strides. The two Belgian passeurs fell in behind him, followed by the airmen and the rest of the Belgians. The first few miles were fairly easy, but as the slope increased, so did the struggle to keep up with the big man. Gaps opened up and Dédée had to prod the men to close them. She was particularly concerned about the oldest hiker, a Belgian doctor in his mid-forties. Although he trooped on without complaint, he was already breathing hard and they hadn't even reached the strenuous part of the climb.

She stole up beside him and asked softly, "How are you doing?"

The doctor nodded, too out of breath to speak.

"We will take a break in a little while."

He nodded again and slogged on, a little quicker now, to catch up with the man ahead of him.

Watching him struggle, she realized how difficult it was going to be for her sixty-year-old father to make this crossing. Although he walked around the city moving men, that was not enough to prepare him for hiking up a mountain. But with a million franc bounty on his head and the Gestapo and Secret Police in two countries closing in, he could not stay in France. He would need to cross in winter when the extra hours of darkness would give them a little more time.

Suddenly, Florentino threw his hand up and crouched.

"Down!" Dédée whispered. The men fell flat, burying their faces in the frigid rocks. Although she heard nothing but the wind through the trees, she had come to trust Florentino's cat-like senses in these mountains. She never knew what had made him stop.

Their mutual trust made them a great team. No guide would dispute

Florentino's prowess in these mountains. He could navigate the trails in total darkness. Up here, he was in charge—she would never hesitate to put her life in his hands. And his admiration and respect for Dédée was unbounded. He accepted the little dynamo without question. She was the boss, and anyone who felt otherwise would have to answer to him.

After a long hard uphill slog, Florentino called a halt near the top of the first peak. The men collapsed on the ground. Dédée sat down next to Spiller and Smith. "How are you two doing?"

"Okay so far," Spiller said hesitantly as he gazed out at the peaks ahead. "Do these mountains ever end?"

"That was the hardest part of the hike." She patted his leg like he was her apprehensive little boy. "You have done well. It will not be long now until we go down to the river. That is the borderline and the most dangerous part of our trip." Dédée bolstered him with a motherly smile. "You are my strong brave boys. You will make it."

Florentino led them through the thin cold air for another hour before they began to descend. Hiking down-slope stressed muscles differently than the climb. The mist-soaked trail became slippery, requiring more care in braking with the poles. Half way down the slope to the river, one of the silhouettes dropped from sight with a thud. Dédée hurried down to find the doctor being helped to his feet by Spiller and Smith. The doctor shook a leg to show it was all right.

She positioned herself in front of him, working her pole with one hand and extending the other for the doctor to grab if he needed. As the rushing water grew louder, she worried about his ability to make it across. He possessed the determination, but it would take strength and balance to fight the current, and right now, she doubted if he had either.

They huddled in a thicket thirty feet from the bank to remove their trousers before crossing the river. This time Florentino secured one end of the rope to the base of a tree then slipped in, stretching the rope as he went.

"Go!" Dédée pushed the men one after the other before wading in herself. The freezing water sucked the breath out of her and stung her bare legs and midriff. Turning into the current using her rear foot as a brake against the force of the water, she wrapped one hand in the trouser leg of the man in front of her and locked her other arm around the rope. Despite her being smaller and lighter than the men, it was up to her to anchor the tail end while Florentino anchored the front. The strong current forced her to take small shuffling steps as lifting her legs too high could knock her off balance.

The rope ended near the middle of the river. The second man in line grabbed ahold of Florentino's trouser leg, and the guide let go of the rope and moved the human chain forward. The line swayed as the men fought to maintain their footing. Then Florentino suddenly waved them down and everyone sank until only their heads remained above water. Lights appeared on the road above to their left, growing brighter then dimming as the automobile motored past heading toward the coast. The red tail lights disappeared. Florentino continued on.

After the midpoint, the current eased a bit and progress became quicker. But by the time they reached the cover of the bushes on the other side, the doctor was white as a ghost. The struggle had unnerved him.

"Rub your legs," Dédée whispered to the group. "You must get circulation back." After they had wiggled back into their trousers, the men followed Florentino, pulling themselves up the slope grabbing whatever bushes they could. She followed, keeping an eye on the doctor. Silently, one by one, they made a light-footed dash across the railroad tracks and ducked into the brush where Dédée issued more instructions. "When you get to the top of the slope, wait until Florentino gives you the signal to go. Once you've crossed the road, climb up to a large rock and hide behind it."

This time, she could not go last. In the doctor's shaky state, she would have to run with him. The best cure for nerves was to take charge. "*Monsieur le docteur*," she whispered, "you and I will go together. You do not think. You just stay with me. Do you understand?"

The doctor nodded.

She helped push him up from the bottom of the slope while Spiller and Smith pulled him from above. After the two airmen dashed across and disappeared into the woods, she grabbed ahold of the doctor's coat sleeve and together they loped over the tracks to the next slope.

Florentino's eyes were focused down the road to the guard area when she and Monsieur le docteur climbed up and lay beside him. Street lamps set at intervals provided a low level of light, but enough to see a figure crossing the road if the guards were looking in their direction. It required patience to time each crossing for just the right moment when the guards strolled back in the opposite direction. The big man raised his arm. Dédée and the doctor rose to a crouch. Then Florentino dropped his hand, and Dédée gave the doctor a gentle push and hurried him across into the cover of the woods.

"Welcome to Spain," she whispered when they were all gathered behind the rock. "That was the most dangerous part of our journey. Eat and drink a little. We still have a long way to go, but the walk will be much easier."

Leaving France behind renewed the energy of the hikers. The trail grew more visible as the darkness lifted and soon they were on a hillside field looking down on a little farmhouse. Florentino went on ahead and knocked at the door. Lights came on inside. Dédée and her renegades were welcomed warmly in a language that neither she nor they understood. The matron of the house chatted away with Florentino as she went about lighting the stove and filling pans with bacon and sausages. The men hung up their wet clothing to dry by the fireplace while they ate. But there was no time to sleep once their bellies were full; they would be picked up within the hour. Dédée led them down to the road where the Belgians departed to make their own way. When the diplomat's car arrived, Spiller and Smith gushed out thank-yous.

"Quickly now," she said, cutting off their hugs with a light shove. "You must hurry and get in the car before another vehicle happens along." She sighed as she watched the vehicle disappear down the road. How she wished she could have hugged them a bit longer. For the past sixty hours she'd looked after them like they were her children. And just like that they were gone.

She walked on to Renteria and took a tram to San Sebastian to rest at Bernardo's apartment before going back over the mountain tonight. But the plan had been changed.

"I have already told Florentino we will not be returning tonight," Franco advised his boss.

"Why not?" Dédée asked.

"Because it is Christmas Eve."

She hadn't actually forgotten—the holiday presented the best opportunity to travel while guards relaxed in their merriment.

"I want you to come to midnight mass with me."

"I do not want to ruin your Christmas," she said half-kidding.

"Why are you so negative about God?"

"I'm not negative. I just don't believe. If God exists, where is he? How can he allow the Germans to kill without cause? Why are so many good people made to suffer from oppression, hunger and illness?"

"God does not cause his people to suffer. He gives us free will. People make people suffer. Illness makes people suffer. When you ask for his help, he may not cure your illness or free you from oppression, he will not smite your oppressors, but he will stand beside you and help you bear it … Bernardo and Sarasola are coming with us. It is Christmas…"

"All right. All right. I will go to mass with you. Now can I just get a little sleep?"

It seemed like half the city was out on the streets as midnight approached, all heading to the *Catedral Del Buen Pastor*. You didn't have to be a believer to be roused by the striking neo-gothic church with its towering spires rising majestically above the city. Dédée swept inside among the hundreds of devout men with hats removed, women with *mantilla's* on their heads, and sleepy-eyed children clinging to their mother's skirts, energized by the excitement for the coming holiday. Sweet voices and silvery notes from a grand pipe organ lifted to the tall pointed arches and filled the long hall with songs of joy and praise for the blessed event. From so far back, the priest was only a tiny white figure amid a backdrop of red poinsettias in the yellow glow of candles, but that didn't seem to matter to the throngs of worshippers who followed the mass through the Latin words and the tingle of bells. Perhaps it was the familiarity of the Latin, the smell of burning incense, or the warmth of so many bodies crowded so close together, but here among these strangers a calm washed over her. For a little while she forgot about this terrible war.

"*Feliz Navidad*," Franco said at the conclusion of the mass.

"*Feliz Navidad*," she replied.

CHAPTER EIGHTEEN

At a corner booth in a Paris bistro, the young Belgian with the tumultuous blue eyes tapped the ash from his cigarette into the glass tray and flashed two fingers for the waitress to bring another glass of wine for him and a beer for the pimply-faced young Luftwaffe trainee across the table. "It is just a matter of time, my friend. We are witnessing the birth of a new world order." Jacques Desoubrie rested his outstretched arm across the top of the wooden seat back. The note in his pocket gave him reason to swagger.

Although only two weeks past his twentieth birthday, he had matured more quickly than the nineteen-year-old seated across the table—thanks to a wealthy doctor who wouldn't acknowledge him and a mother who abandoned him. "Your French is very good," Desoubrie said. "And I understand your English is good as well."

"Thank you. I have studied a long time."

"At university?"

"No," the lad said with apology in his voice. "I was going to go for my degree, but it is more important to defend my country."

"Young men who speak English and French are of great value to Germany." Desoubrie rested a forearm on the table to let his diamond studded cuff show beyond the sleeve of his custom-tailored suit. His green polka dot tie expressed his intrepid individualism. Despite the doctor's lack of interest in his illegitimate son, there was one thing Desoubrie had inherited from his father—a keen mind.

"A degree is nothing more than a piece of paper," he said. "Hitler does not possess a college degree. I have not spent one day in college and I have outsmarted doctors, lawyers, priests, college professors—all of those so-called intellectuals who think themselves above us because they went to university. Hitler is beloved, not because of some pretentious degree or royal blood, but because he is wise, bold and fearless." Jacques crushed out his cigarette as their steaks arrived. "I eat better steaks and wine than doctors or lawyers can get. Germany rewards me for my talents. You and I, we fight for the same cause—to win the war and save our country from communism and from those who would keep us down by controlling the money."

The young man across the table nodded agreement.

Desoubrie smiled to himself. Another pint and a bit more encouragement and he'd have this young fellow ready to jump on a grenade for his country. "We are fighting for our very survival. The French say the Germans have started this war, but that is a lie. Germany was forced into it by financial burdens imposed by the English, the French and the Americans in order to destroy Germany's economy and keep her subservient. But Hitler has broken the chains that shackled Germany and the slave has now become the master.

Desoubrie carved off a piece of meat, but paused before putting it in his mouth. "The French people have allowed their love of fashion and elegance to weaken them. The English believe they can rule the world by conceit and snobbery. And the Belgians have shown their stupidity by having no defense against German invasion."

"You forget about the Americans," the German boy said. "I have seen their planes—they attack by the hundreds."

"That is merely for show. The Americans are fat and lazy. Their Pacific fleet has been destroyed by the Japanese. The Luftwaffe and Wehrmacht will destroy them and push them back into the sea like they did with the English. When this war is over, the Germans will be the ones left standing."

The young German raised his glass. "Long live Germany!"

"Long live Germany," Desoubrie echoed and clinked his glass against the boy's. "Those hundreds of planes over the fatherland—suppose you could easily eliminate dozens of them—would you do it?"

"Of course."

"Good. Germany needs people like us who will use their skills to help bring down the enemy." Desoubrie pulled the note from his pocket and waved it without opening it. "This is the address where I am to deliver supplies for an underground organization that helps Allied airmen. Once I have earned their trust, I will learn everything about them

—who their leaders are—where their safe houses are—who are the guides and helpers." Desoubrie watched for the boy's reaction as he spoke. "My job is very dangerous. If I succeed, I will destroy the underground and save thousands of German lives. But if I am exposed, I will be killed."

The boy's wide eyes revealed that he was enthralled by Desoubrie's bravery.

"I pose as a French patriot. If you are brave enough, you will be trained and dropped into Belgium or France and a reconditioned English plane will be crashed nearby so that you may pose as an English flier who needs to be evacuated."

"So," Jacques sat back and held his glass a moment before taking a swallow. "Are you brave enough to risk your life in order to save thousands of your countrymen and women?"

"Yes."

———

Back in Paris on December twenty-seventh, Dédée wasn't taking any chances. Franco and Robert Aylé accompanied her to interview a pair of 'Americans'. She was also told that a Scot, Hawthorn Reid, who had already been verified, was staying with them and could provide the extra muscle if needed.

"Bonjour, *Madame Noel*," Dédée said addressing Madeleine Dumont by her underground name.

Franco slipped behind the Americans as Dédée introduced herself. "We are going to accompany you on your trip to the south," she said. "But first, please raise your arms out to the side. "I am sorry," she added as Franco patted the American men down, "but you understand we must be careful."

Franco nodded okay to Dédée, but she wasn't finished. She gestured for the men to have a seat. "I'd like to ask you some questions. First, please tell me a little about yourselves."

"I'm Jack Williams from Detroit, Michigan, U.S.A." Jack tipped his head toward the guy seated to his left. "Gilbert and I were part of the crew of a B-17 Flying Fortress, the *Wulfe Hound*. We were shot down on the twelfth near Melun."

"It is a pleasure to meet you, Jack." Dédée looked to the other fellow. "And you Gilbert?"

"Yeah, I'm Gilbert Schowalter, from Milwaukee, Wisconsin, U.S.A. I was the navigator and Jack the co-pilot."

"What squadron do you belong to?"

"303 Bomber Squadron, 360 Bomber Group," they answered in unison.

Dédée turned her head toward the third airman.

"*Ahm* Sergeant Hawthorn Dalrymple Reid, from Arbroath, *Skawtlan*," the man said with a thick Scottish accent.

"It is nice to finally meet you, Hawthorn," Dédée said. "Sydney Smith told me you were not in his regular crew."

"No. That's my luck—their navigator got sick and I filled in."

Dédée offered him an empathetic frown, then turned her attention back to the Americans. "Jack, please tell me how many are in the crew of a B-17."

"Ten," Jack answered.

"Can you tell me what is meant by *carrying the can*?"

Jack shrugged as if it was obvious. "It means I'm taking full responsibility. If anything happens it's my fault."

"Gilbert, do you know what a dry run is?"

"It's a flight for practice. We rehearse our jobs and prepare for the real thing."

Satisfied, Franco and Dédée took Jack and Gilbert for their photographs, then collected another American, John McKee. The fifth fugitive, René Coache, was a thirty-eight year old safe house keeper whose cover was blown. René being *burned* meant the Gestapo was getting closer to her father.

Upon her return on December 31, she hung up her coat and scarf then stole up behind her dear father. "Papa," she said leaning over and kissing his cheek. "I love you, but it is time we talk about you going to England."

———

Once Airey Neave and his bride had settled down in a flat at Elbury House near Victoria Station, his wife graciously insisted he welcome returned airmen to their home where he could interview them in a more pleasant setting than the dreadful Great Central Hotel. Despite her enthusiasm, Airey made his way to the office still wrestling over whether he was the right man for the job.

"Good to see you back, Airey. You're looking cheery," Jimmy said. "Have you come to a decision about the job?"

"I believe I've married the most intelligent and supportive girl in the world." She had told him no one could do a better job than he could, but that she would support any decision he made. "She believes that what we are doing is important and has really lifted my spirits. She's even insisted I should conduct my interviews in our flat to make the men feel welcome."

"Splendid. How would tonight be for your first interview?"

"Tonight?"

"Yes. There's a lovely young lady I'd like you to meet."

"Lovely young lady?" Airey laughed. "You *do* remember I've just been married?"

"Yes, of course. Otherwise I wouldn't let you interview her."

Airey puzzled for a moment then caught on. "*Ahhh*, do I detect a bit of amour? If I didn't know better, I'd say you sound rather smitten."

"I am indeed. And I will wager this—if this young lady doesn't rekindle that fire in you to help the underground, then I will put in for your transfer myself."

Airey went home to prepare for the interview, filled with anticipation and curiosity. The doorbell rang promptly at the appointed time.

"Airey Neave?" a beautiful redhead asked.

"Yes."

"I'm Peggy van Lier."

CHAPTER NINETEEN

Airey found it surreal to have standing before him the girl with the magnificent bronze red hair whom dozens of airman evaders had described as spirited, beautiful, and fearless. "It's nice to finally meet you, Peggy." Airey showed her to an arm chair in the living room and poured her a glass of sherry and one for himself. "You should know you are held in very high regard by the men you have helped. I'm so glad you made it safely out."

"Thank you," she said, but her down-turned mouth and sad eyes hinted at a troubled mind.

"Is everything all right?"

"I'm sorry," she said despondently. "I guess I am relieved from some of the stress of possible capture. But it makes me sad thinking about those who were arrested. It's difficult to feel happy when so many are still in the hands of the Gestapo or in grave danger."

"I understand. I was a prisoner of the Germans myself." He told her of his own imprisonment and narrow escape. "There isn't a day that goes by that I don't worry about my friends in the underground that got me out. I sit here protected by Allied armies and the English Channel while they're living like a hare a half-step in front of the hounds. Some of my friends have already been caught. For others, it's just a matter of time."

"Are you trying to cheer me up?"

"Sorry." He gestured toward a platter of finger sandwiches on the coffee table. "Would you like a sandwich? My wife insisted I give you a proper welcome." Airey set a triangle of bread on a small plate and sat back in his chair. "It's because of my experience that they put me in charge of all the escape lines. Comet is by far the most successful. It's just damn frustrating not knowing how to help. There's so much we don't know. Tell me about Nemo. What is he like?"

She sipped her sherry contemplatively. "He is handsome, slender and has short wavy light brown hair. He is very organized. He ran a coffee plantation in the Belgian Congo. He's tough. He's decisive. But he is also very caring. He's a good leader. We were all young people in our group, and we all looked up to him. We would do anything for him."

"Does the Gestapo know about him? Should we try to get him out?"

She shook her head. "He wouldn't come. He's absolutely devoted to his wife, Bernadette. She just gave birth to their second child."

"Can you tell me what happened in Brussels? How did the Gestapo infiltrate your sector?"

"It was the Secret Police of the Luftwaffe. I read it on the door when I was arrested."

Peggy took another sip. And as she related the experiences of that terrible day her eyes glazed over. Airey could see she was reliving the horrors as if it was all happening now.

When she spoke of the note slipped into the Maréchals' letterbox and the suspicious 'Americans', Airey wished he'd had a radio operator in place to expose them as German agents. Would it have mattered? Or had events simply moved too quickly to allow them time to check? He would never know.

Airey jotted some notes as she talked, but mostly he listened, enraptured by how calmly she recounted what had been an extremely traumatic experience. She didn't merely run down the facts, but instead told the story as she had lived it—the waiting at the Swedish Canteen for word from Elsie—her bold trip to the Michiels' home—the blazing terror when she discovered the key in her pocket—the icy shock when she learned that Victor had been shot and killed—the helpless dread at not being able to warn Elvire Morelle then finding the girl in the hands of the Secret Police—her persistence in speaking in German to persuade the police to release her....

As Airey listened, his own experience and the prickly fear returned. He shifted uncomfortably in his seat, still feeling his German interrogator's vicious blue eyes upon him; eyes that raged like a devil when the agent discovered a tiny hand-drawn airfield map on him. He felt again the cold sweat, the overwhelming fear at the realization that he was about to be killed or tortured. Fortunately, the Gestapo found the prisoner who had given him the map which cleared him of being a spy. He could only imagine how frightening it would be without a soldier's protection under the Geneva Convention.

When Peggy reached the part where she was finally released, Airey looked down at his plate and realized he hadn't even taken a bite of his sandwich. He was full of admiration for this beautiful girl and those around her. To dare to expose themselves to save others as Peggy and Victor had done left him awe struck. An image of Claude Dansey flashed in his mind, aggravating him. To Dansey it was just a bunch of numbers. The man had no idea what kind of courage it took to keep Allied airmen out of the hands of the Germans.

"It seems a bit of irony," Peggy said as she finished the Maréchal saga, "that Georges, Edouard and I would have to use the same escape line that we had sent so many men down."

"You may be the only Comet members outside of Dédée herself to see the entire line from Brussels to Gibraltar. And you crossed the Pyrenees with Bee Johnson and Florentino?"

"Yes."

"Tell me, did you see Dédée when you came through Paris? What do you think will happen to the Comet line?"

"I stayed with Dédée and Paul until it could be arranged for us to travel to the south and into Spain. Dédée is determined to rebuild the line. Her father is looking much greyer these days and she is concerned. He is public enemy number one. The reward has been upped to two million francs. But she will not stop. She believes, as we all do that we must do our part, however small, to defeat the Germans."

Airey lit her cigarette then his own. "I bring repatriated airmen back to their bases. If you could see how it lifts the spirits of the men when one of their comrades is returned, you would understand that what you do is no small thing. You should know Nemo has somehow kept the Belgium sector going."

"Yes, I know." She reached into her bag and handed Airey a piece of paper. "Nemo sent me this note with the airman, Jock Brazill."

When Airey finished reading, she was looking down sadly at her cigarette shaking her head. "I should have stayed … I should have moved to Paris … I…"

"No," Airey said firmly. "You had no choice. You had to come out. If it is any consolation we just brought out René Coache of the Paris sector. I know you wanted to do more, but once you've been burned your presence would only lead the Gestapo to others." He looked encouragingly into her eyes. "You should also know we are trying to convince Paul and Dédée to come out as well. Peggy, the line is still working and delivering pilots back to England because of the example that you and Nadine and Dédée have set. You have inspired others to fight on."

Peggy smiled for the first time during the serious interview. She had suffered so much anguish, Airey felt happy he could provide positive reinforcement.

"But another infiltrator could disguise himself as an Allied airman and slip in somewhere," he said. "I have a Belgian radio operator, Sergeant Henri Decat, ready to parachute into Belgium to help Nemo. If we can authenticate Allied fliers more quickly we can protect everyone better. Perhaps once the Belgian sector is secured, we can convince Nemo to leave. Do you have any idea when it might be safe to drop him in?"

"Nemo will be very cautious. He will suspect anyone he does not know personally."

Peggy thought for a moment then rummaged inside her bag and pulled out a small medal. "This is from my church. It is a medal of Notre Dame de Halle. Before I left, I gave each member of our group one to protect them. I still have some more. Have your radio operator show this to Nemo. He will know it came from me."

Airey decided to prepare Decat to go in without delay. A radio operator was needed as soon as possible: they would have to work quickly to prevent another catastrophe.

But Airey wasn't quick enough.

———

"Funny," Nemo said as the aroma of rich real coffee rose from the tray Dédée set on the little table, "I spent all of my life on a coffee plantation, and now the only coffee we have to drink is smuggled in from Spain."

Paul received a cup and saucer from his daughter. "Thank you, my Darling," he said. "It's too bad, Jean, that you didn't stash some sacks of coffee beans away before the Germans came."

Dédée sat down opposite Nemo with her cup. "How are you holding up?"

"I'm all right, but I have a letter for you that confirms what we have feared. Our line has been exposed, not just the Belgian sector, but all of it."

Dédée unfolded the paper. "It's from Suzanne! How in the world did you get this?"

"I don't know," Nemo said. "She somehow smuggled it out of Saint Gilles Prison."

As Dédée silently read the note, her father sat up eagerly.

Dédée summarized for him. "She says that Charlie had all his papers on him when he was caught. They tortured him, but they have now stopped and he is left alone. She says he is in good spirits and he has tried to escape twice. She says the Germans have known about the line to San Sebastian for a long time." Dédée looked to Nemo as if to acknowledge what he had said. "She said that Nadine was beaten but revealed nothing until they began to beat her mother. Then all she admitted was that she was involved. It doesn't look good for Nadine's father, but they might release her mother. She says they are able to communicate with each other. Elvire swallowed the lease paper and is holding up well. Suzanne says things look very bad for Madame Maréchal and for her husband—impossible. Elsie was severely beaten, but she is mending. She told them nothing." Dédée turned directly toward her father. "Suzanne says she is doing all right and not to worry about her. She is thinking of us and says to try not to join her there."

Dédée handed the note to her father who lifted his big round spectacles off his nose to read the tiny print for himself. She turned to Nemo. "You must stay away from the Canteen, Jean. Even though they have not broken Nadine, Elsie or Elvire, it cannot be safe. The Germans do not make meaningless threats. But I wish there was something we could do for the Maréchals. They are dear friends. If only there was some way—"

Nemo cut her off. "We tried that with Lawyer Y who was supposed to have secured release for Charlie Morelle. All we accomplished was to get the lawyer and Suzanne arrested. Dédée, you told me I had one chance in ten of surviving. You have given every helper proper warning. Now you must accept that we have made our choice freely knowing the risks. Many will make the ultimate sacrifice. It is simply unavoidable."

Dédée nodded agreement. She had no concern for herself. But it was one thing to risk your own life. It was quite another to feel that someone else could lose theirs for following you.

———

Nemo gazed down at the swaddled infant sleeping peacefully in the cradle and wished that his son would stir and wake up. He watched the tiny chest rise and fall, rise and fall. He wanted to hold him once more before he left, touch his little bitty fingers, kiss his chubby cheeks. Warmth on his arm let him know that Bernadette had awakened and was standing beside him. Without saying a word, she picked up the baby and placed the sleepy-eyed infant in her husband's arms. There was no question that his wife understood his torment and loved him in spite of his obstinacy.

Last night, she had expressed her fears through tears and angry words. But he had stood firm. The trouble was she was absolutely right: it *was* sheer madness to continue, and he *was* a damn fool. She had begged him to escape to England. So many in Brussels had been captured it was just a matter of time before the Gestapo found him. He had told her about Suzanne's letter to remind her of the sacrifices others had made, but she said it was more proof that the Gestapo would stop at nothing to get the chief of the Belgian sector.

Even if Nadine and Elsie and Madame Maréchal didn't talk, it would be naïve to think the Gestapo had not pieced together the identity of the Belgian chief. She tearfully begged him to think of his wife and his little girl and boy. And he *did* think of them. The thought of his children fatherless tore him up inside. But he also thought of their future if the Nazis weren't stopped.

He had considered stepping aside and letting someone else do the fighting, but when he did, his mind presented him with images of Elsie and Nadine and Victor. They were his children too, his responsibility. While he could escape to England and raise his family, what kind of man would he be to let Elsie and the others suffer so greatly while he ran away? Dédée's words came back to him—his chances of surviving were one in ten. He knew it. He accepted it.

He held the newborn close, smelling his warm skin, the gentle soap in his fine hair, the mother's milk on his breath. He kissed the sleepy baby's forehead and handed the infant back to his mother. Bernadette kissed him once gently on the lips. No words were spoken. Everything had already been said. He pulled his collar up and across his face, tipped the brim of his hat down and left for his secret flat at Place Blyckaert.

CHAPTER TWENTY

A parent never stops watching over his children. Dédée loved her father for wanting to look after her, but they both knew that he couldn't protect her. His presence might actually make it more dangerous for her: with the price on his head recently doubled, and with so many people being tortured for information, it was only a matter of time before they found him. And when they found him, they would find her. With one daughter already in a German prison, Frédéric de Jongh could not bear the thought of the Nazis getting their hands on his Little Cyclone too. Reluctantly, he conceded that he must leave.

On Wednesday, the thirteenth of January, after collecting two airmen from the flat of Aimable Fouquerel, Dédée met up with her father, Franco and a third evader.

French gendarmes and German police openly patrolled the Paris stations while Gestapo and secret field police might be anywhere. Some were sure to have seen her father's photograph. Paul shuffled along the slow-moving line several places ahead of his daughter, with his *certificat de domicil* in hand and the bored look of a commuter. Wearing a heavy workman's coat and beret, he no longer looked like the well-groomed headmaster from Brussels. A cold rain provided a reason to turn up his collar, allowing him to cover the sides of his face. Dédée exhibited no interest, though her nerves were primed like popcorn on a hot stove.

The group made it through without incident and settled in for the long overnight journey. Dédée tried to sleep, but her mind was restless. The rain dancing across the window in the darkness reminded her of how hard the hike would be on her father. She walked her mind through the most punishing stretches of the mountain, the treacherous climbs up craggy slopes, the rock rubble, the rushing icy current of the river and the ever present threat of the Guardia Civil. But there was no point in second guessing their decision to go. The mountain would be cold and unpredictable, but each day they delayed, the danger of her father's capture increased. Now, with the extra hours of winter darkness, was their best chance.

At half past ten, Jean and Lulu Dassié, Bee Johnson, Janine and Tante Go met them at the Bayonne station. Huddled under umbrellas, the two pretty girls each took an airmen by the hand and set off across the Saint Esprit Bridge. The third flier followed with Franco. Monsieur Dassié walked with Paul, while Tante Go, Dédée and Bee followed at a distance.

"Some of my houses are being watched," Tante confided to Dédée as they walked. "I've shut them down."

"How do you know they are being watched?"

Tante Go smiled slyly. "The Secret Police all wear the same tie so they can recognize each other."

Dédée chuckled. "Too bad the Secret Police aren't so obvious about everything else."

"*Monsieur* Dassié has learned that the police have been asking about him as well. Any word from Brussels?"

"Brussels is all right for now. Suzanne smuggled out a letter to Nemo. All of our friends are in contact with each other. They are coping well. I wish I could see my sister."

"That is one wish I hope is not granted."

Dédée laughed. "Not that way. Only for a short visit."

"You know it has been raining for days down here," Tante Go said not so much as a weather report, as to update her *general* to the conditions. "The trail will be treacherous. There could be mudslides. The Bidassoa will be high."

"Florentino will know which way is best. We might have to go by way of the suspension bridge."

Tante Go looked sharply at her youthful friend. "That's an extra five hours! Your father is not a young man."

"But how can I leave him?"

"You know he will not be able to keep up."

Dédée watched him gamely striding thirty paces ahead. There was no risk he wouldn't take for her, but men half his age struggled with the mountains in good weather. He could not be trusted to make this decision. He would act strong and say he could do it. Dédée sighed.

"I will tell him, Dédée," Tante Go said as if reading her mind. "He will stay with Jean until your next trip."

Tante Go waited to break the news until they had nearly finished lunch at the Gachy restaurant. "It has been raining for days," she began. "The wind on the mountain will be terrible. The Bidassoa is running high and fast. It cannot be crossed." She advised with express focus toward Paul. "That means this trip will take an extra five hours and the crossing of a suspension bridge."

Paul regarded Tante Go, not quite comprehending what she was trying to convey.

She leveled her commanding grey-green eyes directly at him and spoke bluntly. "Dédée will have to take the men over while you wait here. The mountain is hard when the weather is good. The rain and wind will make it terrible. *Monsieur le professeur*, at your age, you simply will not survive."

Paul opened his mouth as if to protest, but Tante Go continued. "You will stay with the Dassiés. This is the way it must be. Franco will not be needed. He will go back to Paris and you will go to Spain when he returns with the next group." She stated it with such finality, he had no choice but to obey.

He sighed resignedly and took his daughter by the hands. "Goodbye my Darling," he said in a fatherly way, "I shall come with you next time."

Tante Go mounted her bicycle and pedaled off from the Dassié home in Bayonne with the three evaders and Dédée following at intervals. Cold wind-driven rain blurred their vision. Their coats turned into sails, catching gusts of wind that threatened to sweep them and their bicycles into the deep, flowing roadside ditches. Dédée chased after the struggling children, coaxing, cajoling and teasing. "You are strong young men. Can you not keep up with a middle-aged woman?" Of course Tante Go was no prissy lady. She was a hardened bicycle rider with incredible stamina. Dédée knew how tough this was for them. She had a time of it herself in this nasty weather, but she had to keep them moving. Their lives depended on it.

Navigating backroads in the driving rain wore them down like fighting a gale in a fishing boat. Two hours later, soaked and exhausted, they reached Saint-Jean-de-Luz where they stashed the bicycles behind a barn and continued on foot.

Despite the miserable weather, their spirits remained high, roused by the nearness of the mountains. Shoes *schlumped* through the rain and mud up the old farm road to Urrugne. Wending their way past white stucco houses with red shutters and red tile roofs, they marched on to Bidegain Berri. Frantxia welcomed them in the back door.

The men peeled off their wet clothing down to their underwear and hung them by the fire to dry. Looking at their worn faces, Dédée knew she had made the right decision leaving her father back in Bayonne. They had made a pact that if anything happened to either of them the other would carry on. But despite her father's assurances that he was in this of his own volition, the law abiding headmaster would never have defied authority, let alone dueled in the shadows against such a cunning and powerful foe, if not for his devotion to his Little Cyclone. She had to get him out of this country before it was too late.

After a meal of hot soup and fresh baked black bread, the men moved into the big room with the children while Florentino drank wine and described the conditions in the mountains. "The trails will be slippery," Frantxia translated. "Mud washing down the slopes will make them very difficult to climb. The river is high and raging. It cannot be crossed."

"What about the bridge?" Dédée asked.

Florentino shook his head and said in his limited Spanish, and a pantomiming of running and climbing, "*Mucho dificil.*"

She understood. Trying to dash across the bridge and climb up the mud-slick slope on the other side before the guards spotted them would be risky.

"*Yeeeha!*" came the shout of one of the pilots.

Tiny voices squealed *yeehas* in response as the children bounced about on the backs of the airmen like they were riding American bucking broncos. Their screams of joy and laughter drowned out the howling of the wind outside. Dédée smiled. "I don't think the children will mind if the men stay here tonight and leave tomorrow."

Frantxia laughed. "They will all sleep well tonight."

The sound of the dog barking in the yard put everyone on alert. A minute later there came a knock on the door. Frantxia's little boy hopped off the airman's back and ran in his bare feet to answer. There hadn't been time to shoo the men upstairs. The little boy opened the door a crack and called back to his mom, "It is Donato."

A sudden gust blew the door out of the boy's hands, flinging it wide open.

Dédée locked eyes with the farm hand—but only for a moment as Frantxia hurried to the door and closed it most of the way as if to block the wind, but really to conceal who was inside. Frantxia didn't invite Donato in. Dédée didn't trust the young Spaniard who had worked as a guide on several crossings. She had dismissed him months ago when she discovered things missing from her rucksack during a mountain crossing.

Frantxia spoke with him in the Basque language. Dédée couldn't understand what they were saying, but she could tell from Frantxia's tone that the conversation was not friendly. Donato's phrases sounded brusque and accusing. Frantxia replied in kind, her free hand shooting up into the air punctuating her words. Florentino pushed his chair back, but Donato's voice lowered as if he was satisfied by what Frantxia was saying. It sounded to Dédée like they had struck some sort of bargain.

After Donato left, Florentino finished off his glass of wine, said a few words to Frantxia, and issued Dédée a two-fingered salute off his forehead.

"Florentino is going to his home in Ciboure tonight," Frantxia explained. "He will be back tomorrow to take the children across the mountains."

By the following morning, the storm had subsided, leaving behind a silent, tranquil mist. The men could scarcely contain their excitement. In just a few hours they would be crossing the frontier into Spain. Frantxia made a late breakfast and everyone was in high spirits, laughing, joking, sharing bread and filling their stomachs, giddy as little children at Christmas time.

The sound of an automobile engine interrupted the laughter.

A chill ran through Dédée as she heard what sounded like a second vehicle.

Stan, one of the evaders, jumped to his feet and grabbed the bread knife. "It's the Gestapo!" he joked.

The other two airmen laughed.

Dédée caught a glimpse of a dark blue képi cap passing by the window. "Get upstairs. Quickly!"

Boots sounded on the porch steps.

The men's laughter stopped.

The door burst open. "Hands up!"

A gendarme pointed his Schmeisser machine gun at Stan.

Stan gently set the knife down on the table and raised his hands.

Dédée's heart pounded. They were trapped.

The children ran to their mother's side. Maiye, the eldest had already left for school.

Ten brawny gendarmes hustled in. A few remained in the kitchen, their guns trained on the captives and the others tramped through the house. Dédée could hear their angry *shlomp, shlomp* on steps and the sound of doors being ripped open. Furniture thunked. Tables and lamps crashed. With a wave of their weapons, the police in the kitchen marched the pilots and Dédée outside into the cold drizzle. A gendarme grabbed the littlest boy's arm yanking him away from his mother. Dédée and the others were made to line up against the wall with their hands clasped behind their heads while the gendarmes inside continued their search. A few minutes later, Frantxia, emerged with several guns trained on her and joined the prisoners at the wall. Dédée could almost feel Frantxia's heart breaking listening to the children inside the house crying for their mother.

An angry-faced gendarme swept his machine gun from one end of the line to the other, threatening to shoot them as saboteurs.

The dog barked furiously at the end of the chain that stopped him from protecting his family.

Stay calm, Dédée told herself. She studied their guards. They were French policemen, not Germans and young—underlings, anxious to wield power. Perhaps when the higher-ups came out, she thought, things might go better—if they found nothing in their search.

A stern officer emerged from the building, shouting, "Where is the fifth person?"

No one spoke.

"Oh you will talk my friends," he assured them with a resolute smile as he pointed his weapon from person to person up and down the line. "You *will* talk."

All hope of playing on the sympathies of patriotic Frenchmen vanished. These were men who did their jobs even if their government was now run by the Germans. Still, if there was a loyal Frenchman among them, he would have to keep up the pretense. Dédée remained optimistic.

The officer stepped toward Dédée and pointed his gun directly at her face. "Where is the fifth person?"

She met his gaze but said nothing. She felt only contempt for Frenchmen who did the Germans' bidding.

Following her lead, no one spoke.

Her fisherman's trousers protected her legs somewhat, but they hadn't been allowed to put coats on. With her hands behind her head, Dédée could feel the cold trickle running down her arms, sending shivers through her. The nasty weather and uncooperative captives further eroded the officer's disposition, especially when one of his men reported that they had found no one in the attic or cellar.

"Where is the other man!" he demanded. If the police were searching for a fifth person, it had to be Florentino. There was only one person who could have known there were five people in the house—Donato!

The dog barked and growled to no avail.

"We can stand out here all day if you like … or perhaps I should just shoot one of you…"

The search and threats went on for an hour. Then the captives were marched in single file out of the yard and down the street, the children left alone in the house to fend for themselves. The mist and chilling wind bit hard as they tramped down the road with five gendarmes on either side. In front of Dédée walked poor Frantxia, hands clasped behind her head and water dripping off her drenched black hair. Her mind must have been a wreck with worry over her children. Dédée thought of her father and was thankful that he hadn't been with her.

They trekked down the foothills until they reached the watercourse between Ciboure and Saint-Jean de Luz. As they crossed the bridge, the river beckoned Dédée to dash to the side and leap over. She hesitated. Before she could decide whether to chance it, they had reached the other side. She breathed a sigh of relief at not giving in to her impulse. It would surely have resulted in a bullet or broken bones and probable drowning.

The prisoners were locked in cells at the town police bureau and grilled in turn. From the questions, it seemed the police didn't know much about the line, only that they had caught two women in the act of aiding Allied airmen. Dédée admitted nothing. If the police didn't know who they had, there still might be a chance.

In the afternoon, Florentino went to Frantxia's house as planned. The children told him what had happened. He committed them to the care of a neighbor and hurried on to Villa Voisin in Anglet where he informed Tante Go. Then he started out over the mountain to get word to the British.

Paul went pale at the news.

Bee jumped out of his seat pacing as if he didn't know what to do.

Tante Go took charge. She comforted the distraught Paul who was scratching his scalp, his eyes welling up with guilty tears. "She is only in the hands of the local police," Tante Go said. "We will use every means at our disposal to find out where they are taking her and get her out before she is turned over to the Gestapo."

In the morning Tante Go set her agents scurrying about to locate the girl she had come to love like her own niece. A disturbing report came back from the telephone exchange. The night before the arrests, Tante's agent there, who was supposed to warn her of any danger, had inexplicably fled to Paris. She put out the word to locate Donato who Florentino said had been at the house the night before. Information came in slowly.

Then, Jean Dassié received a note from a Red Cross worker who had been in Villa Chargrin Prison in Bayonne when the prisoners were brought in. "The little cousin is sick," the note said.

Tante Go sprang into action: arranging for Frantxia's children to be looked after by Cyprienne Dassié's brother, Robert Lapeyre, and his wife, Yvonne, up in Bayonne; sending for Franco to come back down from Paris to help with planning the escape; and banishing Paul, despite his protests, to the home of the Dassiés. The back room at the Chez Gachy in Bayonne became her headquarters. Plans would have to be made quickly if they were to get to Dédée before the Germans did.

CHAPTER TWENTY-ONE

"Good morning!" Jimmy Langley breezed by like his feet were in Fred Astaire's dance shoes. He tossed his hat at the hook and with a flick of the hand unwound his scarf from his neck. "Good morning, Airey."

"Good morning." Airey sat back from his paper work as his friend popped about the office like the virile young man Airey had known before Jimmy lost his arm. There was no doubt about it. The old boy was in love. Airey grinned at Jimmy's attempt at a businesslike façade. "So how was dinner last night?"

"The food was quite good," Jimmy answered still trying to contain his mirth.

"I'm not talking about the food."

"The company was good as well"

Airey raised an eyebrow. "Go on." If he didn't know better, Airey could swear Jimmy was blushing.

"H-Have you arranged Henri Decat's drop into Belgium yet?" Jimmy asked Airey as the secretary delivered his tea.

Airey nodded. "It's all taken care of. Now out with it."

"What?"

"The company," Airey said. "Miss van Lier."

"Peggy is an extraordinary girl. I've never met anyone quite like her. She's at once vivacious like a cat, charged up like a spark plug, forthright... witty ... brave..."

"Not to mention beautiful," Airey added.

"By the way, I owe you for sending that Sussex chap, William Brazill, around. That letter from Nemo really lifted her spirits."

"That reminds me," Airey said handing Jimmy a typed report. "When I debriefed Brazill, he talked about being taken to a new safe house right after the Maréchal affair by a very young, sweet-voiced little girl called

Lily. Her name has come up several times now, but we still don't know who the devil she is."

"There are so many," Jimmy said. "How does one keep track?"

"You and I may have a time sorting it all, but the returned airmen swear they will never forget Lily. She's only fifteen, but she is cunning well beyond her years. I've sent word round to Monday to ask Dédée about her."

Jimmy shrugged. "Perhaps Peggy has heard of her."

"Yes, perhaps you should call on Peggy and see what she knows," Airey said with a sly smile. "How did your meeting go with Dansey?"

"Well you know Uncle Claude. I gave him the information Madame Anne's people managed to gather about the coastal defenses, but all he did was grumble that civilians should stay the hell out of intelligence work."

"Did you tell him aerial recon has already confirmed past reports?"

"Most definitely!" Jimmy humphed. "Then I told him the chief who passed this information on knows the workers and trusts them or she wouldn't be sending it."

"Oh good grief!" Jimmy, in stern-face, mimicked Dancey's gruff voice. "The entire Allied force is planning a major invasion of the continent and I'm supposed to tell them it is okay because a housewife trusts that her information is correct?"

Jimmy flipped open a brass case and drew out a cigarette. "I said it's just more pieces of information, Sir, I'm sure you have other means to confirm it." He stuck the cigarette between his lips and flipped open his lighter. "Of course," he said drawing in the flame, "what I wanted to add was, or you can cram it and hope that no one comes to find you had intimate details of gun emplacements all along the coast and you ignored them." He blew out a great breath of smoke.

Dansey was still taking jabs at them for the November arrests. "The fact that he's provided us scant resources matters little to him." Airey frowned and reached for his cigarette pack. "I'd like to see him do..."

A rap on the door jamb interrupted Airey. "Excuse me, sir," the secretary said. "Cable from Monday,"

Airey read it aloud. "Saturday from Monday. Deeply regret

Florentino reports Dédée arrested with three pilots at Urrugne. Imprisoned Villa Chargrin at Bayonne. Attempts being organized for her escape."

Airey handed the note to Jimmy and slumped back in his chair. All the energy had suddenly been sucked from the room. He and Jimmy had known this day would come, that one day she would be caught. But she had slipped through the Gestapo's hands so many times they'd nearly forgotten she was only human. His logical mind told him it was inevitable, but deep down to his heart and soul he felt like the fates had gotten this one wrong. It was as if the Sheriff of Nottingham had killed Robin Hood. It wasn't supposed to happen. But this wasn't a Hollywood film. And Airey had never felt more useless so far away from those who needed his help.

———

Staying overnight in the local police station was sobering, but it was nothing compared to the apprehension one felt passing through the big arched doors into the Villa Chargrin Prison in Bayonne. Dédée could see the dread in the eyes of the *children*. So far, they had said nothing, but the strain was apparent in their gaunt faces. It was a mistake to show fear. Dédée felt sure the gendarmes would see their anxiety and exploit it. But the prisoners were silenced and she could say nothing to bolster their resolve. They were taken away to separate cells. Dédée told the warder nothing but the name that appeared on her identity card—de Tonga.

The superiority and arrogance of the French guards who escorted her to her cell, and the promise that a few days in the stark lonely room would loosen her tongue, only spurred her defiance. She inhaled deeply and sang out opera to show that her surroundings didn't bother her in the least.

The guard shouted for her to shut up.

She sang all the louder.

. . .

A parent's love for his child can make a wise man a fool. Once Tante Go had found out where they had taken Dédée, she bicycled around Bayonne warning all of her shelterers not to take anyone in unless the request came directly from her and to make certain there were no traces of past evaders lying about. She had to get her agents working on gathering information. She had to speak with the owner of Chez Gachy, René. And in the middle of all this rushing about, she had to stop what she was doing to deal with Paul.

Tante Go did not mince her words. "What were you thinking going to the prison? Can't you see how foolish that was?"

"I just thought I could see her. I didn't tell them I was related in any way."

"You mustn't be seen anywhere near there. You mustn't be seen anywhere!" She scolded him as if he were a little boy. "You must go to the Dassié home and stay hidden."

"I can at least help you with the planning."

Tante Go shook her head emphatically. "No you cannot! Do you not understand that they do not yet know who she is? Can you not see that if you are caught and they link her to you, she will be put to death as will you?" She glared at his stupidity. "If there is any chance to get her out it must be done quickly. We have no time to waste on these debates."

Tante Go contemplated the high walls as she bicycled past the Villa Chargrin prison on her way to the Chez Gachy. She tried to think of a way to use the Red Cross worker who had slipped the note about the ill cousin to Jean Dassié.

The bar's proximity to the prison just across the way made it a good place to observe comings and goings, but it was also close enough to be frequented by gendarmes and German soldiers.

"*Monsieur le patron*," Tante said softly when owner René Gachy joined her at a table off to one side. "You have heard that my niece is not feeling well?"

"Yes."

"Men from the prison come here to eat. Are there any guards that you trust who might help us with a very dangerous venture?"

René nodded. "I know of one. He will come here tomorrow."

When Tante Go returned the next day, René and the guard were already discussing possibilities. René pointed to rows of large soup containers against the wall of the kitchen. "Do you think your niece could fit in one of those?"

"She is not too big, and she is very limber. I think she could."

"We make the soup here and bring it to the prison. We could smuggle her out in one of the cans. We must act quickly, though, before the Boches take too much interest in her."

That brought a bit of relief. If they hadn't taken much interest in her, it meant that the Gestapo was not yet on to her. Tante Go thought it over. "But you cannot take the soup can to her cell. You would somehow have to get her out of her cell and to the kitchen at just the right time. This would take a lot of preparation, and assistance. Would it not?"

"Yes." The guard's shoulders slumped. "I suppose you are right. Although most of the employees are French, I cannot trust them."

"Then we need a different plan," Tante Go said. "Can you leave a door unlocked so she might slip out before anyone notices?"

The warder nodded. "We can try that. Be here at three o'clock tomorrow. She must be taken out of the district immediately."

"I understand." Tante Go said. She left the restaurant and bicycled away furiously. There was much to do. She needed to get some boys' clothes about Dédée's size, and a beret. Most of all she needed to have a motor boat ready to whisk her down river and a place to hide Dédée until she could be taken over the mountains.

Three o'clock the next day, Tante Go, Jean Dassié and Bee Johnson, sat at the window at Chez Gachy watching the door of the prison. Anxious minutes passed. Half an hour past the appointed time there was still no sign of her. Then suddenly a black car screeched to a stop in front of the prison door. A prisoner was brought out to the car, and they could tell from the blue fisherman's pants that it was Dédée. They were too late.

CHAPTER TWENTY-TWO

Tante Go *tsked* sorrowfully at the photograph in her hand. "It is such a shame. He was such a handsome boy." She handed the photo back across the café table to the disconsolate grey-haired woman. "This war has taken too many of our children. We have lost so many loved ones. That is why I wanted to talk to you. I am told that as a Red Cross worker you may visit the prisoners whenever you have something for them. I have a dear friend who is locked up in Villa Chargrin for trying to help young men like your son escape from the Germans."

The woman's mouth quivered in anticipation of what she thought Tante Go was about to propose. Her face took on a pallor.

"Yes?" Tante Go pressed.

"Yes … but … I … I am watched. I … I just try to comfort them. That is all. I cannot do anything other. I am searched when I go in … and when I…"

"Oh I wouldn't ask you to do anything wrong. But I would just ask if you could look in on my friend once in a while ... see if she is all right. Do you know the one of whom I speak?"

The woman nodded.

"I call her my niece, but she is more like a daughter to me." Tante Go spoke sincerely as one mother to another. "I worry about her. You know how it is. The Red Cross is allowed to bring food and clothing, are they not?"

"Yes…" The woman's tone lifted at the end of the word as though she were afraid to ask what was coming next. "But they check everything I bring in … someone brought in a cake and the guards cut into it and found—"

"A file and a hack saw blade. Yes I know. How unfortunate that someone tried to slip that past the guards. But I won't ask you to bring any contraband in. I just want to send the girl some food and perhaps a warm skirt. I understand it is quite cold."

"I cannot carry messages either."

"I understand. Can you at least bring her a loaf of bread?"

The woman shrugged but nodded.

"And can you tell her that her friends miss her? But do not say the message is from her aunt. Where in the prison is her cell?"

"It is on the side near an outside wall."

Tante Go took out a pen and a scrap of paper and drew a box. "Say this is the front door over here. About where would her cell be?"

The woman pointed.

Tante Go smiled and tucked the paper into her pocket. "Thank you. If I buy a loaf of bread tomorrow, will you take it to her?"

Another nod.

Tante Go thanked her again. Now she had something to tell Jean and Bee when she met them later at Chez Gachy. Hopefully Franco had arrived from Paris as well.

———

They waited until the night of the third quarter moon. Franco, in a dark sweater and beret, one-armed Jean Dassié wrapped in a huge ebony cloak, and Bee and Tante Go in coal black clothing trudged out into the crisp air carrying a long pole and thick rope with heavy iron baling hooks fashioned into a makeshift grappling hook. Large billowy clouds drifted across the sky, obscuring the moonlight—a boon to the night raiders in their clandestine operation. Franco, the former Belgian officer candidate and the youngest member of the group led the way to the area of the prison the Red Cross worker had pointed to on Tante Go's sketch. They still didn't know how they would break Dédée out of her cell once they had gotten over the wall, but Tante Go had brought a hack saw and crowbar and said they would figure it out as they went.

At the selected spot, Franco fastened the grappling hook to the end of the pole and hoisted it up. The stupidity of their miscalculation smacked them in the face. The pole reached a little more than half way up the wall.

"Now what?" Franco whispered.

Tante Go scowled at the wall as if it had betrayed them.

After a few minutes of hushed debate, Jean hurried off into the night. Tante Go and the others hunkered down in the cold shadows and waited.

A half hour later, a huffing, breathless Jean Dassié returned carrying a long wooden ladder. With the rope over his shoulder and pole in one hand, Franco climbed up. He still couldn't reach the top.

Bee rushed up to assist. Locking one leg in the rungs, he supported Franco's back so the young man could stand on the top rung where there was nothing to hold on to.

Franco cautiously set the hook on top of the pole and raised it up. Suddenly, heavy boots sounded on the frozen ground at the far end of the building.

Bee pressed himself against Franco and the two men froze in the shadows that they hoped would hide them.

The *thrump thrump thrump* of the patrol grew louder. If the Germans caught them they would soon be imprisoned within the walls they were trying to breach.

Jean whipped off his cloak and wrapped it around himself, the bottom of the ladder and Tante Go. Then he grabbed her with his single arm and pulled her passionately close. They embraced. They kissed. Tante Go listened nervously as the *thrump thrump thrump* grew louder. Jean peered over her shoulder. The Germans were so close now; she could hear the rustle of their uniforms. Jean put his passion into high gear.

A cloud dropped by to lend a hand; covering the moon at just the right time. The Germans glimpsed the amorous couple and politely looked away as they passed without ever looking up. Tante Go and Jean clung tightly to each other until the sound of boots faded and the patrol turned the building corner. Then with a chuckle, Tante Go separated from Jean.

Bee relaxed his hold and returned to his former position. Franco, rolled his shoulders to relieve the soreness from clutching the rail. Quietly, he raised the pole until the hooks caught on the top of the wall then pulled himself up hand over hand. He just managed to get his fingertips on the top and chinned himself up the rest of the way to peer over. The sight deflated his energy. "I'm coming down," he whispered.

"It is no use," he said once they were all huddled together on the ground. "There is another wall inside this one. Even if we could get over the first wall, we do not have the materials necessary to climb the second."

Back at the Dassié home, the quartet sat warming their chilled bodies with brandy and laughing at Bee's colorful account of the bungled operation to Madame Cyprienne Dassié and Lulu. "—And there I was, my nose pressed up against this buggar's arse, while your husband and Elvire are locked together like teenage lovers down below with a German patrol marching not fifteen feet away."

"Teenage lovers, huh?" Cyprienne gave her husband a playfully cross look.

"Yes, Madame," Tante Go shrugged with pretend aloofness. "I apologize if he gets a little frisky with you tonight. He may not be able to help himself."

Jean ducked as Madame laughed and swatted him playfully upside his head.

———

The strapping German agent slowly rose from behind his desk. "You can stop pretending, Mademoiselle de Tonga," he said coolly as he swaggered around his desk with his hands behind his back. He bent down to eye level with his hands on the arms of her chair until his face was close enough for her to smell the knockwurst and cigar smoke on his breath. But he spoke softly as if they were having a private conversation. "We know you help the enemy. Do not think that because you are a woman we will go easy on you. One way or another, you *will* tell us what you know. If you cooperate now, we will take that into consideration. If we have to beat it out of you there will be no leniency."

Dédée stared back into his dangerous blue eyes without flinching.

Finally the German broke it off and stepped back around the desk. He slapped a pad down on the wooden surface. "We know all about the homes in Bordeaux where your friends shelter enemy fliers."

Dédée regarded the names and addresses. She didn't know all of Tante Go's contacts, but she had no doubt the Germans had *coaxed* it out of one of the airmen.

The German waited until Dédée stopped reading and looked back up at him. "Now you will tell me. Who is your chief?"

"I don't know who the chief is," Dédée said. "I get my instructions from a man called Gustav."

"Where do you meet this Gustav? What does he look like?"

"I have not met him. He leaves me notes."

"Where does he leave these notes?"

"The Saint Esprit Bridge. Under a rock."

The German jotted that down. He seemed pleased with his cleverness in playing the address card. What he didn't know was that she had been emboldened by the loaf of bread sent from Tante Go by way of Madame X, the Red Cross volunteer. Although the prison guards had cut and prodded the baguette, they had been so preoccupied with searching for files and hacksaw blades that the folded paper baked into the bread had slipped through undetected. It simply said, *Kiki tucked in under the covers*. Knowing her father was safe gave her courage to resist.

"You follow instructions from a man you have never met?"

"Yes, of course. I am just a guide. I would not expect to be told who the leaders are. Why should such information be entrusted to a *passeur*?"

Her reasoning seemed to appease him for the moment, but she knew it would buy only a little time. Since the Germans had gotten at least one of the pilots to talk, they wouldn't relent until they had squeezed out every drop of information.

"Your headquarters is in Bordeaux?"

Dédée nodded affirmatively and shrugged.

"What section of the city?"

She shrugged again. "I don't know. I only know it is somewhere in Bordeaux."

The agent paused a moment to look back over his notes. "These messages which you receive—they tell you where to meet the airmen?"

"Yes."

"But if you don't speak with this Gustav, how do you know there is a message waiting for you to pick up?"

"I check periodically."

The German rubbed his finger across his chin for a few moments. Then he went to the door and called out into the hall. Dédée heard footsteps and soon her agent and another man were speaking in German. Although she conversed fluently in German with her Austrian brother-in-law, she found it difficult to make out the muffled words now. She managed to catch *bridge*, *messages* and *rock*, and surmised that the assistant was being dispatched to find the fictitious message drop.

The German returned and the questions began again. "I do not believe you do not know the name of your chief. Give me the names of other people in the line."

Dédée said nothing.

"Names, Mademoiselle."

Dédée maintained her silence.

"Torture will make you talk."

"I don't know if it will," she responded with indifference. "I have never been tortured before."

"It will be most unpleasant. We will do what is necessary to make you talk."

"And I will do my best to resist."

"Then we shall begin." He spoke with menacing calm.

She remained defiant although she didn't know where she was finding the courage.

"Are you ready?"

Her heart pounded. "Yes."

The German picked up a mean-looking leather strap. His expression grew fierce. "All right then, if you are ready."

"I am ready." She inhaled, held her breath and tightened her muscles.

But the German didn't strike. Instead, he laid down the strap and left the room.

She didn't know if it was because they believed she was only a lowly passeur, or because she had bluffed them into thinking she wouldn't break, but there was no torture that day. She was returned to Villa Chargrin.

———

Tante Go wasted no time. She and Jean Dassié, Bee Johnson and Franco spent the night after the failed attempt debating their next move. There was simply nothing else for it—they needed to get someone inside the prison.

Tante Go figured that if anyone knew how to get inside the prison, it would be one of her smugglers. Since coming to Anglet, she had built up a tight black market, and the smugglers had quickly learned she was the boss. She paid them well and demanded loyalty in return. She had connections on both sides of the frontier, smugglers who carried the food and goods for her back and forth over the mountains. In France, aristocrats and German officers coveted the sumptuous food in this time of rationing, and they were willing to pay high prices for it. You didn't cross Tante Go or you were cut out of the business.

The man sent to meet her was a big man, a plumber, and a patriot. His round cratered face had earned him the nickname *Moon*. Payment for his services would be a hamper of black market goodies that he could sell.

Tante Go wasted little time on pleasantries. "I am told you are a brave man. You fought against the Germans in your home country, Spain, and you hate the Nazis as much as we French and Belgians do. And I'm told you are a man who can be trusted."

Moon responded with a slight nod indicating that he agreed with the characterization and was ready to hear her proposal.

She slid her wine glass to the side and leaned in over the table, fixing him with her serious grey-green eyes. "A very dear friend of mine is being held in Villa Chargrin Prison for leading Allied pilots out of France. My friend has risked her life time and again to do this. She has forced the Germans to expend valuable resources trying to stop her. We need to learn as much about the prison as we can in a short time. We need someone on the inside." She studied Moon's face. His eyes remained steady, solid, unwavering—he seemed eager to support whatever she had in mind that would disrupt the Nazis. "The danger is great," she said, "but we must get her out before the Gestapo takes an interest in her. I have already arranged for the regular prison plumber to feign illness and take leave for a while. I can arrange for you to replace him."

"Yes," Moon said. "I will help you."

Tante Go held up her hand. "Before you agree, you must completely understand the risk. If you cannot fully commit to this, I need to know right now."

Moon spoke plainly. "I have not been back to Spain since the Germans helped to overthrow my country and put that fascist pig in power. I have no love for the fascists or the Nazis. My friends respect you and say you would not have asked for this help if it was not absolutely necessary. The girl must be very important."

"She is." Tante Go spoke conclusively, but without overemphasizing so as not to give away Dédée's real significance. After all, Moon was a man for hire.

Moon was inserted into the prison and soon reported back that he'd made an excuse to be in the prison governor's office and peeked at papers to learn her cell number. But she was not there. The next day she was back and he brought distressing news to Tante Go.

"I have been in her cell," Moon said, "and she is not looking too well."

"What do you mean?"

"The stress of the prison must be too much for her. You say she is young, but her hair is turning grey."

Tante pictured the vibrant young girl. *What have those monsters done to my friend?* she thought. "Are you sure it was her?"

Moon nodded. He used his fingers in his own hair to demonstrate. "By the scalp I can see grey hair coming in."

Tante Go suddenly realized what Moon had actually seen and laughed with relief. "She dyed her hair black to fool the Germans. Her blond hair is growing back in. Did you see any way to get her out?"

"There is a one-story building outside her cell. She is slim. If I can loosen the bolts on the ventilator she might be able to wriggle through and drop down onto the roof and from there to the ground."

"She is strong and very limber," Tante Go said. "I'm sure she could squeeze out. She could hide in the shadows until we create an opportunity for her to dash through the gate. Go back in and work on that vent. I'll figure out how we can create a diversion."

While the grey hair turned out to be a false alarm, the news that Madame X brought later that day was cause for real concern. "I will bring food and clothing," the woman whined to Jean Dassié and Tante Go, "but I have told you I will not be a messenger." Madame X pushed a folded paper across the table as if it had been a hot coal in her pocket. She dragged her shaking fingers through her grey twists of hair while Tante Go opened the note from Dédée.

Tante Go read it out loud to Jean. "The children are talking and telling what they have learned."

"Oh dear." Madame X took a hanky from her purse and dabbed at the perspiration on her forehead and cheeks.

"Thank you for bringing this," Tante Go said dismissively. "We will not ask you to do this again."

Later that evening, the group of rebels got together in the kitchen of Chez Gachy and devised a plan. "Jean," Tante Go said. "You have severed all ties with your people?"

"Yes."

"If the children are talking, you should not stay in your home."

Jean shrugged. "Where would I go? Everyone in Bayonne knows me. If the Gestapo wants to find me they only have to go to the telephone exchange."

"We at least have to get Paul out. If he is caught they are both finished." Tante Go laid a crude hand-drawn map of the prison on the table. "Now, our biggest obstacle is the three German guards. Two have accepted Fernand's invitation to meet him for drinks here around eight o'clock on Monday. He will make sure they have much to drink. Franco, you and Bee will dress in German uniforms, which Fernand and Freddy have acquired, and go to the prison and request entry. The remaining guard should be relieved to have company."

"What if he refuses to let us in?" Franco asked.

"Then you act like stern German officers and demand entry. Threaten to report him if he does not let you in immediately. Keep demanding. Do not give him time to think about it."

"Does Dédée know the plan?" Bee asked.

"Moon will sing the plan to her. She will go through the vent at nine o'clock. The Germans should be drunk by then. She will drop down to the roof and then to the ground and hide in the shadows until there is an opportunity to run out the gate. I will be waiting for her and get her down to the boat the instant she emerges. Jean will have a car waiting on the other side of the river."

The first part of the plan was put into action the next day. Moon, working in the hallway outside Dédée's cell, sang his Spanish songs but slipped the details of the plan in here and there.

Tante Go was surprised to see him only hours later. "I sang the plan, but when I sang the word, tomorrow, I heard her say through the door, no, Sunday. I sang it again and again she said, no. Sunday." "No, Sun ..." Suddenly it hit her. Tante Go jumped to her feet. "The Gestapo, they know who she is! We've got to get her out tonight!"

CHAPTER TWENTY-THREE

T ante Go wasn't the only chief working furiously. Up north, Baron Jean Greindl *Nemo* and his wife, Bernadette, were shaken by the news of Dédée's arrest. But despite her pleading, *Nemo* refused to quit. How could he? If he didn't keep the line running, Dédée's sacrifice would be in vain.

Like most Belgians, he secretly tuned in to the BBC broadcast every night. Unlike the others, he paid particular attention to the series of *"messages personnels"*. The seemingly nonsensical phrases were coded messages to resistance fighters and underground members in the Netherlands, Belgium and France. Each time the BBC's *messages* confirmed that another group of evaders had made it, his heart soared and he was filled with renewed resolve.

He'd recruited new helpers, worked out new routes and reestablished communications with Franco who had returned to Paris to firm up that sector. Despite the anguish of so many losses inflicted by the Abwehr, the Gestapo and the Secret Police of the Luftwaffe, there was one bright spot—agents Decat and Lieutenant Boeuf, dropped in by MI9, had brought enough money to cover food, clothing and transportation costs for a long time. They also brought a radio to quickly verify airmen. But more importantly, they each carried a tiny religious medal—the Notre Dame de Halle—signifying that Peggy van Lier, and Georges and Edouard d'Oultremont were safe.

Maybe once he had restored the line Nemo could turn the reins over to someone else and find a place to hide with his wife and babies, but for now there were too many airmen waiting to be evacuated. Fliers would become restless, and restlessness could lead them to take careless chances to relieve their boredom. Madame Anne, Lily, Monique and others moved the men around to different houses so they wouldn't be in one place for too long, but that provided minimal relief.

In his new flat at Place Blyckaert, Nemo busied himself with studying train timetables, coordinating guides, moving evaders around, forging identity cards, and distributing clothing and food, but it did little to ease his loneliness. He missed his family dearly. After the November arrests, he couldn't chance living at home. But it had been three months since the Brussels arrests, and Nemo was beginning to wonder if working from the flat at Place Blyckaert was necessary. German interest seemed to have died down. They hadn't even visited the Swedish Canteen to question Commandant Bidoul, Nemo's boss. Suzanne's letter had assured him that despite beatings she, Nadine and Elsie had given nothing away.

He had spent the night with Bernadette just before Dédée's arrest and no one had knocked on the door. Now he wondered if he was being too cautious—if the Gestapo knew Nemo and Jean Greindl were one and the same, they would have visited Bernadette looking for him. And if they hadn't made the connection, his absence from the Swedish Canteen might arouse suspicion. Perhaps, he thought, it was time to dip a toe in the water. It certainly would be easier to run the operation from there.

His questions were answered on the evening of February 6, 1943, as he, Commandant Bidoul, and Jean Naus, sat in the Canteen office making plans for Comet's future.

The door burst open.

"Hands up! German Secret Police." A man in a heavy raincoat leveled his revolver at Nemo, motioning for him to stand up. "No sudden moves," he warned as uniformed soldiers with automatic rifles fanned out to his left and right.

Nemo's body prickled in cold sweat as he rose on unsteady legs with his hands in the air. The gravity of his mistake in coming here glared at him through the barrels of loaded German guns.

A sneer spread across the sallow face of the German. "Well well, Nemo, we have you at last."

A tidal wave of panic drowned Nemo's mind. Light-headed and dizzy, he teetered near to passing out.

Across the desk, Commandant Bidoul's face grew red and blotchy, his eyes floating uncontrolled, jarring Nemo to get a grip on his own fears. He thought of Elsie, Suzanne and Nadine. Those brave women had the strength to get through this: so could he.

With his hands above his head and a German revolver aimed at his heart, Nemo stood motionless as the agent extracted his watch and wallet.

"What's this?" the man said delightedly, holding up a folded piece of paper.

"It's not mine. I'm just passing it along." Nemo tried to sound convincing in denying the note he had written to Paul.

The agent smirked as if amused by Nemo's folly. "We will find out soon enough."

Drawers banged and dishes crashed as agents searched the building. Thankfully, there was nothing else here for the Germans to find. All the identity cards, money, and contact information were still at his flat at Place Blyckaert.

The prisoners were marched outside and shoved into cars. Nemo was taken to Gestapo headquarters on Rue Charles Legrelle and prodded into a waiting room where he faced the terrible consequences of his blunder. On the far side of the room stood the woman he'd taken every precaution to protect. The long separation, the hidden apartment—it had all been for nothing. Ignoring the guards, he crossed the room and took Bernadette's hands in his. He looked into her worried eyes and gave her a slight shake of his head to signify that it was all over for him. The moisture in her eyes said that she was fighting back tears. He wished there was some way to comfort her, but they both knew there simply was no hope. She pulled a rosary out of her pocket, but as she tried to hand it to him, brawny hands gripped his arms and yanked him away.

They were taken to St. Gilles prison, her to the infirmary and him to a cold black cell with Bidoul and Naus. Two hours later they were taken back to Gestapo headquarters. Naus and Nemo were handcuffed back to back. Soon, they came for Naus.

Although well aware of the odds, he'd somehow convinced himself he wouldn't be caught. Now alone in the room he prayed and silently bolstered his nerve by telling himself he could withstand the torture without revealing anything as long as they didn't hurt Bernadette and the children. But there was no guarantee that the Germans wouldn't use them to make Nemo talk. And even if he *did* talk there was still no guarantee they wouldn't hurt his family anyway. But *if* he talked, his brother Albert would likely be caught. He had to stop thinking about it or it would drive him insane.

Sitting in this small room, staring at the wall, he could only think about his stupidity for going back to the Canteen and of those who would suffer because of his error.

Boots sounded in the hall. The door swung open and Naus was prodded in. As he passed by Nemo, his face battered and bruised, he clamped his swollen lips together to indicate that he had given them nothing.

"Let's go," the guard said to Nemo. "Your turn."

He was shoved onto a hard wooden chair in a darkened room with his arms handcuffed behind him. Five goons sat around him in a semi-circle. Two bright lights shown directly into his eyes.

"We can make this easy, or we can make this hard," a German somewhere on the other side of the lights said. "The choice is yours. Now, where is this Paul that you have written this note to?"

"I told you, I was just passing it along."

The first punch came flying from the German to his right, striking Nemo's cheek. He yelped at the pain.

"Let's try this again," the voice behind the light said in a tone of indifference. "Where is Paul?"

"I don't know."

The man to his left stung Nemo's face with a short wooden cudgel. The man to his right did the same. Nemo cried out in anguish.

Again, the German spoke with the blithe manner of one asking directions to the park. "We know you hide enemy airmen, and we know you help them escape. Turn them over to us and the beatings will stop."

Nemo remained silent.

Pain exploded on his face from both sides. With his hands bound behind him, there was no blocking the attacks.

"These men are nothing to you. Why would you choose to suffer such pain to protect them?"

Go to hell, his mind said, but with each strike, the words yelped out through his battered jaw and swollen lips sounded more like the cry of a black backed jackal than anything human.

The German to his left held up his hand to call a pause. "I'm sorry," he said overly politely. "Did you say something?"

Nemo articulated the words as well as his mouth would allow. "Go—to—hell."

The chief interrogator turned off the spot lights and stepped forward issuing a nod to the others who took it as their signal to let their cudgels fly. Nemo struggled to suppress his screams of pain, but he had no control over the sounds coming out of his mouth each time the clubs struck his face.

"Who is the head of the organization?"

Clubs struck.

Nemo cried out.

"Give us the names of your associates."

They mauled him again and again as if punishing him for eluding them for so long.

"Tell us where you have hidden the enemy fliers … Give us the names of others in your organization … Who is Paul?"

Nemo refused to say a word. After a while he stopped trying to straighten up. His face throbbed with pain. One big German pummeled him and then a second took over. Blood ran down from his nose and dripped off his chin.

"The pain will stop when you tell us what we want to know."

Nemo desperately wanted the pain to stop. He knew it wouldn't because he couldn't give in. He couldn't let them inflict this pain on someone else, his brother Albert maybe, because he had spilled out a name. He struggled to hold his head up again, but the sting of a steel spring shut his body down. Barely conscious, he heard the leader say, "Take him back to the prison. Tomorrow we will begin again."

———

Seeing Moon returning to Chez Gachy in less than an hour filled Tante Go with palpitations—it could only mean bad news. He could not have filed down the vent screws in such a short time.

"She is gone," Moon said. "This time I fear it is for good. They have taken her name off the door. All her clothes are gone and the mattress is rolled up."

———

Days later, Tante Go unconsciously twirled her pencil as she studied the map spread on the table in front of her. "There are too many damn roads in Biarritz to cover," she said. She had hoped that going back to the comfort of Villa Voisin would inspire her to develop a brilliant plan. It wasn't working.

"Why don't you take a break," Bobonne said as she opened the oven door, letting out a mouth-watering cloud of baked apple, cinnamon and butter.

"That smells delicious." Janine set cups on the counter out of the way of her mom's map.

Bobonne grinned proudly and ambled to the coffee pot.

"Too many roads and no damn river," Tante Go grumbled. "Even if we got Dédée past the prison guards, how would we smuggle her out of the city?" She threw the pencil down on the map and sat back rubbing her temples. "Janine, please go see how much coffee we have left for bribes."

Soft whistling trilled at the back door.

Bobonne peeked through the blinds, then let Bee in.

"*Ummm*," Bee said as he wriggled out of his woolen coat. He popped the oven door open to steal a look. "I knew I smelled apple tarts!"

Bobonne slapped his hand playfully and shooed him away from the stove.

"What is the news from Brussels?" Tante Go asked.

"Nemo has been taken to St. Gilles Prison, so I'm afraid there is little hope of springing him. His brother Albert went to his flat and grabbed what papers he could—he got away just as the Gestapo arrived. Eric de Menten wasn't so fortunate. I'm told the desk clerk had a Gestapo gun against his temple when Eric rang him up to see if the coast was clear. The poor lad walked right into their trap."

"What about the line?" Tante Go asked.

"Fragile, I'm afraid, but not lost. Jacques Cartier has stepped in."

"Cartier?"

"His real name is Antoine d'Ursel."

Janine returned with two tins of coffee. "This is the last of it."

"You've located her then?" Bee asked.

"Yes," Tante Go said. "We knew by the next day. You had already left for Brussels. She is in Maison Blanche Prison in Biarritz."

"Have you made contact?"

Tante Go nodded. "A friend of Dassié's has a house overlooking the exercise yard. We signaled Dédée with a mirror. She smiled to let us know she saw it. Madame X has gone in to see her, but the woman is very nervous about being questioned by the Gestapo. When we break Dédée out, we will have to abduct Madame."

"They've also taken Dédée's mother and Tante Ninnie and are holding them as hostages," Bee said.

"We can't tell Dédée that until we get her out."

Bee looked over the map. "Paul and Franco have a group in Paris nearly ready to travel. I was planning to help cross them, but if you need me on this…"

Tante shook her head no. "Dassié has been at the exchange telephoning everyone he knows, recruiting shelterers and learning which officials might be receptive to bribes. I'm just stuck on how to hide her once she is out of the prison. The Germans will throw up road blocks and search house to house." She looked up from the map. "Does Paul know about the hostages?"

Bee shook his head. "I thought it best not to say anything yet. In his present state, he would likely do something foolish."

"Good," Tante Go said. "That is best."

"What about a decoy?" Janine asked. "I could dress like Dédée and let the Germans chase me while you take her away in the boot of the car. When they catch me, I will tell them I was rushing to get to the restaurant."

"I'd be afraid the Germans would be all too happy to arrest you in her place," her mother said. "Besides, Franco will need your help bringing the children down. Is this all of the coffee—just two tins?"

"You gave some to the Kommandant, remember?"

Tante Go sighed. "We will have to throw in some hams and cognac as well—that is once I find out who to bribe." She wasn't worried she would be turned in for it. Once an official accepted a bribe she would mark it down on a piece of paper right in front of him, then smile and tell him she kept track of what each person liked. He would understand her meaning: if she was caught—he was caught."

"How about we block the street ourselves?" Bee offered. "We get a flatbed truck, load it with timbers and as soon as the car with Dédée passes we pull out the chocks and let the logs roll into the street?"

Tante Go pondered a moment. "There are too many ways to go around it. And we need to figure out where to hide her where the Germans won't look."

Bobonne set the hot tarts on a towel on the counter. "The only place the Germans won't look is in the police station."

"*Hmmm*," Bee said. "Maybe we can bribe a police official to hide her in the boot of his vehicle."

"Whatever we do, we will have to do it quickly," Tante Go folded the map and shoved it aside like she was mad at it. "Dédée has sent out word that the children are talking and telling what they know."

Everyone fell silent at the sound of a car door. Fernand and Freddy walked in and the group relaxed.

"You're just in time for coffee and apple tarts," Bee said cheerily.

Fernand's somber face and the shake of his head darkened the mood. "The Germans are organizing arrests."

Tante Go took to her bicycle. She managed to alert safe house keeper Yvonne Lapeyre in time for her and Robert to get away, but she was too late to save the Dassiés. One of the airmen led the Gestapo to the Dassié home and positively identified Jean, Cyprienne and sixteen-year-old Lulu. All three were arrested. Jean's seven-year-old son was torn from his parents and left crying for his mother and father.

CHAPTER TWENTY-FOUR

A great big potato with creases for eyes and cheeks—that's what the big German's face reminded her of. Glaring down from his lofty height, he regarded her seated in a wooden chair like she was nothing more than a cornered mouse.

"Now, Mademoiselle de Tonga ... or should I say, Mademoiselle de Jongh..." He spoke in French with haughty nuances as if he considered himself master of the language. "The game is up." A strong inhale expanded his already powerful chest. He bent down and gripped her hands speaking slowly and directly. "Where ... is ... your ... father?" His scorching blue eyes threatened to unleash restrained evil.

Dédée didn't flinch other than to shrug one eyebrow to show he didn't scare her.

"I'll ask you again. Where is Monsieur de Jongh?"

His hands enclosed hers in a vise-grip. Pain grew as though her fingers were about to crack. She gritted her teeth, fighting not to cry out, and stared defiantly back. Their eyes locked in a battle of wills. He squeezed harder, his neck muscles tightening along with his grip. A barely audible moan escaped her, but she refused to show weakness.

His arms began to quiver and finally he released her.

She wanted to rub her hands together to relieve them, but she would not let him see how much it had hurt.

He stepped back and laughed at her foolish attempt to defy him. "We don't have to physically beat you, you know. There are other ways to make you talk." He retrieved a manila folder from the desk and showed her a small photograph. "This is a good picture of you and your father." He reached out and let a bit of her blond and black tresses drape over his fingers. "But I think your hair looked better in the lighter color than it does now in two tones."

She expected him to close his hand around her hair and yank hard, but he didn't. Instead, he returned the photograph and took out another. "Do you recognize these ladies?"

She tried not to react, but her eyes gave her away.

"That is correct; it is your mother and your aunt. This photo was taken when we took them into custody. If you tell us where your father is, we will set them free."

"My mother would condemn me if I told you where he was."

"We will get this information even if we have to beat it out of you. Your stubbornness will do you no good. In the end, we will find him and prosecute him for his crimes."

"You do not need him. He is not the leader of the escape line. I am."

The German laughed. "I understand you wanting to protect your father. It is very noble of you."

"It is the truth! My father only assisted me. I organized the escape line. It is me you want!"

He chuckled with amusement. "Yes, a twenty-five-year-old artist—oh yes, mademoiselle, we know where you worked before the war—a twenty-five-year-old *girl* has organized safe houses and guides for a thousand miles from The Netherlands to Spain." He laughed mockingly at her story. "It is no use trying to protect him. We know all about Monsieur de Jongh. We know all about Baron Greindl. And we know that one of them is the leader."

"You are wrong. I am the leader. Neither Baron Greindl nor my father is responsible for the escapes. I am. I organized the safe houses. I organized the guides."

"You realize you are admitting to a crime which is punishable by death."

"Yes, but it is the truth."

"Very well, Mademoiselle, you keep to your pretense … and we will keep you in prison while we find the real leader."

———

Franco stared out the farmhouse window at the cold grey sky. The steady rain showed no sign of letting up. But it would soon be twilight. The decision had to be made now.

Mountain guide Martin Orhategaray had advised that it would be a day or more before the Bidassoa would be low enough to cross. Crossing at the suspension bridge would take an extra five hours. Franco couldn't help thinking how Dédée faced nearly the same dilemma the night before her capture. Her decision not to go might have cost her her life.

Everything had gone right so far. The children had slipped unnoticed through the Bayonne station, taken a tram and walked about two miles to this farmhouse in the foothills where they changed into overalls. Now they sat bursting with anticipation, unaware that Franco was considering aborting the crossing.

Bee, with a mug of coffee in hand, joined him at the window. "We can take a chance and leave before dark and cut down the time."

Franco looked back to the men seated at the table. The two Americans, Sidney Devers and John Spence, had only been down three weeks and looked in fairly good condition. James Chaster, a Canadian, had been in hiding for six weeks. Albert Greindl, Nemo's brother, was young and fit ... but the children would have to be pushed hard and none of them were in the kind of shape needed to take on the exhausting mountains.

"We couldn't gain enough time to matter," Franco said. "The bridge cannot be crossed before the guards have fallen asleep. And we wouldn't be able to make up the time lost and get down the other side of the mountain before dawn."

"I suppose there's nothing else for it," Bee said. "We either risk getting to Spain after daylight or wait out the weather."

Rain drops pelted the window. Franco drew a slow contemplative breath and blew it out through barely parted lips. "The risk of waiting a day or two is too great. If we are caught again on the French side I am afraid the English might give up on us. I would rather chance being caught on the Spanish side. At least then they will know we are still able to get past the Germans. We must convince the English—and the Germans as well—that the loss of Dédée, the Dassiés and Nemo has not stopped us. We go tonight."

"I like your reasoning," Bee said. "Too bad the Belgian army capitulated so soon. You would have made a fine officer."

Franco chuckled. "I learned more from Dédée than from officer training. She never second guessed herself. She said you simply make the best decision with the information you have at hand. Regretting it afterward serves no purpose. Everyone would make the right decision if they knew the outcome."

Franco closed the blinds and told the men to get some rest. But he knew they were too keyed up to sleep. He understood their excitement. By dawn they would be exhausted. He instructed the men on the importance of keeping quiet and keeping up as he and Martin checked each man's alpargatas and made sure that the rucksacks had shoes, a bottle of wine, a chunk of cheese, some bread, and a spare pair of the rope-soled espadrilles.

"Once we reach the woods this rain will make it very dark," Franco advised them. "Keep close to the man in front of you—hold on to his clothing if you cannot see him. Martin is in charge. What he says —you do."

The fugitives slogged single file through mud-washed roads, over rain-slickened goat trails and around foul-smelling cow pastures. They wound their way higher and higher. Although drenched and breathing heavily, the men trudged on. Somewhere around four in the morning, Martin raised his hand and halted in sight of the suspension bridge. A dim light shone at the barracks of the Guardia Civil on the other side of the river. After a few minutes with no visible movement, Martin signaled for the men to follow him, and dashed onto the swaying slats and ropes.

If they were spotted crossing the bridge, a jittery guard might impulsively shoot. Franco sent the men at short intervals so as not to give them time to think about it. There could be no hesitation. Their lives depended on quickly getting over the river and out of sight before the guards roused themselves to await the morning replacements.

One by one the men scurried under the window and up the slope to the railroad where Martin waited, Franco bringing up the rear. After they had all mustered Martin whispered to Franco that the rain had softened the ground and plant roots so much that the steep slope could not be climbed. Instead, they would follow the railroad tracks.

The rope-soled alpargatas muffled the sound of their footfalls, but their backpacks rustled like a platoon of trainees off to the rifle range. Crouching, they stepped lightly along for several breath-holding minutes with Franco checking over his shoulder for signs of activity at the guard house.

Only when they could no longer see the dim lights did they stand upright and settle into a rhythmic march. The level tracks weren't as strenuous as climbing and it felt good to be on the move again.

They came to a dimly lit tunnel. The sound of their footfalls echoed in the hollow cavity, but they didn't need to worry—the guards weren't about to venture this far from base so close to the end of their shift. After slogging uphill for several more hours, Martin called a break on the downhill side. Franco sat down beside the Canadian, Chaster, who was trying to make out distant lights flickering in the rain. "Elizondo," Franco said. "It won't be long now. How are your alpargatas holding up?" Chaster lifted a foot. "You should change those," Franco said. "Everyone change your shoes," he added. "Tie them tight and put the old ones in your bag. Do not leave them on the trail for the Guardia to discover."

They tramped down the slope for another hour. The strain of the march showed on the men as dawn lit their faces. Franco felt naked out in the open field, but they could only press on and hope no early risers were looking their way.

Finally, they arrived wet, cold and exhausted at a small farm hut on a hill above Elizondo. The men ate what was left of the bread, cheese and wine from their sacks and dropped off to sleep.

Franco rose before the airmen and hiked down to Elizondo to telephone Bernardo in San Sebastian. It was mid-morning by the time he returned to the hut. He kicked the men's shoes and called their names to wake them. "It's time to go. We have a taxi to catch."

Back in the cold miserable rain, they hiked down the hill and along the road to Doneztebe. Franco couldn't wait to get to San Sebastian and into some dry clothes. The sight of the taxi filled the airmen's faces with joy and relief. Franco climbed into the front while Bee ducked under the back door frame waiting for the men to slide over and make room.

Shouts exploded from the woods behind them. Two *Carabineros* yelling in Spanish burst from the bushes. The airmen froze, not knowing what to do.

Bee leaped out of the taxi and made for the nearby trees. Albert followed.

"HALT!"

One officer covered the near side of the vehicle while the other rushed around to the far side and aimed his rifle.

Franco slid across the seat and slipped out the door, but the officer caught his movement out of the corner of his eye and wheeled on him. "HALT!"

Franco froze and raised his hands, but it had distracted the policeman just enough for Bee and Albert to get away. They sprinted into the woods and kept on running.

The Carabineros raged in rapid Spanish at having let some rabbits escape.

Commanded at the point of a rifle, the airmen eased themselves out of the taxi with their hands raised. The driver, with arms up, nervously talked so rapidly in Spanish that Franco couldn't completely follow him, but guessed he was trying to convince the policemen that he'd simply been called to pick up these French tourists.

"Tourists?" the smaller officer said as he looked the men up and down. "I think you are not tourists," he said while holding his rifle at the ready. "I think you are trying to come illegally into our country."

"*No no, tourista—tourista francés,*" the driver insisted.

"Shut up!" The officer pointed his weapon at the man's head.

The driver's mouth clamped closed and the officer turned to the fugitives. "Show me your papers!"

The forged cards identifying them as French citizens didn't appease the officers who debated back and forth in between warnings and threats directed at the captives standing in the rain.

Apparently, the short officer won the debate: he left the taller one to guard the fugitives while he went to telephone for assistance. An hour later more officers arrived and the rain-soaked "tourists" were carted off to Pamplona where they were thrown into a wretched-smelling jail cell. Franco, seeing that the single narrow bunk was already claimed by three foul-looking Frenchmen, put his back to the wall and slid down to sit on the floor. The pilots were taken away to be questioned.

Soon it was his turn to stand before the unsmiling captain. With the haughtiness of rank, the officer looked him up and down puffing on a braided black rope cigar that smelled like burning horsehide. "What are you doing in Spain?"

Franco hesitated.

"You were picked up near the border. Your papers say you are all French. But the others do not speak French. I know you have crossed the frontier. Now what are you doing here in Spain?"

Now that the Americans were fighting in North Africa and massing in England, Spain was no longer so "neutral" in Germany's favor. "We are Allied pilots," Franco said. "We've just escaped from the Germans and are trying to get to the British Embassy in Madrid—we are Americans."

The officer scoffed at him. "Your fellow travelers might be American, but you are French. You are their guide."

"My comrades are American, and I am French-Canadian," Franco said indignantly. "I am a pilot in the Canadian air corps." He really didn't know whether the Canadians called it an air force or an air corps and hoped the captain didn't either.

When Franco was taken back to his cell, the French prisoners gathered around him. "We are pilots," one of them said eagerly. "We want to go to England too, and fight with the Allies. Have you flown the new Mosquito planes? What are they like?"

"They are very nice," Franco said, "good airplanes."

"I have heard they are very fast."

"Yes, very fast."

"How fast do they go?"

"I don't know the speed."

The pilots looked at each other questioningly.

"How many cannons do they have?" the youngest man asked.

Franco looked away as if tired of the questions.

The young man shifted so he was directly in front of Franco's line of sight. "Do you know the answer?"

"You will learn all that when you go to England," Franco said dismissively.

"You don't know, do you? You are not a pilot. You are a spy."

"I don't have to answer to you!" Franco huffed and moved to the opposite side of the cell.

The Frenchmen muttered about him loud enough for him to hear, but he kept quiet. He didn't close his eyes until sometime near dawn.

The next morning, Franco was questioned again. He stuck to his story. This time when he was returned to his cell, the Frenchmen openly snubbed him. He sat back down against the wall, aware the French pilots would have no qualms about beating him up if given the slightest reason.

In late afternoon, he was again taken out of his cell and brought before the police captain. This time, the three Allied pilots were there along with another man in suit and tie.

The captain scribbled on a paper in front of him before looking up. "You are free to go."

The man in the suit and tie ushered them into a big black sedan and drove them to the British Consul in Bilbao. Greeting them there with welcoming grins were Bee and Albert.

"Good to see you, lad." Bee heartily pumped Franco's hand. "We feared we'd lost you. Are you all right? Did they rough you up?"

"They didn't do anything to me, but the place was disgusting. I'm glad to be out. How did you manage it so quickly?"

"Once we got deep enough into the woods, Albert and I followed the mountain west until we thought it safe. Then we caught a tram and came here. I have to tell you, lad, I've never seen such effort. London, Gibraltar, Madrid … nothing was spared in securing your release."

The warmest feeling spread over him. Dédée had always said how much Comet's work was appreciated, but knowing the lengths they would go to rescue him erased any doubt he may have had about the British.

After some time to clean up and rest, he was led to a room with cushioned arm chairs. "It's good to see you, Franco." Michael Creswell, Monday, the attaché to the British Embassy in Madrid, shook Franco's hand and motioned him to a seat. He chuckled as he poured two glasses of wine. "A year ago this would have taken us months to arrange. The Spanish have softened since Hitler's conquest of England has failed. Tell me, how is it going in Belgium?"

"They are getting on. Nemo's arrest was a great loss."

"Yes, I've told Albert we will do everything we can for his brother, but I don't know if our efforts will do any good. What about Paris?"

"Paul has moved some of the men to other lines while we recruit new helpers."

"We have always been in awe of Comet's resilience," Creswell said. "You've been soundly beaten up time and time again, yet you never give up."

"Dédée never quit and neither will we. We will not stop until the Germans are defeated."

Monday nodded agreement and sipped his wine. "Dédée spoke very highly of you. Bee has said you would make an excellent leader. We agree. There needs to be an overall chief. If you are willing, we will support you one hundred percent."

Franco suddenly felt uncomfortable. Did the English think it was up to them to choose Comet's leader? he wondered. Did they think that if they supported him, they would gain some control over him? He didn't try to be diplomatic. "Comet was begun by Belgians. It has always been run by Belgians. And it will always *be* run by Belgians. I appreciate your support, but Dédée would not have it any other way; nor will I."

"And we have no intention of changing that. We simply want to provide what assistance we can. After all, many of the boys you've been saving are English." Monday lifted his glass. "Let us drink to Comet remaining Belgian, and to England remaining a dear friend."

CHAPTER TWENTY-FIVE
February 23, 1943

"I thanked Monday for getting us out of the Pamplona jail," Franco said as he bicycled beside Tante Go on the road to Biarritz. "He told me that England and the United States are immensely grateful and that the underground is now rescuing more than fifty percent of downed airmen."

"Very good," Tante Go said. "I was afraid that without Dédée the British might abandon us."

"He wanted to know if there was any news on her. I told him we have not given up."

She frowned. "Since the arrest of the Dassié family everyone is afraid to help." She stopped talking as they rode past two women standing at a tram stop, then continued softly, "Our opportunities are slipping away."

"Monday has encouraged me to assume leadership of the line," Franco said. "I don't know how anyone else feels about that, but I told him it must remain a Belgian line. We will not let the British control us."

"But of course you must run the line," Tante Go said. "I cannot accompany the children over the mountain. Bee is too English—too recognizable. Paul is too broken hearted over Dédée's arrest. You are the most logical choice."

Franco accepted with a shrug.

"But you must fortify the Paris sector. With both of his daughters arrested, I fear Paul is taking too many chances. He doesn't seem to care if he is caught."

Franco nodded.

"While you are doing that, I will work on finding new routes and safe houses farther to the east. The coastal region is being watched more closely since the capture of Dédée and Frantxia. Robert and Yvonne Lapeyre are still willing to help although they are very upset over the arrest of Robert's sister, Cyprienne Dassié."

"It must be so difficult for them to continue."

"I don't worry about myself," Tante Go said as they turned the corner and pedaled toward the train station, "but I am concerned for Janine and Fre—" She suddenly stopped talking and nodded for Franco to look ahead to the train station. "That looks like the lorry from Maison Blanche."

They leaned their bicycles against a storefront and strolled casually to a better vantage point. French guards were standing by the truck as if waiting for something. Franco and Tante Go loitered near a lamp post pretending to chat.

From inside the station came four German policemen. After a brief exchange of words, the Germans stepped back with rifles at the ready while the French guards opened the back of the lorry and commanded the prisoners out. Jean Dassié stepped down, then Cyprienne, Lulu, and finally Dédée. Clearly, they were going to be transported somewhere. But where?

"Take care of my bicycle," Franco said. He walked right in front of Dédée but without looking at her. She too made no sign of recognition.

One train car had been fitted with bars. He boarded the car behind and watched out the window to see them directed into the same train. At each stop he looked out to see if they were taken off. When the prisoners remained on the train all the way to Paris, Franco had to accept the bitter reality that she was now beyond reach —she'd be locked away in a well-guarded prison, Fresnes. Worse, she would be in the custody of the Gestapo. Franco followed them off the train at the Austerlitz station where Dédée was prodded into the prison van with the others. Franco passed by the van, this time casually glancing over. Dédée winked to let him know she had seen him.

———

Getting summoned to see Colonel Claude Dansey, the buzzard in charge of MI6, made Airey feel like a schoolboy being sent down to the office of the headmaster. It nearly always meant you were in trouble. Airey took a deep breath and opened the door for Jimmy to go in first.

Brigadier Crockatt, their boss at MI9, was seated beside the desk with his dress hat in his lap.

They quietly took seats while Dansey, with eyes flaming, read a cable his aide had placed in front of him. The Colonel dashed down his reply and returned it to the aide, who looked at his boss questioningly. "Send it just like that!" the Colonel thundered.

"Blasted fliers," he grumbled to those seated before him. "Nothing but a bunch of pampered children expecting to be coddled." He shoved a stack of aerial photos out of his way as he spoke. "I've had enough of this nonsense. The blasted prima donna pilots are getting restless waiting to be moved. They're disregarding the directives of their hosts and venturing out. The Germans have had extra men watching the railway stations. Just because the RAF can't seem to keep their planes airborne over enemy territory, we're supposed to spend what little resources we have rescuing them. In the Great War, if you got shot down behind enemy lines you made your *own* way back. These spoiled little striplings expect to be given a teddy bear and tucked into bed at night."

Airey listened attentively as was expected of him, although Uncle Claude's rants tended to be rather repetitive.

Dansey glared directly at Airey. "We are spending entirely too much time on these so called escape lines. Arrests in the north … more arrests in the south … I've warned you about putting too much reliance on these people playing at being spies. Our real spies are being fouled up while Room 900 plays nursemaid to a bunch of spoiled pilots and civilians. Why is it that we still have no British agents on the ground? What happened to those two we sent in with all that money?"

"Ducat and Laboeuf," Jimmy said in a servile tone. "We received just one transmission announcing Baron Greindl's capture."

"Unconfirmed word is they have both been killed, sir," Airey added.

Dansey shook his head in disgust.

Airey knew without Dansey saying it that he blamed room 900 for that too.

"I would like to get out of this escape business altogether," Dansey boomed, "but if we must be in it, we need British agents running the lines. I never trusted this O'Leary chap or that girl."

Airey bit his lip. The Pat O'Leary line had gotten him safely through France and into Spain … and that 'girl' Dédée had done more for morale in France, the Netherlands, Belgium and England than a hundred of Dansey's agents could.

"Civilian lines are too easily infiltrated," Dansey said. "What does an eighteen-year-old girl or her mother know about ferreting out an infiltrator? We need trained agents, Neave. The escape lines are in shambles. The girl was the heart of the line. Well, they cut out the heart … and the arrests in the north have severed the head as well. Key persons in the south have been arrested, and now I'm told that another chief was arrested in Spain…"

"We have already obtained his release," Airey said.

"Yes. Fortunately, it didn't happen in France or he'd still be in jail. The point is these people are going to keep getting caught. It is inevitable. They are untrained. They are easy prey for German intelligence. They simply are not equipped to duel with professionals."

Airey fumed. Dédée and her organization and O'Leary and his had smuggled scores of airmen past German professionals. They had done it under all kinds of conditions, in all kinds of weather, and against a very determined enemy. There had never been such an effort to hunt down resisters as in this war. Notices had gone up in every occupied country warning that men who helped Allied airmen would be shot, and women sent to work camps in Germany. Yet despite the efforts to crush the lines, the underground insurgents persisted. In fact, owing to Dédée's brave example, other escape lines had emerged. *Not equipped?* Airey thought. *Indeed.* But he knew it was futile to contradict the boss.

"I'm going to end this blasted babysitting service. You boys will become part of MI6 where you can do some real good for the war effort."

The words hit Airey like a mortar round. Dansey had threatened before, but never had he been this adamant. Airey had just promised Franco that the British were behind him one hundred percent. He didn't dare say what he was thinking—that he would rather resign and go into France himself to help the underground than tell them that the British were abandoning them.

Brigadier Crockatt didn't say much, only enough to let everyone know where he stood on the issue. "Sir, without the escape lines, our sabotage and intelligence networks would be tempted to step in and aid the airmen. We need those escape lines."

The trio was dismissed. Crockatt assured Jimmy and Airey that he was convinced the escape lines were doing a lot of good: he would do what he could to keep room 900 operating. They lingered a moment in the outer office. Airey glimpsed the cable that had just been received, lying on the desk of Dansey's aide. It said that the airmen in Paris were getting restless and wandering out despite their hosts' efforts to stop them. They asked what they should do. Dansey's two-word reply: "SHOOT THEM!"

———

Clang clang clang clang clang. Wooden clubs dragging across iron bars echoed throughout the prison hall. Dédée felt a hand tugging her off the bed.

"You must get up, Dédée," Celine, her young cellmate said. "If they find you lying in bed they will beat you."

Frigid air stunned her as she sleepily shed the covers. It was February and Fresnes prison, a modern facility in Paris equipped with heating radiators, was as cold as a morgue. To save coal for the war, the heat was not turned on except in the staff areas. Concrete walls and floors retained the cold like an icebox. The bitter chill did nothing to allay the putrid stink of the place. Dédée pulled on the woolen skirt and sweater that Tante Go had sent when she was in Villa Chargrin Prison. She still shivered. With nothing on the fourth wall but iron bars, body heat could not be conserved.

"If you think it is cold now, wait until they take us out into the yard for our two hour recreation. Women have frozen to death. If the sun is out, it will be a little warmer in here when we come back." Celine said cheerily. "Tonight you can sleep in the middle where it is warmer."

Charlotte, their sour-faced middle-aged cellmate jerked her head dismissively toward Dédée. "Why should *she* sleep in the middle?"

Celine withered and said in a docile tone. "Because we should take turns."

"She has warm clothes," Charlotte said as if Dédée wasn't standing right there in the room. "Let her sleep in those.

Celine's mouth opened as if to protest, but she said nothing. Clearly, sweet, perky Celine was afraid of the woman.

"I have only been here one night," Dédée said flatly, "so I can wait for my next turn. But if we are to survive this, we must work together." She looked Charlotte directly in the eye, daring the woman to bully her.

Up the cell block aisle came a woman inmate pushing a trolley, watched closely by a stern-looking female guard toting a big wooden truncheon. The inmate poured "coffee", an awful-tasting liquid made from barley. This was breakfast.

After four hours of huddling together to keep their lips from turning blue, the women received their noon meal—a hot, colorless soup served with cold potatoes.

Who would have thought that being brought to Gestapo headquarters in a prison van could provide a bit of relief? Dédée was apprehensive of course, but at least she would be warm for a little while.

Dédée was ushered into a small room with three simple wooden chairs and a wooden table, and was soon joined by her interrogator. "Good day, Mademoiselle de Jongh, I am *Obersturmführer* Arnold Schneider." Resplendent in a flawless grey-green uniform the man cheerily introduced himself with a smile as if they were meeting at a social event. His spirited blue eyes conveyed intelligence and confidence. She'd expected the stern threatening approach used by the gendarmes and Gestapo in Bayonne, and had been prepared to make up more lies to drive the officials back to their notes to try to make sense of her assorted stories. She wasn't quite ready for Schneider's tactic.

"You and I have a great deal in common," Schneider began. "Our work has been very similar."

"Oh? That would be quite surprising to me," Dédée replied.

"No, no." Schneider laughed. "I don't mean now. I mean before the war. You worked for the art department in the advertising business. I used to sell paints. I worked for Faber Paints. Belgium was my territory."

"I like Faber Paints. They are good quality."

"I used to deliver to the Sofina Company. We may have even met."

Dédée shrugged. "Perhaps. I don't remember."

"Well, no matter. I was surprised that you didn't become a teacher like your father. Your grades were certainly good enough."

Dédée was beginning to understand Schneider's approach. Unlike her previous interrogators, he wanted to show that he knew everything about her. "I never liked math very much," she said.

"Do you know why you are here?"

"Yes, of course. You want me to tell you what I know."

"You don't have to tell me everything. Just tell me where your father is and we will be done. I won't bother you again."

"I have already told the others. My father has nothing to do with it. I run the escape network that you are interested in. And now you have me."

"Yes, I know what you have told the others. Don't you know how ridiculous that is? We know it is impossible. So why don't you just tell us the truth?"

"It *is* the truth."

"Why are you being so obstinate? Don't you know you could be put to death for this? Isn't a cold dark cell enough for you? Tell me what I need to know and I will have you moved to a more comfortable cell with warm blankets."

"I have told you. I am the leader of the escape line."

Schneider threw up his hands. "I have never met anyone so stubborn!"

He drew a calming breath and began again. "Perhaps if I asked in Spanish or Italian, or Flemish …"

"Why? Do you speak Flemish?"

Schneider spoke to her in Flemish. "If you don't cooperate, we will have to torture you. Aren't you afraid of being tortured?"

"Of course I am. I'm scared to death. Wouldn't you be if you were in my shoes? But it changes nothing. Kill me if you want. There is nothing I can do about it."

Schneider sat back exasperated. She could see he was a decent fellow who didn't want to have to hurt her. But she would rather die than give up her father to save herself.

———

"I love your dress," Tante Go teased Yvonne Yribarren-Lapeyre. "Is it new?"

"Yes it is." Yvonne set her tea cup down on the café table and playfully modeled the outfit. "I needed something for those special occasions —like when my other one is in the wash."

"Yes," Tante Go agreed. "It is still a bit chilly to walk about naked."

Yvonne giggled, covering her mouth and looking coyly around the café.

It was nice to see her friend smiling again. Tante Go thought. When the Gestapo mistakenly raided the apartment below theirs, Yvonne and Robert had escaped with little more than the clothes on their backs.

Fernand had forged new identity cards for the Lapeyres and found a new flat for them to live in. Tante Go provided money and ration cards for them to go shopping. But the many personal items, the family photographs and keepsakes, simply could not be replaced. Still, Yvonne trooped on, making light of what they had lost. Tante Go said little about the Dassiés. Franco had sent word back that they were all in Fresnes Prison, and while everyone tried to remain optimistic, Yvonne and Tante Go knew their release was highly unlikely.

"You know," Yvonne said, "it is the silly little things I miss the most, my favorite tea cup … my bath robe. I had these soft pink slippers … our flat has cold wooden floors and I really miss them now. And my nightgown—I don't even have a nightgown to go to bed with…"

"I'll bet Robert is all right with that!"

Yvonne's cheeks turned pink.

"Ah, poor Bee," Tante Go said peering through the window at the approaching figure, "he tries so hard to pass for French, but he still looks like a slouching Englishman with a beret."

"Hello, ladies," Bee said as he sauntered up to their table. "Are we ready for our outing?"

"Definitely!" Yvonne said. "I've been so looking forward to getting out of the apartment."

"Have you decided where we are going?" Bee asked Tante Go.

"With the coastal routes being watched so closely now, I thought we'd have a look around Ustaritz. What have you learned from Paris?"

"Paul has sent some of the pilots to the Burgundy and Val lines and is working on getting Comet moving again. Robert Aylé has learned of a Belgian lad working with the Brandy line who could help us conduct the children from Brussels to Paris. Madeleine Bouteloupt will lead them south."

Before they boarded the east bound train, Tante Go handed Bee a tiny slip of paper which he tucked into his jacket. "These are homes in the area that are working with us." She sat down beside Bee and across from Yvonne and pulled out a ball of yarn and a partially knitted sweater.

"The trees are beginning to bud," Tante Go noted glancing out the window. "I can't wait for spring."

"It isn't spring until I see asparagus growing in the fields," Yvonne said.

"No," Bee said. "It isn't spring until I see Bobonne's asparagus soup in my bowl."

Tante Go looked up, pausing her needles. "Did you have anything to eat? I should have asked you before we left the café—" Tante Go stopped short when she noticed Yvonne's eyes grow large. "What is it?"

"Germans," Yvonne whispered. "Tossing the train."

Tante Go continued her knitting without concern. Their papers had been checked before and it was not the first time the Germans had done this. She nonchalantly showed her documents to the two officers. Bee and Yvonne did the same.

An officer regarded Bee suspiciously. "You do not look French. Where have you come from?"

"Paris," Bee answered. He pulled out his train ticket to confirm it.

The officer looked at the ticket and his papers and then back at Bee. "Empty your pockets."

"Oh," Yvonne's head wobbled down as if she was about to pass out. "It is so close in here. I feel faint."

Bee chivalrously rose with his hands on the window catch, and glanced back to the German for permission to open it to give her relief.

The German nodded.

Bee opened the window and as he sat back down turned out his pockets as the officer had requested. There was nothing to be found of any concern. Bee had already let the paper with the names fly away when he opened the window.

The German turned to Tante Go. "I believe this man is English. What do you say?"

"No. He is Belgian," Tante Go said flatly. "His mother is English. His British looks come from her."

"I think he is an English airman and you are helping him escape across the frontier," the German declared in haughty French. "We have caught other women who do that."

"That's ridiculous," Tante Go scoffed.

The German turned back to Bee and held the identity card before him. "This is a fake. I know you are English and you have come down here to cross the border into Spain."

"I have come down here to see a doctor," Bee said with conviction.

The trio was taken off the train to the town of St. Jean Pied de Port with a number of other suspects. Tante Go remained calm as they were marched to a small hut to await questioning. But before the group had settled in, a Basque man dashed through the open door. The Germans gave chase.

Tante Go nudged Bee. "Quick! This is your chance!"

Bee shook his head no. "If I do, they will know they were right and that will make it worse for you." He remained steadfast.

Poor Yvonne, Tante Go thought. Yvonne had hoped that this little outing would be a chance to relieve some of the stress from the arrest of her brother and sister-in-law and her own narrow escape. Now Tante Go watched her softly weep. Then she pulled out her knitting to assure Yvonne that being detained by the Germans was nothing more than an inconvenience and they were going to be fine.

The Germans returned fuming about the Basque man who had gotten away. They relieved their anger by shouting at those that remained.

Tante Go maintained her calm—until they ordered Bee to come with them. "Where are you taking him?"

"That is not your concern."

"It is my concern," Tante Go said. "This man is sick. We were taking him to a doctor. You will make his condition worse."

The German brushed her aside and shoved Bee in the direction of the door. When they returned without him, she demanded again to know what they had done with him. They ignored her.

The next morning, when the Germans entered the hut for more questioning, Tante Go immediately demanded, "What are you going to do with us?"

"Sit down and be quiet!"

"I will not!" Tante Go said. "I will report you to Kreis Kommandant of Biarritz!"

"You do not know the Kommandant."

"Oh no? Then ring him up! I provide the Kommandant with black market goods."

"So what were you doing with an Englishman?"

Tante Go spoke slowly and pointedly, showing annoyance at having to repeat herself. "He is not English. He is Belgian. His mother is English. He is ill. He has tuberculosis. We were taking him to a sanatorium in Ustaritz."

"We found addresses on him."

She realized he'd had the names of her suppliers on a separate piece of paper. "They are the people who help me gather the black market goods. I buy hams, vegetables, eggs, butter, chocolate ... all on behalf of the Kommandant. Telephone him. He will tell you I buy these things for him. Go to those addresses and tell them I have sent you to pick up the goods."

The Germans left again, and Tante Go wondered if they would consult the Kommandant. Hopefully, he would just say he knew her and let it go at that.

When the Germans returned, they had a hamper full of black market food and grins wider than children eating candy.

"You cannot keep this food," Tante Go warned them. "The Kommandant will be angry. When he asks me, where are the things I bought for him, I will have to tell him you took them from me."

Tante Go's threats worked. She and Yvonne were driven to a hotel and released. The next day Bee was released as well.

"You are good friends and patriots," Tante Go told Robert and Yvonne, "but you can no longer work for the line. It is time you went to England. Bee, you will take them across the frontier as soon as it can be arranged with Florentino. And when you cross over, you will go to England as well."

CHAPTER TWENTY-SIX

Two grey-uniformed officers with swastika armbands invaded the tram like foxes stealing into a chicken coop. The airman stiffened like he was the plump hen. Jean Masson, the young passeur, whispered "I will distract them. You get off at the next stop. Wait for me in the shoe store on the corner."

Masson stepped into the aisle and purposefully peered out the window beside the Germans. "It looks like spring is here at last. The daffodils are in bloom."

The Germans politely regarded Masson while the airman slipped out the rear of the carriage.

"Are either of you soldiers from Aachen?" Masson asked.

"No."

"Oh, that is too bad. I have friends who live there. Well, have a nice day. Enjoy Paris," he said and exited the tram.

Masson strolled into the shoe store. "Hello, my friend. Did you miss me? Come. Let us walk."

They could have waited for the next tram, but it was a beautiful March day, sunny and warm, perfect for strolling through Paris. Besides, walking would give him a better opportunity to impress the airman. "We were very fortunate. The soldiers were on the tram to hunt for fugitives. I think it is best to walk."

"Look," Masson said softly to the pilot as they reached the Arc de Triomphe, "German soldiers pretending to be tourists. They are looking for anyone out of place. Act casual. Do not admire the landmarks."

Masson chuckled to himself as the airman sweated it out until they were well past the soldiers who never even glanced their way. Eight blocks later they reached a residential neighborhood where Masson led his charge into the apartment building on Rue Perronet in Neuilly-Sur-Seine. "I am sorry to be so late," he told Camille Spiquel, his next contact in the Brandy underground line. "We had to exit the tram hastily to evade German officers."

"It is better to be late than to take unnecessary chances," Camille said. "Have you eaten? I've made a pot of soup."

"Thank you very much." Masson made himself at home, draping his coat over a peg and carrying hot bowls to the table. "You know," he said after swallowing a spoonful of soup, "we could get many more men through if we take a different route."

"Oh? You know a different route?"

"I grew up in Tourcoing and I have many contacts in the Quiévrain and Blank-Misseron region. I know a reliable route across the frontier."

"There are too many gendarmes in that area."

"They are not a problem when you have passes with the stamp of the *Feldgendarmerie* for Lille."

Camille said nothing, but her eyes widened with doubt.

Masson laughed heartily. "I told you I have contacts."

"How many passes can you get?"

"As many as we need." He smiled conspiratorially. "How many pilots are hiding in Brussels?"

"Our line does not have very many, but I know of a line that does."

"Let me know if I can be of service to them."

―――――

Out the taxi window, storefronts faded in the distance as Airey recalled Nemo's brother, Albert's dejected words. "It should have been me who was caught, not Jean." He thought of the young man's eyes tearing up and his slumping shoulders. "Jean was chief in Belgium. I'm only a helper." Airey wished there was something more he could say to ease Albert's anguish.

"You have done more than anyone could have expected of you," Airey had told him. "You were lucky to come away with Nemo's papers only seconds before the Gestapo got there. Your quick action gives your brother a chance to defend himself. At least it would in any *civilized* court. The Germans may still convict him, but you did all you could."

"If there is any possibility to free my brother …" Albert's words trailed off in resignation.

"I promise we will do everything we can," Airey said. "We're trying to confirm if he is still being held at St. Gilles. I've made arrangements for you to stay at the Great Central Hotel until we can find you an apartment. Is there anything you need right now?"

"Yes. You can send me back to Belgium."

As Airey rode the lift up to room 900, he marveled at the valor of brave souls like Albert who had narrowly escaped the most frightening experiences yet were willing to face them all over again. The first step to fulfill Albert's wish would be to enroll him in a parachute course. If he passed that, then they would think about an assignment.

But also eating Airey was the sickening news that *Pat O'Leary*, real name Dr. Albert-Marie Guérisse, and Louis Nouveau had been arrested. These arrests were painfully personal to Airey as it was the O'Leary group that had smuggled him from Switzerland to Gibraltar after his escape from Colditz Prison. Louis Nouveau and his wife, Renée, had lodged him in their apartment and shared their meals and wine. They had toasted to the future liberation of France and the overthrow of Hitler. Guérisse had taken over the O'Leary line after its founder Ian Garrow's arrest. Now Guérisse and Nouveau were in a German prison because of a British traitor.

A somber *good day* from the secretary as he passed, forewarned Airey that more disturbing news awaited him. Jimmy regarded Airey through fatigued eyes, shaking his head, holding out a cablegram for Airey to read.

The wire advised that the man responsible for O'Leary's arrest was an infiltrator, Roger le Neveu, also known as Roger le Legionnaire, an associate of the British traitor Harold Cole.

Jimmy growled out what Airey was already thinking. "We had him dammit! We had the blasted dodger within our grasp and let him slip through our bloody fingers! Now there are fifty odd people in German prisons because our loggerhead colonel simply could not believe that an English sergeant would go rogue. *Sunday* had Cole pegged as a bad hat right from the start." The lines flanking Jimmy's nose flared deep and angry. "Damn that Dansey!"

Airey pumped his hand downward gesturing for Jimmy to lower his voice. The secretaries were loyal, but if someone walked in and heard his friend deriding a superior officer....

Jimmy shouted all the louder. "I don't give a damn who hears me! The bloody bugger gets sod off at us when one of our underground is arrested. Here we've lost the whole bloody line because of his stubborn refusal to let the Résistance liquidate this bastard."

Airey couldn't remember ever seeing Jimmy this upset. It was a good thing, he thought, that they weren't in the same building as the Colonel.

Jimmy seethed. "We could have disposed of Cole long before this, but no, we can't make a bloody move without Dansey's bloody approval. He doesn't trust O'Leary and Dédée—two people who between them have delivered more than a hundred bloody airmen—and lets this no good scoundrel go." He paused, his body taut with anger.

"What worries me," Airey said during the lull, "is that with the Pat line gone, the Gestapo will focus more attention on Comet."

"You'd better wire Sunday."

———

"Wait here," Jean Masson said motioning for the two airmen to walk their bicycles off the road into the woods. He pedaled leisurely further on over a little stone bridge and up a country lane between the brook and the railroad tracks, calling, "*Bonjour*" as he passed two gendarmes posted at a small railroad station.

"It is no good," he said when he returned to the airmen. "Two policemen are at the station. We will have to find an alternate route." He consulted a map from his bag and led the men in a new direction. "That is the problem with these outlying areas," he explained later, while they waited in a café in the next town for the bus to arrive. "A little interruption like gendarmes at the station can change the whole plan. But do not worry, my friends. One way or another, I will get you to Paris."

One of the pilots, a curly-haired fellow, leaned forward. "Thank you,

Jean. We can never repay you for your help and the risks you and your people take on our behalf."

"We are all in this together," Masson proclaimed. "I was in university studying to be a doctor like my father when the Germans invaded. The sooner we rid our country of the *Boche* the better."

"Once you get us back to England, we'll do our best to hurry that along."

Masson tipped his head and flashed a V with his fingers. "Excuse me one moment. I must advise my associates that we will be delayed."

Jean closed the door to the telephone booth and turned toward the wall in case anyone was a lip reader.

"Hello?"

"This is Jean," he said simply. "I have the two pounds of margarine you ordered, but things have gotten busy at the store, so I will be about three hours late."

"Very well," came the reply. "We will see you then."

That done, he deposited more coins and made a second call. "Jacques here," he said. "I'll see you at Jimmy's around ten."

With a self-satisfied smile, Masson returned to the table. "The rendezvous is all set. I let my wife know I will be late so she wouldn't worry. She is nursing our newborn son—my second."

"Congratulations. You risk much, my friend. We will never forget your quick-thinking and courage."

———

That evening, Jacques Desoubrie, strutted into Jimmy's Bar for some well-earned libations.

"We were beginning to wonder if you would show up," Prosper said as he signaled for the bar tender. "You have some catching up to do."

"I encountered gendarmes at the train station and rode on to the next town. I could have showed the police my card and had them disappear until we boarded, but this worked out so much better. The stupid airmen think I am the bravest man they ever met. They raved about my quick thinking to Madame Spiquel." Jacques sloshed the ice about in his glass and knocked back a large gulp of the glorious burning liquid. "Now, I am not only guide for the Brandy line, Madame has arranged for me to meet with Robert Aylé tomorrow."

"Who is that?"

"He is the assistant to the Chief of the Paris sector of Comet," Jacques said proudly. "I am one step closer to finding the elusive chief, Monsieur de Jongh."

"Well done, Jacques." Prosper clinked his glass against Jacques'. "Be careful not to move too quickly."

"Don't worry. My net will be spread out with plenty of agents around it before I shake the tree. There will be only one place for them to go —down."

———

A tiny desk lamp shone down on the kitchen table at the Brusselmans' home—a single bulb that couldn't be seen outside through the thick drapes. Anne, hunched over the table with drafting triangles and scale, worked off the dimensions provided on the tiny hand-drawn sketch.

"Darling, it's two in the morning," Julien said as he came sleepy-eyed from the bathroom. "Come to bed."

"I'll be there soon," she said. "I just have to finish going over these lines."

"Can't it wait until morning?"

Anne shook her head. He knew it couldn't be done in daytime when the risk of a visit from the Germans would be much greater. If caught, she would be executed as a spy.

Julien pulled his robe closed against the chill of the unheated room as Anne worked. "I thought they would have begun the offensive by now."

"British Intelligence wants additional information on the coastal fortifications, so I think the invasion will come soon. I will not let our boys go into battle without a complete picture of what they will be facing. They will be sacrificing their lives. I am only losing sleep."

"It seems to take you longer and longer," Julien said sympathetically.

"It does take longer. I have twelve workers feeding me information now." Anne leaned in and blew on the paper. "Besides that, they've provided this special ink and paper, so I have to go over every pencil line in ink."

"Shall I fix you something to eat?"

"No. This is the last one."

In the morning, Anne dressed in a plain skirt and spring jacket, and set out with her large cloth bag slung over her shoulder. Not wanting to chance the trolley being stopped and searched by Germans, she walked the dozen or so blocks to the rendezvous, pausing three times along the way to powder her nose. Of course she only pretended to do so, using the compact mirror to check for *guardian angels*. Since the arrests of Dédée and Nemo, she went round to collect all parcels herself. Nothing was to be delivered to her home. She carried forged papers so if caught she could not be easily connected to Julien and the children, giving them time to get away.

"Ah, good morning, Madame," her contact greeted her when she reached the café. He was dressed in a common grey business suit so as not to stand out either. "It is a lovely day. The tulips are in bloom."

"It is indeed, Monsieur," They never used names, although she was sure the name given her was not his real name, nor was the one she had given him. She had confirmed his authenticity using a phrase she had sent through him which was broadcast by the BBC, and further confirmed by her contacts in the Résistance.

The gentleman ordered two coffees and when the waiter walked away, asked if she had seen the news that morning. "There has been an uprising in Warsaw," he said. He passed a newspaper across the table.

Anne read with interest while removing the envelope from her bag and slipping it between the newspaper pages. "I am surprised they were allowed to print this."

The fellow set the paper aside and stirred sugar into his coffee. "I am sure the true story is different from what the Germans are admitting to." After chit chatting about the weather and fictional dogs and children, he casually glanced around to make sure no one was near and said softly,

"We need snaps of the guns in sector B. Do you think your fellows can manage that?"

"Carrying a camera into the restricted zone would be difficult," she whispered.

The man slid his hand across the table and lifted it slightly to reveal a tiny object no larger than a cigarette lighter. "This one is pre-loaded."

She reached out and shook his hand, palming the small camera. "It has been so nice to see you," she said. "I hope your wife is feeling better. Perhaps next time she can come along."

———

April 20, 1943

Airey sloshed the ice around before lifting the glass to his lips. With any luck, the burning liquid would dull the blade of guilt that stabbed his gut.

Jimmy ambled up, laid his hat on the bar and with nothing more than a flick of his hand ordered his usual and another for Airey. "One of those days?" he asked more cheerily than Airey was in the mood for.

"Aren't they all?"

"I've got some news that might cheer you."

"Has Hitler surrendered?" Airey asked dryly.

Jimmy laughed. "I'm afraid it's not as good as all that. I've had a sit down with Crockatt. It seems our favorite uncle has gotten a bit of come-uppance." Airey raised his eyebrows, and Jimmy smiled. "Uncle's bid to cut room nine hundred has backfired."

"Oh?" Clearly Jimmy's teaser was meant to create suspense. It was working.

"It seems our Major Crockatt has more friends in the Air Ministry than Uncle Claude imagined. Word has gotten back to Churchill. Instead of cutting our budget, the prime minister has increased it. He said it costs Britain fifteen thousand pounds to train a fighter pilot, and twenty-three thousand pounds to train a seven man Lancaster crew. In the past six months alone, the underground has returned nearly two hundred airmen —more than fifty of them by Comet."

Airey tsked. "I'm afraid with the arrests of Dédée and Nemo, and the demise of the Pat O'Leary line the numbers have slowed considerably."

"Now we'll be able to hire more agents."

"Splendid," Airey said dejectedly into his drink.

"All right. Out with it. What's eating you?"

Airey let the burning alcohol wash down his throat before speaking. "I interviewed an airman today—a French Canadian, Pierre Alphonse. Now I know why we only got the one transmission from Drew and Boeuf informing of Nemo's arrest. They're dead. Drew was found in a pond with two bullets in his back. Pierre was told the White Brigade silenced him because his boasting jeopardized their existence."

"That was his own doing," Jimmy said. "Why are you beating yourself up over it?"

"I should have trained him better. I knew he was prone to brag. I should have cured it or cut him from the program."

"You had to assume that the man had some bloody common sense."

Airey frowned and sipped his drink.

Jimmy looked him straight in the eye. "There's only so much we can control—the rest is up to fate. Slow-downs are to be expected. We provide what support we can, but in the end it's up to the lines themselves, isn't it? You should be happy you're not involved in the Pacific theater. Crockatt tells me that other than providing jungle survival training there's little one can do there to aid airmen. They are completely on their own." Jimmy lit a cigarette. "Now—let's figure out who is left to run the line and how we're going to put this extra money to work."

"All right." Airey sat up, inhaled deeply and let out a cleansing breath. "We've extracted Bee Johnson and Robert and Yvonne Lapeyre. Franco is handling the crossings and Denise Houget is helping conduct men to Saint-Jean-de-Luz. Up in Paris, we have Paul—but I'm not sure for how long. Franco is worried he is taking too many risks. There is a young Belgian fellow working in Paris, a Jean Masson, conducting men from the north, and *Jacques Cartier* has taken over for Nemo in Brussels."

"What about that girl, Lily, we had been hearing about? "Jimmy asked. "Neither Georges d'Oultremont nor Peggy have any idea who she is, but they doubt she is fifteen as the airmen believe."

"Nothing's come up about her of late. I've received no word that she has been arrested ... Perhaps with the difficulties in Brussels, she is just lying low."

"How is it going with d'Oultremont's parachute training?"

"I'm awed by the bravery of these chaps," Airey said. "Despite having narrowly escaped capture—he was at an aunt's funeral on the day of the Maréchal arrests—he is ready to go back and risk his life again. I'm sending him in with the French Canadian radio operator, Conrad LaFleur. Since they have both escaped from the Nazis, they should be a little smarter than the last pair."

"Very good." Jimmy laid his hand on his friend's shoulder. "We've saved hundreds of airmen, Airey. Let us not allow our losses to interfere with our helping those still waiting to be saved."

———

"Well, what do you think of my apartment?" the tall gentleman asked in nearly perfect French as he turned about in the living room.

Jacques Desoubrie strolled the room with hands clasped behind his back, considering the eggshell-colored walls with a strip of gold filigree trim just below the ceiling. The oil paintings of people looking into shop windows and water colors of Paris street life were perhaps a bit more than one would usually have in their home, but not too distracting. "Who are the people in these photographs?" Jacques asked picking a frame off the walnut buffet.

"They came from a home we tossed during an arrest," the man said with heartless glee. "Nice touch, *n'est-ce pas?*"

"And what if someone recognizes them?" Jacques sat down on the couch and picked up a copy of *V* magazine off the coffee table.

"Good point," the man said folding down the frames.

"And while you are there," Jacques said while flipping through the pages of nudes and art, "change the wireless setting."

"It is set on the BBC ... The French listen to the BBC, do they not?"

"Of course they do. But people are not so stupid as to leave the wireless tuned to the station when they know it means automatic arrest if German police come to call. And get rid of this *Paris-Soir* newspaper. Everyone knows it is run by Germans now." Jacques thumbed aside the *Voila, Detective, Cinémonde* and other magazines on the table. "These may stay."

The man changed the tuner.

"Do you have a tenant yet?" Jacques asked.

"Yes. We have a French woman who believes she is really aiding evaders. She will pretend to live here when we have men for her to host. When we arrest the others, we will arrest her as well."

"If it is a woman, you should get rid of *Detective* and buy some fashion magazines—perhaps *Le Petit Echo de la Mode, La Femme Chic* or *Votre Beauté.*"

"I will take care of it. Now, when will everything be ready on your end?"

"Patience, my dear Helmut, I have only just been introduced to members of the Comet line. Monsieur Robert Aylé has vouched for me to a Monsieur Moreau."

"Monsieur Moreau!" The Gestapo colonel's eyes lit with surprise as Jacques had known they would. "Do you know who that is?"

"But of course. It is our dear Monsieur Frédéric de Jongh." Desoubrie replaced the magazine on the table and stood up. "I will need to be given a free hand, of course. I will bring fifteen airmen down from Brussels to earn their trust."

"Fifteen! Why do we need to allow so many to escape?"

"It is but a small price to pay to crush the entire Paris sector of Comet wouldn't you say?"

"Well done, Jacques."

"Monsieur Jean Masson if you please."

CHAPTER TWENTY-SEVEN

"Anny, my dear," Prosper Dezitter said when Anny Lall answered the door, "I'm sorry to drop by so early, but Flore and I have a busy schedule today and I wanted to pick up that letter before we got involved in other things."

"It is very much all right." Anny offered an affable smile. "You would like some tea, yes?" She dumped a pile of pinned and chalk-marked trousers and oddly shaped material scraps on the floor and carried the sewing machine chair into her kitchen. "Have seat. I get letter that is belongs to you right in cupboard." Anny sparked the flame under the kettle and brought out three cups and the envelope.

"What is that you are making?" Flore asked conversationally.

"I make a chapeau." Anny went back to the sewing machine and returned with a partially completed woman's hat. "What do you think?"

"This is beautiful. Look Prosper," Flore said turning the hat around in her hands. "Isn't it a pretty violet pastel?"

"Lovely." Prosper gave it a brief glance before returning his focus to the letter, which confirmed that the Gestapo in Paris was ready to take delivery. He stuffed the letter inside his jacket and took out his billfold. "Thank you for holding the letter." He pressed twenty francs into her hand.

Anny hesitated. "This is much money just for to getting your mail."

"Not at all, my dear." Prosper loved to hear Anny speak with her cute Estonian accent, and she wasn't bad to look at either. Although closing in on forty, the tall blonde had a slender figure and a rather attractive face. Under other circumstances he could see himself making a pass at her, but he reminded himself that this was strictly business. She was struggling to make her rent payments which made her the perfect patsy. "You do me a great service letting me have letters sent here. And you could use the money, could you not?"

"Thank you," she said accepting the bills with a grateful smile.

"In fact"—Prosper said as he reached into his billfold once more—"here is another ten for the meeting next Tuesday evening. You are sure it is all right for us to use your place?"

"Yes. I will go to movie. Do you like for me to make food for you?"

"No. That won't be necessary. You are kind enough to let us use your apartment. Besides," he said with a laugh, "I don't want to spoil my friends or they will want to meet here all the time."

Flore checked her watch and raised her eyebrows at Prosper.

"Yes, yes, my love," Prosper said. "We must be mindful of the time." He stood up with cane in hand. "Anny my dear, I'm sorry, but we really do have to be going. Thank you again for welcoming us into your home."

As they settled into the black Citroën, Prosper said to Flore, "I'm glad you ran into your old friend." Prosper cranked down the window. The cool June breeze was perfect for a suit jacket—refreshing as a spring morning in Canada. "I don't believe Anny knows what we are about and she doesn't ask questions."

"She believes we are part of the underground helping Allied airmen."

"Yes," Prosper said contemplatively. "She will be very useful to us." He drove a dozen blocks humming a tune. "Ah, here we are," he said easing the car to the curb. "Be a good girl and put our Swiss Embassy signs in the window, won't you love, while I go up and have a chat with *Monsieur Pollock.*"

"Hello, my friend," Prosper greeted the British soldier who opened the apartment door. "We will come for you shortly. Your role is that of a lieutenant captured in Greece. You have just escaped from a German POW camp, and we are taking you to the Swiss frontier. Are you ready?"

The man nodded somberly.

"Good. Get all the information you can from the pilots. Remember, we will be watching."

"Will he do it?" Flore asked Prosper when he returned to the car.

"Of course he will," Prosper said loftily. "He greatly prefers the comfort of a furnished flat to a cell in St. Gilles Prison. He knows if he crosses me he will be in Gestapo hands quicker than he can say London Bridge. Now let us go find this Nurse Collet."

The nurse opened the door startled to find Flore on her step. "I am with the Captain," Flore conspiratorially advised. "Your friend must come quickly. The Captain is waiting."

Although flustered by the surprise, the airman said a quick goodbye to his host and followed Flore out the door. Prosper had been right. An evader had no choice but to come without question. For obvious reasons, the underground didn't operate on a predictable schedule.

As he pulled away from the curb, the 'Captain' welcomed the new arrival while checking his rearview mirror with the staged caution of an underground operative. Next they picked up *Lieutenant Pollock*, the British soldier captured in Greece, and finally two Canadian pilots. Prosper stashed the automobile in the garage at 369 Avenue A.J. Slegers and led the four passengers up a stairway to the flat above. "Make yourselves at home."

"I'll leave you to your own introductions," he said as the new arrivals joined the five airmen already seated in the large L-shaped living room. "Give these men a good lunch," he instructed the cook, "they begin a long journey tomorrow. Gentlemen—" he turned to the men—Flore and I will see you first thing in the morning. Tomorrow, we go to Paris, and in three days' time, you will be crossing the Swiss border." A cheer went up from the men and with that, he and Flore left them alone, secure in the company of compatriots. It was the best way for Pollock to learn what he could.

The next morning Prosper and Flore gathered the group and passed out fake identification papers and train tickets. "Flore will go through the gate and board first," he told them. "Follow at a distance and act like this is a routine trip. We have booked two private cabins. You are not to speak—not even if you speak French. If anyone comes to our cabin, pretend you are asleep. Flore and I will do all of the talking. If you must use the cabinet, I will monitor from the hallway in case someone comes by. Are there any questions? Good luck to all of us."

Prosper chuckled to himself at the men's nervousness. They needn't have worried; the precautionary lecture was strictly for show.

The rhythm of the train and the monotony of field after field lulled the airmen to sleep. Prosper smiled at them lying against the seat cushion innocent as children. They looked like unsuspecting babies, he thought, little slumbering lambs.

Prosper awakened them as they neared Paris and watched the eager pilots taking turns at the window in boyish wonder gazing at France's famous landmarks. He especially enjoyed Lieutenant Pollock's performance—clamoring at the window as if he was also seeing Paris for the first time. The train *shushed* to a stop at the Gare du Nord where Prosper maintained his ruse, instructing them to follow him and Flore without getting too close. He led them down the avenue to a café and turned them over to the next helpers. "You will be taken to a safe house," he said. "Tomorrow you will journey east to Switzerland. Good luck."

As the scenery passed by on his trip back to Brussels, Prosper tried to imagine their surprise when their new 'helpers' pulled out revolvers and announced that they were secret police. He'd love to have seen the expressions on their faces.

——————

Jean Masson brimmed with anticipation. It had taken two hectic days to coordinate the helpers, photograph each evader and have identity papers made up, but finally everything was ready. He collected the group of seven airmen at various safe houses in Brussels and led them to the train station. "Stay close together," he whispered. "Keep your eyes on me and do what I do." He handed train tickets to each evader instructing them to show their papers when they passed through the check point before boarding. "You may be asked to show them again when you are on the train. This is normal. Do exactly what I tell you to do without hesitation. Everything depends upon it."

Masson strode ahead of the airmen, proud as a mother hen, struggling to maintain a serious face. He'd engineered a brilliant deception. Not only would it be the greatest number of subversives ever rounded up, some of the biggest fish in the entire underground were about to swim into his net. He couldn't wait to reach the station. If Comet helpers were there, then Messieurs Aylé and de Jongh had taken the bait.

He strutted boldly across the terminal building at Lille, paying little attention to the nervous evaders following him or the gendarmes they passed. He could hardly contain his mirth at the sight of Comet helpers, Raymonde Coache and Madeleine Bouteloupt standing against the far wall, their faces apprehensive. Perhaps they sensed what was coming. It would do them little good. They were already trapped.

Raymonde said nothing when he assigned her to take charge of a young RAF pilot, but she clearly was not comfortable taking orders from him. Neither was Madeleine when he paired her with a short Londoner with a heavy Cockney accent. They were likely put off by him issuing orders when he was so new to the organization. He wished he could see their faces when the trap was sprung, but he would make up for it when he netted the bigger fish. He left Raymonde and Madeleine and instructed his large group to follow him to the lounge.

"I don't like this," Raymonde whispered to her RAF pilot. Masson's bravado seemed bound to attract attention, and staying in the open like this would expose them unnecessarily. An alert gendarme would quickly spot foreign mannerisms. "Come with me." She shepherded her airman across the street into a café and took a table near a window where she could watch for the train's arrival.

She was peering cautiously through the glass when a hand gripped her shoulder.

Three very big Germans had surrounded the table.

"Luftwaffe Secret Police," one of the men announced while holding a revolver at his waist. "Do not move."

Raymonde and the pilot froze.

"Hands on the table and stand up slowly."

She and the airman were patted down by two of the Germans while the third kept a finger on the trigger of his gun. Waved into a back office, they sat in silence under the threatening eyes of three guards. Clearly, coming to the café had been a grave mistake. The loud whistle of the arriving train amplified her error.

"Watch them," the German leader said. "It is time to collect the others."

Raymonde fidgeted in her seat regretting her decision. She had no way to warn Masson and Madeleine. The glaring eyes of the guard with the gun in his lap warned her that putting his reflexes to the test would not be wise.

As she listened to the train whistle and the *hissss* of discharged air, the words, *It is time to collect the others,* replayed in her mind. Suddenly, it became all too clear—the Germans hadn't just happened to spot her. Someone had tipped them off.

On the train, Madeleine and her Cockney airman settled in for the two-and-a-half-hour ride to Paris. Twenty minutes in, German officials entered their car and proceeded up the aisle checking person after person. Madeleine calmly took out her identification papers and made sure her charge did the same. But when the official reached her, he said, "These are not right", and tucked her identification papers into his pocket. "Come with me."

She obediently followed. The moment she stepped inside the compartment at the end of the train, the fist of a big blonde woman struck her hard in the face. "You are under arrest," the brute declared in guttural accented French. Handcuffed and shoved onto a bench, she was then hauled off the train at the next stop where she saw her airman also in the custody of gendarmes.

Paul inhaled the hearty aroma of onions, carrots, potatoes and beef as he stirred the pot of stew. He believed, as Dédée had, that the airmen should be fed well to maintain the strength needed to cross the mountains. Hunger made one restless, and a restless pilot might draw attention. As he sat down at table to fill out *certificats de domicile* and identity cards for the arriving airmen, he sighed heavily, remembering his Little Cyclone laughing while making up occupations to match each pilot's photo. How he missed her—not only because he worried terribly about her, but because she was so wise and intuitive. He'd been bothered by this Jean Masson fellow and wished she were here now to consult.

Masson had been introduced to Robert Aylé by a friend in the Résistance. He had been helping the British-run Brandy line and was vouched for by local priests. He'd made two very successful trips bringing down fourteen evaders from Belgium and was very reliable and usually polite. But his attitude before making this trip had left Paul unsettled. Masson had said in a commanding way, *I am bringing a large group of evaders down from Brussels on the sixth of June. Have all of your people ready to help.*

That was quite brash for someone so young and new to the line. After discussing what Masson had done to help them, Paul and Robert decided his brusque behavior was just the eagerness of youth, and his desire to prove himself. With the Americans and British bombing day and night, airmen were dropping from the sky like rain and they could certainly use the help.

At four o'clock Paul set aside the identity cards, gave the stew one last stir and shut off the burner. Then he pocketed his papers identifying him as Monsieur Moreau, positioned his beret at a casual angle, and took a tram to the Gare du Nord where Robert Aylé and his wife, Germaine, were already standing on the platform.

The whistle sounded. Paul checked his pocket watch. The train was on time. In the stream of people, Masson appeared followed by only five evaders. There should have been two more. And where were Madeleine and Raymonde? Paul wondered. Before he could react, ten gendarmes swarmed around them.

He and Robert were shoved into one car, Germaine in another. He couldn't see where they had taken Masson or the airmen. At the Gestapo offices on Rue des Saussaires, Paul and Robert were conducted under guard to a bench in a small room to await interrogation.

The door swung open. In walked Jean Masson.

Robert's face brightened at the sight of his friend. He stood to greet him.

Masson stepped toward him and spat on the floor. "You stupid fools!"

Paul was confused. Masson seemed to think it was their fault that they had been captured.

Masson smiled.

Robert's face flushed with sudden understanding. "You filthy bastard!" He lunged forward and punched Masson in the face.

A guard stepped in and yanked him away.

Masson touched his chin, laughing heartily as he left the room.

CHAPTER TWENTY-EIGHT
June 1943

The girl's gaze bounced from person to person like a rubber raft on the Atlantic, her mind adrift somewhere between disbelief and panic, faint and flight. Excitement coursed through Jacques Desoubrie like a drug. This was the hands down best part of the job, he thought, the payoff for months of undercover work. There was nothing he liked better than watching the color drain from a victim's face when they realized they were trapped like a fly in a web with the spider drawing near. He smiled as her fearful eyes took in the revolver he held by his waist.

"As you can see, my dear, your time of aiding enemy airmen is finished." Jacques motioned with his gun for her to step away from the door and back into the room. Three thugs followed him in. "Where is your husband, Madame?"

"H-he's not here."

"Oh, that's too bad." Jacques jerked his head to the left, signaling the goons to search the other rooms. The men soon returned shaking their heads. Jacques sighed. "I suppose we will have to wait for him."

She sat helplessly on the sofa guarded by two Germans while he wandered about the room smugly admiring family photographs. "Ah, The Eiffel Tower," Jacques said turning a snow globe over to watch the white flakes swirl. "Too bad *you* will not be going back to France any time soon." A couple of steps further he bent forward to take a closer look at a framed Belgian service medal from the Great War. Her fearful eyes followed him as he poked nosily through her things. He knew the girl was nothing more than a lowly helper—the gravel upon which the underground pyramid rose. But if he removed the gravel, the pyramid would topple. They thought they could fool the Secret Police. Now they were the ones fooled.

Jacques pulled a book off the shelf and slowly leafed through it. He never looked toward a watch or clock. It was important for them to see he was in no hurry lest they get the idea there was a chance that he would get tired of waiting.

Less than half an hour passed before the German peering through a slit in the window blinds raised a hand to alert the others. One officer followed Jacques to the door while the other pressed his revolver into the woman's cheek.

The door lock clicked. The knob turned.

"Ah, Maurice," Jacques greeted him when the door opened. "How nice to see you. Come in. We have been expecting you."

There was that moment of confusion followed by the sobering realization that he was caught. Poor Maurice looked like he had touched a wet finger to an electric socket. Jacques simply couldn't contain his mirth. "My friends will keep you company, while I pay a little visit to some of *your* friends." Jacques turned to two of the officers. "Take them away."

———

Franco covered a yawn with the back of his hand. It seemed as though Paris had gotten much farther away from Bayonne than it used to be, but perhaps it was just the heat inside the coach and his eagerness to get home and change into some clean clothing. He'd been gone for nearly two weeks. Using the inland crossing took a lot longer than the route near the coast, and there was really no way to get a good night's sleep while traveling with the *children*. Every creak of an old farm house, every bark of a dog, even the jingle of a sheep's bell put him on alert listening for sounds of car doors and jackboots. He needed some quiet time in his own apartment and a good meal to restore his energy. Wilting in the late afternoon heat, he walked to the apartment on Rue Vaneau and wearily unlocked the door. Paul had apparently stepped out, perhaps to the market or to conduct a pilot. A balmy breeze blew in from an open window ruffling the blank identity cards and airmen's photos on the table. He knew Paul wouldn't have gone far with those left out.

Franco hung his beret on the back of a chair and changed out of his work clothes disguise. He thumbed through the rack in his closet, but his favorite tie didn't seem to be there. Paul must have borrowed it for an airman's photograph.

He returned to the kitchen annoyed that Paul hadn't used one of his own ties. Opening the refrigerator, he caught a whiff of something sour, but closed the door when he noticed the pot on the stove. He lifted the lid to peek inside. Green cottony mold and a fetid smell of foreboding jolted his mind. He blinked himself alert.

Franco went back to the refrigerator and opened the milk bottle, recoiling from the odor. It was all too clear—the open window, the pot, the sour milk, the papers on the table. Paul had left expecting a brief absence, but he would not be returning.

He staggered back from the window, his mind racing. The Gestapo could be watching the place right now. He might already be trapped. His only chance was to get away quickly. He made for the door, but turned back. If the police didn't know that Monsieur Moreau was actually Frédéric de Jongh, the papers would incriminate him. Franco snatched the papers off the table and whatever money he could grab.

He eased the door open a crack to peek out. Seeing no one, he snuck into the empty lift, quietly closed the metal gate and rode down. After a check of the street, he slipped out keeping his head down as he quickly walked from the building. After a number of evasive turns down small streets and alleys, he came to the only place he knew would be safe—the apartment of his friend Michel Roger *Max*. Max had taken the trip south with him, so he wasn't in Paris when the arrests were made.

He stayed the night and over morning coffee they decided to learn the extent of damage.

At the home of Germaine and Robert Aylé, they found Gestapo seals on the door and turned away. Next, they visited the flat of Aimable Fouquerel, the hospital masseur in whose apartment many airmen had stayed. Gestapo seals said they weren't the first to visit.

They decided to return to Paul's flat to make sure no secrets had been left behind, but as a precaution, they exited the lift at the floor above the apartment. Male voices carried up from the landing below. Franco and Max froze, listening to the guttural German dialect, scarcely daring to breathe. They waited until they heard a door close and the voices stop. Cautiously, they slipped into the lift and rode the car back down.

Back in Max's apartment they calmed their nerves with a bit of brandy. Franco finally broke the silence. "I have to go back to the apartment."

"You're crazy!" Max said.

"You're probably right. But maybe the Gestapo hasn't had the time to do a thorough search yet. If they find everything they will have all the evidence they need on Paul. It will mean his death. And who knows who else it might lead them to."

They slipped out after curfew with two small flashlights, racing hearts, and a pen knife. They cut the seal and searched every known hiding place for papers, identity cards and money. Franco still couldn't find his tie. But good providence had been with them, and they weren't about to press their luck. They rode the lift back down and vanished into the night.

———

"I'm going to the dog races tomorrow, so we could have lunch today if you'd like." That was René Ponty's code signifying he needed Anne Brusselmans to come and question a new evader. After the June arrests, men were backed up all over Belgium and René had asked Anne if she could help move them. She agreed on the condition that she would interview each man herself before she allowed him to be moved to her home or the home of any of her safe house keepers.

"Please turn around and raise your hands to the side," she told the airman. She smiled inwardly at the look of surprise when she patted the young fellow down, including the insides of his thighs. "Thank you," she said. "Now please have a seat while I ask you some questions. You are a pilot in the RAF, correct?"

"Yes, that's right."

"What type of plane do you fly?"

"Hurricane."

She frowned to herself. It was easier for Germans infiltrators to claim to be fighter pilots so they didn't have to make up names of bomber crew members.

"Can you tell me what a mahogany spitfire is?"

The fellow blinked several times, apparently in shock that she knew the term. "It's a desk for penguins—officers who don't fly."

"How about a fruit salad?"

"It's a big cluster of different color medals a highly decorated fellow wears on his uniform," he said making a circular motion in front of his chest to indicate the area.

"And who is Pilot Officer Prune?"

"Oh my God." The fellow laughed. "You even know about Prune? He's the chap in our training manuals. He shows us what could happen if we don't follow procedure."

Anne smiled. "I'm sorry. But you understand we cannot take any chances that you might be a German agent. Tomorrow someone will take you to a department store for photos for your identity papers. After that, just sit tight and we will extricate you as soon as possible."

———

"*Bonjour*," Michou said to the six-year-old boy with tear stains down his grimy little cheeks. His pant leg was torn exposing a skinned knee. "What happened to you?"

"He fell off his bicycle," his mother said.

"That is too bad. Do you think you can make it up on this examining table so I can have a look?"

The boy nodded, his face scrunched up with exaggerated pain as he hoisted himself to the cushioned top and sat with legs dangling over the edge.

"Now you are taller than me!" she said with pretend surprise. "Of course it isn't hard to beat me."

A smile nearly broke through the little boy's frown, but he quickly recovered his pained look.

She gently pulled his trouser leg up over his knee. "Oh my," she said.

"You certainly scraped it good, but we will fix it up. I will have to clean it." She filled a bowl with warm soapy water.

The boy recoiled even before the wash cloth touched his skin. She smiled to comfort him. "I will be very gentle," she promised. "You are such a brave boy." She dabbed at the wound then opened a packet of sulfa powder. "This is going to sting a little, but you can take it. You are brave, right?"

His eyes widened as if he wasn't too sure of the answer.

"You know I fell so many times when I learned to ride my bicycle, I wanted to give up and never ride again. But I didn't give up. I eventually learned and you will too."

The boy let out a slight gasp at the first touch of the powder, but he held his leg still and let her work.

"You are being so good," she said. "Just one more thing and we will be done."

He looked ready to jump off the table at the sight of the hypodermic needle. "This is going to hurt just a little," she said as she swabbed his arm with alcohol, "but not too much for a young man who endured such a hurtful scrape."

She plunged the needle in before the boy had a chance to react, and he held back his tears. "There," she said. "We are all finished. You have been a very brave boy."

Michou checked the clock. It was nearly noon, the end of her shift. She worked quickly to fill out the boy's release papers so she wouldn't be late.

"Michou, do you want to come with us to the club?"

She looked up at the three nurses gathered around her. "I'm sorry. I cannot go tonight."

"You work too hard. It's time for a laugh," her friend said. "Just come for one drink."

"I will join you some other time."

"*Aaahh*," a second nurse said knowingly. "I think our little Michou has a boyfriend."

"A boyfriend!" Michou laughed. "Men don't just drop from the sky!

There is no one left in Belgium to date except the Boches and who wants them!"

The first nurse sighed. "That is why we have to go to the club alone."

"You should have lied and said you had a date," the second nurse said sadly. "Then we would have felt our chances of getting a man were only one in four."

If they only knew about her date! She hurried home to the apartment of Hélène Camusel, a spinster in her sixties, who let Michou stay in her two-bedroom flat in Laeken.

Michou dashed through the kitchen, dropping a pocketful of leftover cloth dressing and tape into a cardboard box in the cupboard. Her blouse was unbuttoned and her skirt unzipped by the time she reached her bedroom. Off came her nurse's stockings and in ten minutes all traces of makeup were gone. She wiggled into a short green and white checked skirt, pulled on a pair of bobby socks and slipped on black saddle shoes.

Standing at the mirror, tying her hair with a green ribbon, she thought of her father. He hadn't even let her date until she was in nursing school. She wondered what he would think if he knew *whom* she was dating today. He would worry about her of course, but he would certainly approve. Although she had been on her own since enrolling at university, she had never felt truly alone until the arrests of her family. Now she had to rely on herself. She hadn't seen her parents or Andrée in months—not since they were taken from the local jail to St. Gilles Prison.

Lunch was a hit-and-run bowl of corn flakes. Then she was off. She'd nearly gotten to the lift when she realized she'd left her algebra text book behind. She caught the tram just in time, but to her dismay the only seat left in the carriage was next to an impeccably uniformed German lieutenant. The handsome officer smiled in welcome and shifted over to make room. She accepted with an obligatory nod.

Soon she felt his gaze drifting in her direction. She ignored him for as long as she could, but after a while he stopped sneaking peeks and looked directly at her. When she turned toward him, he was smiling pleasantly.

"I see you are studying algebra," he said nodding toward the book in her lap. "That was a favorite subject of mine when I was in school." His

French was very good. Like many of the homesick German soldiers, the lieutenant was well-mannered and well-disciplined. His warm blue eyes and gentle voice conveyed genuine friendliness.

But he was the enemy.

"I do not like mathematics very much," Michou answered courteously.

"Do you not like school?" he asked.

"It is all right."

He nodded knowingly. "I used to feel like that when I was your age. Now I wish I was back in school."

Michou chuckled to herself. She was probably as old as the young lieutenant, but being petit she didn't look it. He seemed like a nice fellow —not arrogant as some were. Like many of the young German soldiers, he was lonely and longed for companionship.

"You will see," the soldier continued, "after you are out of school for a while you will miss it."

Michou didn't want to be rude, but at the same time she didn't want to encourage him. With so few men left, some Belgian girls made the best of it and dated German men. But Michou couldn't bring herself to think of the Germans as anything but evil butchers—slave masters of the Belgian people.

"What lesson are you up to? I could help you if you are having difficulties."

"Thank you, but that won't be necessary." She presented an appreciative smile, but turned back to face the front to let him know she wasn't interested in further conversation. She said nothing more but a polite goodbye when she reached her stop.

As Michou walked past the shops she thought back to the time when their windows were filled with displays. Now a sign in the grocer's window advised, 'No meat today'. Streets once filled with automobiles now were choked up with bicycles and pedestrians. Large leather handbags no longer existed as French leather was now shipped to Germany for the army. Gone were the leather-soled shoes—replaced with wooden-soled sandals and wooden sabots that made an annoying tapping sound when you walked.

Michou sighed as she thought of her last days shopping with her sister Andrée. She missed her sister. She missed the silly faces Andrée would make sitting on a bench watching odd characters pass by. Her sister could find humor in almost anything. Perhaps what Michou missed most was having her to talk with and share secrets, although not all secrets. She knew Andrée had been passing out pamphlets and delivering clothing for the Résistance, but only after the arrests did she learn from Anne Brusselmans just how brave and daring her sister was. Michou didn't want to think about how those Nazi butchers might be torturing poor Andrée.

Working in the hospital, she saw firsthand what the Boche were capable of. She'd treated people for cigar burns, broken fingers, gunshot wounds, bruised and battered faces ... How everyone's lives had changed since this war began. There was no cheer in Belgium anymore.

Leaving the commercial district, Michou walked until she found the appointed house number. She hesitated before ringing. *Blind dates* always made her uneasy and the recent rash of arrests meant this one was especially risky. She drew a breath, steadied her nerves and rang the bell. "Bonjour Madame," she said when the door opened. "I am here to get some help in algebra." Michou held up the book.

The woman nodded. "I can help you with your mathematics." She looked beyond Michou to the street as she welcomed the girl in.

Michou waited in the front room while the woman went down the hall to a room in the back. A moment later, she was followed out by a tall young man. Michou had hoped that her new 'boyfriend' would have been better dressed with pants that didn't end six inches above his shoes.

"May I present John," the woman said.

"Hallo, John." Michou shook his hand and smiled. "I am your *passeur*. You may call me *Lily*."

————

Anne, tea cup in one hand, touched the map on the table with the other while pondering aloud to Michou. "Our guides can lead the puppies to Mons where Julien has made arrangements for a customs official to get them across the frontier into France. Others will conduct them from there"—she took a contemplative sip—"but with the Paris guides all arrested and Jacques Cartier gone into hiding, how the devil are we going to reconnect Brussels to Paris?" Anne stopped talking at the sound of the door latch and looked to the clock. "Half past four already?"

"Hello, my darlings," she called. "How was school?"

Little Jacques and Yvonne ambled into the kitchen and dropped their books on a chair.

"Good," Jacques said unconvincingly.

Anne laughed and planted a kiss on his forehead. "You've only a few days left. Then it will be summer recess."

"Hello, Michou," Yvonne said.

"Hello, my friend. That is a lovely necklace you are wearing."

Yvonne gave her mom a sour look as she removed the string and tin can from around her neck. "Mother makes us wear these in case our school is bombed and we are buried under rubble."

Michou gave little Jacques a hand taking his off. "*Oooh*, Let me see," she said with pretend excitement. "What is in here?" She twisted off the lid. "Ah, one, two, three, four lumps of sugar… a whistle … a little bottle of water …"

"It's a nuisance during recess," Yvonne grumbled.

"Yeah, It's a nuisance," Jacques echoed.

"I can't help it," Anne said with a laugh. "I'm your mother. It's my job to worry about you."

"Do you want to play table tennis?" Yvonne asked Michou with hopeful anticipation.

Her mom cut in before Michou could answer. "Why don't you and Jacques run down the cellar and fetch some potatoes for dinner while I talk with Michou?"

"I'll play in a little while," Michou promised.

Anne chuckled as the children ran off. "They miss you. You've become one of the family."

"I miss them too. I am so grateful to you for taking me in when my family was arrested."

"How are you doing at Mademoiselle C's? Are you eating well? You need to start eating better."

"Hélène makes sure I do," Michou said with a laugh. But they both knew that with Michou constantly on the move guiding men it was nearly impossible. "I believe she enjoys the company. She especially loves feeding the airmen. She treats them like they are her children. And what about you, Anne? What did the doctor say?"

"He said to rest." Anne shrugged. "I have three more men scattered about the countryside to interview tomorrow."

"Be careful in the provinces, Anne. I've heard many friends have been arrested there as well. I hope they find that bastard, Masson. I still do not know how a Belgian could do that to his own people."

"I've had enough of these infiltrators," Anne said angrily. "I will not let any evaders come to Brussels until I have met them myself. While I go question those men tomorrow, can you take the puppy at Monsieur P's for his photographs?"

"No problem."

"I still don't know what we are going to do with these men once we get them to Brussels if we cannot find who to contact in Paris."

CHAPTER TWENTY-NINE

Prosper took notes as the skillful German interrogator plied his trade, tossing the British pilot's military discs on the desk like an old candy wrapper. "These mean nothing. You were caught in civilian clothes. Yet you expect us to believe you are an English airman. Spies are not covered by the Geneva Convention. Spies are tortured. Spies are shot!"

Dark wet circles grew under the arms of the handcuffed lad in the wooden chair. Fear glistened on his face. Ragged breaths—taut neck muscles—quivering chest—the boy was nearly in tears and the Abwehr officer hadn't even laid a hand on him. "What can you tell me to convince me you are truly a flier and not a spy?"

"I—I've told you the air base I was stationed. I've told you where my plane went down. There must be reports of a Hurricane down in that area. It was only one week ago. Surely there must be reports—"

"Anyone can claim to have parachuted out of a plane that crashed and burned beyond identification. You could have dropped in to be inserted as a spy."

Every time the interrogator used the word, "spy" the pilot swallowed hard.

"Who helped you?"

The airman looked at Prosper.

"Before *Captain Jackson* picked you up," the interrogator growled. "Where did you get your clothing? What did you do with your uniform?"

"I stayed with an elderly lady. I don't know her name."

"Where does she live?"

"I—I don't know." his fearful eyes pleaded for the German to believe him. "I was led down many blocks before we got to her home."

"How did the underground know you were a British pilot?"

"They asked me questions about the plane I flew, where I was born, and what school I attended. They gave me identification papers and moved me to the house where Captain Jackson picked me up."

The interrogator paused and jerked his head to the side for Prosper to follow him out into the hall. "Tell Captain Kohl we have just confirmed that the underground has a radio in Brussels. That is the only way they could have authenticated the airman's information so quickly."

A week later, Abwehr Section chief, Rudolf Kohl, gathered a team of agents around a map of Brussels and pointed to a spot where two blue pencil lines intersected. "We have a fix on the underground's radio. One squad will move in behind the building. A second squad will contain the front. Prosper, your team will toss every apartment in the building until it is found."

"HANDS UP!" They charged with guns drawn into apartment after apartment. In the fifth flat, two men sat at a table eating bread simply too relaxed to be innocent, Prosper thought. They could not have missed the banging on the other apartment doors, yet here they sat pretending they had heard nothing. Prosper sat down across from the men with his revolver in hand, admiring his manicure while the three SS officers turned over furniture, ripped out drawers, and tore the place apart.

Prosper could tell the two Belgian occupants were doing their best to suppress their urge to look over and see what the Germans were into, but they knew they couldn't risk Prosper reading their faces. A German stepped out of the bedroom shaking his head.

The Belgians sat unmoving, staring forward.

Prosper stood up with gun in hand, watching the faces of the suspects as he strolled the room thinking. He was sure these were his men, but their eyes gave nothing away. They showed no concern as one German stood on a chair to check the tops of the cabinets or when he rapped his knuckles on the wall listening for any change in timbre.

A thought struck him. "Get up! Stand over there," he ordered with a wave of his revolver. "*Schieb sie den Tisch zur Seite*," he instructed the Germans.

As the agents moved the table to the side, Prosper watched the suspects closely. He thought he saw a slight tightening of the facial muscles. He walked across the empty space tapping his heel on the floor as he went.

Tunk tunk tonk There it was. Prosper repeated his steps. *Tunk tunk tonk tonk—tonktonktonktonktonk.* "*Unter den Dielen,*" he said.

The German officer pulled a pen knife from his pocket and pried the floor boards up. And there it was, the prize they had been searching for, the radio transmitter.

————

I must be crazy, Anne Brusselmans thought. It had sounded so easy when she proposed it to Michou. She would simply borrow Michou's little sister Francine's *schein*, her allowance to appear at the prison to visit their sister, Nadine, and learn how she and Michou could reconnect with Paris. It certainly felt different than taking bread to friends in prison. If caught communicating about the underground, Anne's trip to the prison would be one-way.

St. Gilles Prison, an imposing fortress, was guarded by both professional Belgian warders and German overseers. Anne took a deep breath and marched to the gate before she could talk herself out of it.

"*Schein,*" the official demanded with outstretched hand.

Anne handed over the appearance permission paper and waited several heart-palpitating moments while the guard examined it. If he lifted his gaze from the paper, she was sure he would see the thumping of her heart. But, with no more emotion than a cinema ticket clerk, he issued her a blue card and instructed her to wait.

Thirty long minutes ticked by before a serious-faced German sergeant came out to scrutinize her blue ticket and replaced it with a numbered tin disk. Another half hour passed. The door swung open and the sergeant called her number. She followed obediently, but the *thrunk* of the heavy door slamming behind them blanked her mind like a gunshot. She fought the impulse to flee, repeating to herself her alibi: *Francine was ill so I came in her place.*

"Fifteen minutes." The warder ushered her into a small cubicle before stepping back to stroll up and down keeping an eye on the visitors.

Loud voices emanated from neighboring cubicles as people tried to communicate with their loved ones through the thick glass and heavy iron bars. As Nadine took her seat, her face lit up with curiosity and delight at the surprise visitor.

Anne smiled back and said a loud, "Hello."

"Hello."

"How are you getting on, Andrée?"

"I take it day by day."

Although Nadine smiled bravely, Anne could see in her gaunt face that the year spent in prison was taking its toll. But there was no time to waste. Anne wrote quickly on a slip of paper, *Line down – need contact.* She flashed the paper just long enough for Andrée to read it. "Is there anything I can bring to you?"

Nadine closed her eyes a moment to remember. *Tante Go—Villa Voisin,* she mouthed, then said aloud, "A toothbrush would be nice."

Anne listened to the footsteps of the guard behind her. She waited as he passed and glanced over her shoulder before writing her next question. "I will send it in a Red Cross packet," she shouted through the glass as the word *Where* flashed on the lifted paper.

"That would be wonderful," Nadine shouted back. *Anglet—south of Bayonne,* she mouthed.

"I will send cookies and bread, too," Anne bellowed.

"Thank you," Nadine said.

"Stay strong, my friend." Anne wrote down one more message. *Michou sends love.*

Nadine put her fingers to her lips and blew a kiss through the glass for Anne to take back to her sister. Then she said with resolve, "They have not broken my spirit!"

The next day, Michou was on a train for the south of France.

―――――

The beagle pup didn't seem bothered by the hot August day, sniffing his way down a row of border shrubs, pausing every now and then at the curiosities of a butterfly or bug. Comfortable in the shade of the chestnut tree in the back yard of Villa Voisin, a gentle breeze blowing in from the bay, Tante Go stretched out her bare feet on a chaise longue while working knitting needles through a length of yarn from the bag on the ground. The dog pranced to her side and she scratched him behind the ears. "I'm sorry, Dickie, it is too hot. Maybe Janine will play with you."

The dog turned hopefully to the girl in the other chair.

"Sorry, Dickie," Janine said leafing through the pages of *Votre Beauté* magazine. "I'm busy looking at all the dresses I cannot buy."

The dog's ears perked at the sound of knocking on the front door.

Tante Go regarded her daughter questioningly.

Janine shook her head to indicate that she had not been expecting anyone. She went inside to answer while her mom slipped on her sandals.

"Is Madame Elvire de Greef at home?" a German field police officer asked.

"I am Elvire," she said as she came in from the back.

"You must come with us, Madame," the officer said. "The Gestapo would like to interview you."

"All right," Elvire said in an unconcerned tone despite the alarm hurtling through her mind. "I'll get my rain coat," she said maintaining her façade of innocence.

As she passed Janine, she whispered, "The papers."

The officer ushered Tante Go ahead of him and turned back to Janine before leaving. "Tell your father when he gets home to come to the station. We would like to speak with him as well."

Janine remained still until the car left, then found her mom's black book—the one with the names of the evaders they had helped—and hid it under the floor boards. She stuffed all the blank identity cards, evader photos, lists and stamps into her bag, slung it over her shoulder, and bicycled to the office of the Kommandantur where her father and brother worked.

"Your father is not here," the secretary told her.

"What about my brother, Freddy?"

The girl gently touched Janine's arm. "He has been arrested."

Janine pedaled quickly to the apartment where Franco was staying with a friend and told him what happened.

"Give the papers to me," he said calmly, "and make sure there is nothing else in your bag that might be incriminating. Go back home to warn your father. Look through the house again. Make sure you have gotten rid of everything. I will send someone to watch for your father in case he returns to his office."

When her father got home, he didn't go to the police station as instructed, but instead to his friend, the officer directly under the Kommandant. "I am a poor interpreter just trying to make a decent living for my family," Fernand said indignantly. "Yes, we make a little extra money on the black market, but you already knew that. Most of the goods we get are obtained for the Kommandant and other German officers. My wife and son should not be arrested for helping German officers."

The officer patted him on the shoulder. "I am sure this is just a misunderstanding. Let me see what I can do." The officer made a phone call and asked to speak to the agent in charge.

"Of course she bicycles all over town," he heard the officer say. "She runs errands for the Kommandant himself."

Freddy and Tante Go were released at midnight.

CHAPTER THIRTY
September 5, 1943

B*OOM BOOM BABOOM BUMBALABOOM BOOM.* Anne
Brusselmans jumped out of her seat. It was eleven at night and this
was what she had come here for. She ran to the window of her hotel
room, but saw only darkness. She was on the wrong side of the building!
Why couldn't the raid have come last night before the large contingent of
soldiers requisitioned ten rooms? she thought. But she hadn't come down
to Waterloo and paid for a hotel room just to *listen* to the cannons. She'd
have to take the chance.

Comet had once again reorganized. Before going into hiding, fifty-
year-old Antoine d'Ursel, *Jacques Cartier*, helped Jean Serment take
over the Belgium sector while Michou, with the information provided by
Nadine, reconnected to Paris. Once Serment had the reins, d'Ursel
headed south, but it wasn't to run away from the fight. He had already
begun assembling Belgian helpers for a new line—one to evacuate partisans like himself who were wanted by the Gestapo. Next, he would do
the same in Paris then hike over the Pyrenees to share his plan with the
British Consulate.

Infuriated by the number of airmen still getting away, the Germans
sent more trained agents and doubled the patrols at the Belgian-French
border. Although Comet was forced to hold men in safe houses until new
evasion routes could be found, Anne wasn't sitting idle. With Julien
away working at the farm in the Ardennes, she decided to do a bit of
spying and investigate the source of the wicked flak around the village of
Aerschot that American fliers had told her about. So, she packed off the
children to the Baroness, threw some clothing in a valise, and took the
train down to Waterloo.

Saturday night had been quiet. But as luck would have it, the hotel
had filled up with Germans just in time for the raid. Despite the threat of

twenty soldiers a floorboard creak away, she had to do what she'd come here for.

Raucous noise spilled out of the German rooms as she tip-toed past. Perhaps with their partying they wouldn't notice a woman out of her room after curfew, but just in case one of those doors opened, she would say that the bombs had frightened her and she wanted to go down to the cellar.

Down the hallway past the German suites, Anne cast one last look behind her, slipped inside a room she knew to be empty and locked the door. Through slightly parted drapes she watched the flashes of light bursting in the sky. Counting out seconds between the flash and the boom, Anne figured the guns to be maybe five miles away. She mentally noted the relationship of the red bullet traces to a nearby chimney.

As she watched, a white search light beam swept across the sky and locked on a silver plane like a spotlight on a stage performer. Since it was a night raid, there were likely English boys in that plane. Projectiles streaked upwards, exploding in deadly flashes around it. Anne quietly rooted for the little plane trapped in the beam. "Go! Go! Get out of there!" In the darkness, she couldn't tell if the missiles might be finding other planes: all she could see was the little silver bird in the circle. "Come on, miss, you lousy bastards!"

Allied bombers had no defense against the German anti-aircraft fire. They couldn't drop bombs indiscriminately hoping by chance to take out one of those pesky cannons. Too many civilian lives were at stake. Bomber pilots had no choice but to set their jaw and fly straight on through.

To Anne, that plane was more than some nameless craft in the sky— it represented Edward and John and Bill and all the fine young boys she had come to know since joining the underground. She couldn't bear to watch the projectiles of death exploding all around them. Nor could she look away. Riveted by the drama, she held her breath as the little plane plodded on.

The spotlight crept across the sky. Then reaching the end of its tether, it stopped. But the silver bird continued on, breaking through the circle of death and vanishing into the night.

. . .

The next morning Anne returned to the vacant room with a small compass an evader had given her. At the window she aligned her compass with the chimney and noted where she had seen the tracers last night. Downstairs and out in the street, she followed her compass.

She came to the town of Oolen. There, under some camouflage netting, she found the battery of guns and soldiers. Two days later her sketch was on its way over the mountains to the Allies.

It had been three days since she dropped the children off with the Baroness and she couldn't wait to see them. The intense hug from her daughter left no doubt that Yvonne had deduced that their mother had gone on a dangerous mission. What a sad thing to see her little girl's childhood robbed by this war, Anne thought. But Yvonne never complained. Wise beyond her years, she watched over her little brother while they stayed with the Baroness: she even helped her mum conceal airmen. She delighted in acting in her mother's charades, like pretending to be a family when they were really taking a fellow for his identification photos.

That evening, the peaceful quiet in Anne's living room was broken by the drone of heavy planes. The English were apparently on another night raid. Anne sipped her wine and turned a page of her magazine.

A thunder of bombs shook the apartment. Lights flickered. Dust rained down. Jacques leapt into his mother's arms. Yvonne drew nearer. "It will be all right," Anne assured them. "The bombs sound closer than they really are. Yvonne, go get the torch. We'll go down to the basement."

It wasn't hard to find the bombers' objective the next morning. Anne simply followed the smoke and devastation to the Etterbeek Barracks, where German soldiers and members of the Belgian Nazi party were lodged. She felt no sadness for the Germans or the Belgian Nazis, but the bombs also destroyed nearby homes.

Later she heard that seven hundred people had been killed in the raid, most of whom resided in the targeted barracks. But she also learned that despite the rules of war, a civilian had been imprisoned there—Baron

Jean Greindl, *Nemo*, the beloved former chief of the Belgian sector of Comet and the father of two little babies. He was killed instantly by an Allied bomb.

————

Prosper bowed over his plate, closing his eyes. Tantalizing scents of garlic and clam billowed upward. He tweezed out a succulent steamer, relishing the melted butter, the chewy texture, and the garlicky oils that danced across his tongue. After a few more bites, a sip of wine and a dab of his napkin, Prosper leaned in and spoke softly. "I've come up with a plan to deliver our products much quicker."

Jean Marcel Nootens, and the bloated-faced Charles Jenart, stopped gorging themselves to give him their attention.

"We've been moving our products down to Paris so nobody gets suspicious. Right? But why do we have to go all the way to Paris? As long as we get the packages away from Brussels, we can accomplish the same thing."

"You mean take them only part of the way?" Jenart asked.

"No." Prosper spoke like a teacher instructing his students. "Suppose we don't go into France at all? What if we say we're bringing them to a secret air strip where they will be flown to Switzerland? We take them out of Brussels to a backroad in the provinces where we say a car will pick them up and drive them to the air strip. As long as they are completely alone when the Abwehr agents arrest them word will not get back to the underground."

Flore snapped her thumb and forefinger together to warn them to shut up. "Yes," Prosper said with a smile toward the approaching waitress, "Canada has its maple syrup, Rome its pizza." He lifted his pair of shells as if to toast with them. "But in Brussels we have our mussels."

"How is everything?" the waitress asked.

"Delicious," Prosper said for all.

A man paused in the restaurant doorway until the waitress left the table. It was the British soldier who worked for Prosper.

"I'm afraid you are too late," Prosper said leaning in to look inside the pot as the man approached. "Have a seat. We will order more."

"I didn't come to eat. I need to talk to you. In private if you please."

Prosper wiped his mouth with his linen and excused himself.

"We have a problem," the man said when they stepped outside. "It seems our friend, Anny Lall has told someone in the Résistance that she suspects you are running a phony escape line."

Prosper exhaled his annoyance wondering how long she had known —and who else she had told. "Thank you." He patted the informant's arm to show appreciation and dismiss him at the same time. "I shall go have a little chat with Anny."

———

Tuesday, October 19, 1943

Michou swooped into the kitchen and lighted on a chair to pull on her white ankle socks.

"Are you ready for me to cook your omelet?" Hélène asked.

Michou frowned. "I am sorry, but I will not have time for breakfast."

"You must eat." Hélène Camusel, the trim-figured, white-coifed matron of the home said wielding a fork and spatula. She never 'mothered' Michou or questioned her hours or activities, but she tried to see to it that her young protégé ate well and felt comfortable staying in her apartment.

How nice it would be to sip a cup of tea and talk with the young airman, John, about his aerial exploits and his home and family in Indiana U-S-A, Michou thought. "I'm sorry," she said, "I have to meet a potential host today and I don't like to eat much before I travel."

"How about some toast and jam?" Hélène asked. "That is quick."

Michou conceded with a smile. Hélène was an angel of calm in these chaotic times and cared for each of the pilots like they were family, even keeping English language books on the shelf for them to read. No matter what time of day they arrived, she made sure they had a good meal.

Staying a minute longer for a bite of bread, Michou thought, was the least she could do to show her appreciation. She pulled out a scrap of paper as she ate, memorizing the girl's address *66 Allée du Beau Chéniat in Loverval*. "Don't wait dinner for me. I will be back late."

"Is there anything I can do to help?"

"Maybe you could take John for his photographs if you wouldn't mind."

"Certainly."

"Ah, Michou," Yvon Michiels *Jean Serment* greeted her when she arrived. "I've arranged for René Ponty to drive you to Loverval. But before you go, I want to make sure we are on schedule. There are so many men in hiding it is difficult to keep track of them."

Michou came around the desk to look at the ledger. Serment had done a magnificent job setting up a network of chiefs and sub-chiefs since taking over for Antoine d'Ursel. She dragged a finger down the names in the book. "After their dinner with René tonight, I will take Paul Shipe and Harold Penny to Anne's for questioning. Clary is at a café in Schaerbeek and James Berry is staying with Madame Bienfait. John Connell is staying with me and will be conducted by Monique to France tomorrow. These two, Kellett and Street, are staying at René's ..." She paused to allow Serment's scribbling to catch up then continued. "I am taking Geoffrey Madgett to René's today. Lawrence, May and Hudson, I will collect tomorrow ..."

He tapped his pencil on the remaining names. "Ashcraft and Whitlow are in the Netherlands waiting to be smuggled into Belgium, and we still have Wallington in Ghent, Burgin in Limburg, Dix in Luxembourg, Ward in Geel, and seven or eight more that we have heard of but have yet to confirm. If they keep falling from the sky at this rate, we will never keep up."

Michou shrugged. "We will do what we can. We can move some to other lines if we have to."

"Those lines are probably overloaded as well. I worry that the Germans will take this opportunity to begin more false lines."

Both fell silent at the sound of the door. Michou's body relaxed when René Ponty stepped inside.

"Please excuse my tardiness, but I parked several blocks away and around the corner."

"Make sure the girl knows the risks," Serment reminded Michou as she left with René.

"Do not worry," Michou said. "If she is too afraid of the danger, I will reject her anyway."

The quiet community of brick homes in Loverval was far enough from the urban areas so as not be frequented by the Germans, but as René drove around the loop street looking for number sixty-six, Michou surmised that everyone on the block probably knew each other. A host would have to be especially careful—yet an airman *had* been hidden here a long time.

A young woman maybe in her twenties opened the door. "Mademoiselle Gazet?" Michou said. "May we come in?"

The woman nodded cautiously to what must have seemed an odd pair —Michou looking like a fifteen-year-old did the talking while René, old enough to be her father, said nothing. She led them into a sitting room where the girl confirmed that they were alone.

"I am called Lily," Michou began. "And this is my associate, René. You are Simone Gazet?"

There was hesitation in her voice. "Yes."

"You know a friend of ours—Rolande—a nurse. I am also a nurse." Michou read the skepticism on her face. "I am not as young as I appear. This is my disguise when I guide Allied airmen. One of those men, a Spaniard, Arthur Kellett, was sheltered by you and is now in our care in Brussels. Arthur said to tell you he will miss your sausage and stoemp."

Simone's shoulders relaxed. If caught by the Germans, Sergeant Kellett might have had her name and address tortured out of him, but there would be no reason for him to tell them about the dish he had delighted in eating. Simone smiled proudly, reflecting on a happy memory. "Would you like a cup of tea?"

Michou offered a warm smile. "That would be nice."

Simone poured the tea and asked after Kellett. Michou told her he was staying with René and would be evacuated in a few days.

"He was concerned for the other men in his crew. Do you know of them?"

"Three men we believe were part of his crew fell victim to a false escape line." Michou grimaced. "It's run by a man with a missing little finger who calls himself Captain Jackson or Jack the Canadian. This man speaks English and tells the fliers he can get them back to England quickly which gives the hosts a sense of relief and they turn over the men. When the airmen arrive in Paris or Bordeaux, they find that their guides are really secret police. If the hosts become suspicious, they are arrested as well."

Michou watched Simone's face for signs of nervousness, but the girl listened with only interest. "You can see how important it is that we only work with people we can trust. You sheltered Arthur eight weeks and did not turn him over to an escape line until you felt sure that it was safe to do so." Michou tipped her head to express her admiration for what Simone had done.

"We know we can trust you. I am sure you have guessed by now that we have come to see if you would be willing to help us. But before you give your answer, I have to warn you that this is a very dangerous business. The Germans are relentless. There have been many arrests of our friends, but we go on. British and American pilots now go into battle knowing that if they are shot down, there are people here who will help them. No matter what happens to us individually, the Belgian people must show the British and Americans that we are not afraid to defy the Germans to aid Allied pilots."

Michou could feel her passions rise as she spoke. "My sister and my father are in jail. They are sentenced to death. I will not let that stop me. I would rather die fighting the Germans than bow down to them."

Simone sat up straight as if taking an oath. "I will do whatever you need of me."

"Giving shelter to men shot down in this region is all we ask. The risks of moving men are taken by us for now. If we need your services, you will be contacted by René, Rolande or myself. Trust no one else."

. . .

By early evening, Michou had recruited Simone, gone to Schaerbeek to visit two airmen, conducted a flier to René Pirart's apartment in Anderlecht, and collected two more at René Ponty's and taken them over to Anne's apartment in Ixelles. And before she could go to bed tonight, she still had to paste several photos and prepare identity papers.

"*Bonsoir Madame Anne. J'ai amené les chiots pour interrogatoire.*"

"*Bienvenue.*" Anne welcomed them in.

A handsome dark-haired young man of about twenty-five said as he extended a hand. "*Je m'appelle* Paul Shipe."

"*Bonsoir*, Paul." When Anne finished shaking hands with Paul, the second man reached out.

"Harry—Harry Penny, here."

"Hello, I am Anne," she said with a welcoming smile.

Harry's eyes grew wide. "You're English!"

Anne grinned at his shock. The younger fellow, Harry, had straight starched posture, perfectly groomed short-cropped hair parted on the side and a genteel British face that would make it difficult to pass him off as French or Belgian. But he also had an air of easy confidence that might help him blend in with the crowd. "How was your dinner?"

"Splendid," Harry said. "René is a most gracious host."

"Nearly worth getting shot down for," Paul quipped.

"Before we sit down, please raise your arms so I may search you." Anne didn't wait for permission. They blushed a trifle as she ran her hands up their chests, down their backs, outside and inside their legs and up their backsides.

Understanding their embarrassment over her rather personal search, she spoke casually as if it had been as ordinary as a handshake. "Come have a glass of wine." Anne motioned to the table. "As a precaution, we are moving you to a different house tomorrow. Tonight, you will stay here. Lily, have you had any supper?"

Michou shook her head. "I was so busy I forgot about food. All I have had since breakfast was a handful of grapes while I waited for the tram to Schaerbeek.

"I left a potato in the oven for you. And there is ham in the refrigerator. I'm sorry you cannot heat it. The gas is off for the night."

"It is fine," Michou said as she stood on tiptoes to pull a plate down from the cupboard.

Anne poured four glasses of red wine and set out a bowl of dried chick peas for the men to snack on. She offered them cigarettes and lit one for herself. "I'd like to ask you a few questions if you wouldn't mind. Paul, you were part of an American bomber crew?"

"Yes," Paul nodded, "a B-17-F Flying Fortress."

"How many men were on your plane?"

"Ten."

"And what was your job on the plane?"

"Mechanic and gunner," Paul answered with a questioning tone that said he didn't quite understand why he was being quizzed.

"Can you tell me what G.I. stands for?"

"Government issue."

"And what is a Mae West?"

"It's the life jacket we wear in case we have to ditch in the water. It keeps us afloat like a pair of ..." Paul motioned with open hands in front of his chest, but stopped short of saying it. "You know, like the front of the actress, Mae West."

Anne laughed at his somewhat red-faced description. "And you, Harry, can you tell me what a tail end Charlie is?"

"It's the last plane in the formation—the one who gets hit first if the Germans attack from the rear." Harry continued with noticeable annoyance. "I already filled out a form with the information about my plane and crew—Form E. I'm a radio operator in a Halifax Mk II with RAF Bomber Command thirty-fifth Squadron. There are seven men in my crew ...the pilot, co-pilot, browser ..."

Anne touched his hand for him to stop. "I am sorry Harry. But you must understand that many of our friends have been arrested for helping Allied fliers. We have to be careful."

Harry sat back in his chair a bit embarrassed by his testiness. "Yes, of course. You are risking your lives for us and we are in your debt."

"It is we who owe you our sincerest gratitude. You are up there in the sky every day battling the Germans. We are just trying to keep you alive to fight them some more."

Paul raised his glass. "To our mutual hatred of the Germans. May Hitler rot in Hell."

Anne translated for Michou who swallowed her mouthful of ham so she could join in the toast.

"Just leave the dish on the table," Anne told Michou after she had finished eating. "You'll need to get back home before curfew." she called for Yvonne to show the men where they would sleep. Anne accompanied Michou to the door. "You will be back in the evening tomorrow?"

"Yes. Two more will be dining with Madame and Monsieur Ponty and then I will bring them here for you to question … and search." Michou grinned as she wiggled her fingers.

Anne laughed and whispered, "I think they would not have minded so much if I was ten years younger. Until tomorrow night then. Be careful going home."

CHAPTER THIRTY-ONE

"Well?" Prosper Dezitter was hovering at the door before Flore even took her jacket off. "Did you find out anything?"

"I told her you were being very secretive and that I was worried that you might be involved in something illegal. Once I had her confidence, she told me everything. She suspects we—you—are running a false escape line. She has learned that airmen we have housed have been arrested."

"Has she told anyone?"

Flore nodded. "She has passed word on to the Résistance."

Prosper's pallid lips turned contemptuously down. "She said she does not know anyone here. How is it she knows someone in the Résistance?"

"I can stay close to her until we find out."

Prosper let out a ragged huff. "No. I will handle this."

He could see the resignation on Flore's face. This was not something he could put off. They both knew it. Although Anny had been her friend, she acquiesced with a nod.

He found what he needed in a kitchen drawer and went out into the night. Anny's apartment was dark, but with the curfew she would have to return soon. He stepped back into the shadows.

The next morning, the newspapers reported the body of a woman found lying on the sidewalk in front of her flat stabbed twenty-two times with an ice pick.

———

Elsie Maréchal let the knitting needles and square of stitched wool slip off her fingers into her lap. "I cannot do anymore." She sat back on her jail cell bunk and rotated her neck to stretch her aching muscles.

"Is your back hurting?" her mother asked.

It hurt day and night, sitting, standing, lying down—it didn't matter what she did. The terrible beatings had left sores on her back that refused to heal. But without medical provisions what could her mother do? She would not depress her mother further. "It's not too bad. I'm just tired of knitting and crocheting."

"I know." Her mother sighed. "But it's better than sitting here doing nothing. We should be grateful that Bobby was able to sneak these things in."

"I am grateful. I'm just bored. I'd even read Bobby's geometry book."

"I'm so happy they let him go. At least one of you is safe." Lines creased Madame Maréchal's face. "But I worry about him smuggling things in to us. If he is caught, the warders may not release him again." She lowered her needles and looked over her crocheting at Elsie. "And I worry that when he turns seventeen they'll deport him to Germany to work in their factories."

Elsie set her needles aside, moved to the other bunk and hugged her mother. "Don't worry, Mum. As long as the Germans believe Bobby is slow witted, they will have no use for him."

Madame Maréchal sighed. "I hope you're right. He's a good boy. It's bad enough that you are here."

Elsie squeezed her mother's hand. "Bobby will be okay. He's smart. He has Dad's temperament and he can take care of himself. He has even learned to cook," she said with a giggle. "And who would have thought my little brother would ever do laundry for me."

Her mum relinquished an uneasy smile.

"And you shouldn't worry about me either. Whatever they do to me, it was my choice. I have no regrets. I have already taken all of their punishment. And they have not broken me."

She gave her daughter a one-armed hug and a kiss on her cheek.

Elsie laid her head against her mother. "One day, we will be a family again. We just have to keep believing that our lawyer will win us a reprieve." Although Elsie said the words with conviction, she didn't believe them herself. Their trial had been a sham, conducted in German with their appointed lawyer offering no real defense. She and her parents had been found guilty of crimes against the Reich and sentenced to death.

The sound of boots echoed in the corridor. Elsie lifted her head. It wasn't time for a meal and it wasn't time for exercise. That could only mean one thing—they were coming for somebody—but who? She and her mother stashed the needles and supplies under the mattresses and sat up innocently.

The door lock clinked. The bolt screeched.

Elsie hadn't been beaten in months, yet the unexpected visit prickled her back and bathed her in a cold sweat. Her muscles tensed, a conditioned response to the terrible beatings she'd received. She closed her eyes, drawing in slow deep breaths and telling herself to stop shaking. If she showed fear they would be quick to exploit it.

"Step out," a Belgian guard commanded them. Another guard waited for them in the hallway.

It had to be a room search, Elsie thought. Her legs became shaky again. If the guards found the knitting and crocheting materials, they would be punished for having contraband.

But to her confusion, the guard simply closed the cell door and said, "Come with me." A few dozen steps and a hundred heartbeats later, he unlocked another door and motioned them inside. Elsie took a deep breath and entered. Her eyes flew open as her father dashed across the room and grabbed her up in his arms. His hug, urgent, emotional and strong, stung the sores on her back, but she didn't care. She hadn't seen him in months and months—not since that sham of a trial. Her mother joined in the hug and the three stood locked in an embrace until nudged by the guard to separate.

Each assured the other they were holding up well. They talked about the Allied air campaign reaching farther and farther into the continent, pounding the Luftwaffe and dominating the air space. Elsie felt sure this reunion was arranged because the Belgian guards were encouraged by the Allies' progress.

Back in her cell, she lay down with renewed hope that the Germans were weakening and that release from this awful place might become reality.

Michou pasted photos and filled in identity papers long into the night. The next morning, she arrived at René Pirart's in Anderlecht clutching her algebra book. "*Bonjour*, Harry. Are you ready for *za* travel home to England?"

"Quite." At thirty years old, Harold Street, a Halifax gunner, was a model of British seriousness, but a twinkle in his eyes gave his excitement away. Lily had visited Harry often since guiding him down from Arnould. It was important to visit and talk with the men to keep their spirits up and to assess their tolerance for inactivity. Boredom invited risks and carelessness. After six weeks of being cooped up, unable to so much as look out the window at the shops and people on the street below, Harry had to be bursting like a kid going to a carnival.

Affectionately regarding Lily like she'd been guilty of mischief, Harry told René, "When I first saw Lily skipping rope, I said these Belgians must be daft sending a little girl to guide me. She bloody well fooled me."

Lily laughed and brushed a bit of lint off the sleeve of his dark jacket. "Have you any news on my crew?"

Lily tried to explain in her limited English. "Some *aviateurs* were fooled by a false escape line. Your team mate, John Damboise, was arrested in Bordeaux."

"Damn." Harry shook his head sadly.

"*Zis* imposter promises *za aviateurs* he can get *zem* home quickly. We know him as *l'homme au doigt coupé, za* man with *za* missing little finger."

"If you know it is a fake line, can't something be done about it?"

"We are trying." She didn't want to go into details. The Comet organization maintained their *fight without hitting policy* that Dédée had insisted upon from the beginning, but the matter had been turned over to the White Brigade who had no such reservations.

"Before we go," Lily said, "you must empty your pockets, please."

Harry raised an eyebrow. "My pockets?" He shrugged a shoulder and set the contents on the table.

Lily separated his things into two piles. "You cannot take *zeese*. When you cross into France, you must not have *anysing* to show you have come from *Belgique*. You cannot take *zeese* cigarettes. *Zey* are *Belge*."

"You cannot smoke on the tram anyway or you will be arrested," René added.

Harry raised an eyebrow. "Arrested for smoking?"

René chuckled mischievously. "German dress uniforms must be perfect—crisp, creased, immaculate." He clicked his heels and snapped to attention. "Their shoes must be polished. Their brass must shine ... So of course," he said with an impish grin, "we do whatever we can to embarrass them." René mimed lighting a cigarette and slyly looking away as he press it to a German officer's coat. "When the soldier returns to his billet, he finds little burn holes in his tidy grey uniform." René laughed with pride. "Now cigarettes are banned."

After the trip to Mons and a short ride on a local train, Lily delivered Harry to Henriette Hanotte, a tall, sturdy, dark-haired girl, who would guide him through fields across the French border.

"*Hallo* Harry. I am *Monique*," Henriette said, handing him a French Baguette wrapped in deli paper. "I am sorry we do not have time to sit for lunch. I hope you like ham and cheese." She looked up to the darkening sky. "It will not be long before the storm begins."

"The sandwich is fine," Harry said. "Do you want some? We can split it."

Monique shook her head. "You eat while we walk, yes?"

"Most definitely. Let's be off." Harry took one step then turned back and threw his arms around Lily. "Thank you. Stay safe."

"*Bonne chance*, Harry."

They had gotten only few steps when Lily called, "Monique." She ran up and pressed French francs into Monique's hand. "Please tell Diane to buy Harry some cigarettes when they get to Paris."

Lily sighed as the pair disappeared down a path in the woods. It was hard to let them go, but she had no time to linger. She hurried back to Mons to conduct four more, including Arthur Kellett, the Spanish airman hidden by Simone Gazet. She didn't waste time toying with these fellows. "Do not worry. I am not a child. I am twenty-two years old. *Zis* is my costume to fool *za* Nazis. I am called Lily. You are wounded?" she asked one fellow.

"It's just me hand." He raised it for her to see his bandaged fingers.

"*Hm*. It is not yet cold enough for gloves. You will have to keep your hand in *za* pocket. You will follow me, but not too close—two by two. If I stop and look into shop windows, you stop and wait for me to move again. But you act—what is *za* word?" She mimed strolling slowly while glancing about.

"Casual?" one of the men offered.

"Yes, casual," Lily said triumphantly. "You walk casual. Sorry. My English is not so good."

Lily slung her cloth bag over her shoulder and clutched her school book to her chest. Heightened awareness was needed when leading men whose foreign mannerisms might be detected by a trained observer. Two blocks before the train station, she took her compact mirror from her purse—a trick she'd picked up from Anne. A man in a grey suit across the street seemed to be loitering without purpose. She walked another two blocks and repeated her surveillance. Satisfied that the man hadn't followed, she led the children on the train to Brussels. Next, they took a tram to Laeken and reached the flat at 160 Rue Marie-Christine in early evening through a roundabout walk. As always, Hélène Camusel was ready with fresh bread and a pot of thick beef stew to fortify the men before their journey to France.

Meanwhile, Anne Brusselmans, conducting airmen, Penny and Shipe, took a seat on the tram two rows back from the evaders. Her mind on her intelligence information gathering, she'd taken her eyes off the *children* for not more than a few seconds, when she glanced up. Shocked into action Anne hopped off at the next stop without looking back and walked a half-block before turning to see if the bloody idiots had followed.

"Why did we take the tram if we were only going a few blocks?" Shipe asked confused.

Anne tried to calm her nerves. She knew the airmen simply didn't know any better, but she couldn't hold her tongue. "You will get us all arrested!" she said in a harsh whisper. Then, seeing their puzzled faces, she added, "You cannot smoke cigarettes on the tram. If a German sees you doing that, he will drag you and everyone close to you off the tram and haul you down to the police station and search you!"

The men apologized profusely.

They arrived at Hélène's flat fifteen minutes behind Lily's group. Leaving them to Hélène's hot stew, Anne went home, poured a tall glass of wine and waited for Lily.

That evening Lily delivered to Anne two more men, Americans who had taken dinner with René Ponty. Once Anne put the newcomers through her series of authenticating questions, they relaxed in the living room.

Lily slipped off her saddle shoes and put her feet up on a hassock. "I hope my feet do not smell," she said wiggling her toes in their white ankle socks. "If they do, I apologize. But it has been a long day."

Anne poured wine for the boys and brought a glass to Lily. "A long and harrowing day," Anne said as she refilled her own glass. "Let me tell you boys right now so we have an understanding. There is positively no smoking on the tram. Remember that." Then she broke into laughter and retold the story of the two pilots who couldn't understand why they had gotten off the tram at only the first stop.

"Thank goodness it wasn't us," the pilot from California said. "We're beholden to you. There ain't a pilot who hasn't heard of what you're doing. Everyone who makes it back says how wonderful you folks are."

"*Zey* must be anxious to meet us," Lily said. "Your friends *zey* are falling from *za* sky faster *zan* we can return *zem*."

The pilot from California snickered. "Yeah—it's not because the Germans are shooting us down. We just drop in for the wine and cheese and the conversation."

His buddy laughed and lifted his glass as if to toast.

"Perhaps we should make an arrangement," Anne said. "You stay up there and shoot down Germans and we'll send you wine and write letters."

The conversation stopped abruptly at the whir of the lift in the hall.

"Quickly," Anne said to the men. "In the closet in the bedroom. Michou, the glasses."

Michou grabbed up the airmen's glasses, rinsed them quickly, twisted the dishtowel inside and out and set them in the cupboard just as a knock sounded in the hall.

Anne glanced back to see that everything was out of sight before opening the door. "Pasteur Schyns." She exhaled and relaxed. "Come in." She checked the hall and closed the door behind him. "You gave us quite start I must say. Would you like a glass of wine?"

"Perhaps something a little stronger if you please," the Pastor said.

"Of course." Anne returned with whiskey and a water glass. She had a feeling that whatever he had to report would require more than a shot glass.

"I'm so sorry for stopping by at this late hour, Madame, but I have some bad news." He took a large gulp of liquor before continuing. "We have gotten word that a number of our friends were executed this morning by firing squad at Tir National Rifle Range."

Lily gasped and covered her mouth.

Pasteur Schyns pulled a slip of paper from a coat pocket and read, "Eric de Menten de Hornes ... Jean Ingels ...Albert Marchal ... Henri Rasquin ... Ghislain Neybergh ... Gaston Bidoul ... Robert Roberts Jones ... and Georges Maréchal."

"Oh my God," Anne said. "Poor Elsie and Madame Maréchal."

Lily's face had gone pale. Anne knew instantly what her young friend was thinking. The shooting of Georges and the others meant the Germans were carrying out their death sentences; and her father and sister had been condemned to death.

"Mummy?"

Anne turned toward the soft voice. Seeing a worried Yvonne standing in the archway, Anne reached out and summoned her over. Yvonne curled under the protection of her mother's arm. The young girl's eyes were filled with tears. As Anne hugged her little girl and kissed her forehead, Lily turned her face away so the girl couldn't see her dab at the corners of her own eyes.

"I hate to bring this up after delivering such bad news," Pasteur Schyns said, "but I've gotten word of several more airmen down. One is seriously injured. He is being protected by the White Brigade, but he may not survive his wounds. Nurse Rolande and a doctor are tending to him. I know you already have your hands full …"

"We shall handle it," Anne said resolutely. "But no one steps one foot toward Paris without me questioning them first." She looked toward Lily.

Lily palmed away the wetness from her cheeks and nodded. "We will be ready."

CHAPTER THIRTY-TWO
October 27, 1943

Franco lay curled up in total darkness, his shirt wet from sweat, his knees nearly touching his chin. He hadn't hidden in such a tight space since he was a child playing games. But this wasn't a game. He was in the trunk of a black sedan on his way to Gibraltar at the request of British intelligence. They had accepted him as the successor to Dédée, but now he wondered whether it was because they considered him the most capable, or because at only twenty-three years old, they thought he might be easy to manipulate.

The airless trunk of the car was hot as a can of spam in the desert. He struggled for air. Sweat dripped from his cheek and basted his neck. The car slowed, then stopped. Lying perfectly quiet he tried to make out the muffled exchange of voices between *Monday*, and the checkpoint guard.

Fifteen minutes later, the car stopped and the trunk cover lifted up.

"Welcome to Gibraltar," Monday said. "I'm sorry we had to put you through that. I'm sure the deplorable condition of the Spanish roads did not help."

"It was not so bad," Franco lied, shielding his eyes against the bright sunlight while climbing out. The warm breeze against his wet shirt actually felt refreshing. And how could he complain about a little discomfort when so many of his compatriots were being tortured in Nazi prisons? As his eyes adjusted, he realized he was in a courtyard in the midst of three and four-story buildings. Rows of fishing boats gently rocked in the bay below. High above, a huge bright Union Jack gallantly waved.

A big chap greeted him with a warm firm handshake. "Nice of you to come, Franco," he said. "I'm Donald Darling—*Sunday*, if you will. I hope the trip wasn't too unpleasant."

"It was fine."

"Good. Come along then and I'll drive you to a flat where you can relax and freshen up. I'll even let you ride in the front seat," Darling said teasing a bit.

Franco was well aware of Darling's importance to the Comet line. He was the Gibraltar chief of escape and evasion operations. His dark complexion, black combed-back hair, thin mustache and deep set eyes gave him a serious look. But although Darling was a straight-forward sort of fellow, he didn't come across as staunchly military.

"I have heard so much about you from the pilots that I feel we are old friends," Darling said in fluent French as he ushered Franco into a modest apartment. "Make yourself at home. I'll be back at four to show you around a bit and we'll have some supper."

Gazing out over the untouched city with the warm breeze blowing in from the bay, Franco thought how wonderful it would be to go exploring in those little shops, maybe see some of Gibraltar's famous apes, or just stroll in the bright sunshine and forget the war for a while, no airmen to shuffle about, no intelligence information to smuggle, no winter mountain crossings … With a heavy sigh, he went back and lay down on the bed watching the ceiling fan blades endlessly spin. There was too much to be done before he could ever relax.

Donald Darling returned and acted as tour guide as they walked. "You know since the British won Gibraltar from Spain in 1713, they tried to take her back three times. Without control of Gibraltar, the North African campaign would not have been possible." Darling flicked his head toward the water. "Have a gander down there."

Franco gazed at the shimmering bay where an awesome fleet of ships, each flying the British Union Jack lay at anchor. From this height, deadly artillery could be poured on any enemy ships foolish enough to dare to attack. And everywhere he looked, there were men and women in uniform.

As if reading his mind, Darling explained, "We've sent most of the civilian population to England to make room for military personnel. Gibraltar is the gate keeper to the Mediterranean. The Germans will pay a heavy price if ever they try to take it from us."

Franco's heart was energized. From the proud flags to the unblemished storefronts to the fleet in the harbor, it was clear that Great Britain was not the beaten nation German propaganda portrayed. "It's nice to walk in a city where there are no swastikas."

After a bit more walking, Darling stopped and inhaled deeply. "Ah, smell that? This place has the best seafood and beef dishes." He held the door with one hand, while sweeping Franco inside with the other. "I often bring the airmen here. I believe a nice steak helps to restore them after their trek over the mountains."

"We also give them steak before we take them across," Franco said, "but it nearly got Tante Go arrested."

Darling raised an eyebrow. "How's that?"

Franco laughed. "Meat is rationed so people stretch the little they have in stews and such. But because German soldiers eat at Chez Gachy, they serve steaks. An American didn't like the way his was cooked. He grumbled, 'This is raw. I cannot eat this! It is not fit for a dog!' He set his dish on the floor and whistled for the dog. The Germans took immediate notice. Obviously a Frenchman would not give his whole steak to a dog! Shocked, Tante Go quietly said, 'Get up. We must leave.' But before she could get away, a German captain marched straight to their table. Tante was sure they were going to be arrested. But the captain said to the American, 'It is nice to see a man who thinks of the poor animal.' Tante politely said, 'I am sorry, Captain, but we are late for an engagement,' and she hurried the men out."

"Good God!" Darling shook his head, astonished. "Ignorant pilots must give you some anxious moments."

"Dédée called them little children," Franco said. "In Dax, it is so common for workers to ride bicycles to their jobs, I didn't think to ask an American pilot if he knew how. He could not keep his bicycle steady." Franco acted out the scene, faltering side to side on an imaginary bike. "Two German soldiers came riding in our direction. The more the nervous pilot tried to steer away, the more the bicycle wobbled straight for them. He crashed into the soldiers, falling right on top of them."

"Good God. What on earth did you do?"

"I began yelling at the pilot." Franco punctuated his words with arms waving as he had done that day. "'You stupid oaf! Look at what you have done! You should be beaten for running into these men!' Then I took a flask from my pocket and said to the Germans, 'Look what this fool has done. He has drunk a whole bottle of whiskey in one gulp!' I helped the Germans up and brushed them off and said to the American as I set him back on his bicycle, 'You should be shot you drunken idiot!' The Germans were not pleased, but accepted the explanation and let us ride away."

"Very quick thinking." Darling chuckled. "While we can laugh about these episodes now, I know how difficult it must be for you and your friends, but I assure you, your work is not in vain. The Allies *will* defeat Germany."

"Will the invasion come soon?"

"We'll talk more about that in the morning. After dinner, I will take you back to your flat so you can rest up. The Governor would like to personally greet you tomorrow."

Franco wiggled a finger inside his shirt collar. The tightness and oppressive heat irritated the boils on his neck, but it was important to make a strong impression. He wished he had found his favorite tie—the one he lost when the Gestapo sealed his apartment. His age would work against him, but he had the advantage of Dédée's mentoring. Of the many things he had learned from her, one of the most important was to show confidence. She scoffed at those who lacked decisiveness. Times like this reminded him how remarkable she was. Her name had not appeared among the executed—he had to believe that she was still alive. Going into the meeting, he resolved to draw on her strength and tell the British in no uncertain terms that Comet would always be run by Belgians.

"You know *Monday*, of course," Darling said, leading Franco around a sunny, spacious room overlooking the glistening bay. "This is Colonel Codrington of the War Office, and Airey Neave, *Saturday,* of Military Intelligence."

"Nice to finally meet you, Franco," Neave said. "You should have seen the confused looks back in the office when the wire came through that *Saturday* was going to Gibraltar on Wednesday to meet with *Monday* and *Sunday* to talk with *Franco*."

After a few more pleasantries, Franco was asked about the day he discovered that Paul had been captured. "Tante Go and I implored Paul to go to England, but he refused…" Franco's voice trailed off dejectedly. "He no longer cared what happened to him."

"I've got to hand it to you," Neave said. "You and Max had a lot of courage going back to that apartment to get the papers. I've been a guest of the Gestapo myself. They are a frightening lot."

"In our countries people live every day in fear of what the Germans may do. I—we do what we must so that one day we will no longer have to live in fear of them."

"You are one of the few remaining who have worked with both Dédée and Paul."

"I saw her at the train station," Franco said heavily, "but there was nothing I could do to help her."

"I know." Neave laid his hand on Franco's shoulder. "Paul wanted us to negotiate for Dédée's release, but if we had done that, we would have signed her death warrant. As long as they think she is nothing more than a guide, they may allow her to live. If we tip them off to how important she is, they will torture her and make an example of her."

Neave poured water for Franco and himself. "You've been at this for about a year now. You've made fourteen crossings and evacuated nearly as many men as Dédée. It is time you took a break. Come back to England with me and rest a while. We have a number of your friends there who would be happy to see—"

Franco shook his head without even waiting for Neave to finish. "I must return to France."

"You have done enough," Darling said. "Comet has suffered many arrests and executions. We do not want to see more lives of the underground sacrificed to help us."

"There are too many airmen to bring out. If they are not moved, they can pose a great threat to the Résistance."

"Someone else can take over while you rest," Neave said. "I am sending in a man to help handle things—"

"What do you mean someone to handle things?" Franco glared at Neave. "This is a Belgian line! It will be run by Belgians!"

"Yes, of course. We have always honored our commitment to Dédée. Comet is a Belgian line and it will remain a Belgian line. Our fellow can help Max run things while you rest. It would only be until you are back."

"Who is this man you want to send us?"

"For now, let's just call him Mr. Lewis."

Franco scowled.

"You have my word. My intention is to provide communications, finance and assistance and nothing more." Neave looked straight into Franco's eyes to assure his sincerity. "We have begun another line, Shelbourne, which will be run by French Canadians and will evacuate men by sea. I will also be sending men in the coming weeks to help organize camps for hiding the airmen."

"Camps?"

"Yes, when the invasion does take place, it would be disastrous to have fliers running about trying to rejoin the Allied lines. We are looking for sites of no strategic importance to the Germans where we can hide the airmen until we can reach them. We will need the underground's help to move the men. The operation is code-named Marathon. Only your key people should know about this."

"In the meantime," Darling said, "is there anything we can do to better assist you?"

"You can let the White Brigade handle our Brussels problem."

"If it were up to me," Neave said, "he would already be dead."

Colonel Codrington looked quizzically at Neave, who explained. "A collaborator in Belgium called Captain Jackson or Willie, or the man with the missing little finger has lured many fliers with a phony escape line that promises quick evacuation. His cohorts have infiltrated the real lines resulting in many arrests of our underground friends." Neave looked apologetically to Franco. "The White Brigade was to eliminate this man and his group, but the Belgian Government in exile would not allow it."

When they concluded, Franco followed Darling to meet Lieutenant-General Sir Noel Mason-MacFarlane, the Royal Governor of Gibraltar. Instead of the highly decorated and polished military uniform Franco expected, the head of government greeted him wearing a bush shirt and khaki shorts.

A tall greying man with an intelligent forthright look, MacFarlane spoke excellent French in a warm and genuine manner. "It is a pleasure to meet you, Franco. Welcome to Gibraltar. On behalf of Great Britain, I want to commend you on the work you and Comet have done for the war effort. Although King George is a prisoner of war, his cabinet in exile has asked me to express their gratitude for what Comet is doing. Your organization is making quite a difference. I congratulate you and thank you for your bravery. The day of liberation is coming and we will celebrate victory together."

A lump rose in Franco's throat. "Thank you, Sir."

The next day, Neave and Darling followed Creswell's car to a garden café about two miles over the border into Spain where Franco was let out of the boot. Neave tried one last time to convince Franco to stay. "Since the day of her arrest, I have regretted not being able to persuade Dédée to come out in time. I implore you to reconsider. You know the Secret Police *must* be on to you by now."

"I will leave when I find a suitable replacement," Franco promised.

"Perhaps Mr. Lewis will fill that need."

"This Mr. Lewis, when can I expect him?"

"He injured his back during parachute training, so he will have to come in over land. I will send him back with you on your next crossing."

"I still wish you would reconsider," Darling said.

"Thank you, but your fliers need to know they have a good chance of getting away and no escape line can help them better than Comet."

Darling somberly nodded and extended his hand. "Please take this. It is a medal of Our Lady of Europe to protect you. May God be with you."

CHAPTER THIRTY-THREE

"There. Now, Monsieur Longette, you are a broom maker." Franco chuckled as he pasted the miniature photo onto an identity card.

"What is so funny?" *Max* sliced a wedge of apple with his penknife and popped it into his mouth.

"I was just thinking that Dédée would say I hope no one asks Monsieur Longette how to make a broom."

"Oh." Max cut another wedge of apple. "So are we really going to give this *Lewis* fellow full access to all of our contacts here in Paris?"

Franco felt a little guilty about Max's resentment which probably came from his own attitude toward having a British fellow in the line. He decided to keep his negative thoughts to himself. "Monsieur Lewis cannot succeed if we do not give him our full support. He does not have to take this risk. He could stay safe in England."

"But how do we know we can trust him?"

"The English are not going to betray us. It is their men who are being rescued."

"That is not what I mean. No one had more passion for our cause than Bee Johnson, but he could not conceal his English looks. This Monsieur Lewis will probably stand out like Little Lord Fauntleroy. Then there's the radio. The Germans will pick up his transmissions and eventually locate him—and us!"

"Yes, the radio may be a problem, but the Allies must have quicker communication as the day of invasion approaches."

"And when will that be?"

Franco sighed. "I don't know."

"How do we know that this Mr. Lewis isn't being sent to take over the line for the English?"

"They have given me their assurances and I must trust that. Monday was among the first to believe in Dédée's plan. His faith in her and us has never wavered. When I was arrested in Spain, he used every possible resource to get me out. I trust him and he assures me that Saturday and Sunday are men of their word."

"All right." Max frowned and cut another piece of apple. "We will do our best to work with this Mr. Lewis." He shook the wedge at Franco. "But if he turns out to be an idiot, I will escort him over the mountains myself and give him back to the English!"

Two days later, Franco met the early morning train in Bordeaux. Four 'packages' rode with him to Dax where Denise Houget waited with six bicycles. Denise, a stylish, easy-going, Belgian woman, had taken on more responsibility to allow Tante Go to minimize her visibility in case she was still being watched.

Franco fell into a moderate rhythm down Avenue St. Vincent de Paul with the warm November sun on his face and a lazy breeze fluttering his dark wavy hair. The throng of pedestrians and cyclists traveling to work provided cover, but also made it difficult for him and Denise to keep an eye on the *children* spaced two by two at long intervals.

They had gone just four blocks when Franco spotted a police commissaire on a corner monitoring traffic. With a shrug of her eyebrows and a return to a straight-ahead look, Denise acknowledged that she had seen him as well but there was nothing else for it but to keep riding as if nothing was wrong.

French gendarmes were supervised by the German police who dealt harshly with those who neglected their duty to arrest suspicious persons. If caught aiding enemy airmen or underground helpers they would be executed and their entire families arrested.

Franco and Denise pedaled past without looking at the officer, but stopped several hundred yards beyond them where Franco pretended to check his bicycle chain while they waited for the children to catch up.

The first two arrived moments later, but there was no sign of the others and after ten uneasy minutes it became painfully apparent that the remaining parcels were not coming. Franco gave it two more minutes then told Denise to go on with the two men. "I will go back and see if I can find out what happened."

Pedaling slowly, scanning for the blue and grey workman's jackets the men were wearing, Franco rode back to the intersection. Neither the gendarme nor the airmen were anywhere to be found. Chances were good that the *children* had been arrested. Franco cycled down several side streets hoping against hope that they had spotted the gendarme and tried to detour around him. He bicycled slowly up to the train station and back past the intersection. Nothing. It had been an hour. Clearly, the worst had happened.

He paused his bicycle with one foot on the ground while he made mental lists of the people the airmen had had contact with so they could all be warned. Would the children admit they were part of a larger group? Were Denise and the other two evaders in danger? One thing was for sure, if Franco lingered in this area much longer someone was bound to take notice. His mind still mapping out damage control, he rode on around slow-moving motorcars and cyclists. As he veered around a parked car, a pair of cyclists in familiar clothing came into view. Franco stood on his pedals and veered around other bicyclists and vehicles to catch up. It was the missing airmen!

They looked happy to see him, but not stressed or alarmed as might be expected from strangers lost in a perilous land. "What happened to you two?"

The men looked at each other and laughed, and the Canadian, Ed Bridge, spoke. "The commissaire stopped us. I guess he detected an accent in my French. He told me I didn't sound like the person on my papers. So I told him we were RAF pilots and we were trying to escape from the Germans. He told us to come with him to the police station. We thought it was the end of the line, but when we got inside the station, the officer slapped us on the back and pulled out a bottle of wine. He poured drinks and toasted to the next Allied victory!"

The next evening was crisp and clear, perfect weather for hiking over a mountain, fortunately for them since they had to take the longer route over the suspension bridge at Endarlaza because the Bidassoa was flooded. Franco had taken this route before, but experience never made it any easier. Crossing the rope bridge took less than thirty seconds—but they were intense, dangerous seconds, like dashing over a train trestle just ahead of the locomotive. Franco crouched down with the airmen in the bushes. Not only did they have to scramble across the swaying bridge past the Spanish Guardia post in seconds, but they had to do it wearing a pack with their shoes draped around their necks and a blinding light aimed toward them instead of lighting the path.

Fatigue showed on the faces of the men as they reached the farm pastures above Oiartzun, Spain in the grey dawn. Franco was exhausted as well, but allowed himself just four hours of sleep before hiking to town to notify the British Consulate. He worried about the return trip and whether the injured Mr. Lewis would have the speed and agility to negotiate the slopes and bridge quickly.

When the diplomatic car arrived, Franco went with them to Bilbao to meet his would-be replacement.

He was led out to a small patio garden, where a tall, blond man rose immediately. "You are Franco. It is wonderful to finally meet you. I have heard so many good things about you." The man had a polite soft-spoken manner. His French was flawless.

"I am pleased to meet you, Mr. Lewis."

"It is Legrelle—Jacques Legrelle. Mr. Lewis sounds much too English, do you think?"

"Yes, but your code name should be short."

"I know. I was thinking I would use Jérôme. Have a seat. Would you like something to drink? Some tea?—or perhaps a glass of wine?"

Monday joined them.

Jérôme filled three glasses of wine and lifted his. "To a quick end to Hitler and Germany."

"Hear, hear," Monday responded.

"I greatly admire what you and your friends are doing for our country," Jérôme said. "I am proud to be allowed to join you."

"And I thank you and your country for helping us," Franco said.

"You think I am English?" Jérôme chuckled a bit. "I am Belgian like you."

Franco's eyes widened like he'd suddenly been awakened. "You are?"

Jérôme nodded. "I was a lieutenant in the Belgian army," he added somewhat apologetically. "Many of us were evacuated to England with the British when Belgium fell."

Franco could hear in Jérôme's voice a sense of shame at being part of the defeated army, but he knew Belgium had neither the weapons nor the manpower to repel the well-equipped German fighting force. Jérôme wasn't at all what Franco had expected. He was quiet and reserved, perhaps even a little shy, and when Jérôme did speak, Franco found him polite and charming. Some might take his politeness for weakness, but as they battled the formidable mountain on their return to France, Jérôme proved to be anything but weak. Perhaps it was the army discipline, but even though it showed on his face that his back gave him pain, he carried the extra weight of the radio without complaint.

Back in Paris that evening, Franco, Max and Jérôme retired after dinner to the living room with their wine glasses and Franco laid it all out. "Our organization is set up so no one knows everyone. Each chief, sub-chief, safe house director and group leader knows only those within their own circle of people they trust. That way if someone is arrested, they can only identify members of their immediate group. It gives us time to alert the others to sever ties and get away."

"That's brilliant," Jérôme said.

"That's Dédée," Franco said, "and she *is* brilliant. Basically, you will be in charge of the Paris sector and Max and I will conduct the men south and over the mountains. We have a young director of safe houses here, Henri Crampon, who will help you conceal the packages while they wait for evacuation."

"Are all chiefs selected by you?"

Franco shook his head. "No one applies for the job of chief or group leader. It is simply a matter of valor. When one is arrested, someone steps up to replace him or her. It is like when an officer falls in battle and the next in line takes command." Franco set out a plate of cookies and refilled the wine glasses. "The line was infiltrated in June. Hundreds were arrested. But those who evaded capture rebuilt the line and recruited new helpers, some of whom may one day take over. I was already running things in Paris with Frédéric de Jongh, so when he was arrested I was able to rebuild the line. The probability that we will be caught is very high."

"It's a wonder anyone steps up to replace those arrested." Jérôme selected a cookie. "Tell me about Dédée. She must be some woman."

"She is an amazing person and I love her dearly, but she can be rather obstinate at times." Franco chuckled. "We've certainly had our share of lively debates—especially about religion. She is a natural leader, perhaps the bravest person I have ever known."

"Have you any word on her whereabouts?"

"I don't even know if she is still in France or if she has been sent to Germany." Franco sighed deeply. "I know you have been given a code to communicate directly with London, but messages to Brussels and to the south are still carried by courier. Diane, Lily and Monique are our usual couriers. If you need to communicate with Brussels, Henri, Max or I can arrange it until you are established."

Max raised his glass. "To the rapid defeat of Germany."

Franco raised his. "To Belgium and France."

"And to the safe return of Dédée," Jérôme added.

———

Lily knew that the man in the light grey jacket, standing in front of a clothing store with a book held at chest level, was only pretending to read. It was the book she had given the helper who had guided the airman back from Tournai to Brussels.

Several stores to the left, three German soldiers milled about in front of the grocer's. To the right, two men in suits strolled by conversing in German and eating pastries wrapped in white paper. Lily waited for the two to pass before attempting the pick-up. She'd recently had a close call, a random tram search by German police. Luckily she had dropped off the false identity cards and intelligence information prior to the search.

Once the suits were gone, she made her move. Rolling a large wooden hoop in front of her down the sidewalk, she counted on the Boches to dismiss her as a child, even though she looked more like she was in her early teens. She pushed the hoop with the stick, deftly navigating around pedestrians until she reached the clothing store where she let it fall. As she reached down for the hoop, she said softly to the airman without looking up, "I am Lily, a helper." She glanced up as she retrieved her hoop. "Follow me, Monsieur. But not too close."

She continued on, plying her hoop with her stick and making her way past the shops and businesses, pausing only once to make sure the *puppy* was following. After several blocks, she turned down a side street and waited for her evader to come around the corner.

He was at least a foot taller than she was and looked apprehensively at her little blue coat, white ankle socks and black saddle shoes. She smiled and nearly broke into a laugh. "Do not worry, *Monsieur*. I am not a child. *Zis* is my costume. We will take *za* tram at *za* next corner. Follow me, but we do not sit together. Get off when I do."

The industrial neighborhoods in Shaerbeek, having no shops to attract off-duty Germans soldiers, were a little easier. Lily walked beside her airman without need of her hoop game, and soon had delivered him to the family that would harbor him for the next few days.

She visited another airmen hiding in Shaerbeek, and dropped by to say hello to a fellow in a safe house west of the city. By the time she returned to her flat, it was already getting dark and she was tired and hungry.

Hélène met her at the door, taking her coat while anxiously filling her in on the condition of their latest arrival. "It took a little time to get him up the steps. I believe he is in pain, but he has not complained much about it."

Still wearing her little girl clothes, Lily proceeded to the bedroom "*Hallo*, Bob. I am Lily."

His quizzical look said Bob Grimes didn't know what to make of his new visitor.

Lily didn't chuckle at his confusion. His condition was too critical for her to poke fun. "I am a nurse. I am twenty-two years old. Can you sit up?"

"Yes."

"Good. Where are you wounded?"

Bob touched his upper thigh.

"We have to take your trousers off so I can clean and dress your wound." She removed the bandage and examined his thigh, touching it gently. He winced, but didn't cry out. The area was very tender. He was clearly in great pain. "I am sorry. I will try to be gentle."

"It's not so bad now. You should have seen it a week ago. I was out of it with a fever for a couple of days. Two different doctors probed for it —like to send me through the roof."

"I do not understand *za* roof."

"It's an expression. I just mean it was real painful. My leg had swelled up like a balloon. Do you know balloon?"

"Yes. I know balloon."

"Well anyway, a nurse, Rolande, cleaned it every few hours and sprinkled some powder on it and that seemed to help it a lot."

Lily nodded understanding as she continued her examination. The wound was high up and the color was good. But he could lose his leg if he didn't have an operation to remove the bullet. He could not be evacuated in his condition. "Your fever is gone and *za* powders have helped with *za* swelling, but I believe *za* bullet needs to come out."

"That's what both doctors said. But neither of them would do the operation."

"*Za* doctors are watched by *za* Germans and *za* drugs are closely monitored. But I know a doctor who might be willing to help us."

Anne Brusselmans didn't know the chemist down the block all that well. She had made the occasional visits to the store, exchanging the usual pleasantries about the weather and such. She didn't know his politics or his views. But he had always seemed a genuine fellow, a decent man. And she had heard nothing about him to make her think he had Nazi sympathies. She saw no choice but to take the chance.

Anne looked around to make sure there were no other customers before approaching him at the counter.

"Ah, Madame. How are you today?"

"I am well," she said. But she had no time to spend on things of little importance. She had to speak to him before anyone could overhear. "Monsieur V. I need bandages fifteen centimeters wide, iodine, ether, cotton wool and sterilized lint, and I haven't a doctor's prescription."

The man's face grew serious his eyes unblinking. What she was asking of him could get him shot. He gave her a slight knowing nod— "Just one moment"—and returned minutes later with a small, neatly wrapped parcel.

"How much do I owe you?"

"Nothing."

"Thank you." Anne turned and walked away.

The chemist called after her, "Come back if you need more."

Doctor Rouffart, a longtime friend of the Dumon family and a colleague of Michou's father, had examined Bob Grimes' leg and agreed to do the operation. But there could be no hint of what they were doing—not even to his staff. The doctor, who had studied in England, explained in perfect English, "We cannot go to the hospital. We will take out the bullet at my clinic, but I will not be able to put you to sleep. We will have to be quick and you will have to leave on your own feet."

Bob scratched a thoughtful hand through his hair, sighed, then nodded that he understood and agreed to the procedure.

The doctor arrived at the apartment at the appointed time and wound a scarf around Bob's neck. "We will say you have a sore throat."

Doctor Rouffart and Lily helped Bob down the stairs and into the doctor's car. Once inside the clinic, the doctor set to work x-raying his patient with a fluoroscope to locate the object then laying him down on the operating table. The doctor and Lily scrubbed their hands. "I can only give you a light dose of chloroform," the doctor said somewhat apologetically. He twisted a towel and had Bob bite down on it.

"Ready?"

Bob clamped his jaw on the towel and his hands on the sides of the table. He nodded.

Lily watched Bob's grimace as the doctor cut into the leg. She anticipated the doctor's needs, attentive to the procedure, but from time to time checking Bob's face. He clenched his teeth so tightly, his cheek muscles quivered—he seemed near the end of his endurance. She was proud of him for being so brave.

"There," Dr. Rouffart said handing Bob what turned out to be a two-inch long piece of shrapnel that looked like a fragment from the plane.

Bob's face relaxed.

The leg was sutured up in minutes and Bob made his way on his own power to the car, walking slowly so as not to reveal a limp. The doctor drove back to Hélène's where he and Lily helped Bob up the stairs.

"You were very brave," Lily said as she eased him back into bed.

Bob smiled up at her as she fixed his pillow. "It wasn't so bad."

He had a beautiful smile.

CHAPTER THIRTY-FOUR
Saturday, November 20, 1943

Lily sewed papers into the lining of her coat—papers that would guarantee her a death sentence if discovered. She laid the coat on the couch and followed the sweet aroma of blueberry muffins into the kitchen. "*Bonjour*, good morning," she said brushing past Hélène to the cup of coffee awaiting her across the table from Bob. While his finger traced the list in front of him for the right phrase, she stole a look at his gentle eyes and soft brown hair combed back like Jimmy Cagney—only she thought him more handsome than the actor.

"*Comment ça va?*" he asked uncertainly.

She smiled. "*Très bien.*"

"I see you are wearing your young girl costume today…"

Seeing her in various disguises—one day a child, the next day a woman or a teen—must have intrigued the dashing young pilot. "I know you are curious about where I go, but it is better if you do not know what I do."

"I just thought it being Saturday and all…."

His look of disappointment melted her. She broke off a bite of muffin and offered a sympathetic pout for his sad puppy dog eyes. He was lonely and bored sitting around all day. Hélène did her best to keep him occupied, speaking French words and phrases for him to repeat and practice. She said that he was polite and uncomplaining, but often restless and dispirited; and that he perked up so much when Lily was due to return that if he had a tail it would have been wagging. In his limited French and her limited English, he and Lily would talk long into the night.

"When I return home tonight, we will go for another walk to strengthen your muscles for your journey home. Your team mates should be back in England soon. We will listen for their message on the BBC."

In the eighteen days since Bob's operation, Lily and her group had aided more than two dozen airmen and there were more waiting up in the provinces and elsewhere in the system. Evasions were running like a factory assembly line. As soon as one package was sent on its way another dropped from the sky to take its place. Just this past Wednesday, she had helped escort four airmen down to the French border where *Monique* guided them across the frontier along back roads and through woods and farms and delivered them to *Diane* who conducted them by train to Paris.

Lily popped in another bite of muffin and slipped into her blue coat. "Practice your French, Bob. I will test you when I get back."

She rode the tram to the center of Brussels, walked two blocks and ducked into a book shop where she browsed at the back of the store. Minutes later, a perky, dimple-cheeked brunette wandered in. Lily closed her book and exited the store paying no attention to the girl. Several shops away, the girl caught up to her and they walked together toward the train station.

"*Bonjour*, Jeanne," Lily said.

"*Bonjour*, Lily, How is your puppy?"

"His paw is still tender, but he is mending well." Once they had reached an empty stretch of sidewalk, Lily abandoned the coded chatter. "Thank you for coming with me. The zinc and lead mines of Vieille Montagne are very important to the Germans, so our boys must stay hidden. I cannot explain well in English."

Jeanne Macintosh, a Londoner whose father was Scottish and mother Belgian, had been visiting an aunt and uncle in Halle when the Germans invaded. She was already helping her uncle Francois Hanssens, a Résistance operative, with passing messages and hosting airmen when she was sent to Liège to guide Arthur Kellett, the Spanish RAF pilot aided by Simone Gazet and Rolande Crusiau. It surprised her to realize she'd met Kellett when he was a student in Herne Bay, England. That made her to want to help other airmen too.

Lily hoped Jeanne could interrogate the evaders to make sure they were truly English airmen. But Jeanne had told Lily in a doubtful tone, "I have never interrogated anyone."

"Just ask them what someone from England should know. I can help. Things I have learned from other pilots you can translate to English."

The girls sat at Madame Morimont's kitchen table as the two airmen were led into the room. "Hello, I am Jeanne, and this is my friend, Lily."

"You speak English!" The first airman's face lit up like a little boy with a brand new bicycle. "I'm Sergeant Andrews—Frank. And this is Lieutenant Albert Pepper."

"Nice to meet you both."

"Nice to meet you," Frank gushed. "I was really beginning to regret that I had not taken French class in school." Despite his sergeant's rank, Frank exuded boyish charm, with his light curly brown hair, handsome face and warm captivating eyes.

Lily cautioned Jeanne in French not to reveal that she was not Belgian. If an evader was caught, it was better if he did not know too much about his helpers.

Jeanne agreed with a nod. "Tell me, Frank, what type of plane do you fly?"

"I'm a mechanic on a Halifax Mk II. I was shot down two weeks ago."

"And you, Albert?"

"I am a browser on an Avro Lancaster Mk III. I was shot down two nights ago."

"Where in England are you from, Frank?"

"Brisley originally."

"What would I mean if I said I was one over the eight?"

Frank laughed. "It means you are drunk."

"And you, Albert, what if I said I have more front than Brighton?"

"I'd say you were pretty bloody sure of yourself."

"All right then." Jeanne laughed. "Now, in case Madame M. has not told you, there are many Germans in this region. To get you out you must do exactly as we say. Understand?"

"Yes, of course."

"*Parlez-lui de son identité militaire.*" Lily reminded Jeanne.

"Yes. Once you have your identity papers, Madame M. will sew your service discs into the sleeve of your coat. If you are stopped by the Germans, you will show your papers and pretend to be mute. Do not panic. Act like you do this all the time and don't let your eyes wander to any of your helpers—they will not be able to assist you. If the Germans arrest you, show them your identity discs and tell them you're British airmen. They will put you in a prisoner camp, but it is better than being shot as a spy."

"Yes, I believe that would be rather unpleasant," Frank said drolly.

"You will remain here while we make arrangements for your travel. Someone will contact you in a few days. Do you have any questions?"

"Yes," Frank said. "Do you have a boyfriend?"

Jeanne blushed.

Lily followed the airman's eyes as they opened wide to invite an answer. But Jeanne gave none.

That didn't dissuade the airman from pursuing it. "I swear, if I'm captured and the Germans want to know your relationship status, they'll have to torture me to get it out of me."

Jeanne laughed at his bravado. "I am unattached. And you? Do you have a sweetheart back home?"

"Nah. I'm footloose and fancy free."

Lily nudged Jeanne who jumped a bit. It seemed she'd been so wrapped up in the charms of the grinning aviator she'd forgotten Lily was there. Lily spoke in Frangliais— half-French, half English. *"Je ne comprends pas celui-ci footloose and fancy."*

"Fancy free," Jeanne said. She regarded Frank coquettishly as she told Lily in French, "It means he is single." Jeanne tried to reinstitute a commanding tone, but her face was still a bit flushed. "Today, we will take you for snaps for your identity papers. We will go as couples." Frank's eyes begged her to pick him and she conceded with a smile. "Albert, you go with Lily. Frank, you are with me."

On the way back to Brussels, Lily teased Jeanne. "That new puppy has taken a liking to you. He will be very disappointed if someone else returns to fetch him."

"And how about you?" Jeanne asked. "Are you going home to take your puppy for a walk?"

Lily smiled. "Yes. I walk him every night. Otherwise he will make a mess in the house."

Jeanne laughed at the innuendo.

Thinking about the way Frank Andrews's face brightened when he heard Jeanne speak English, gave Lily an idea to chase away Bob's blues. "Would you like to meet him? I know a place where we can go later."

"Bob," Lily said after they were ushered to the back room of a friend's café, "*Je voudrais vous presenter á Jeanne.*"

"*Enchanté.*"

Jeanne shook his hand. "Nice to meet you, Bob."

Bob's eyes widened with the delight Lily had hoped for.

"I understand you were badly wounded," Jeanne said. "How are you doing now?"

"I'm doing a whole lot better." Bob grinned at Lily. "Thanks to my wonderful nurse."

"You sound like you have a southern accent," Jeanne said.

"Virginia," Bob said. "You don't sound like you're from around here either."

"I'm from London. My mum's Belgian. My father's Scottish." Jeanne covered her mouth and looked apologetically at Michou. "Oops. I shouldn't be telling you where I'm from. Oh well." She shrugged. "Now that I let that cat out of the bag, you're probably wondering what I'm doing here."

"Wrong place, wrong time," Jeanne said with an affable frown. "Mum and I were visiting my uncle when the Germans invaded. It's going on four years now."

"We are winning this war," Bob drawled. "We're kicking the shi— the crap out of the Germans. They can't even mount a full scale attack on our bombers anymore. It's just a matter of time."

"Not too much time, I hope. So tell me, Bob, what would you be doing if you were in Virginia tonight instead of here?"

"*Hmmm.*" Bob thought for a moment. "I guess I'd be getting ready for Thanksgiving."

"Oh that's right," Jeanne said. "I forgot that Americans celebrate Thanksgiving this time of year."

"It would be this Thursday, the day after my birthday."

Seeing Lily's quizzical look, Jeanne translated what he had said.

"*Sanksgiving?*" Lily asked.

"It's a feast, right?" Jeanne looked to Bob for confirmation.

"That's right. We eat turkey until it is coming out of our ears."

Jeanne translated gesturing with the roll of her hands outward from her ears.

Lily laughed as Bob continued. "My mom would make a big stuffed turkey with all the trimmings—sweet potatoes, cranberry sauce, turnips … and for dessert there'd be pumpkin pies, pudding, apple pies, nuts, figs … we'd eat and eat and eat …"

"*Jusqu'à ce qu'il sorte de tes oreilles,*" Lily said whimsically with her hands circling from the sides of her head.

"That's right," Bob chuckled. "'til it's coming out of our ears."

"I bet you wish you were back there now instead of in the middle of this mess," Jeanne said.

"It's not so bad. The Belgian people are great. Lily has taken me to see a lot of the city."

"I used to love coming to Brussels this time of year." Jeanne gazed wistfully as she lost herself in a memory. "Streets were filled with people for the winter festival. All the way from Place Sainte Catherine to the fish market was a Christmas Market lit up like a fairyland. There was music and toys and gifts … my mum would do all of her Christmas shopping here … and the food, my God what food. For Belgians, food is a celebration, a social event, a time to enjoy life and each other's company —but that was before the Germans came. Now Brussels is like a flower that has withered on its stalk, not quite dead, but not living."

On Wednesday, Lily cut her visits with other evaders short and rushed back to Hélène's apartment. "Put on your coat, Bob. We are going out."

Bob had gotten used to following her without question. They rode the tram, sticking to their usual practice of taking separate seats and paying no attention to each other. Bob had become comfortable riding crowded trams shoulder to shoulder with Germans, bumping against them with no more concern than if he were riding a trolley back home. Yet she couldn't help worrying that at any moment he could be singled out by an alert German who picked up a mannerism that didn't appear Belgian. She feared for every evader of course, but Bob was different. He was her wounded little puppy that she had cared for and nursed back to health.

Sensing that she had special feelings for him, Bob had told her he didn't want her to take unnecessary risks on his behalf—if he was caught she was not to try to help him. She was too important to the cause, he had said, and she couldn't help him anyway.

She had promised him she wouldn't, but she didn't know if that was a promise she could keep. She felt more protective of him than anyone she had helped before.

Bob gave her a questioning look now when she changed trams for the second time. Their usual outings were limited to locations from which they could easily get back to Madame Camusel's flat. Tonight they were traveling out of the city proper to a neighborhood Lily knew very well. She smiled to herself. He would find out soon enough where they were going. For now, she would let him wonder.

At the stop, she dallied until the tram had disappeared into the night, then grabbed Bob's hand and set off at a brisk pace. Several turns later and up the hill on a quiet street, they reached their destination.

The door opened and a young mademoiselle with a smile bright as sunshine threw open her arms. "*Bon anniversaire, Bob!*" She kissed both his cheeks and moved over to Lily as another young lady took her place.

"Michou," the first girl said as she led them through the living room to a dining table set with china plates and trimmed with colored paper, "you didn't tell me that your friend was so handsome. Does he speak French?"

"He is learning," Michou said. "Bob, these are my good friends, Jeanne and Hermine."

"*Enchanté.*"

Jeanne and Hermine Biard were longtime friends of the family. Their sister, Madame Marshall had lived near the Dumons in the Belgian Congo, where Michou's father, Eugene, had worked as a colonial doctor when Michou, and her sisters were children.

"They have made you a party and a *Sanksgiving*." Michou beamed.

"This is a wonderful Thanksgiving." Bob, his eyes still wide with surprise, hugged each girl in turn. "*Merci beaucoup*."

Hermine opened a bottle of red wine.

Her little party idea was just what the pilot needed. Jeanne removed the lid of the serving dish and a delicious aroma of beef roast filled the air. Their host served up generous portions of savory beef and mashed potatoes with dark brown onion-rich gravy drizzled over every tender slice. It may not have been the Thanksgiving Bob would have had in the United States, but he grinned so broadly that Michou couldn't help stealing glimpses of his delighted face as they ate. She proudly regarded Bob's properly executed French table etiquette—politely waiting until the hostess had sipped her wine first; cutting his meat and eating without changing the fork and knife in his hand; and resting his hands, but not his elbows, on the table. A slip in etiquette could mean the difference between getting noticed by an alert German and slipping by undetected.

"Your *aéroplane* was shot down?" Jeanne attempted conversation in the little English she knew.

"*Oui*," Bob said. "We were on a mission to Germany, but I had to turn around because one of my engines failed. Before we could make it out of Belgium, six German fighters attacked us. We got shot up and had to bail out."

Michou already knew the story and was able to fill the girls in on the parts they didn't understand.

"And you were wounded," Jeanne said. "Poor man."

"Lucky man," Bob said. He pulled a metal fragment from his trouser pocket and held the shard up for them to inspect. "Shrapnel—hit me in the leg." He patted his upper thigh. "Michou has been nursing me."

The girls took great interest in the sliver of metal, but Michou could see they were more enthralled just having a man, especially a war hero, at their table. Other than the disgusting Boches, young men were rarely seen in Belgium these days. It was also rare in Belgium to have meat, but

Jeanne and Hermine's family owned a grocery store, so they were able to sidestep some of the rationing. Although the girls tried to get him to eat more, Bob insisted he was full. He was being polite, but it endeared him even more to Michou that he was so considerate.

After dinner, the girls carried in another surprise for the young pilot —a birthday cake and real coffee. Bob would never forget how he had spent his twenty-first birthday.

Lily and Bob stayed as long as they dared. If she had figured it right, they could make it back to Hélène's apartment in Laeken before the ten-thirty curfew.

Bob's leg had stiffened up from the hours of sitting, but he kept pace with Lily without complaint. They rode the tram sitting apart without looking at each other, as they always did, and made the transfer without incident. Then the unthinkable happened. The tram stopped. In the dim glow of street lamps lurked shadowy figures in dark trench coats—the Gestapo!

The doors opened and German soldiers entered waving machine guns. *"Raus!"*

Stay calm. Stay calm, Lily's mind cautioned her. But the fear thumping in her chest nearly overcame her. *What are they searching for —or whom?* She mechanically descended the steps telling herself this was all her fault—she should have known better than to stay those extra few minutes. But Bob was having such a good time she hated to leave. Although she had promised not to, she exited the tram and moved in the direction Bob had gone, hoping he'd show his papers without giving himself away. She edged a bit closer to him. He didn't acknowledge her although she knew he was aware she was nearby.

Three soldiers moved through the crowd checking identity papers and patting each person down. "Show me your papers if you please," a soldier commanded in French. Lily produced hers as instructed. The German looked down at her. "It is late for such a young girl to be out alone. Where are you going?"

"Home," Lily said with a shrug as if it should be obvious she was trying to get home before curfew. The German handed back her papers and moved on toward Bob. Then a frightening thought seized her: when he was patted down, the German would find the shrapnel in his pocket! She shifted even closer without being too obvious about it. What could she say if it was found?

Bob stood with his arms raised above his head as the German patted down his shirt and trousers. "Your identity papers," the soldier said. Bob handed his papers over. Many beads of sweat later, the German handed back Bob's documents and moved to the next person, and Lily took her first breath.

After twenty nervous minutes, they were allowed back on the tram. Bob followed the queue, but when he reached the steps, the soldier at the door blocked him with his gun. Lily's heart stopped. "Did you show your papers?" the German asked in French.

"Oui," Bob responded with a nod of tired annoyance. "Oui."

The soldier let him pass.

Lily abandoned her travel procedures and sat in the back seat with Bob for the remainder of the trip.

"Why did you come so close to me?" Bob whispered.

"I was afraid they might ask you something you did not understand."

"But you agreed you would not risk yourself for me."

"I know. I am sorry. I was afraid the German would find the shrapnel in your pocket."

"I held it between my fingers while my hands were up." Bob demonstrated with an imaginary fragment. "In the darkness, he could not see it."

Lily sighed and laid her head on his shoulder. "We will have to be more careful."

CHAPTER THIRTY-FIVE

Nadine leaned back on a sweater to cushion her head against the bumping of the cattle car. Struggling to find enough air to fill her lungs was like trying to breathe through a heavy blanket—a blanket that reeked of urine, body odor and squalid hair. She had no idea where they were going. Crammed into every possible space of the bolted up railroad car, women and girls from all parts of France and Belgium seemed little more than sacks of dirty laundry now, their bodies providing the only warmth against the December cold. Five days of long stops, slow progress, and no food and water, deflated the once vital women.

Try as she might to be polite and not look at the others, Nadine couldn't help wondering about the women in the car. The quiet young miss in the corner stared straight ahead hour after hour, unconsciously twisting and untwisting her fingers through her auburn curls, depression and fear dulling her pretty blue eyes. Although everyone in the train car fretted about their future, this mademoiselle looked particularly broken.

Next to the young lady, a woman with short greying hair stroked the dark tresses of a girl of maybe thirteen whose head lay in her lap. The girl seemed calmer now since the rantings of the magpie had subsided.

Nadine had silently dubbed the woman in the middle of the car the magpie because of her stringy black hair, sour face and dire predictions. She had quieted now, but earlier the woman had scared nearly everyone in the car with her prophecies of doom.

"We will be taken to a German death camp," the magpie had said with certainty.

"Stop trying to scare everyone," a woman next to her said. "How do you know what the Germans will do?"

"You don't believe it? It is true."

"*Paah!*" the woman lashed back at her. "The Germans are not so stupid as to waste all of this slave labor. They will put us to work making uniforms and bullets for German soldiers."

"I will refuse to help the Boches make war on our people," a young voice said defiantly.

"Then they will kill you."

"You are all fools," the magpie said. "I speak German and I have listened to the guards talk. We French have made too much trouble for the Germans. Their need to get rid of us is greater than their need for our services. They have said we will never be heard from again. And that can only mean one thing."

The grey-haired mother pulled her daughter tighter to her chest, muffling one ear against her bosom while covering the other with her hand. "Stop it," she said. "You don't know what the Germans will do any more than the rest of us."

"No? Do you think the Germans have suddenly become civilized? *Psshht!* We will be herded into the shower room, only it will not be a shower we receive but gas. And we will all be dead!"

"You must trust in God," a voice from the middle of the car called out. "We are all being tested. Hitler is the Antichrist, and his followers are the Devil's helpers. We must remain strong in God and do only what the bible tells us to do."

A dark-haired friend nudged Nadine. "She must be a Jehovah's witness."

Nadine shrugged. Her mind was on the woman with the teenage daughter. As the woman stroked the young girl's hair, Nadine thought how terrible it must be for a mother and daughter to have to watch each other suffer. She prayed the guard in Saint Gilles prison had told her the truth, that her mother was being released. She could face the gas chamber or whatever the Boches had in store for her knowing that her mother was safe. Unlike her father who had helped the Résistance with acts of sabotage right from the beginning, her mother was an innocent, doing nothing more than distributing clothing and food and occasionally moving an airman a short distance.

Nadine knew her own fate was sealed the moment she committed herself to the cause. She was fighting for the freedom of her country. She had done everything she could to disrupt the Germans and save English pilots so they could fight again. Even now, with death perhaps only hours away, she would have done it all again without hesitation. She accepted her punishment with pride.

A shrill whistle and the slowing of the train interrupted her musings. Heads picked up. The fingers of the auburn-haired young woman in the corner froze mid-twist. And the teenage girl lifted her head off her mother's chest to listen.

The train stopped with a mighty *woosh* of steam. The women pulled themselves to their feet in anticipation. Guttural voices outside shouted words they could not make out. Was this another stop along the way, or had they reached their destination? More than forty apprehensive, suffocating minutes passed. Then they heard the *barruump, clunk, brrrlll* repeated down the line as ramps dropped into place, wooden bars were lifted, and doors slid open on car after car. The door flung open. Blinding sunlight streamed in.

"*Raus!*" a husky female voice commanded. "*Aufstellen!*"

Nadine shielded her eyes feeling for the person in front of her. Outside, snarling German Shepherds strained at their leashes anxious to be let loose on anyone who dared to disobey. Women straggled out of the train, some with nothing but the clothes on their backs and others carrying armfuls of clothing and dragging leather suitcases.

Soldiers with machine guns blocked every means of escape. Fierce SS female officers strutted through the crowd shoving women and barking orders. The words were foreign, unintelligible, but from the tone and their motioning with their guns, the prisoners gathered that they were supposed to line up. Aching from days of cramped conditions in the airless train cars, the women did their best to assemble themselves into some sort of formation. Each moment of delay angered the Germans who marched back and forth shouting at these inferior creatures who dared to have the nerve to defy them.

"*Stell Dich nicht so an!*" A female guard grabbed the nearest woman by the shoulder of her coat and flung her toward the formation. "*Fünferreihen!*"

"Five rows," whispered the magpie. "Five rows."

A cold breeze chilled Nadine as she stood in formation. Guards tromped up and down the line cursing and shoving until all were assembled. Then the need for hurry ended. The Germans kept the women shivering in the crisp air while they counted bodies—once, twice, three times. Finally, the counting stopped. They were ordered to turn. Carrying all their possessions—packages in brown paper, satchels of clothing, bags of toiletries and whatnot—the women were marched off through a quiet hamlet of gaily colored buildings.

The peaceful beauty of the gentle town—the clean two and three-story German houses with steep alpine roofs and gingerbread trim, the humble homes, the steeple of a Christian church that peeked out above the rooftops, the decorated inns and merry shops—felt as though they were walking through a picture postcard. The sweet scent of autumn filled the air. Mounds of crimson, scarlet, orange and gold chrysanthemums seemed to be everywhere. Flowers skirted mail box posts, burst from pots and planters and adorned buildings.

Nadine tried to read the faces of the inquisitive people who came to the windows and balconies to watch the procession. Did their eyes hold pity for the parade of disheveled women? Did the citizens looking down feel contempt for this mob of foreign enemies of their Reich? Perhaps they simply found them a curiosity. From one of the balconies, the smell of eggs and sausages nearly made her delirious. It had been days since she had last eaten.

The procession passed an inn with pink walls on which a large sign read, 'Fürstenberg'. She'd never heard of the place.

They turned a corner and left the village behind. Even over the *schlump schlump* of the women's feet Nadine could hear birds singing in the woods. On the right side of the road, a line of cottages awaited the morning sun as it rose to reach them through the gentle pines. Beyond the cottages, ducks lazily paddled near the shore of a picturesque lake while two squirrels romped over white sand dunes. Row boats overturned on the beach lay ready for the coming winter, waiting until spring when they would once again gently rock beside the little wooden dock. How nice it would be to just sit on that dock in summertime sipping lemonade and dangling her feet in the cool water.

The daydream burst at the sight of a fifteen-foot brick wall rising up in the distance. Glancing at the dejected faces of the women to her left and right, Nadine knew that just like her, they were evaluating the fortifications. The compound was encircled by a hundred yards of open ground; a *no mans land* where guards would have a clear shot at anyone trying to reach the vast pine forest beyond. And even if they could make it to the trees, they'd never get away from the dogs. Signs on the barbed wire atop the high walls warned that it carried high voltage. The whole place carried a dreadful, desolate emptiness that not even the loneliness of solitary confinement at St. Gilles prison in Brussels could have prepared her for.

The sign above their heads read, *RAVENSBRÜCK.*

Machine gun emplacements guarded the huge entryway to ensure that in case of an uprising the population could be contained inside and no one rushing the gate would get out alive. As Nadine passed through those huge doors, a nauseating sensation rose in her throat. Across the vast expanse in front of her, sat row upon row of dismal grey barracks set on an immense field of grey-black clinker. The air reeked of putrid food, death, excrement and despair. She had surely passed through the gates of hell.

To the left of the entrance, stood clean, white, two-and-a-half story buildings. Through the windows of the nearest one, Nadine could see male and female SS officers casually moving about. In the crowd of women inmates indistinguishable in prisoner clothing and kerchiefed heads watching the procession, she thought she recognized one— Suzanne Wittek. She wondered if Dédée had seen her.

The new arrivals were herded toward a wooden barracks and held up at the door. One by one they were summoned in. Although Nadine didn't understand the German words, she followed the hand gestures inside to a table across the room. First, she had to overcome the shock of what she saw: naked women, young and old, trying to cover themselves with their hands, and others undressing. Never since becoming a woman had Nadine been naked in front of anyone. She proceeded numbly to her station, but her shock increased when she saw that the room contained not only female overseers, but SS men who stood watching the women take off their clothes.

Behind the table, a woman in striped prison garb looked up from her ledger. "Name?" The woman spoke French, but with a pronounced East-European accent.

"Andrée Dumon."

"What are you here for?"

"Pardon?"

"What did they arrest you for?"

"Helping English airmen," Nadine said unapologetically.

"Political," the woman said knowingly as she wrote it down in her book. She also wrote down the letters NN. "Take off your clothes and give them to me. And whatever else you have brought with you."

Nadine hesitated.

The woman lifted her head and said dryly, "Mademoiselle, the SS men would be only too happy to come over here and assist you in taking them off."

Nadine gazed out the window behind the woman trying not to think about who might be ogling her. But what she saw through the window was even more disturbing. The women trudging about the yard didn't look like women at all. They were walking skeletons.

The Czech admissions clerk noticed and looked up from her book again. "In six months, you will look like them," she said with a flick of her head. "In nine months, you will be dead. Unless you are selected before that."

"Selected?"

"When you can no longer work or for whatever reason the Germans want to get rid of you, your name will go on a list. You will be taken away in a truck—the *transport noir*—and only your clothes will return." The woman focused on her ledger, recording each item Nadine had turned in, clothing, toothbrush, shoes and soap.

Nadine stared back at the woman, not knowing whether to believe her.

When the woman again looked up, she nodded to assure Nadine that she spoke the truth. "When you get your clothes you will see that they have been worn before." She handed Nadine a small red cloth triangle. "You are to sew this on your clothes. Now, stand over there and wait with the others."

Nadine leaned in as she received her triangle and asked softly, "Is there a way to improve the chances of not being selected?"

"Do your job and don't give them reason to single you out." She offered a palms-up gesture at the ledger on the table. "Or work for the Germans."

Out of the corner of her eye, Nadine saw an overseer wandering in their direction. She gave the clerk a slight nod and took her place with the others. Like all French and Belgian women, Nadine had been raised to be modest. Now, her humiliation was stemmed only by her sympathy for the grandmothers made to undress in front of their daughters and granddaughters. The older women bore the shame of the snickers and mocking from the cruel SS men that they had to pass. The so-called master race was nothing but a bunch of disgusting animals.

Nadine followed the others, covering what she could with her hands and arms. The Boche pigs grinned with no pretense of hiding their lubricious looks. Nadine could feel their swollen eyes traveling over her, making her skin crawl like she'd fallen into a rotting bog of creepy, slimy insects.

Keeping her chin up, she tried to banish these filthy men and cruel-faced women from her mind—picturing herself somewhere else; in her bedroom reading a book, at the café with friends, shopping with Michou ... anywhere but here. She refused to look at the men, refused to hear their nasty comments, refused to look down in shame like many of the other women. When the line began to move, Nadine followed, numb to everything around her as if she wasn't a participant, but merely a spectator.

They were herded into a windowless shower room, where Nadine remembered the warnings of the magpie. *If I am to be gassed, get it over quickly*, she thought. Swept along with the crowd, she shuffled in until the space was full and movement stopped. The door clanged shut. Women looked to each other and to the fixtures above them. The room grew deathly silent.

Suddenly, the shower heads *woodshed* to life. Cool water rained down. There was a collective sigh of relief. Despite the lack of soap, it felt good to rub off the smell and grime of the week spent locked in the train car. Still wet, and with no towels to dry themselves, they were herded back out where new horrors awaited them.

"Line up," a French-speaking inmate worker instructed them. The women filed along to the next station where they were told to raise their arms. A burning green liquid was sloshed over the front of Nadine's body with a mop. "Turn," the worker commanded, and the process was repeated from her shoulders to her heels.

Next, they took their turns on cutting stools where prisoners clipped away the hair of the newcomers under the watchful eyes of the female guards. In less than a minute, a woman's head was rendered bald. Then, with quick snips and little care as to whether they drew blood, the inmate barbers trimmed away all other body hair.

Nadine watched in horror. She never imagined anyone, not even the Nazis, were capable of inflicting such humiliation on their fellow human beings. The quiet girl with the auburn locks Nadine had seen on the train, sat sobbing while her hair fell down around her. Touching her baldness, the trembling girl could scarcely stand. An SS woman, smiling, yanked the distraught girl off the stool and shoved her toward the other bald women who were no longer individual and distinguishable

Nadine again sent her mind somewhere else, telling herself she would get through this too. She refused to give the sneering SS overseers the satisfaction of knowing that tiny grenades of fear were exploding inside her. She left the stool fighting back her tears.

When she neared the others, three women put their bald heads together. "Look. We are a bushel of peaches!"

Nadine couldn't help but laugh.

A large woman touched her own scalp and said, "My head is too big to be a peach. I would have to find a bushel of melons."

Nadine felt better. The women were right to make fun of themselves, she thought. There was no point in being upset about it.

But the worst was yet to come.

Standing in line nearly two hours, she dared not think about what the dentist might be doing to their teeth. But when her turn finally came, all the dentist did was take a quick look in her mouth, more likely searching for hidden jewels than for bad teeth.

After the examination, one woman quipped, "Leave it to the Germans to make women stand around naked for hours just to look in their mouths."

They stood for another hour. Her feet and legs ached terribly, but they were not permitted to sit on the floor. Then an SS guard walked down the line announcing that the doctors had arrived and the examinations would begin.

Nadine soon learned what that meant. To her horror, women young and old were subjected to crude gynecological exams conducted in the open with no privacy and no cleansing of the instruments between exams. For some, it was the breaking point. More than a few were led away sobbing uncontrollably after the doctor finished with them. While there might have been a smidgen of medical purpose to it, once again it seemed more a search for jewels than anything else. Nadine turned away. It struck her that making the prisoners stand naked before their conquerors and subjecting them to the most humiliating examinations was the Nazis' way of driving it into these women, many of whom had defied them with resistance and underground activities, that they were mere slaves and the Germans could do with them as they pleased. Not even one's most private body parts were her own.

Women of the Résistance and underground were accustomed to danger; clenching their jaws closed and when it was over walking away without a whimper. Nadine numbed her mind and got through it, but others—especially those who had never taken part in seditious activities—trembled with fear. Instinctively, the stronger women comforted the weaker ones.

The afternoon shadows had grown long. An inmate clerk handed Nadine a coarse grey shirt, a blue-grey striped dress, a half-apron, a bandanna, and a worn out pair of wooden shoes. Slipping the stained dress over her head, Nadine remembered what the Czech clerk had told her about the transport noir. With no lining, the dress would allow the winter wind to blow right through. She slid her feet into wooden shoes that were much too roomy, but she knew better than to complain about them or she'd likely be sent away naked and barefoot. An inmate issued her a blanket, a bowl and a wooden spoon, warning, "Do not let these out of your sight or they will disappear."

They were herded outside like cattle and shouted into formation again. A starched, spit-shined *Oberaufseherin* delivered long instructions punctuated with crisp guttural words. Nadine felt the intensity of her directions and sensed the severe repercussions for failing to obey—but she had no idea what the woman was saying.

Once the overseer was satisfied that she had covered the important points, the women were split into groups and assigned a *Blockova*—a block senior.

The blockova spoke French with a Russian accent. She led them into a large dingy room with bare light bulbs hanging from the ceiling in what she called a quarantine building. The barracks was a long one-story building, divided so half the women's beds were on one side in wing A and the other half in wing B. Each wing had a day room with a table but no chairs. Situated between the day rooms was a washroom area of about twenty sinks and ten toilets.

After Nadine's group was given a bowl of thin turnip soup and a ration of bread in the day room, their blockova explained, "Tomorrow you begin instruction. You learn how to conduct yourselves in Ravensbrück. You learn the prison rules. After a few weeks, you will move to permanent barracks."

Hearing a commotion outside, the blockova paused a moment to peer out the open window, then returned her attention to the group. "Probably someone being beaten. The overseers will not hesitate to beat you if you give them any reason."

One of the French prisoners asked, "I didn't understand what the overseer said when we were in formation. Something about mail and packages."

The blockova nodded. "All mail is read before it goes out. It must contain nothing about the camp or the conditions. A notice will be affixed to each letter informing your loved ones that all mail and packages received will be opened in front of you and any contraband will be removed before it is passed on to you. If letter does not follow the rules or if it contains news about war, it will be confiscated. You may receive clothing and food from home and Red Cross packages—unless you are NN."

"What is NN?" someone asked.

Nadine remembered the clerk writing those letters next to her name in the ledger.

"Those who are NN live in separate block isolated from the others. They are not permitted to send or receive mail. They are not permitted Red Cross packages. They can have no contact with outside world."

"Why?" Nadine asked. "What does NN mean?"

"*NACHT UND NEBEL*—NIGHT AND FOG."

"Those who have defied the Germans in Résistance or underground are considered too dangerous to let out of sight. They are not permitted to leave the camp—not even to work. Their friends, their family—they will not know if they are alive or dead. The Germans believe this will deter others. Those designated NN are to completely disappear—lost in the night and fog."

The sound of the door interrupted the blockova. An overseer called her outside. Moments later, she returned to the day room. "It seems one of our new arrivals didn't want to stay in Ravensbrück. She committed suicide falling onto electrified fence."

After the long march, the examinations and the hours and hours of standing, they should have been exhausted, but Nadine couldn't sleep. The beds were nothing but wooden planks hung three high on the wall. There was no mattress or cushioning of any kind. But it wasn't the stiff bed that kept her awake. It was the terrible feeling of despair and the stories passed on by older inmates—the executions, random beatings, transport noirs, and working until you dropped dead. The emaciated women in the yard seemed to attest that it was all true.

The stories crashed in her head like breakers on a beach. But she wasn't the only one thinking about the terrors they had yet to face. Nadine lay there in the gloom, breathing in the putrid odors and listening to sobbing from around the room. In the darkness, women who had shown such strength all day through the horrors and humiliations, could no longer hide their emotions. Nadine couldn't hold back her own tears.

———

After release from formation the next day, Nadine found Dédée who had been on the same train as her. "Did you see who was here?"

"Who?" Dédée asked.

"Come with me," Nadine said.

They hadn't gone far when the woman Nadine went looking for, found them.

"Suzanne!" Dédée exclaimed. "I never thought I'd see you again!"

"Nor I you," Suzanne said as the sisters held each other in a long embrace. "I had hoped you had escaped to England."

"I am not happy I was caught," Dédée said, "but it is only fair I should suffer the same fate as all those who have followed me."

"Your mother has been released," Nadine told Suzanne. "I shared a cell with her for a while in Saint Gilles, but we didn't know what happened to you."

"*Nacht und Nebel,*" Suzanne said with a sigh. "Too dangerous, no mail, no Red Cross packages, nothing."

"What about the work here?" Nadine asked.

"The Russians, the Poles, they work in the kitchens and fields where there is food to steal. The Czechs work in the offices and the supply areas. The Jehovah's Witnesses are the house keepers because they keep themselves clean and do not steal."

"And us?" Nadine asked in anticipation.

"Because we are the most educated, we have better book keeping and office skills than other groups," Suzanne said, "but most French and Belgians would rather go hungry than help the Germans. So we are given jobs digging trenches, building roads, mucking out the shit from the toilets." Suzanne flicked her head to signal that they should walk with her so as not to stand out from others strolling the yard. "Filth and disease are rampant in some blocks. We keep our block clean and we do not steal from each other. But not every woman in our block thinks as we do. Some women never had to work before they came here. You must be careful. Some women talk like staunch patriots, but they will do the Germans' bidding for a crust of bread."

"Is it true what we have heard about medical experiments on women?" Dédée asked.

Suzanne nodded. The Germans had performed horrible experiments on a number of women, most of them were Polish, some as young as fourteen years old. Five had died immediately after the operation, but the others were maimed for life. They were called the rabbits.

In August, ten additional women had been summoned to the *Revier*. They were to report back the next day but refused. *Oberaufseherin* Binz had surrounded the block with machine guns and demanded the ten to surrender or everyone in the block would be shot. Five women had given themselves up and were operated on. But the block stood together and refused to give up the others. Binz had sealed the buildings, allowing no food, no light, no fresh air. After four nights, she had offered through loudspeaker that anyone who opposed the revolt and came out would be given no punishment. She had even offered them food. But no one came out. Five hundred women were being kept from working, so Binz finally had had to give in.

"Binz is pure evil," Suzanne said. "Watch out for her. And be careful what you say. You never know who is listening."

CHAPTER THIRTY-SIX

Prosper Dezitter eased the Peugeot into the garage at 16 Rue Forestière and the portly Jean Nootens quickly waddled out to close the bi-fold doors. After all of the trouble of moving, Prosper certainly didn't want some fellow spotting his car in the street.

He could hear the prancing of little feet before he even reached the top of the stairs. The moment he entered he was nearly bowled over by a menagerie of dogs dancing about and jostling for position, trying to get noticed by the master. "What are you looking for?" Prosper asked, tousling the head of a German shepherd. He laughed at the wire-haired terrier standing on its hind legs with its paws on Prosper's trousers trying to peek at what was inside the small paper bag. "Do you think I have something for you?"

The terrier's barks were enthusiastically echoed by two Scotties.

"Well, let me in the door you mangy mutts," he said affectionately as he dragged them forward.

From her perch on the back of the sofa, a shiny black cat looked on with mild interest. Sprawled out on the cushions below the cat and paying even less attention, Serge, Flore's tall, overweight, thirteen-year-old son, reclined with a magazine leaning against his raised knees and a bowl of pudding in his lap. His black wool coat lay in a heap beside him on the floor.

The terrier lost his balance as Prosper pushed his way into the room. "Let me see," he said peering teasingly into the bag. "*Ummm*, this looks good." The terrier pranced excitedly on its hind legs again. "Do you want some?"

The dogs barked the affirmative.

"All right." Prosper laughed as he handed out biscuits. "One for you … one for you …" He sniffed the air as he moved farther into the kitchen, inhaling the succulent aroma of deep sea scallops and sautéed mushrooms. "Emily, my dear; do I detect coquilles Saint-Jacques? It smells divine."

The cook thanked him without taking her eyes off her cutting board. She wasn't much to look at, Prosper thought—narrow grasshopper face, black lifeless hair and horn-rimmed glasses—but she cooked well enough. And most importantly she knew to keep her mouth shut.

"Serge," Flore snapped as she emerged from a back bedroom, "why is your coat still on the floor? I told you to put it away."

"I will," the boy replied, but he made no effort to move.

"That is what you said a half hour ago."

"I am busy." Serge turned a page.

"Is that the coat we just bought you?" Prosper asked. "If you cannot put it away, we will take it back to the store and you can wear your old one."

"He has outgrown his old one," Flore said in her son's defense.

"No wonder with what he eats. Make yourself useful, Junior, and go downstairs and bring up a couple of bottles of wine."

"I am not the maid," the boy said curtly. "Send Emily for the wine."

"Emily is not the maid either. She is the cook."

"I will get the wine," Flore said. "Which ones would you prefer?"

Prosper frowned at Flore's lazy son. "Bring the good stuff. Leave the cheap wine for American pilots. They do not know the difference anyway."

"Here," Prosper said pressing a stack of francs into Flore's hand when she returned. "Buy yourself a nice Christmas present."

Flore's eyes widened. "You got this from the pilots!"

"So what? Are they going to report me to the Germans?" Prosper shrugged. The evaders he and Nootens had taken out to the Ardennes this morning hadn't suspected a thing until the guides pulled out their guns. "They will not be needing money where they are going. Besides, it is not their personal money. The English give it to them for their escape."

The dinner conversation returned to mundane topics—sleigh riding as a child, driving a thirty-two Ford in a Canadian snow storm, Serge's need to get more fresh air—The real discussions didn't begin until Emily had been dismissed for the evening and Serge had gone off to bed.

"Goering has berated the Luftwaffe Secret Police for not doing enough to stop enemy pilots from escaping," Prosper told Nootens and Jenart. "So Abwehr is planning a raid."

Jenart snorted. "We've turned over plenty of airmen since starting this safe house."

"Yes," Prosper said, "but the underground is still rescuing more men than we are capturing."

"If we move too soon," Nootens said, "we might spook the helpers."

Prosper nodded his agreement. "I told Kohl that. I told him we have a better chance of finding this English woman if the pilots trust us. But he believes he can torture the information out of those we capture."

Nootens shook his head. "I think that's a mistake."

"It doesn't matter what we think," Prosper said. "It's not just the English woman. We haven't found this Jacques Cartier, or Lily, or Monique ... all we have are suspicious characters—a girl with reddish-blonde hair, a little girl who has not yet led us to her parents, a possible chief in Halle ... Kohl is planning a raid in a suburban town. He has already picked up the photographer, Eli Miroir, and the town will be sealed so no little fishes can escape."

———

Franco stood on the corner in Bordeaux peering over a newspaper until Max, Marie-Louise and Rolande disembarked. Then he tucked the newspaper under his arm and joined the queue for the train to Dax. No words were exchanged as they rode. The 'packages', dressed as common laborers, were revealed by brief eye signals from the helpers.

"One at a time, you will follow Marie-Louise," Franco said once the men all had bicycles, "keeping at least a hundred yards apart. I will be a minute or two behind. If one of you is stopped, the rest of you must go on. You show no recognition of the man stopped. Understand?"

The men nodded and Marie-Louise set off.

Franco stood beside Max with one foot on the pedal waiting for his turn to follow. "How is our friend, Jérôme, getting on?"

"He is not Paul, but I think he will run Paris well enough for you to stay down here. That will make it a harder for the Boches to find you. I've warned him not to discuss any of the Comet members with the English and that he is to follow your orders or he will be shut out."

"Good," Franco said. "What about the reorganization?"

"He has recruited a young man, Pierre Boulain, who comes highly recommended by a village priest. Henri Crampon is acting as chief of housing using his parents' psychiatric hospital to hide evaders. Brussels warns that the Germans are increasing efforts there."

"Monday has warned me of that as well," Franco said. "Comet is their number one target."

Max mounted his bicycle, Franco pedaling alongside. "If the Germans are going all out to stop us, it can only mean one thing—we are having a great impact."

"It also means they have become more dangerous. I worry about the Germans tracking Jérôme's radio signals. Be careful in Paris, my friend."

———

Lily gazed out the bus window at the lazy farm fields slumbering under a blanket of fresh white snow oblivious to the war all around them. The day would come when that peaceful world would be ripped apart, the smooth, unblemished surface cratered by bombs and foxholes. At some point, two mighty armies would battle here as they had done in the Great War. People were saying it could be this spring, but that might be wishful thinking.

She smiled at Anne sleeping peacefully on the seat beside her. Tension and late nights had exhausted the poor woman, but Lily was grateful Anne had come along. Trying to manage six puppies alone with hand signals and her limited English would have been quite a challenge.

The bus slowed upon entering the city and Anne's eyes fluttered open as it rumbled down the cobblestone streets. She sat up and peered out. "I am sorry. I guess I haven't been such good company."

"I am glad you came. You have such a way with the puppies—they understand you and do what you say."

Anne laughed. "When they get out of line I find a smack on the snout with a rolled up newspaper does the trick. What about your *rebel* puppy? He must be better by now, no?"

"Yes, the veterinarian said he is well enough to travel." Just speaking the words out loud made Lily sad inside. She had been taking care of Bob Grimes for nearly two months—tending his wound—walking with him every evening to strengthen his leg —talking long into the night. It would be hard to let him go.

Anne finessed the six evaders with her usual directness. "Raise your arms please," she commanded in the Queen's English and patted them down from head to toe.

One older mustached fellow raised an eyebrow. "Is this really necessary, Madame?"

"You do not have to submit to this," Anne said matter-of-factly, "but if you do not, this is where your journey ends." She turned to Lily and said in French, "I think they would not mind so much if I was fifteen years younger."

Lily laughed. "They are more embarrassed that you are doing it in front of me. They think I am a child."

Next came the usual questions and when Anne was satisfied, she had them empty their pockets. "You may take with you cigarettes only if they are Belgian. Cigarette lighters are not to be used and there is no smoking on trams. You will each find your own seat. Pretend to sleep or read. If someone talks to you, pretend you are mute. I will sit toward the front of the car and Lily toward the back. When I stand up to leave, you follow. Any questions?"

"Are you English?" one man asked.

"Any other questions?" Anne said without answering him. "Good, then we are off. Follow us singly or in pairs, but not too close. You do not know us."

"*Bonne chance*," Lily said.

Although the return trip went off without any problems, by the time the men had been delivered to their new temporary homes, Lily was exhausted.

Anne walked with her to the tram stop. "We have to get rid of some of these puppies before they get restless."

"I know," Lily said, "but what are we to do? We are moving two groups a week. Hélène's flat is not big enough to take more."

"We will figure something out," Anne promised. "Say hello to the rebel for me."

Lily returned to Hélène's apartment. Little did she know that in less than a week, she and Bob Grimes would be running for their lives.

CHAPTER THIRTY-SEVEN
Saturday, December 18, 1943

Anne felt a gentle hand on her shoulder. "What is bothering you?" Julien's comforting voice broke her reverie. She hadn't been aware she was staring out the window into the darkness. She reached back for his hand to let him know she appreciated his thoughtfulness, but sighed into the black night. "Nothing but this damn war." She turned and offered him a tired *I'll be all right* smile. "This will be our fourth Christmas of the war—four years now with no real Christmas for the children."

"I'm sure they understand."

"Yvonne yes. She is thirteen. But Jacques is only eight. He has never even known a real Christmas."

"We haven't much money left," Julien said," but I think we can afford to buy a few little—"

"I went out this afternoon determined to buy some little toys for him. There was nothing but a few toy soldiers—soldiers in German uniforms with swastikas on their arms! I'll be damned if I will buy such things."

Julien took her hands in his. "The boy will be fine. Children do not need a lot of toys. All they need is their imagination."

Anne conceded with a tip of her head. "I guess you're right." She sighed. "It just brought back memories of my own childhood during the last war. I had no presents for Christmas when I was little either."

"Think of all of the fliers who will have a wonderful Christmas because of your help. Think of the Christmas present Bud's and Lorne's families will receive when we get them home."

Anne laughed. "If they pull another stunt like the other night they'll be spending Christmas in Germany!"

Two nights ago, the drone of airplanes rattled the house. Anne and Julien had rushed out to the balcony to watch seven Spitfires, ascending and diving pursuing a twisting turning Messerschmitt 109. As the fighters swooped in and out, Anne heard shouting from her left. She turned to find the two English pilots poking their heads out of the windows cheering the RAF fighters on. Anne had rushed to the bedroom and pulled the pilots back inside, explaining how their indiscretion could get the whole family arrested. With everyone looking toward the skies, the airmen probably hadn't been seen, but it had kept Anne up all night with worry.

"Well, they will soon be on their way," Julien said. "Let's not take any more in, at least for the holidays."

In his gentle way, Julien was telling her to rest a bit as the doctor had prescribed for her stressed heart. "Yes. I agree," she said, but they both knew she would not turn men away.

The downstairs bell buzzed—three dots and a dash—V for victory in Morse code. Anne looked to Julien. It was the signal of a trusted comrade, but who would be calling this late? It was nearly nine o'clock at night. The children were down in the basement playing ping pong with Bud and Lorne. Hopefully, they had heard the bell and hidden.

Julien went down the lift to answer. "Michou. It is nearly curfew. Is everything all right? Come in."

They rode the lift to the top floor where Anne greeted her with a motherly, "Are you hungry? I have some ham."

"No thank you. May I use your phone?" Michou asked. "I need to make a trunk call."

"Of course," Anne said. But as she listened to Michou, she realized she should have asked the nature of the call. Someone had been arrested —Jeanne Macintosh.

"I hadn't heard from her in days," Michou said, staggering backward upon hanging up. "I knew something must be wrong. That was her aunt. Jeanne and her uncle have been arrested, and the two airmen as well."

"My God!" Julien burst out. "You will bring the entire Gestapo down upon us! Their telephone is surely tapped by the Germans!"

Michou covered her mouth. "I didn't think."

"No," Julien growled, "you didn't think! The police probably left the aunt alone so they could watch her house and listen in on her telephone calls!"

"I-I am so sorry," Michou stammered, trembling in guilt and worry. "All I was thinking about is that Jeanne had my address in her coat pocket."

"All right. It is done," Anne said. "Michou, I suggest you gather your belongings and get yourself and the rebel out of Madame C's as quickly as possible."

Anne put the children to bed and warned Bud and Lorne. "Keep your clothes on and your coats next to you," she said. "Be ready to run out the back if the police come."

Then she set about burning identity papers. She hid her diary under a big flower pot on the balcony, and while Julien scoured the house, Anne checked coat pockets, pocket books, under chair cushions and beds and any other place she could think of. Finally, the curfew left them in the dark with nothing to do but lie in bed worrying.

"I have told Yvonne that if we are ever arrested to contact her grand-parents and Baroness H. I hope she remembers."

"Yvonne is a bright girl. She will know what to do."

At two in the morning, the sound of an automobile on the street below broke the silence. With the curfew, it could be no one but the Germans. Anne reached for Julien's hand. She scarcely breathed.

The doorbell rang.

Anne jumped, her heart in her throat.

Julien released her hand and went down the lift to answer.

The door buzzed angrily once, twice, three, four, five, six times.

Julien opened the door, and was met by agitated Germans. "Why has it taken you so long to open the door?"

"It is the middle of the night," Julien said with annoyance.

Anne kept the door to the flat open a bit, straining to listen, ready to chase the pilots out the balcony if the Germans entered the lift. Abrasive voices snarled at Julien. He argued back. It went on for several minutes. Then the door closed and the hall went quiet. The silence was broken by the metallic squeal of the lift. Anne opened the door when Julien emerged by himself.

"They saw a light on," he said. "They thought it came from our apartment."

———

Was it her imagination, or did the man in the long dark coat and black fedora avert his eyes as she passed him? Lily wanted desperately to look back, but that would only draw attention. She walked on, trying hard not to show emotion, trying to move quickly without running though she felt like a field mouse dodging the shadow of an eagle.

She slipped down the first cross street, quick-stepped halfway to the next block and crouched behind a green Citroën to watch. While her eyes focused on the crowd, her mind mapped out an escape route in case she had to run for it. Her nerves might have gotten the better of her again. The recent arrest of Jeanne and others had her imagining Gestapo agents behind every lamp post, tree and opened newspaper.

Jeanne must be scared out of her wits, Lily thought as she used her mirror to peer around the vehicle. *I haven't even been caught and I'm a wreck.* She drew a deep breath trying to get ahold of herself. She had no time to dwell on such things. Evaders had to be moved and helpers had to be warned.

After one last look, she hurried to the tram stop. But instead of queuing up with the others, she slipped inside a fabric shop until boarding was almost done, then rushed to be the last one on. No one followed. Still, as an extra precaution, she changed trams in center city and made her way to Woluwe-Saint-Pierre on the eastern side of the capitol, taking several evasive turns before reaching Avenue du Val d'Or.

Marie Maca answered her knock. "Michou. Come in. What is wrong?"

"We have some puppies that need a good home. Can you take them?"

"Yes. Of course."

Marie checked the street behind Lily as she ushered the young girl in and closed the door behind her. "Are they with you?"

"No. Can you go to Anderlecht and collect them? I have to get Bob and Hélène out and warn others."

"How bad is it?"

"Jeanne Macintosh has been arrested, her uncle and aunt as well, and two airmen they were sheltering."

"You look shaken. Would you like a drink for your nerves?"

"I am all right. I nearly visited Jeanne and the airmen that day. I could have been there when the Gestapo came to call."

"Tell us where the puppies are and Henri and I will go straight away."

"Number eight Rue des Tournesols. René Pirart is a professor of art at the university. I moved the three men there a week ago when Elie Miroir was arrested." She hated to expose her friends to this danger, but having to scramble again so soon left her no choice but to enlist their help. "When René answers the door, say you have heard that Professor Pirart gives classes in clay. He will say, no, but I know someone who does. If he says yes, or gives you some other answer, it is probably the Secret Police pretending to be René. Once you are sure, tell him Lily says tally ho, and he will bring the puppies to you."

"We will go at once."

Lily hurried off, worrying that she could be sending Marie and Henri into a trap, or that she would walk into one herself. She wanted to take the quickest route to end the suspense, but went a roundabout way looking out for anyone who might be taking a particular interest in her. She felt a stomach-gnawing fear, yet at the same time it was strangely thrilling knowing that the Nazis were so agitated by what she and her comrades were doing that they put the destruction of the underground above almost everything else. Daring to defy the Nazi bastards was exhilarating—scary—but exhilarating.

"Bob, get your *sings* together. We have to move!" she blurted as soon as she entered Madame Camusel's flat. She called Hélène out of the kitchen and spoke so rapidly in French the young pilot stood motionless trying to understand what was happening. "Hélène, we must leave at once. Jeanne Macintosh, Robert and Mary Goffaux and two pilots have all been arrested. Brussels chief, Serment has been burned. Pack what you can quickly. You must leave with us."

Hélène brushed it off with a shake of her head. "No. I will not leave."

"You do not understand," Lily said. "The Gestapo will come here. Jeanne had our address in her pocket. Even if she does not talk, the Germans will find the paper. You must leave."

Lily rushed into the bedroom and jammed skirts, blouses, slacks, sweaters and underclothes into a paper bag. Bob, grasping that they were going on the run, began filling a second bag with her shoes and hats. There was nothing of his to add except his shaving kit.

"I have a valise you can take," Madame Camusel offered.

"Thank you," Lily said, grabbing money from a drawer. She stuffed it in a shoulder bag along with combs, brushes and toiletries. "But we do not want to draw attention. Hurry and get your things. Do not use the valise. Put your clothes and jewelry in bags and Bob and I will help carry them."

"I am not going to leave."

"You must!"

"They will not bother me. I am an old woman. As long as there are no men here, the Gestapo will take no interest."

"Please, Hélène, you must get out."

Hélène shook her head again. "I will be all right."

Hermine was shocked to find Lily and Bob on her doorstep, but seeing their bags, she immediately understood. "You are in trouble," Hermine pulled Michou inside and waved for Bob to follow. "Jeanne," she called for her sister.

Hermine and Jeanne only occasionally took in evaders, so there was little chance they would be on any police or Gestapo list. "It is just for a day or two," Michou said.

"Jeanne," Hermine said when her sister entered the room, "help Bob with their bags while I prepare something to eat. Now, Michou, tell me what has happened."

Michou explained quickly while Hermine scurried around the kitchen pulling meats and cheeses out of the refrigerator. She ushered Michou to a chair and set a cup of hot tea in front of her. "You and Bob can stay here as long as you need. It is so sad about Jeanne."

"Yes. She and the pilot, Frank Andrews, were becoming amorous. And now they are both gone."

Hermine sat down and laid her hand on Michou's. "You are speaking about Jeanne, but you are thinking about yourself and Bob."

"I am going to find an apartment for us. If I do not use it for anything to do with the escape line ... If I can keep it separate from our activities ... maybe Bob can hide there until the end of the war." Michou looked for support in Hermine's face. "It cannot be long now before the Allies come back to the continent, right?"

Hermine nodded, but Michou could tell by her disingenuous smile that she was just agreeing to be kind.

Jeanne led Bob back into the kitchen, chatting happily with him like he was simply a house guest here on holiday instead of a fugitive hiding from the Gestapo. He probably understood very little of her words, but he smiled along with her congeniality.

Jeanne and Hermine kept up the conversation while Bob and Michou ate. But Michou's mind churned with schemes to make it work for her and Bob. By the time they had finished the meal, she had convinced herself that perhaps it was providence shepherding them to their own apartment. Despite the pall of recent events, the adventure of her next move excited her.

In the morning, she and Bob moved their sparse belongings to a small furnished apartment. For the next couple of days, she carried on her underground activities by day and came home to dinner with Bob at night.

Then came the disastrous news—Madame Hélène Camusel had been arrested.

———

Dax, France, December 21, 1943

Franco stood inconspicuously beside the bicycle shed as the train shushed to a stop. Dax wasn't the busy station that Bordeaux was—fewer guards and attendants watching the local trains—but it was still far from safe. Max spilled out with the throng of commuters. Following at a distance were the four evaders—two with more zip than the typically indifferent laborers, a tall man with light-colored hair, and an older-looking fellow with a slow deliberate gait. They were all too easy to recognize as Americans.

Franco observed from a distance as Max passed bicycles to the airmen. Periodically leaving sacks of Spanish delicacies on the desk of the Station Manager, allowed Comet members to collect their bicycles without receipt. The men departed at one-hundred yard intervals with Max leading.

Franco gave them a moment to pedal off, then mounted his bicycle and followed. One of the men glanced back wary of the suspicious bearded man who was following them. Franco pedaled faster and over-took their moderate pace. Surprise filled their faces as he pulled along-side and spoke in his French-accented English, "It is very dangerous here. I will lead."

Once Franco made it to the front, Max dropped back to look after the men from behind. They kept a casual speed through the narrow streets. After several months of using this route, Franco had come to know these streets well; with gas severely rationed, they could blend in among the throng of people pedaling to work. Still, with each trip, his odds of getting caught increased. Only when they passed the edge of the city where the landscape opened up to fields and long distances between houses did he breathe a little easier. But after five minutes of cycling on an open country road two of the airmen began falling behind.

Franco slowed a bit, but the gap remained. Stopping here on this narrow lane flanked by roadside ditches would leave them dangerously exposed should an unfriendly car pass by. He had no choice but to ride on until he found a suitable place to stop. Up ahead, a thin hedge of scrub and trees separated the road from a farm field. He signaled back with a wave and exited the road down a short slope that led to a cart track concealed by the roadside trees.

"I am called Franco," he said when the last two cyclists caught up.

As the men introduced themselves, Franco was surprised to learn that it wasn't Bob Grimes, the man with the leg wound, who had been lagging behind. It was bombardier Lloyd Stanford and co-pilot Jim Burch, crewmates on a B17 Flying Fortress.

American, Art Horning introduced himself with a laugh. "*Ik ben doof.*"

"How's that?" Grimes asked with one raised eyebrow.

"I bailed in the Netherlands and that's about all the Dutch I know." Horning snickered. "It means I'm deaf. Every time I had to figure out how to get somewhere or buy a train ticket or something, I'd go up to some kind-looking person and say, *Ik ben doof*, and point to what I needed and they would help me."

After the men had rested a bit, Franco said, "I know it is difficult for some of you, but we have a long way to go and must keep to our schedule, so you must try to keep up."

Burch somberly nodded agreement.

"We'll do our best," Stanford said.

Franco understood the problem. He and Dédée had discussed it before. After weeks or months of inactivity, hiding in safe houses, the men were out of shape. Still, neither he nor Dédée could understand why they didn't try harder.

Even on these back roads, a procession of bicycles would attract attention of the passing motorists. The sooner they reached Bayonne the better. But despite their promise to try, Burch and Stanford fell behind again.

Franco rode on at a dangerously slow pace. Max pedaled up alongside him. "At this rate we will be lucky to reach Bayonne by nightfall."

Max was exaggerating, but making the next safe house by noon was no longer possible. Franco sighed. "I'm more concerned about the mountain," he said glancing back over his shoulder. It was crucial to cross in one night and be on the Spanish side and far away from the Guardia Civil by dawn.

By the fourth time they had to stop for the pair to catch up Franco could read the annoyance on the faces of the other two airmen, Grimes and Horning. Clearly, they were fed up with the delays as well.

Finally, nearly an hour late, they reached Bayonne and rode through the city to the southern suburb of Sutar. Keeping an eye out for German vehicles, Franco led the airmen to a two-story chalet style building with the white stucco walls and reddish trim and shutters common in the southern region.

"Wait here for my signal." Franco entered by the front door, scanning for Germans.

Marthe Mendiara, owner of the Restaurant Larre, signaled okay with a slight nod. Franco still believed in Dédée and Tante Go's practice of making sure the men were well fed before attempting the mountain crossing. Hearty soup, warm bread and tea fortified the men. They were less than fifteen miles from the border and their spirits were high.

But on this crossing, fate would not be kind.

———

Jacques Desoubrie leaned back in his desk chair, an interrogation transcript in one hand, a cup of coffee in the other, and a smirk on his thin lips. *American pilots,* he *tsked* to himself as he read. *They are so brave miles above us with fifty millimeter cannon at the tip of their thumbs, but become scared little rabbits when face to face with the German Gestapo.* Captain Schnurr said this one had nearly wet his pants before he even touched him. He hadn't even finished setting all the implements of persuasion out when the trembling pilot began stammering out every detail he could think of to save his petrified ass.

Jacques drew a pencil from the drawer and underlined several words. Even when the pilot didn't know the name of the street where he had been taken, he gave enough landmarks that his movements could be followed. Jacques spread out his map. It was just as he suspected.

Now he could pay Comet back for the humiliation. Two weeks after he had boasted how he had shut the line down, the bastards were up and running again. *No one makes a fool out of Jacques Desoubrie,* he thought. He took his plan to his boss.

"Ah Jacques, I have just received word that the last of the agents in the Brandy line was picked up one hour ago."

"Excellent. That should finish them. Now, how would you like to finish Comet?"

Jacques could read the skepticism on his boss's face. Heat rose in his stomach. "They slipped through my hands once. It will *not* happen again. This time I will burn Comet down and blow its ashes to the winds."

"You have located Franco?"

"Not yet. And I am still looking for the Belgian girl that Prosper calls Lily. But I will have them soon."

"How do you know?"

"Look at this," Jacques said using a pencil to point locations out on his map. "The pilots were caught here, here and here. Do you see the pattern? This building is the one the captured airmen have described. I am sure of it. We will set up surveillance here." Jacques tapped the map with his pencil. "And here. Captain Schnurr will squeeze the information out of the airmen like grapes in a press. Then we will have Franco and his entire sector."

"That will take care of Paris, but what about the rest of the Comet line?"

"A snake cannot live with its middle cut out." Jacques broke his pencil in half and held the ends apart. "I underestimated their ability to continue without their chiefs. I will not make that mistake again. This time we will get all of them—every chief—every sub-chief—every group leader—every safe house coordinator. We will do more than just cripple Comet. We will drag them out from every stinking rabbit hole and rub out their footprints so no one can follow."

"And Belgium?"

"Once I have dealt with Paris I will join with Dezitter in Brussels to crush Comet in Belgium."

That evening, Jacques strutted into Jimmy's Bar with a pocket full of money he'd earned for taking down the Brandy escape line. Within minutes three pretty girls were seated beside him laughing and drinking. A few more rounds, he thought, and he'd have his pick. He had the best of all worlds, beautiful girls to take as he pleased and a loving mistress who didn't care if he had some fun to relieve the tensions of his work.

Two girls and a tall, broad Luftwaffe captain with dark hair and greying temples sat down at a nearby table. Jacques smiled to himself at the superior air of the officer. He called the waitress over and sent them a round of drinks.

When the waitress pointed out Jacques, the officer bowed toward his benefactor. "Won't you and your ladies join us, Captain?" Jacques said.

They butted the tables together and Jacques circled his hand in the air to order another round of drinks.

"It's Jacques' twenty-first birthday," a buxom blond informed the officer before planting a kiss on Jacques' cheek.

"Ah youth," the captain said wistfully. "Happy birthday, Jacques," he toasted.

"Long live Germany!" Jacques replied.

"Long live Germany!" The captain drained his glass and ordered another round. They drank and partied until tomorrow became today and the German sloshed into patriotic songs, with a loud robust voice, but virtually no melodic talent.

With a hand on Jacques' shoulder to steady himself, the Luftwaffe Captain wobbled to his feet and staggered toward the men's room like a sailor on a stormy ship. "Shoot straight," Jacques called after him.

When the captain returned, he dragged his chair closer to Jacques. "I have twenty-two kills." He slapped Jacques on the back and laughed with gusto. "I always shoot straight, my friend."

The moment Jacques had waited for had finally come. He chuckled. "Well, when you shoot down those pilots, I find them, arrest them and persuade them to tell me where I can find more. You say you've shot down twenty-two enemy planes? I've captured more than seventy airmen and over three hundred underground enemy helpers. Not even your best ace can beat that!" He took a large swallow of drink to punctuate his bravado.

The captain nodded that it was certainly impressive. Then he broke into a belly laugh and nudged Jacques in the ribs. "But you couldn't capture them if I didn't shoot them down first."

Jacques lifted his glass to toast. "You're right. You knock them out of the sky and I will pick them up." He clinked his glass against the captain's. "And together we will defeat the English and Americans."

As the night wore on Jacques grew heavy headed and bleary eyed.

But a Belgian could not be out-drunk by a German. He forced his hazy mind to focus. "So, Captain, tell me, how did you shoot down so many planes?"

"Patience," the Captain said tipsily acting out sitting behind the controls of a plane. "We wait in the sun for the pigeons to come to us. With the sun in their eyes, they cannot see us until—*brrrrrrr*," he mimicked the firing a machine gun.

"As long as you shoot straight," Jacques quipped.

"That's right." The captain laughed heartily and drained his glass.

Jacques sat straight up. His mind cleared. "Captain, you have given me an idea! I know now how I will capture all of the underground helpers in Belgium."

CHAPTER THIRTY-EIGHT
December 22, 1943

After spending the night in the cellar of the Restaurant Larre, the airmen mounted their bicycles and followed Franco and Max through the meadow across the street to a narrow dirt path along the murky River Nive. Although this route was less direct, grey fallow fields and pastures separated the trail from the roads which made it a little safer for escaping airmen.

Storm clouds gathered. Franco set a modest pace hoping to reach the paved road a few miles down before the impending rain turned the dirt to mud, but once again Stanford and Burch began falling behind. Franco dropped back. As Grimes and Horning passed him, Grimes grumbled, "I hope we don't have to keep to a tight schedule with those two."

"It will be all right." Although he was frustrated himself, Franco didn't feed their discontent. Coordination and cooperation were essential. An attitude of *if they can't keep up it's their problem* could jeopardize the entire escape line if airmen were separated and left behind. Dédée had regarded the airmen as children, saying it was up to the helpers to keep them on task. He slowed to ride beside the stragglers.

"How are you doing?"

Burch nodded okay and pedaled faster, but his pained face said he was having great difficulty.

Burch was the oldest man in the group, but not so old that he should be so out of shape. Franco worried about the difficult mountain trek ahead. The ground would be wet and muddy, the air would be thin, the weather harsh and unpredictable. The uphill hike would be exhausting. But Comet was making two crossings a week now, delivering more than forty airmen, military operatives, and French and Belgian fugitives each month. They had no choice but to push on.

They left the trail just north of Herauritz, and reached Usteritz fifteen minutes later. The pedaling grew more strenuous on the uphill grades of the foothills. Burch and Stanford fell farther behind. Franco led them to a farm north of Espelette, and laying his bicycle against the wall motioned the men inside the barn. "We will rest here a while."

The old stone building stank of horse, hay and leather, but the men were too beat to care about its aroma. Burch, lay back with a slight grimace and closed his eyes. Stanford stretched out his leg muscles then collapsed down on a mound of straw near Burch. Bob Grimes rubbed the soreness out of his wounded upper thigh. While the men rested, Franco went up to the house and returned with Denise Houget and a platter of sandwiches.

Food restored the men's energy and they were swapping stories of their last missions when the clatter of a wood-fueled truck engine interrupted them.

Max peeked out. It was just the local baker who had come to take him and the bicycles back to Bayonne. "*Bonne chance*, my friends. *Au revoir.*"

Late afternoon, Franco and Denise gathered the men in a circle. "We will be crossing a bridge guarded by Germans. You will follow Denise. Walk casually. Slouch like you are tired after a long day's work. If you are stopped, show your papers, but do not speak."

Denise held the men just before the bridge over the River La Nivelle to let Franco go ahead. Smiling with one hand casually in his pocket, Franco strolled right up to the German private posted at the entrance to the bridge. "*Bonsoir, comment allez-vous?*"

"*Ça va*," the private replied.

"Have you been in the army long?" Franco continued in French.

The German seemed to be mentally counting, remembering his French numbers. "Thirteen months," he said proud to show the French he knew.

"I wanted to join the army," Franco said slowly, "but I did not pass the physical exam. I guess it is best that I did not."

The German nodded along delighted with himself for understanding. "Yes, it is good that you did not."

Franco kept up the conversation until the last of the airmen had passed. In a world where nearly everyone hated you, a pleasant conversation was welcomed by the young soldier far from his home. "It must be tiring having to stand here for hours."

The German shrugged. "It is not so bad."

"Well, I do not envy you, my friend. Have a good evening. *Bonsoir.*"

Denise had already led the men across the bridge and down the hill to the three-story Basque chalet style house of Kattalin Aguirre. Franco greeted the stout, silver-haired woman who opened the door.

Kattalin let him inside shaking her head in annoyance. "There are too many men. Three others are already here." Fiery hands punctuated her exasperation as she spoke. "So many men in my house will draw attention. I cannot have this!"

"I am sorry, Kattalin," Franco said, "but what else can we do? Two are taking intelligence information to the English and Americans. *Cartier* is going with me to meet with the British Consul."

"You must bring smaller groups," Kattalin said.

"There are only four airmen," he said apologetically. "I cannot take less than that. More are already on the way down here."

Kattalin stirred a pot on the stove, her face sour. "It is too many—too risky." She threw up her hands as she turned around and shot at him again. "If we are caught by the Germans, we will not save four men. We will save no men."

After the arrest of Frantxia, Franco wouldn't have blamed her if she wanted to quit, but she was too valiant to run from the fight. Taking better care not to expose her was the least he could do. "I am sorry," Franco said. And he meant it.

Kattalin relented with a sigh. She had made her point.

Franco hung his coat on a hook by the door. "You have papers for me to take, no?"

Kattalin wiped her hands on her apron, left the room and returned with a small flour sack. She poured out some flour into a bowl, then reached into the sack and pulled out a pouch of papers. "We have Christmas presents for the Allies," she said as Franco peeked inside. "Maps, locations of artillery, bunkers, photographs of new German weapons, armored vehicles…"

Franco looked questioningly at a photograph of two smiling German soldiers.

Kattalin pointed out the beach obstacles in the background of the photo and laughed. "A little girl took these. The stupid Germans never even suspected she had a camera inside her coat. She has taken many pictures of German defenses in that way."

"Very clever," Franco said, "but very dangerous for the girl."

"We have details of German camps, aerodromes, estimates of troop strength, location of telephone lines…"

"And this?" Franco asked pulling out a picture drawn in pencil.

"A German SS insignia. The Allies will copy it for their agents."

"You have been a busy lady. Our friends will certainly be pleased with their presents."

Kattalin smiled proudly as she stirred the pot. "I hope the English and Americans deliver a big present to the Germans soon." She called up the stairway, "Fifine."

Her fifteen-year-old daughter came down and after filling bowls for the visitors, Kattalin handed a bowl to Fifine with instructions in Euskara.

Franco didn't understand the Basque language, but did catch one word. "You said something about Florentino?" he asked in French.

"He is in bed with influenza." Kattalin handed Franco a loaf of bread and a serrated-edged knife. "I have already sent for other guides."

The thought of taking so many men over the mountain without the number one guide worried Franco as much as the number of men had worried Kattalin. The rain and fog would make the mountain especially treacherous. He mulled it over during lunch, but there was no other option. Not going would be certain disaster.

By the time Franco finished helping Kattalin with the dishes, Stanford and Burch were already asleep. He sat down with his glass of wine next to his old friend Antoine d'Ursel—*Jacques Cartier*. A mustachioed man in his fifties with a long face and bags under his eyes, Antoine had served as chief of the Brussels sector until he became too hot. He was now on his way to Spain to work out an escape line with the British to evacuate underground members like himself who were wanted by the Gestapo.

Daniel Mouton, real name Albert Ancia, a heavy fellow with a broad smile strolled over by Grimes and Horning. "You are *Americain*, no?" he asked in heavily accented English. "In what State do you *leeve*?"

"I'm from Virginia," Grimes said.

"Ohio," Horning said. "What part of France are you from?"

Daniel laughed. "I am not French. *Je suis Belge*. We are all *Belge*—Cartier, Franco and myself."

"The Belgian people have been very good to me," Grimes said. "I owe them my life."

"Ah *très bien*." Daniel offered a jovial smile. "*Zare* are over seven *Sousand* in *za* Résistance and underground, but if Jacques, Franco and I were ever taken … eeee." Daniel rattled a hand in the air. "Comet would be *fini*." Daniel delighted in the Americans' attention. "I have escaped from *za* Germans *zree* times—once from a moving train car. You will tell your friends *zat* many of us are helping, no?"

"Yes, sir, I sure will," Grimes said. "We will never forget what your people have done for us."

"Especially the girl on the train!" Horning added with a suggestive grin. He let them wonder a moment before explaining, "There was some mix-up with my French identity papers, so this dark blond girl with the most gorgeous blue eyes sat on my lap and made out with me all the way to Paris. I had to keep reminding myself that it was just an act." Horning closed his eyes, inhaling deeply. "I can still smell her sweet perfume." He opened his eyes, and grinned. "Man! I had all I could do to keep my hands to myself! No sir, I'm not going to forget *my* helpers—especially *Diane!*"

In the morning, Franco tucked the intelligence packet under the clothes in his backpack as Kattalin wished each fugitive *bonne chance*. Crossing the mountains with such a large conspicuous group without Florentino, would be challenging, but they could not delay without endangering the next group. The big man had tried to get out of bed to lead the party, but Kattalin pushed him back down and threatened to come back with the rolling pin if he tried to get up again.

Franco blessed himself, kissed his crucifix and fell in behind guides Manuel and Ramon. A cold mist blurred house and village lights as they worked their way up dirt roads and farm fields into the foothills. Even though he had taken this route before, Franco had to reach out blindly for the man in front of him as the woods plunged them into near total darkness.

As they left the woods and followed a narrow path through an open meadow. Franco tuned in to the dull footfalls, the jingle of cow's bells and the bleating of sheep, listening for anything that might sound out of place, trying to compensate for not having Florentino who always had a sixth sense about German patrols.

Breathing grew heavier as the slope rose. Unseen tree branches slapped their faces. Slopes of loose rubble scraped up palms, shins and legs. The mist turned to a light rain that slickened the trail further. Stanford had to help Burch back to his feet several times.

Breaking near the peak, the men struggled out of their backpacks and ate sandwiches and drank the wine that Kattalin had packed for them. "Going down to the river the ground will be slippery," Franco advised while he checked their alpargatas. "Use your walking sticks to keep from tumbling down. You must be very quiet. Spanish border guards will shoot if they hear a noise."

He assessed Burch's haggard face. "Are you all right?"

Burch nodded.

"We're good," Stanford said speaking for both of them.

"Just a little longer." Franco patted Burch's leg.

A slight grimace and a fabricated smile was Burch's only response.

Slowly, carefully, they felt their way down to the rushing water of the Bidassoa. Manuel and Ramon crept ahead to the river and reported back. Franco, holding a hand just above his waist translated. "The water is this deep. The current is strong. Take off your trousers and tie one leg around your neck. Hold onto the loose leg of the person ahead of you to form a chain."

The river was normally only seventy-five feet wide, but water stampeding down the canyon chased by mountain rains had swelled the stream to nearly twice its size. Manuel went first, followed by Horning and Ramon. Franco sent Richard, Grimes and Stanford next. Then he sent Burch in with the sturdy Mouton to anchor him, and he and Antoine d'Ursel slipped in behind them.

The plunge into the frigid water always took his breath away. But there was no time to ease in like an old lady at a swimming pool. Struggling to keep his own balance, he tried to steady d'Ursel.

Thrashing erupted mid-river. Franco strained to see only *Richard* Roland Bru, a Résistance fighter still standing. Then Stanford surfaced and slogged to the shallower water on the Spanish side. Grimes, emerged grabbing onto Richard's coat, but before Grimes had fully regained his footing, Burch lost his. The pilot flailed at the water, grabbing the leg of the trouser tied around Daniel Mouton's neck, but he couldn't hold on. Daniel lunged after him.

Franco watched helplessly, too far away to do anything.

Daniel grasped the pilot's clothing and dragged him back up to the shallow water near the French bank. He stayed there a moment letting Burch catch his breath. The pilot looked exhausted, but nodded that he was ready to give it another go. Daniel waded out, even more slowly and carefully than before.

Franco waited with d'Ursel until Daniel and Burch reached the middle. He'd only taken a step or two when he again heard splashing and this time Burch's yells for help. Daniel dove after him and managed to grab a bit of the pilot's coat, but he couldn't hold on. Both men disappeared under water. Daniel struggled up for air. The thrashing continued downstream. Daniel swam toward him, but this time there was no catching up to the pilot.

Prowng! A rifle report echoed off the canyon walls, then another and another. One round zipped into the water somewhere in the darkness. Bullets whizzed through the brush along the French river bank. "Wait here!" Franco called to d'Ursel. He waded across, and ducked down with the men crouching on the far bank. "Ramon," he said, "take the men up to the road. Manuel, you go back and bring d'Ursel across. I will wait here for you."

Manuel disappeared into the darkness. Franco waded a few steps in making ready to help Manuel when the two neared.

Prowng! Prowng! Two more shots rang out. d'Ursel screamed. Franco waded farther into the water, listening for sounds from his friends. He heard splashing, gurgling and cries for help, but could make out just one head. Then more of the body emerged as the man reached the shallower water. It was Manuel. Franco took another step and grabbed an arm. Chest heaving, Manuel made it to the side and with Franco's help climbed onto the bank where he lay on his forearms and knees catching his breath. He shook his head side to side and pointed downstream.

Franco slipped off his rucksack and handed it to Manuel. "Give this to Richard. Tell him if I am not back in a few minutes to go on without me. I'm going back to look for d'Ursel." He waded across to the shallows on the French side and whistled a bird call. Climbing onto the bank, his wet body and bare legs numbed by the cold air, he whistled again. His eyes searching the land and water, he hurried downstream, periodically pausing to whistle and listen. There was no reply.

Franco replayed the scream in his mind, trying to determine whether his friend had been shot or just startled. He worried that he had overestimated d'Ursel's physical ability. Although not as strong as when he was a young man serving as a soldier in Southeast Asia, d'Ursel was still a determined and courageous figure. But Dédée wouldn't let Paul cross under similar weather conditions. Franco wondered if he should have told d'Ursel to wait back at Kattalin's. But neither he nor the guides knew how high the river was until they got here, and once here, the decision was made to cross. Franco shook it off remembering how Dédée hated when people second guessed themselves. He slogged back upstream and over to the Spanish side whistling at intervals in case d'Ursel had managed to cross on his own. As he stood in the dark considering what to do next, there came a whistle. Franco sent his bird call into the wind once more. A response came from the French side, and tired but relieved, he slipped back into the water and waded across.

When he found his friend, the man was shaking uncontrollably. "Malaria," d'Ursel explained. "From my days in the jungle."

"We will go back to Kattalin's and cross in a few days," Franco said.

"No. I will be all right. The shakes will pass."

It wasn't just the shivering—the man looked exhausted. "The water will be lower in a few days," Franco said. "It will be easier then."

"No. We go tonight!"

"One of the pilots has disappeared. I do not want to risk losing you, too."

"Tonight," d'Ursel said firmly. "I am not going back. Either you go with me, or I will go by myself. But, I am going to Spain tonight!"

The two men plunged back into the swift current. They reached to mid-calf, then waist level. Another two steps and they were in over their mid-sections. One more step and Franco felt a tug on the trousers around his neck, then nothing. Franco lunged after d'Ursel, but came up empty. There was no sign of him. Franco swam to the Spanish side and frantically whistled. Nothing. He repeated it several times working his way downstream. He crossed back over to the French side and continued his call.

Lights appeared on the Spanish side. They were not shining toward the river, but toward the roadway. Had the Spanish Guardia caught the group? To the east, the sky was now a faint grey. Dawn was nearing. If he stayed here, he would be caught as well. Franco had no choice but to stop his search and go back to Kattalin's.

Before Franco even finished telling what had happened, Florentino was pulling on his pants and issuing a stream of expletives. He cursed himself for being talked into sending Manuel and Ramon in his place.

Franco wanted to go back with him, but they all knew he could not. While Florentino was hiking into the mountains, Franco would be on the train to Bordeaux to meet the next group.

———

Prosper had a good idea why he had been summoned to Abwehr headquarters. Rudolf Kohl, his boss, had been quite busy interrogating the Allied fliers Prosper had delivered to him. Prosper's brainchild, the phony escape organization, had netted more than a dozen Allied airmen. By now, Kohl had probably questioned the last group he had turned in. He only wished he could have seen the loathing on their faces at having been so fooled. Prosper couldn't wait to hear if Kohl had been amused by his latest con which Prosper considered positively genius. Sometimes Prosper even amazed himself.

After the formalities of the Heil Hitler greeting when Kohl entered, Prosper asked with anticipation, "So, *Kommandant*, did the enemy airmen tell you about the letters?"

"Letters?"

Prosper had to stop himself from laughing so he could speak. "You always enjoy when the enemy shows their stupidity. I provided pen and paper to the last group of airmen and told them to write to their families that they were safe in Switzerland and I would post the letters for them. Then I took the letters back to show the safe house keepers to convince them that my escape line was real."

"That *is* amusing." Kohl shifted papers on his desk and found the one he wanted.

"Jacques Desoubrie has thought up a good plan as well," Prosper said. "After he has vanquished the Paris sector, he will continue to collect airmen in Brussels and take them to Paris as if nothing has happened—"

Kohl held up his hand. "I am sure you and Desoubrie have great plans for capturing airmen, but that is not why I sent for you. The General has demanded that we catch the organizers of the escape line, not merely the airmen who ride along it. You have located a number of hosts, but I am not looking for house-keepers—I want the leaders. We will make examples of them. Catching the big fish will scare all the little fish away once they learn that they cannot hide from us."

Kohl handed the paper to Prosper. "I want you to go to this address. We have observed enemy airmen following a little girl of about thirteen or fourteen. She is often seen in a blue coat and skipping rope or playing with a ball or hoop."

"You want us to bring her in for questioning?"

"No. I want you find out whom she reports to. If after two days she has not led us to her boss, we will pick her up and *persuade* the information out of her."

———

Lily crossed the street for a better look. There were at least two, and she was pretty sure she had spotted a third. Sure enough, a man in a dark trench coat and grey fedora ducked behind a building corner. That made three guardian angels.

A knot suddenly twisted in her stomach—four fake identity cards were hidden in the left sleeve of her coat. So far, the angels were just following her, but she couldn't take the chance. If caught with forged papers she could not talk her way out of it. The problem wasn't getting them out: the lining had been sewn so she merely had to pull a thread to unravel it. She had to get rid of the cards without being seen.

The cold winter weather narrowed her options. Crowds were thin and there were no fruit and vegetable carts, no street vendors. She regarded the trash bins outside the food market. But if she so much as paused there, the Germans would have the bins thoroughly searched. Then again, she thought, maybe the trash bins would help after all.

Down the street was a newsstand and two blocks farther a sandwich shop with counter service. Her first step would be to make an obvious stop beside the market and make like she was throwing something into the trash bin. Hopefully that would keep one of the Germans busy, leaving only two to shake.

After playing out the scene at the garbage can, she strolled on to the newsstand. One hand reached for a magazine while the other palmed the identity cards and slipped them in the back of the rack. The whole con took mere seconds. She paid for the magazine and continued on to the café.

Once inside, she peeked through the curtains. Two of the trench-coated men met up across the street. One headed toward the café, leaving no doubt that she was the one they hunted.

She bought a sandwich and soda at the lunch counter and carried it to a small round table. With unhurried movements, she draped her coat on the back of the chair, laid open the magazine on the table and began to read. The man in the trench coat entered and bought a sandwich too, then sat down near the door behind an opened newspaper. Leisurely turning magazine pages, she stole an occasional peek. She found it rather amusing that the man by the door had no more idea of what was in that newspaper than she had about the magazine she pretended to read.

Lily took another unhurried bite and turned the page. When she sipped her drink, she let a bit of soda spill from the straw onto her blouse. She dabbed it with her napkin, but a dark spot remained. Leaving her coat on the chair and her sandwich on the plate, she went back to the ladies room as if to further clean her blouse. Once inside, she locked the door and opened the window. There was no time to be modest. She slipped off her skirt so it wouldn't snag, dropped it to the ground and followed it out. She landed in the loading area behind the buildings and pulled her skirt back on. That's when she noticed a young man of maybe sixteen looking on with interest from the back of a truck he was unloading.

She laid a finger to her lips. *"Ssshhh."*

The kid nodded, probably thinking she was running out on paying the bill.

She strode away until she reached the next street then took off at a run.

Before reaching Anne's flat, Lily circled the entire block to make sure she wasn't followed then rang the bell with her three dots and a dash.

"Well, my friend," Anne said when Lily completed her story, "it is definitely time for you to leave Belgium."

CHAPTER THIRTY-NINE

A few of the prisoners tried to make light of their situation. Some silently battled their fears in the claustrophobic rail car that was carrying them to their grim future. The rest, like Elsie and Madame Maréchal, sat impassively on the hard wooden floor with their backs to the walls bumping and swaying numbly with the movement of the train. From the stench, it was obvious they had not been the first to take this trip.

Three men crowded the small high window near the back of the car, gulping in the cold January air and calling out the town names they passed. Wherever they were going no longer mattered to Elsie. It made no difference where the Germans carried out the death sentence on her and her mother.

She had been told that her father died bravely and that all eight men taken to Tir National Rifle Range in October refused blindfolds and looked their executioners in the eye, shouting, "Long live Belgium!" She imagined herself standing in front of the firing squad when her time came. She would hold her head high. She wouldn't give the bastards the satisfaction of thinking she feared them.

"Do you think Robert got my message?" her mum asked. "I hope he didn't waste money on food for us."

Elsie touched her mother's arm. She knew it wasn't about the food. After months of listening every Friday for the names of those to be deported to Germany, theirs were finally called. Her mother had slipped a note out with a guard, hoping to see Robert one more time before they were taken away. But the only hope left now was that he had received her note—her final goodbye. Elsie squeezed her mother's hand. "Robert is going to be fine, Mum."

Her mother squeezed back. "Do you want to lay your head in my lap? These walls must be hurting you."

Her mum was right. No matter how she tried to lean to one side or the other, and no matter how she tried to bunch up her coat to cushion her back, there was no way to sit without pain. The welts where the Nazi clubs had gashed her skin had never fully healed.

The train slowed then stopped. "Namur," the lookout announced.

Another man at the window added, "It is just a passenger stop."

"I don't suppose they will let us out to use the toilet," a woman said.

"That bucket in the corner is our toilet," said another woman. "Forget your modesty. Do what you have to do..."

"Elsie ... Mum ..." came distant calls from outside the window.

"... we will look away," the woman continued. "Civility is not in the German..."

"*Ssshhh*," Madame Maréchal swung her arm through the air, cutting the woman off as she sprang to her feet.

Elsie jumped up with her and they pushed their way to the window. Elsie stood on tip-toes to see. "Up there!" she said to her mother. "Robert!" she yelled out the window.

The boy was running toward the front of the train and couldn't hear them. He must have gotten into one of the passenger cars before the train left Brussels. Upon reaching the front, he turned and started back, still calling out. Elsie could see a package in his hand. "Over here!" she shouted.

The train bumped to a start.

"Robert! We are over here!"

The train gained speed, Robert chasing after it.

Elsie and her mom watched as Robert ran after the train trying desperately to get back on. It was no use. They watched until they could no longer see him.

————

The clock in the plaza displayed five-forty-five, time to walk back to the Bayonne train station where Max said Franco would be meeting the six o'clock train from Dax. Lily looked for the dark bearded man with a terrible boil on his neck whom Max had described. Shuffling in the shadows trying to make out features, she spotted a woman standing near the bicycle shed who looked familiar. It was Tante Go.

"Lily!" Tante Go said in shock. "What are you doing here? Is something wrong?"

"I am burned in Brussels. I've come to find Franco. Is he here?"

"Yes. That is him walking this way."

"Hello, Franco. I am Lily. I saw you at the restaurant this afternoon, but I didn't know it was you."

Franco's forehead scrunched as if he were trying to recall if he saw her. "Max did not tell me how I was to recognize you."

"I was sitting on the bench next to the restaurant."

"We are cycling down to Sutar," Franco said. "We can talk there. But since I didn't know you would be here, I do not have enough bicycles. You will have to ride on the handlebars of mine. It is only a twenty minute ride."

When the train arrived, Max had only two airmen with him. "We lost one," he said. "He was escorted off the train when he could not answer in French."

Franco turned to Lily. "It seems we have a bicycle for you now."

When they reached the safety of Restaurant Larre and were seated for dinner, Tante Go asked what had happened in Brussels.

Lily leaned in and spoke softly to Franco and Tante Go. "My friend, Jeanne Macintosh and her uncle were arrested. A week later, the Gestapo picked up Hélène Camusel, the woman I had been staying with. I had to shake some guardian angels and have not stayed more than a single night in any one place since." She and Madame Anne had organized new safe houses and guides. Then Michou had spoken to Brussels chief, Jean Serment, and told him she was burned and had to leave Belgium. "He said I may leave, but first I must write down the names and addresses of all of my contacts. I told him I will not do that. If that paper was found, everyone would be arrested. He said I must or he would not let me leave."

Tante Go's fork stopped midway between her plate and her mouth, clearly bothered by what she was hearing. Franco, with raised eyebrows, had stopped eating as well.

"Writing down everyone's name is crazy," Lily said. "Is it not? We will all be caught if we do not use common sense."

Tante and Franco glanced at each other, concerned.

"I left without telling him. I went to Jérôme in Paris and he sent me here to find Max."

"You did the right thing." Tante Go patted Michou's arm. Then she spoke bluntly to Franco. "Someone needs to talk to Serment. We cannot have a chief making such stupid decisions."

Franco nodded. "I will speak to him. Jérôme and I are going up to Brussels in a couple of days to see what we can do to bolster the northern sector." Franco's voice grew somber. "While I am there, I will go personally to d'Ursel's family to tell them what happened."

"Antoine d'Ursel?" Lily asked. "What happened to him?"

"You have not heard?" Tante Go sighed. "He drowned in the Bidassoa."

Lily covered her mouth and gasped.

Franco nodded that it was true. "The night before Christmas, we tried to cross the river between the mountains, but it was too high and fast. Antoine and an American pilot were swept away. I searched and searched but couldn't find them …" He choked up recalling that awful night.

Tante Go took over. "The Germans found the bodies and displayed them under guard in the village of Biriatu as a warning to others. But instead of fear, the villagers showed their defiance, paying tribute with pine boughs and blankets of flowers."

"The American pilot …" Lily hesitated, the worry in her throat making it difficult to even ask … but she had to know. "What was his name?"

"Burch," Franco said. "Jim Burch. He had been lagging behind the whole trip. We thought he was a slacker. It wasn't until after he died that his crew mate, Stanford, explained that Burch was suffering from a severe bone bruise. The man was determined to hide it and press on. Stanford told the British Consul he didn't know how Burch had managed to walk at all."

Lily could hear Franco speaking, but his words dissolved in the air before reaching her consciousness. She closed her eyes and breathed a sigh of relief. Bob Grimes was safe. Slowly, she let the images of Grimes drift away as she tuned back in to Franco.

"… and when Legrelle and I return from Brussels we will figure out where to fit you in the organization—maybe you can guide evaders to the south. In the meantime, you can stay with Tante Go."

———

January 17, 1944

"We have done what we can to fortify the line." *Jérôme* broke off a bite of biscuit thinking aloud. "But we'll need to recruit more hosts, guides and helpers to move all the men piled up in Belgium."

Franco set his coffee cup down and sat back. "With the Allies bombing night and day, the numbers just keep growing. The faster we can get the fliers back into the air, the faster this war will be over."

"We shouldn't chance crossing the border by rail anymore even though it is faster. The Germans are on every train …" Jérôme broke off another bite, but stopped short of his mouth. "—Then again getting off before the border and hiking overland takes longer … and crossing so many men on foot puts strain on our guides. The customs agents working for us are already taking far greater risks than they should.

Franco laughed at him.

"What?"

"I was just thinking of what Dédée would have said to you."

"About what?"

"About your second-guessing yourself. She hated indecision. She drummed it into me that such thinking was a waste of time. She believed you should make your decision based on what you know and trust that doing something is always better than indecision."

"It sounds like she would have made a good army officer."

"If she had been a general, the Belgian army would not have surrendered in eighteen days. To her impossible simply means you have to work a little harder at it."

"I wish I could have met her."

"Be careful with your wishes, my friend." Franco sipped his coffee. "You and I are surely known to the Secret Police, and if our people do not start using more sense, we may all meet her sooner than we would like."

"MI9 knows that I am burned as well. Neave has summoned me back to England." Jérôme shrugged. "I would have been called back in another two months anyway. They only allow their agents to do six months at a time."

"Have you thought about how you will use Lily?"

"Housing chief, Henri Crampon, will take over the Paris sector while I am gone. Maybe Lily can help Max move men to the south."

"I was thinking the same thing. And now, my friend, you had better leave or you will miss your train. After I visit with d'Ursel's family, I'll meet you in Paris."

"Good day, Madame Crampon." The tall, fair-haired man in a dark trench coat spoke in a pleasant tone. Then he flashed his badge. "German Secret Police," he said.

Her face went pale.

The man stepped forward scanning the apartment as he spoke. "We would like to talk to you about your husband."

"My husband is not here." She moved aside so as not to be knocked down by him or the agent who followed. "What do you want with my husband?"

"No. He is not here. He is our guest at the moment."

Madame Crampon reached down with one hand to comfort the tot who had scampered to her side and latched onto her skirt for security. "Why do you have my husband? He has done nothing wrong."

The German smirked. "Come now, Madame. We know your husband is involved with the escape organization, Comet." His gaze fell upon the woman's belly. "You have a young child … and another on the way, I see…"

Madame Crampon said nothing, waiting to see what the man was leading up to.

"You do not want them to grow up without a father…"

Fear filled her eyes, but she remained silent.

"Your husband's life is in your hands."

"What do you want me to do?"

"Nothing." He gestured for her to proceed to the living room. "Take a seat. There is nothing to do but wait." He remained silent until she was settled down. "Take care of your child, Madame."

While the first agent spoke, the second wandered unhurriedly through the apartment, checking rooms, opening closet doors, and looking in cabinets.

"Now, some rules, Madame. If someone knocks, you will not make a sound. We will answer the door. You will not go near any windows. If the telephone rings, you will answer it. You will do nothing to tip off the caller, whether it is Jérôme, Franco, Cartier or whomever…" He watched her face grow paler. "Yes, Madame, we know their names. Your husband has been most cooperative … Now, whoever calls, you will speak normally, and you will assure them that all is right here. There will be no coughing, no inflection in your voice, no hesitation—If you do anything to give us away, your husband will not live to see another sunrise."

More than an hour passed before the phone rang. The German held the receiver down and warned her with one finger before letting her pick it up. His eyes burned into her.

"Hello? Yes—yes it is all right." She returned the receiver with a quiver like she wanted to pick it up again and shout a warning.

"Jérôme?" the agent asked. She didn't speak, but her eyes betrayed her. "It does not matter, Madame, my agents are already there."

Franco felt a gnawing in his stomach. The d'Ursel family had thanked him for trying to save Antoine, but he still couldn't forgive himself for not making his old friend go back to France with him. He knew the river much better than Antoine. As chief of the entire line, he thought he should not have let himself be swayed.

But there was something else that was bothering him—a foreboding that he couldn't shake. Franco tried reading the newspaper to take his mind off it, but it was no use. The barren winter landscape out the train window merely added to the gloom.

He shuffled out of the train with the crowd at the Paris station. It was the one-year anniversary of Dédée's capture and the one-year anniversary of his taking charge of the Comet line. He told everyone who joined that they had six months at best. His number should have been up long ago. It was probably just his imagination getting the better of him, he thought. But just in case, he didn't go directly home. Instead, he took the precaution of telephoning the flat of Henri Crampon.

"Yes," Madame Crampon said, "everything is all right."

Jacques Desoubrie, or *Pierre Boulain* as he was now known, entered the interrogation room and dragged a chair up close to the naked figure whose ankles were tied to his thighs and head submerged in a tank of water. A big German interrogator lifted the man's head out of the water by the hair and slapped him on the back, where a whip had ripped his flesh. The man cried out in agony, coughing and sputtering out water.

Pierre allowed the man a moment to recover before speaking to him. "Hello, Monsieur Legrelle, or should I call you Jérôme?"

The interrogator held Legrelle up by the hair and pointed him toward Boulain.

"Do you know who I am?"

Legrelle's face was bruised black and blue where he had been pummeled. Water ran down his face. Snot dripped from his nostrils. His eyes were swollen, but he managed to open them a bit.

"I am Pierre Boulain, one of your trusted guides," Desoubrie said merrily. "It is I who betrayed all of you. I am also Jean Masson, the one who betrayed Monsieur de Jongh last year and captured over two hundred of your friends."

Desoubrie sniggered at Legrelle. This Belgian trained army officer—

a British-trained agent—the head of the entire Paris sector of Comet was completely at his mercy. The pathetic figure was still dripping and breathing through his mouth, but Desoubrie could virtually feel the hatred rising in the man.

Desoubrie laughed. "You think that because you have been taught by the British you can outsmart me. I do not have such training, but I have outsmarted you. You will eventually talk. Save yourself more beatings. Tell us what we need to know. You say you are not the leader of the organization?"

"No. I am not the leader."

"Then who is?"

"Antoine d'Ursel."

"And where is d'Ursel?"

"Dead. He drowned crossing the river into Spain. You can go check if you'd like."

"What else can you tell me about the line?"

"My name is Jacques Legrelle. I am a lieutenant in the Belgian army."

"Tell me about Monsieur Crampon."

"My name is Jacques Legrelle. I am a lieutenant in the Belgian army."

"Give me Franco's address."

"Only d'Ursel knows where Franco lives."

"If you think your stubbornness will spare the others, you are wrong. We have agents at the homes of the dozens we have in custody. Sooner or later, Franco will contact one of them and then we will have him too. Comet in Paris is finished, and soon I will have Brussels and the south as well." Desoubrie stood up "Now, if you will excuse me, there are more of your friends I have to meet."

CHAPTER FORTY
January 18, 1944

Franco paused outside Jérôme's flat on rue de Longchamps, though still not sure what was making him uneasy. He rang the bell. The door flew open and a stone-faced German smiled with satisfaction, leveling a revolver at Franco's chest. "Hello, Franco. It is nice to finally meet you."

At Gestapo headquarters, guarded and strapped to a chair, Franco offered up a silent prayer that he might be given the strength to withstand the coming interrogation without revealing anything important.

A well-dressed man entered the room and marched up to Franco. Removing his gloves and overcoat like it was just another day at the office, the man manifested the aura of being an expert at his trade.

Franco kept his head up, bolstering his nerve to present an unfazed façade. The Nazi may have been well-groomed, wearing a custom-tailored suit, but he was nothing more than a thug. Franco took a closer look at his silk necktie and began to chuckle.

"Why are you laughing, Franco? Perhaps you do not understand how bad this is for you."

Franco knew full well what it meant to be in the hands of the Gestapo, but seeing his favorite tie—the one he had searched for when Paul was arrested—around the neck of this stylish dresser, was too amusing for him to stop grinning.

———

It was a long drive from the mountains down to Madrid and Lily wasn't quite sure what to expect. She'd imagined the British vice-Consul to be a stoic, formal, English officer. But *Monday* presented no air of self-importance as he greeted the Comet trio with the enthusiasm of a fan meeting cinema stars.

"I know Elvire and Max, so you must be Lily," he said warmly as he pumped her hand and kissed her on both cheeks. "How was the drive? It is rather long."

"I enjoyed the scenery," Lily said. "It is nice not having to look around swastikas to see the buildings."

"I can only imagine how terrible it must be to live under Nazi occupation. You are a very brave woman to do what you do."

Her short stature and sweet high voice often made people dismiss her as being too young. She appreciated Monday's words of respect. "We do what we must," she said modestly.

Monday kissed Elvire's cheeks and Max's as well and led them down to a glass-enclosed terrace with tiled walls and terra cotta floors. He motioned toward a wrought iron table with loaves of bread, meats and cheeses. "I hope you don't mind eating here. It is only sandwiches, but I thought it best that we keep our conversations private."

"Sandwiches are fine," Tante Go answered for all.

Lily nodded agreement. Actually, the simple lunch and Monday's informality put her at ease.

"I am delighted to finally meet you," he said to Lily as they gathered around the serving table. "All of the airmen you have helped hold you in high regard. I feel as though I know you already."

Lily smiled shyly. "They are all very dear to us."

"Thank you all for coming," Monday said as they filled their plates. "I welcome the opportunity to thank each of you personally for all you have done. I know it is a difficult trip over the mountain. This was your first crossing, Lily?"

"Yes. I never really appreciated how difficult it was until I did it myself."

"Dédée crossed the mountains thirty-three times," Monday said.

"And with a pack heavier than that of the airmen," Tante Go added.

"I thought I was in shape," Lily said apologetically as she made her selections from the tray of deli meats. "I feel like a marshmallow compared to her."

"I remember the first time she came to us," Monday said with a chuckle. "British intelligence would not believe that such a young girl could have crossed those mountains—especially at night. It was absolutely astonishing." He slathered mustard on his slice of bread and piled on the meats. "The moment I met her, I knew she was for real. She was passionate about her plan. I knew she was telling the truth, but it took a few more trips with confirmation from the airmen before MI6 was convinced."

"Do you have any knowledge of her whereabouts?" Tante Go asked.

"We believe she is in Germany. Some have suggested we negotiate a trade, but I think *Saturday* is correct. It would only draw attention to her importance and risk her being put to death to serve as a warning."

"Donato is lucky we have not yet found him," Tante Go hissed.

"Do you know anything about my father or sister?" Lily asked.

"No. I'm sorry."

Monday gave it a moment before speaking again. "I asked you to come here because the three of you are the longest surviving members of the Comet organization. The arrests of Legrelle, Franco, Henri and so many others were devastating to the group. The question I have for you is, has the line been damaged beyond repair?"

To Lily's thinking, the line could never be damaged beyond repair. "I sent a courier to Madame Anne in Brussels," she said. "Anne immediately moved the parcels to new safe houses. I am burned there, but before I left I took steps to have others take my place. You know about the man with the missing little finger?"

"Yes," Monday said. "His name is Prosper Dezitter. He also goes by Captain Jackson or Jack Kilanine. He has been tricking hosts and airmen into believing that he runs an escape line."

"Everyone in Belgium is being warned about this man," Lily said.

"What about Paris?" Monday asked. "The Secret Police were waiting for Legrelle and Franco."

"They threatened harm to Henri's pregnant wife," Max said defensively.

"But how did the police know about Henri? The Crampons may have been betrayed by someone in the line. Perhaps it is time to close Comet down. You have all earned your passage to England."

Tante Go eyes narrowed pertinaciously at Monday. "Are you telling us the British will no longer support the line?"

"No, no. Of course we will support the line as long as it continues. I am just saying I understand if you have had enough. We could begin a completely new line."

"You *have* begun new lines," Tante Go said a bit testily. "None of them have had anywhere near the success of Comet. Our friends have paid dearly for our mistakes, but we are still operating. We cannot let their sacrifices be for nothing."

"You thanked us for the work we have done," Max put in. "We have made a difference, have we not?"

"You have made a great deal of difference—not only have you given us back our trained pilots and crews, but when those airmen return to their bases, it boosts the confidence and morale of every other airman. I firmly believe that our boys are fighting with more determination because of your work. The intelligence information carried over the mountains is being put to use to plan for the invasion of Europe."

"Mr. Creswell," Tante Go said, "you asked us if Comet can continue. I believe Comet *must* continue. I knew what I was getting myself into when I signed up. I for one intend to continue my work as long as airmen are brought to me or until I am arrested."

Max sat upright and slapped his hand on the table. "You speak of British and American morale. We have frustrated the Germans for more than three years. We must continue if for no other reason than to let the Germans know that they have not beaten us.

Monday's face grew more enlightened with each declaration.

"I agree!" Lily leaned forward, fists clenched, her emotions fired up. "If the Germans are so determined to stop us—we must be even more determined to continue!"

"Very well." Monday's eyes had now filled with admiration and pride. "Then let us plan how to move forward. Do you think we can keep the Brussels to Paris connection running?"

The trio relaxed back in their chairs.

"Diane and I have worked out a new route to the French frontier through the Ardennes," Max said. "We have been recruiting guides to conduct men down from the north. One of our recruits, Pierre Boulain, is a daring young man who has gotten us identification cards for the border crossing. He had been working with a priest associate in the provinces."

"MI9 is sending in a man to help in Paris," Monday offered.

Max's face tightened as to warn Monday not to attempt and fool him. "What man?"

"His name is Jean de Blommaert—code name *Rutland*. He was recruited from the Belgian army and is a trained agent like Legrelle. They are also sending two radio operators and money to cover expenses."

The three Comet members shared a skeptical glance.

"I assure you," Monday said, "we have kept our word to Dédée and Franco that Comet will always be independent. But I do not think it is wise for Max to remain in Paris. Rutland is Belgian and he is not known to the Gestapo. He could head up that sector while Max continues to bring men down from Paris to Dax."

"Since she is not yet known in Paris, Lily could help Rutland," Max offered. "And she could take the parcels from Dax to the border."

"Fernand and I will continue in the Basque territory," Tante Go said. "I would like to send Freddy and Janine out. Denise Houget will assist me and help conduct the airmen. Kattalin will continue to house them and to gather intelligence and Florentino, of course, will guide the men over the mountains and courier papers."

———

Lily jumped into her assignments with renewed vigor. She, Max and Tante Go were not only determined to show the Germans that Comet had not been defeated—they wanted the British and Americans to know it too. And that meant getting the line moving again as quickly as possible. A few hours' sleep at Tante Go's after the night hike over the mountains, Lily was off again and back in Paris in the late afternoon. She and Madeleine Noel *Martine*, with whom she was now staying, set about recruiting safe houses while de Blommaert *Rutland* and Max worked out the scheduling.

When everything was ready she took the tram to 30 rue Doriston in the 16th *Arrondissement* (district).

"Diane? I'm Lily."

The striking dark blond girl who answered the door let her in and quickly closed the door. "Yes. Max told me to expect you." Amanda Stassart *Diane* led Lily into the kitchen. "It is nice to finally meet you, Lily. I believe we have handled some of the same packages."

Lily understood Diane was testing her. These were dangerous times. "Yes, Monique conducted the men from me to you—Tom Hesselden, Lloyd Stanford, Jim Burch, Ken Garvey…"

Diane smiled and relaxed. "I guided all of them to Paris," She set a bowl of pistachio nuts on the table and poured two glasses of red wine.

"Perhaps you guided Bob Grimes," Lily said.

"Yes … tall handsome fellow … blue eyes …"

"That is the one," Lily said smiling. "It was I who nursed him and got him in shape for the mountain crossing."

"He was with the group I took to Paris, but I didn't escort him. I shared a car with a handsome American pilot who did not get his identity papers in time. We had to embrace and kiss all the way to Paris so the Germans would not ask for his papers. Oh the sacrifices we make for the cause," she said with a playful giggle. "So you are a nurse?"

Lily nodded.

"I was in law school when hostilities broke out," Diane said. "I only just heard about the organization a few months ago. My mother had worked with the Résistance in the last war. When she said she had joined an organization smuggling Anglo-American airmen out of the country, I told her I wanted to help."

Lily cracked open a pistachio. "I knew my father was passing messages for the Résistance, but I was shocked when the German police arrested my whole family. I didn't know my sister, Andrée, had been working with Comet for over a year. The Germans let my mother go, but my father and Andrée were sent to Germany and have disappeared. I'm afraid to think of what might have happened to them." Lily sighed. "I was burned in Brussels so I came to Paris. We need to get the line moving again. Max has sent me to tell you to leave at dawn and begin the new route." Lily pulled a stack of French francs from her pocketbook. "Money for expenses," she said.

Diane sipped her wine contemplatively. "There is one thing." Her face grew serious and troubled. "Henri introduced me to a man—Marc Poulain or Boulain or something like that—he said he would assist me. I will not work with this man. He gives me the creeps. I don't trust him."

———

The next morning Lily joined Martine at the table with good news. "You can pass the word that we will be receiving some packages from the north tomorrow."

"So we are in business again?"

"I hope so."

"Good. After my last appointment today I will visit my hosts to make sure they are ready." Martine brushed the crumbs from her toast into the dust bin and asked jocularly, "And when was the last time you saw your dentist?"

"It has been a while."

"You should not neglect your teeth."

"I know. But I cannot come in right now. I'm meeting with Max today. Then I have to go back down to Spain. I will make an appointment when I return."

"You do not need an appointment. Just tell me when you…"

The ring of the doorbell interrupted their conversation.

Martine opened the door and a courier handed her a note.

Diane has fallen ill, it read. It meant she had been arrested.

———

Nine days later, after her second meeting with Monday in Spain, Lily took the train back to Paris and went straight to the flat of de Blommaert, *Blom*. "I have an urgent message from Saturday," she said. "MI9 says you are being watched and must leave France immediately."

Blom acknowledged the news with resigned acceptance, but his brow furrowed. "I will need a few days to make preparations. "We still must reconnect to the north somehow—you and Max will have to work that out. I will visit Philippe Lake and tell him to step in for me while I am gone—"

"You cannot go to Philippe if you are being watched," Lily said. "We do not need to lose him as well. I will go. Tell me what you want him to do."

Blom agreed with a nod. "Tell him to set up new headquarters and cut ties with anyone he judges to be a risk. Ask his wife, Virginia, to arrange a safe house for me and my radio operator, Willy LeMaitre until it is time to leave. Another radio operator, Conrad LaFleur, is on his way down here from Reims. The Gestapo came to arrest him, but he shot his way out and escaped. Tell Philippe to have Ancia help you reconnect with the North."

She buttoned her coat and turned to leave.

"Lily," he called before the door closed. "Be careful."

She nodded and flashed a two-fingered V.

———

Lily made the arrangements to conduct Blom and the two radio men down into Spain. On February 29, 1944, the day before she was to leave, Martine brought her to a small bistro to meet a new team of helpers.

A restaurant? Lily thought, but said nothing. Things in Paris were certainly different. The Brussels group would never have met in a public restaurant, and here they were seated in a dining room crowded with other patrons. Lily followed Martine to the table wondering how they could discuss private matters in a place like this. A very friendly young fellow across from them politely stood and introduced himself. "I am Pierre—Pierre Boulain."

"How do you do, Pierre? I am Martine, and this is Lily."

Pierre beamed. "It is a pleasure to meet you. He seemed to be an ordinary fellow, yet there was something about him that bothered Lily. Perhaps it was his energetic blue eyes that danced evasively as he spoke or his fly-away hair that made him appear careless.

Martine nudged Lily and whispered as Pierre moved off to greet others, "He comes highly recommended by the priest at the end of the table. He is said to have experience and connections."

He looked a bit cocky to Lily, and a young lad looking for adventure could be dangerous in this business. She wondered why the priest had invited such a young passeur to this meeting.

When Pierre returned to his seat, Lily stared at him. Unconsciously, her rumination spilled out of her mouth. "You're wearing a polka dot bow tie."

His eyebrows flicked up and he gave a little chuckle. "So? What of it?"

She realized she should have kept that thought to herself. Boulain wore a bright purple jacket and polka dot tie. Her father had told her to be wary of anyone dressed in garish clothes. "Oh nothing. I just like neckties better."

Pierre smiled like it was just for show—like he was covering his thoughts with a good-humored façade.

CHAPTER FORTY-ONE
February 29, 1944

Jacques Desoubrie kissed thirteen month old baby Adolph and two-year-old Jacques good night and Marie-Thérèse whisked them off to bed. Moments later, he joined Captain Schnurr, Lieutenant Brandstetter and others in the adjoining apartment.

With a map of Paris spread out on the kitchen table, Jacques laid out the details. "The raids must be coordinated so they do not have time to warn others. We must hit before the morning curfew ends so they cannot get away."

The officers agreed. Since the spectacular netting of Comet's big fish, Desoubrie, now *Pierre Boulain*, was a man of high standing among the secret police. He orchestrated the particulars tapping his pen at locations on the map. "One team will visit safe house keepers here, here and here. We'll send two men to the province to collect our priest friend. One team will pay a surprise visit to Monsieur Rutland and the last will come with me to visit our dentist friend, Martine. We shall see what that smart little bitch, Lily, has to say about my bow tie now."

———

"Hold me down, boys!" Lily half-joked as she staggered against the powerful mountain wind. The snowstorm had come out of nowhere. "Don't let me blow away!"

With their clothing flapping like flags in a squall and their faces turned sideways against the wind whipped snow, Lily, John Oudinot, Blom, and radio operators Conrad LaFleur and Willy LeMaitre fought through the swirling white to keep up with the mountain guides. Despite slips, falls and bruises, they made it down to the Bidassoa River. With her pants tied around her neck, Lily followed the short Canadian, LaFleur, into the icy stream. She nearly screamed at the sting of the freezing water. It took a moment and a great deal of willpower to get her feet moving and she fought for every step as the water lapped ever higher. Each time she lifted a foot, the river buoyed her up and threatened to sweep her under as it had done to Antoine d'Ursel.

Lily teetered a bit, felt LaFleur's firm grip on her arm and knew he wouldn't let go. The men looked after her like she was their little sister, Oudinot and LeMaitre pulling her out when she reached the other side. Fortunately the road crossing went quickly, probably because the Guardia Civil stayed inside figuring that no one in their right mind would be in the mountains in weather like this.

Monday welcomed them to Bilbao with fire-grilled steaks and rich rioja reserva wine. "Good to have you back in one piece," he said to the Canadian. "I'm told you'd had a very narrow escape."

"I had only a moment to drop the signal to alert Saturday and grab my revolvers," LaFleur said. "There were several minutes of pure terror before it was over. I shot into the group coming up the stairs. The lead guy fell back on the others and while they ducked for cover, I leaped over the balcony. I sprained my ankle, but managed to get away while the rest of them went running upstairs toward the sound of the gun shots."

"The Germans have been transmitting on your radio," Monday said. "Saturday has not let on that he knows it has been compromised. He has been sending messages to mislead them. They will catch on eventually."

"This is the problem with radios," Lily said with a tip of her head to signify that she had warned them. "The Germans can detect them. And if the operator is captured without as you say dropping the signal, the Germans can gain information on underground members. I do not like the use of radios."

"Yes. There is a danger," Monday conceded. "But sending messages by courier is so slow and unreliable. Radios allow us to authenticate airmen much quicker."

"Blom is safe because I carried the message to him personally."

"Lily's correct," Blommaert said. "Willy's radio had already been captured."

Monday acknowledged her point with a nod and dabbed his mouth with a linen napkin. "We have a bigger problem. We are without a Paris chief and the line from the north is undependable. Saturday suggests we shut the line down for two months until he can train another operative."

Lily could feel the hairs on the back of her neck bristle. "Comet is a Belgian line! We do not need a British agent to run it."

"No no, we will not run the line, the agent will just help as Blom and Jérôme have done. The dynamic of the war is changing," Monday said laying a map out on the table. "The Allies are bombing farther inland in preparation for the invasion of the continent. Moving airmen will only become more difficult and unreliable and we are afraid that any airmen caught after the Allies have landed will be executed as the Germans will not spare troops to guard and transport them. We need to stop evacuating them and find sites where we can hold large groups until after the invasion." Monday looked directly at Lily, she being the only one returning to France. "We're calling the endeavor Operation Marathon. Collecting fliers from all over France, Belgium and the Netherlands and getting them into forest camps undetected will not be easy. We will need Comet's assistance."

"Comet will help," Lily said, "but the more men we get out before the invasion, the fewer we will have to hide." She looked Monday straight in the eye and spoke slow and plain. "We will decide when we can no longer bring men to the border. We will work with you on the camps for Marathon, but you must trust that we know our countries better than you do."

"Yes, of course." Monday touched her arm to reassure her. "We will only help. Tell us what you need and we will provide it. Do you think you can reconnect Brussels?"

"Certainly. No problem."

"Here!" Blom pointed out an irregular-shaped green area on the map. "*Forêt de Fréteval*. It is between Le Mans, Tours and Orleans so we can transport men from all different directions. The forest cannot be breached with tanks and vehicles so it has no military importance. No armies contesting it makes it a great place to hide men."

"I do not know the area," Lily said, "but I will help Philippe Lake recruit helpers. Paris should remain the primary collection point."

Monday nodded. "Daniel Mouton is being sent to organize sites in

Belgium as well." He sat back stretching is shoulders. "I will send this to Saturday. He will make the final decision. Now before you leave, Lily, I have money and a little something for you to take back."

Lily peeked inside the bag. "Coffee and sugar. Martine will love this. Thank you."

———

Pierre Boulain Jacques Desoubrie smirked at *Martine* every time he passed her sitting in the wooden chair with a *Feldgendarmerie* revolver trained on her. She proclaimed that Lily did not live there, but he knew better. "There are two tooth brushes in the bathroom, Mademoiselle."

"I am a dentist," Martine said shakily.

That made Desoubrie smile more at her folly. He strolled through the apartment, and returned to Martine holding up the blouse and skirt Lily had worn to the restaurant. "Perhaps she gives you her laundry too?"

Martine said nothing.

"Take her away," Desoubrie said. "We have no more use for her. Two of us will stay here to welcome Lily home."

———

March 4, 1944

The wail of the camp siren erupted in Nadine's ears. "*Aufstehen!*" the *stubova* shouted yanking women from their beds. "*Aufstehen!*" Lights burst on. Nadine squinted until her eyes adjusted. Pressed against the wall on the wooden bunk, she could not move until the girl in the middle and the girl on the outside peeled themselves away. And none of them could climb down until the three women crawling out of the bunk below were out of the way. Then they all had to avoid the three climbing down from the top bunk and the bunks in the middle of the room. It had been tight quarters before, but with last week's arrival of 958 French women, they were now packed together like strings of dried figs.

Cold air blew in through the open windows stinging her body awake. The stench of urine and excrement hung heavy in the air. Eighty women stood ahead of her waiting for their turn in the washroom. They had only one hour for two hundred women to use the ten toilets and twenty basins. Only the most audacious braved the cold water showers—there were no towels and the frigid air was the only means to dry off. Nadine and most of the women settled for a splash at the sinks. Those who couldn't wait for the toilets slipped outside of the barracks and squatted, risking punishment if caught.

Nadine brushed her teeth, sharing a sink with two other girls, then slipped her toothbrush back into the cloth bag with all of her other worldly possessions—a wooden bowl, a wooden spoon, and a comb. When the five o'clock siren sounded, she tied on her kerchief and took her place in formation with the other slaves in the cold morning air of northern Germany.

Käthe "Kate" Knoll, the German inmate *blockova* in charge of block 32, the *Nacht und Nebel* block, doled out special treatment to those she liked—potato or meat in their soup bowl or an assignment to an easier job. Most of the French women refused to kiss up to the Germans despite the harder work details and less food. Although she ruled the Night and Fog block, Knoll was a prisoner herself. Her power came from the real queen of the camp, the first assistant to the Chief *Oberaufseherin*, the sadistic Dorothea Binz, whose mere presence evoked chills of fear.

Barelegged and shivering in threadbare dresses and worn out jackets, the women shuffled in place to keep their blood circulating. They had to stand and bear the cold for more than an hour while the *blockova* checked off every person in her book and accounted for anyone in the infirmary or otherwise missing from formation.

Transporting her thoughts from this cold horrible place, Nadine poured the beautiful egg sunrise into a bowl in her mind and whisked in light cream, ham, mushrooms, and a dash of salt and pepper. She closed her eyes almost smelling the soft buttery omelet that would fill her empty stomach.

When the counting was finally done, the women were given their work assignments. Some marched off to work in factories. Others labored on work Kommandos cutting down trees for the expansion of the camp to accommodate the ever increasing number of prisoners. Those not assigned a job, like older women and the ill, were sent back inside to clean the barracks, carry the kettles of soup from the kitchens at meal time and be ready to fill in at the factories when needed. These were "the Availables".

Prisoners that were paraded out through the gates were made to sing bright German marches to give the appearance of being well-treated. But Night and Fog inmates like Nadine worked at the Siemens factory inside the camp because they were considered too dangerous to be allowed beyond the prison walls. After all, they were the ones who had had the guts to defy the Germans.

Not all of the French women in the NN block were underground or Résistance fighters. Some were innocents falsely imprisoned. When the Nazis couldn't come up with a solid case, they simply convicted the person of crimes against the Reich, which could mean anything from disrespecting German authority to infecting German soldiers with venereal disease. Some were simply caught in the wrong place during a German sweep for subversives. Underground and Résistance members tried to protect the weaker prisoners, but sometimes there was no way to help them.

In the Siemens factory, women worked in complete silence assembling precision instruments, and radio and telegraph parts. A row in front of Nadine, a young girl whispered to the woman next to her. The woman ignored her and kept working. The girl tried again. In her mind, Nadine yelled at the stupid girl to shut up, but she could say nothing without getting herself in trouble.

The overseer up on the platform rose from his chair. "*Ruhe!*"

Female guards converged on the girl from both sides, knocking her to the floor, punching and kicking her. "*Halt die Schnauze!*

"I am sorry," the girl pleaded in French. "I do not know how to do this."

The guard slapped her head again. The girl cried out and held up a forearm to protect her face from the vicious blows. "I was just asking how to put this together."

"Auf Deutsch!" the guard backhanded her across the cheek. *"Antworte uns auf Deutsch!"*

"Please. I don't understand what you are saying."

"Steh auf!" The guard yanked the girl to her feet and shoved the prisoner back down into her chair. She addressed the woman next to her. *"Zeig ihr was sie tun soll."* The French woman nodded and showed the girl how to put the parts together. The guards returned to the edges of the factory floor.

On the way back to the barracks for lunch, the women noticed children tossing around a rag fashioned into something more like a doughnut than a ball. The orphaned children had arrived a month ago after an uprising in Warsaw, Poland, which had been sealed up by the Nazis to imprison Jews. Some women, knowing that they might not live to see their own children again, could hardly look at the young waifs. For others, the children were a vision of hope. But it was false hope.

"Keep it moving," *blockova* Knoll ordered as the women filed past the soup kettles. Being German, Knoll was given preferential treatment, better clothing and more food. When Nadine reached the kettle, Knoll teasingly dipped the ladle way down to the bottom and brought up chunks of potato and a bit of meat. Then she poured the contents back into the pot and ladled nothing but liquid into Nadine's outstretched bowl. Knoll smiled goading a reaction.

Nadine said nothing. She wasn't going to kiss the bitch's ass for a bit of potato. Nadine took her bowl to the side of the room where she could lean against the wall to eat. She broke off a piece of bread from her day's ration and dipped it in the thin cabbage soup.

One of the new arrivals sidled up to an older inmate near Nadine. "It is nice to see children," she said.

The woman shrugged.

"Do they put the mothers in another block?"

The older inmate paused her bite of bread and looked up. "Are you pregnant?"

The girl smiled and nodded.

The older inmate sighed. "Yes, child. I suppose they do." The woman's eyes briefly met Nadine's.

Nadine gave a shrug of her eyebrows and moved away. The poor girl would learn soon enough that babies were drowned immediately after they were born, but she wouldn't learn it from Nadine.

On Saturday, instead of being released after the noon meal, the prisoners were called back into formation. Some women feared that it might be a selection where the women paraded in a circle holding their skirts up so doctors could decide who was fit to continue working. Those deemed unfit were sent away and only their clothing came back. Others suspected a room toss or *being controlled*, where they stood outside for hours while guards searched the barracks for drawings, diaries, books, medicines, poetry and other contraband. Fumigation of the barracks was a third possibility, but since they hadn't been ordered to strip naked in the freezing air to await clean clothing, that was unlikely.

Assistant camp director Bräuning marched to the front of the formation followed by his evil mistress, *Oberaufseherin* Dorothea Binz.

Nadine stood at attention with eyes front as Binz prowled through the formation with her riding crop clutched behind her back, no doubt itching for an excuse to use it. Eyeballing the pretty, wicked-faced blond *Oberaufseherin* would earn the looker boxed ears, a lashing of German profanity and a quick sting of the crop. Beatings and public floggings sexually aroused Binz and appearing weak and timid could cost the victim a beating until she was nearly dead.

"*AUFMERKSAMKEIT!*" issued from the loudspeakers. Binz rejoined Bräuning at the front of the formation as baritone voices belted out *Deutschland Über Alles* from the poles above. The song ended in thunderous canned applause which ushered in the expressively charged voice of *Der Führer* Adolf Hitler. All Nadine cared about was how long she would have to stand shivering in the cold.

Binz' dangerous blue eyes swept the ranks making sure everyone was paying attention. Once all eyes were on her, she began rubbing her backside up against Bräuning. She pulled his hands up to her breasts, and writhing with arms raised, smiled at the inmates. The more the women watched, the more aroused she became. She unbuttoned the top of her blouse and shoved his hand inside her bra. Pauses in Hitler's words were filled with loud grunts and moans from Binz and Bräuning.

It took nearly an hour for Hitler to run out of ways to express Germany's superiority. When the inmates were finally released from formation, Nadine took her bandanna from her head and tied it fashionably around her neck. Despite the cold weather, few went inside, having spent enough time packed together in one room.

Most conversations were about food. "… I cut little slits and push chunks of cheese and garlic in. Then I bake them … I slice the eggplant in half, scoop out the middle and stuff it with cheese and chopped meat…" Hunger panged so hard, nearly every waking moment was spent swapping recipes. But a group gathered around Dédée and Suzanne wanting to know about the war.

"What did Hitler say about Italy and the Americans?" a woman asked.

Suzanne waved her off. "You cannot believe anything Hitler says. His speeches are nothing but propaganda."

"But what about the Americans?"

"He said German forces have pinned the Americans down on the beach at Anzio, Italy," Dédée said. "He said it shows how futile it would be to try invading Europe."

"He boasted that more than two hundred of the American elite forces were captured," Suzanne added. "He said that the Americans achieved their goal of entering Rome—but they did it as prisoners of war."

The first woman shook her head sadly. "Even if Hitler is lying, it will be a long time before the Allies reach us."

"It is of no use to think about such things," Dédée offered with a shrug. "Each morning I get up determined to get through one more day. That is all I can do."

———

The hike back over the mountains into France was grueling, but Lily was eager to begin reconstructing the northern line. She couldn't wait to see Anne again when she went to Brussels to work out the details.

She excitedly filled in Tante Go and Fernand *L'Oncle*. "The British fear that having to pull Blom out is a major setback and suggested the line be shut down for two months until they could insert another trained agent, but I told them Phillippe and Virginia Lake can pull Paris back together and I can help Martine organize more safe houses."

"Of course we can do it," Tante Go said. "Trained agents didn't create this line—we did."

Lily nodded agreement. "It is a matter of pride, Tante. Comet is not going to be shut down—not while I have anything to say about it."

"You know."—Tante Go chuckled at her young friend—"you would think the British would have learned by now that we Belgians are a determined bunch. L'Oncle and I will continue as long as possible. Denise Houget and Kattalin will help at this end."

"I'll continue to help Max guide the men south and recruit more help after I go to Brussels and coordinate things with Anne and Monique."

"Do you think that is wise? You are still hot in Belgium."

Lily shrugged. "Some risks must be taken. I will be careful."

The overnight train to Paris only got as far as Bordeaux. After a very long wait, a conductor entered her car, explaining that the tracks ahead had been damaged by American airplanes. After two hours, Lily took the option of continuing to Paris by bus. There she found a telephone booth right away. She was nearly five hours late—and Martine was probably worried sick.

"Hello, who is this?" a woman asked. But the voice was not that of her friend.

A chill ran down her spine. Lily slammed down the receiver. They had gotten Martine.

———

"Stay here and rest a few days," Tante Go said when Lily returned and told her what had happened. "I will arrange for you to go to Spain with the next group. You need to get out of France."

"Yes," Fernand agreed, "I think it is time we sent Freddy and Janine out as well."

Lily sighed. She had no choice but to leave France. If the Gestapo knew about Martine, they knew about her as well. If not for the train delay, she would have been arrested too. But all of the pilots had been verified—she didn't see how the Gestapo could have learned about Martine. "I have to go back!"

"You cannot go back," Tante Go said. "You'll be arrested the minute Gestapo spots you."

"There has to be a traitor in the line. I have to find out."

"But whoever the traitor is knows who you are."

"Which is why it has to be *me* who goes to Paris." Her mind was already considering the possibilities "The traitor must be someone I have met. If I don't find out who has betrayed us, there will be more arrests. They will finish off Comet in Paris, then come for you and everyone in the south."

"You do not have to worry about us. We have managed before."

"We are all at risk," Lily said. "I have to go back."

Tante Go's sideways glance enlisted Fernand's support as she proposed that she and Lily should go to Spain to speak with Monday. But Lily would have none of it.

"Monday will make me stay in Spain. I have to go back."

"Michou, it is suicide," Fernand reasoned in a fatherly tone. "The traitor, whoever it is, is very likely armed. If he discovers that you are looking for him, he will have no choice but to silence you to protect his identity."

"And even if you go back to Paris, how will you find the traitor?" Tante Go asked.

"I don't know. But there is no one else who can do it. I will find a way."

B ritish Intelligence begged Lily to come out—the Gestapo was on to her. Nadine, Dédée, Franco, and scores of others had disappeared somewhere in Germany. Paul was dead. Elsie had been mercilessly tortured. And now Diane and Martine had been arrested. Whoever had betrayed the line knew who she was. But more would be arrested if she didn't stop him. There was only one way to ferret him out. Lily slipped into her juvenile skirt and pulled on her ankle socks. A button-down blouse and saddle shoes completed her adolescent disguise.

Lily sat forward in the seat as Virginia drove slowly around the perimeter of Fresnes Prison searching for some way to get what they needed. "I was hoping we'd be able to see something from the top of the hill."

Virginia stopped the car. "If you stood on my shoulders you wouldn't even reach half-way up that wall. "We've gone around the entire prison. Now what?"

"That way," Lily said, pointing in the direction of the afternoon sun. "Go that way a few blocks and drop me off."

"Drop you off? What are you going to do?"

"I'm going to walk back to the prison and ask to see Martine."

"You're going to do what? Michou, that's crazy. You cannot just walk up to the gates and ask to see a German prisoner." Virginia stared in disbelief as Lily pulled a brush from her purse and touched up her hair. "*Vous avez une araignée au plafond.* You've got a spider on the ceiling."

Lily laughed at Virginia's use of the French phrase. Virginia had completely embraced French ways—lightly applied makeup on her round pleasant face, not garish like American women; soft brown hair cut just to the neckline, rolled back from the forehead on top with symmetrical side rolls in a modern French style—but when she spoke, there was no disguising her American accent.

"What? Did I say it wrong? Maybe you'd rather hear the American translation. *You're nuts!*"

"Exactly! No one but a fool or an innocent young girl would do such a thing." Lily tied her hair back with a bright blue ribbon. "It is what I did when my family was arrested. I went right to the jail and asked to see them."

"What am I supposed to do while you're gone?"

"Just park over there and wait. If I am not back in one hour, leave." Lily finished tying her hair ribbon and opened the car door. "Wish me luck." She walked quickly, fearing that if she hesitated she might talk herself out of it.

"What are you doing here?" a French prison warder demanded.

"I want to see my friend."

"Certainly. We will bring you to her," a second guard said in a condescending tone.

They seized her arms and ushered her into the cell area where she was given over to a female guard. "This girl wants to see the inside of a cell."

Two guards conducted her down a corridor and shoved her into a cold concrete cell that smelled like an outhouse. The heavy iron bars swung closed with a resounding *BRRRUNK*. It was terrifyingly clear that the direct approach had been a miscalculation.

She had gotten lucky so many times, she had perhaps deluded herself into thinking that she was charmed, like someone above was watching over her, keeping her safe. She stared at the drab, lifeless walls. How foolish she felt that after all of the times the Germans had nearly caught her, all the times she had slipped their traps, she had now delivered herself right into their hands.

Sitting on the iron bed, her back against the wall, she resolved not to languish in self-pity. It was too late to think about her mistake. The women guards were French—she would have to try to convince them that she was just a child too stupid to know that going to a prison to ask about a friend would get her into trouble. Then again, if the guards had any idea who she really was, they might just turn her in for the bounty.

She'd heard the talk. When the Allies invaded, all Résistance and underground prisoners would be liquidated to eliminate any threats behind their lines. She had known all along that she would likely pay the ultimate price for defending her country, but what worried her now was the torture. She knew that Nadine and Elsie had been terribly beaten. *Be strong,* she told herself. *Showing weakness will only make them think you can be broken.*

The *tick tick tick* of hard-heeled boots drew near. The door clanked open and two female French guards entered.

"Why did you come here?" one demanded.

"I came to see my friend, to see if she needed anything—food —clothing ..."

"What is this prisoner's name?"

"Madeleine Noel."

"Is she an associate of yours?"

"Associate? I don't know what you mean. She is my dentist."

"Your papers say you are from Anglet. That is in the south of France, no?"

"Yes."

"Then how can your dentist be in Paris?"

"We used to live in Paris. When the war began, my mother moved us to the country because she thought it would be safer."

"Your friend was arrested because she committed a crime."

"I don't know what she might have been involved in. I only know that she is my dentist."

"Perhaps you will remember more when you have had time to think about it."

The guards left and Lily was once again alone.

———

Elsie Maréchal stood on the assembly line sliding copper coils into metal cages and passing them along. Despite the cool temperature in the factory and the threadbare prison clothes, she felt hot and drained of all energy. The lack of sleep didn't help. The cells were cold as a morgue and the walls deadened all sound. Depression smothered her like a grave blanket. She felt like she was treading water and all she had to do was raise her arms and let herself sink. But if she quit, her mother would surely not go on.

She wasn't even sure how long they had been in Waldheim prison. They had been to so many prisons since leaving St. Gilles on New Year's Day that it was hard to keep track. She wanted to forget the horrors she had seen, but at the same time, she wanted to remember. She wanted to live to tell what monsters these Germans were. She wanted to recount all the atrocities—the inhuman treatment of the bloody man in the tiny cage in Frankfurt, the cells without daylight in Aachen, the days spent in the prison train with no food or water and only a bucket in the corner for human waste, the airless cells in Nuremburg, the abscesses on her back from the beatings in St. Gilles, and the indignities of showering in Cologne and standing naked in a room where soldiers passed through.

Her hands worked on, sliding the coils into the cages as if they were functioning on their own, detached from her body and she was merely an observer.

They had been stripped of more than just clothing—little by little the Germans were stripping away their very existence. Moving them from prison to prison had covered their trail, making them disappear in the night and fog. All they had left was a dying ember of hope that the Allies would somehow rescue them before it was too late.

Elsie felt tired, so tired. She picked up a coil. The air was hot and suffocating. The overhead lights began to spin. The coil bounced on the floor and rolled away. Then her body crumbled and the world went black.

———

Moments after the guards' footsteps disappeared down the hall, Lily heard two taps on the concrete partition. She got up and turned an ear to the wall. The taps repeated. There was nothing in the room to tap back with, so she pounded twice with her knuckles.

Two taps responded, followed by a hushed voice. "You are looking for someone here?"

"Yes."

"Whom do you seek?"

"Martine," Lily said.

"We will try to find her when they send us outside for exercise."

"I need to speak with her."

Lily could hear other voices in the cell discussing it. After a while, two taps sounded again on the wall.

Lily tapped back.

"Three taps—" the woman knocked on the wall—"means we have found her. Four taps means she has changed places with someone."

Lily heard the women being marched outside and heard them two hours later when they returned. Filled with anticipation, she listened for the clang of gates in the hallway. It seemed an eternity, but finally there came two taps. Lily knocked back.

Three taps came, then four.

Lily drew in a breath. "Martine! Martine!"

"Who is that? Who is calling me?"

"It's me! It's me! Who betrayed you, Martine?"

"Pierre—Pierre Boulain!"

———

The rattle of steel wheels on a rolling cart woke Elsie up. She blinked several times at the unfamiliar grey walls and line of beds—not the cots of the prison cell but real iron beds with real mattresses. It took her a moment to realize she was in the infirmary. The last thing she remembered was working in the factory.

"Can you sit up?" the nurse asked.

It sounded a simple enough question, but a question instead of a command felt odd coming from a German. Elsie rolled from her side onto her stomach and pushed herself up. She leaned her shoulders against the wall, careful not to let the painful abscesses touch.

"Eat," the nurse said putting the tray on Elsie's lap. "You will need your strength."

The next day she found out why. Stripped of her clothes, she was laid on the bed on her stomach. The nurse twisted a rag and held it to her mouth. "Bite," she commanded.

"Hold her still," the doctor said, and the two male assistants knelt on her legs and pinned her arms down.

Searing pain burned into the right side of her back. She screamed and bit down hard. Her muscles went rigid. Uncontrolled tears ran down her cheeks. The sting of the implement let up, replaced by squeezing fingers. She could hear herself sobbing.

Her taut muscles had begun to relax when the knife struck again on the left side of her back. She clenched her teeth until the muscles in her jaw began to shake. After a short break, they began again on her lower back. Stinging, throbbing, poking, probing, it seemed it would never end. There was a moment of peace when the doctor finally straightened and stepped away. Then a burning liquid was dabbed on her back.

The assistants released their hold. The nurse removed the rag from her mouth. Elsie felt the nurse's hand brush her shoulder, though she couldn't tell whether it was a discreet attempt to comfort her or an accidental brush.

Gauze dressings were applied and a sheet was pulled up to her shoulders. She was left on her stomach to heal or not. The medical crew said nothing to indicate that they cared either way.

———

For a second night, Lily lay on the hard cot thinking of what else she might do to convince the guards to let her go. So far, she had stuck to her story through three more interrogations. But things would be different when the Gestapo came for her. They would be much more brutal than the French guards.

She had gotten the answer she had come for, but that would do no good if she couldn't get the information out. And who was Pierre Boulain really? She had met him at the restaurant and remembered the polka dot tie, but it was hard to picture exactly what he looked like. She closed her eyes and thought about their brief conversation. Before she blurted out her remark about the tie, he had been talking about getting permission papers for crossing the border. As the conversation returned to her, his face began to come into focus—not very tall, unruly dirty-blond hair, a face that tapered down to his chin like an upside down bullet, beady eyes, a mouth that looked like a puppet … He reminded her of someone. She couldn't remember who.

He had been recruited by the priest and said he had gotten identity papers and official seals for Paul … Lily suddenly sat up. She remembered there was a boy who could get passes easily as well and he always seemed to get through check points without any trouble. Whenever he guided airmen through a train station, the attention of the Germans seemed elsewhere. That fellow was also short with blond fly-away hair. He looked a lot like Boulain.

And he had gotten involved with the line just before Paul's arrest and that of more than two hundred Comet members. Masson! Jean Masson! That was his name!

Boulain and Masson were the same man!

The next morning, the door clanked open and two female guards escorted Lily to the warder's office where she was told to sit down on a wooden chair.

"How old are you?" the warder asked.

"Fifteen."

"You came to the prison to talk to a friend?"

"Yes, my dentist. She has always been nice to my mother. I thought I might bring her food or clothing or something. I didn't know you could get into trouble just by asking if you could bring food for a friend."

"These are dangerous times." The warder sighed and glanced at a photo on his desk. It was the picture of a teenage girl, probably his daughter. "You will be a woman soon. You must learn not to do such things." He turned to the guards—"Take her to the front gate"—then looked back at Lily. "The Gestapo are on their way. Get out of here right now and do not come back."

She walked away without looking back, afraid that this wasn't real, that they were only toying with her. As she crossed the bridge, a big black German staff car approached from the opposite direction. She kept walking, watching the car out of the corner of her eye. Big men in grey Gestapo uniforms glanced her way. The car passed without stopping. She let out her breath.

But now she would have to make herself the rabbit and lure out the fox.

CHAPTER FORTY-THREE

"*Je voudrais vous présenter* Lieutenant Abraham Teitel," Safe house host Lucienne said when she called the airman out of the bedroom.

"How do you do, Lieutenant? I am Virginia, and this is Philippe," Virginia d'Albert-Lake said.

"You speak English?" the young man asked with surprise.

"That's right."

"You don't even have an accent. Where're ya from?"

Virginia laughed. "We'll get to me in a minute. First, let's start with you. I know you have been through this before, but I'd like to ask you a few questions if you don't mind." After Lily's warning, Virginia wasn't taking any chances.

"Okay. Shoot."

"What division are you in, Lieutenant, and what plane do you fly?"

"Sixty-eighth *Bommah* Squadron—B-24 Liberator."

"How many men are in your crew?"

"Ten."

"And you're from New York City?"

"Utica Avenue Brooklyn."

"Are you a baseball fan, Abe?"

"Who ain't?"

"Can you tell me what a balk is?"

"Yeah, it's when the *pitchah* makes like he's gonna throw the ball to the plate, but he don't let it go, an' all the *runnas* move up a base."

Every word that fell out of the lieutenant's mouth sounded like Brooklyn. Still, she had to be sure.

"So, are you a Yankees fan—the Brooklyn Bombers?"

"Heck no I ain't no Yankees fan. The Yankees are up in the Bronx. If you ain't a Dodgers fan, you ain't from Brooklyn."

"Who plays short stop for the Dodgers?"

"Arky Vaughan"

Virginia chuckled. "All right. That's enough questions."

"So where're ya from? I know it ain't from around here."

"I grew up in Florida. I got my master's degree from Columbia University in New York—not far from the *Bronx Bombers*," she said with a wink. "I take it you don't speak any French."

"Just the little I picked up in the *fauw* months I been hangin' out here."

"Okay, *Brooklyn*, these are your new identification papers for the south of France. When you travel, you do not speak. Not a word. If someone says something to you, you pretend to be mute. If someone says something in English, you show no reaction. Always remember that you are supposed to be French. You do not comprehend English."

Brooklyn nodded that he understood.

"You will follow your guide, but not too close. If you are singled out and questioned by the authorities, you are on your own. Your guide cannot let on that she knows you. Now please stand up, give me your old papers and empty your pockets."

"French cigarettes ... French money. That is good, but you must leave the change here. It is a nervous habit for Americans to jiggle the coins in their pocket, so we will remove the temptation."

She handed him a folded up pro-German newspaper. "When you go on the train, you pretend to read this. Good luck."

———

A dark grey rain cloud accompanied Lily to the train station. Evaders Glenn Camp and Ray Reeves followed Albert Ancia to one compartment while Lily took Jarvis Cooper and *Brooklyn* into another. They rested comfortably for the first ten hours, but shortly after the train left the Libourne station, just north of Bordeaux, a *Feldgendarme* entered their compartment.

It appeared to be a routine check, but as soon as the Feldgendarme looked at Cooper's papers he said, "You come with me." Then he turned to Lily. "Is this man traveling with you?"

"I am traveling alone."

When the officer left with Cooper, Lily whispered to Brooklyn to get off at the next station." He made his way through the cars to the front of the train while she waited in her carriage for the stop. Lily met up with Ancia in the Bordeaux station. He had only Brooklyn and Reeves with him. "What happened to Glenn Camp?" Lily whispered.

"Feldgendarme," Ancia softly replied.

Lily looked to Brooklyn. "Same one who took Cooper?"

Brooklyn nodded.

"Cooper and Camp stayed with the same host," Ancia said. "I'll take these two to Anglet. You go back to Paris and warn the others."

The next morning Lily learned that Blom and Daniel Mouton had been dropped into rural France and were now back in Paris. She met Mouton at his apartment, and advised him of the airmen's arrests then discussed her bigger concern—the traitor in the line.

"This is a very serious accusation," Mouton said after listening to her story. "Boulain has been a good and reliable operative. It is difficult to believe it is he who betrayed us."

She had gotten the information directly from Martine. Diane didn't trust Boulain either. Lily shook her head emphatically. "You should have seen his eyes when I asked him about his polka dot bow tie. He knew that I knew it was to identify him for others in the Secret Police."

"You know I will have to turn this over to the Résistance. And you know what they will do to him. How can I condemn a man to death from a few words exchanged through prison walls and because he wore a bow tie? We must be sure, Lily."

"What do you want me to do to?"

"You said you have seen both Boulain and Masson. Do you think you would recognize him if you saw him again?"

"Yes, of course."

Though his eyes showed how troubled he was by the matter, Mouton's somber tone said he would do what he must. "I have a meeting with him tomorrow. I was going to give him five hundred thousand francs to set up a Marathon camp in Belgium. Come join us. We are meeting in a café near the Pont de l'Alma."

"No restaurants."

"It is already set."

Lily shook her head. "I am not going to meet in a restaurant." She knew of Mouton's four escapes, but one short stay in prison was enough for her. "Tell me where and I will find a place nearby where I can watch for him."

"We are to meet at the statue of King Albert in the seventh arrondissement."

"I will be there."

The next day, Lily found a bench where she had a good view of the statue. She wore dark glasses so no one could see her eyes peering over her magazine every few seconds. After twenty minutes, a young man and woman strolled up to Mouton like this was nothing more than a relaxed outing on a beautiful spring day. Lily got a good look at him, but just to be sure, she waited until they emerged from the café an hour later. The couple passed right by like they hadn't a care while Lily watched from behind her glasses and magazine. The moment the subjects reached the promenade along the river, Lily rushed up to Mouton. "It's him. I'm pretty sure Boulain is Masson."

"Pretty sure is not good enough, Lily."

"What then?"

"Follow him. See where he goes."

Lily took off in the direction Boulain had taken. An ocean of people swam in her way. She darted in and out, but could see nothing. Finally she pressed up against the railing overlooking the river, sweeping her gaze back and forth over the Pont de l'Alma bridge. There they were! The couple had just about reached the midpoint of the Seine.

Lily hurried to the bridge, weaving through the crowd, bobbing around slow walkers. After being cooped up all winter, the beautiful weather had all of Paris out and about—and they all seemed to be on this bridge. She felt like a calf in a herd of cattle. By the time she reached the end of the bridge, she had lost them again. She paused against the railing, picked them up and continued the chase.

She scurried past shops, markets, a metro station, plazas and gardens. The couple had only been strolling, but they had somehow disappeared again. Had they gone into a store? Had she passed them without knowing it? She side-stepped a group of old ladies window-shopping.

Suddenly, there he was, directly in front of her—not more than thirty feet away—close enough to see the dimple on his chin and the peach-fuzz beard on his pale white face. She stopped short, but it was too late. Their eyes locked. His mouth gaped and his treacherous blue eyes flashed understanding. His cover was blown.

She spun around and quick-stepped away. He followed. She dodged on-comers and darted through crowd gaps. He was still following, his face fierce, his eyes narrow and focused. She glanced back and picked up the pace. Her short legs were nearly at a trot.

His life depended on catching her.

Her life depended on getting away.

Neither could run. If she ran, she'd draw the attention of every gendarme, and secret police in the area. If he caught her, the damage could be contained. Her knowledge would die with her. But if he ran, he'd expose himself.

She looked again over her shoulder. He was gaining like a cheetah closing in on dinner. He was a marked man—a desperate man—a wounded animal—very dangerous.

An idea struck. She slipped around a group of pedestrians to hide her move, then dashed left at the metro station and bounded down the steps to the track level where she burrowed through the crowd. Crouched low behind a businessman and his briefcase, she peered around him to watch the stairway.

When the train arrived and the doors opened, she nearly toppled the businessman over as she scurried past his legs like an unleashed puppy. Keeping below window level, she duck-walked down the aisle and slipped into a seat.

She held her breath as people filed by. The train filled up. Her heart pounded. Seconds passed like hours until the doors finally closed and the train began to move.

Lily lifted her head to the window and risked a peek. There on the platform in the midst of the crowd, stood Boulain turning around and around, angry curses spewing from his pasty lips.

———

Monday, June 5, 1944

Virginia d'Albert Lake rushed into the Paris flat with a basket full of black market food. "I'm sorry, darling," she said to Philippe as she dashed through the apartment with her sack. "The time got away from me." She tossed her handbag on the couch. "Peel some potatoes for me, won't you my love? The gas comes on in eight minutes!"

She cut up a pepper and an onion and tossed them into the pan then grabbed the coil of sausage and began slicing off half-inch pieces. There was no time to bake it properly and sausage couldn't be eaten under-cooked like the many vegetables and potatoes she'd prepared in the past. Cooking enough food for six men, Philippe and herself in a half-hour was a challenge. It wouldn't win any cooking awards, but it was the best she could do in the little time before the gas was cut off for the night.

"I shouldn't have tried to make onions," Virginia told Philippe as she shoved the sausage around in the pan. "They'll never cook in time. These poor men will be happy to get home and eat a real meal."

Philippe kissed her cheek. "It smells delicious, and so do you."

She gave him a backwards glance and chuckled at his flattery.

He planted a quick kiss on her lips. "These men will be gone in a few days."

"And more will take their place," Virginia said, giving the beans a stir. She enjoyed sitting around the table talking with the men and wished she could get to know them better, but most were passed on quickly.

The airmen ate as if she'd prepared them a banquet. No one seemed to care that the potatoes were slightly underdone.

"It was a hang of meal, Virginia—an absolute feast," one black South African said in his well-mannered British accent.

"Thank you," Virginia said. "I wish I could make you a proper dinner."

"You have already done more than we can ever repay, Virginia." The second South African finished his last bite and dabbed his lips with his napkin. "It was delicious—more than I have eaten in nearly a month. I lived on emergency rations for a week before I was given a bit of cheese and some bread by a friendly farmer."

"Cheese and bread! You're lucky, pal." One of the Americans pushed back his chair and lit a cigarette. "I dropped into a field in Holland. For a day and a half, I ate nothing but last year's beets."

Virginia began to rise, but another American from out west laid his hand on her shoulder. "You just have a sit, Virginia. You've done enough. Me and the boys'll clean this up." As he collected plates around the table, he said, "I hid out for three days and walked for two nights before I found someone who put me in touch with you folks."

"Some field hands saved my butt," a young Canadian put in as he scraped off his plate. "I spent the night in an old barn, and the next morning, I started down a dirt road. I waved good morning to some guys working in a field. A couple of seconds later I hear, *Monsieur, Monsieur!* I turn around and this guy's waving like crazy for me to come, *venez, venez.* I go into the field and he sticks a hoe in my hand, slaps a beret on my head and makes digging motions toward the ground. Then I hear it— a truck coming down the road. It was loaded with German soldiers. Those farmers sure saved my bacon."

"We'd all be *sprechen sie* Kraut if not for you folks," the westerner said.

Another man nodded. He'd bailed out nearly a month before and a Dutch teen got there before he even hit the ground. "He pulled me out of my harness and helped hide my chute. I don't even know the kid's name to thank him."

"Thank him by defeating Germany," Virginia said. "Our names are not important. It's better if you don't know your helpers' names in case you are caught."

"Well there's one joker I'd like to see again," one American said. "I was hidden for a couple of days by a Dutch farmer. He brought a school teacher 'round who spoke English. The teacher took my French francs and my wrist watch and said he'd bring me back Dutch money. The bastard never came back. Now, here I am in France with no money."

"Don't worry," Virginia said, "you won't be buying any Eifel Tower souvenirs anyway. Now finish up. The BBC's about to come on."

Huddled in a semicircle on the floor, the airmen listened through the crackling static for the V for victory notes in Morse code that began the BBC's broadcast from London.

One of the Americans shrugged when the program ended. "Same old stuff."

The Canadian laughed. "How do you know? In all that mumbo jumbo they could be signaling Résistance groups all over France to start taking out their objectives."

"You know," one of the South Africans said, "there must be a couple hundred airmen hiding about. If we could get our hands on some guns…"

"Forget it," Virginia cut in. "Military Intelligence is way ahead of you. They thought you might try something like that. Uncoordinated fighters would just confuse things and jeopardize the invasion." She twisted the dial away from the BBC station and switched off the radio. "You gentlemen are going to be hidden away—Allied orders."

Virginia and Philippe left the men and returned to their studio apartment about a mile away where they resided as a precaution. "I've had a word with Blom," Philippe said while Virginia sat by the mirror brushing out her short brown hair. "Mouton advised him that Pierre Boulain has been eliminated and Lily and Monique have made it into Spain."

"Thank God for that."

"Virginia, if for any reason we get separated when the Allies invade, we'll meet at the *maquis*," he said referring to the camp *Saturday* had code-named *Sherwood*. The Fréteval Forest was chosen because the Résistance was strong in the area and could smuggle supplies and guard against German patrols—and it had a freshwater spring.

"There will be room for us?"

"Saturday has planned on two-hundred-fifty. There's just over a hundred there now. "

Virginia set her brush down and turned to smirk at Philippe. "Good luck keeping that many men corralled. The six we have here are itching to go fight."

"An RAF Squadron Leader has been sent in to take command."

Virginia climbed into bed, turned off the light and sighed as she wrapped her arms around Philippe. "Thank goodness Lily and Monique have gotten away."

CHAPTER FORTY-FOUR
June 6, 1944

Virginia felt a kiss brush the back of her neck as Philippe passed on his way to the tea pot. Housing the airmen in a studio apartment a mile away not only let the couple distance themselves in case of a Gestapo raid, it also gave them a place to enjoy being alone together. The little cottage they had been fixing up in Cancaval by the coast was supposed to be their love nest and the place where they would someday raise their children. Then the Nazis had commandeered it to quarter German officers. Even worse, she had turned thirty-four last Sunday; her child-bearing years were passing by and the campaign to take back Europe still hadn't begun.

Her family had urged her to return to the U. S., but Virginia didn't consider that an option. While some might quip that one's spouse was their other half, for Virginia and Philippe it was absolutely true. To run away to America would be to leave half of herself behind.

It had been an anxious three years with frighteningly close calls. Conducting American boys was especially risky as they couldn't help but gawk at Paris landmarks or let an American mannerism slip at the worst possible time. Any little miscue could expose them, and she'd held her breath more times than she cared to count. Yet it was thrilling in a dangerous sort of way. And with every airman she helped—sixty-six of them to date—she felt like she was striking a blow for the freedom of France, her adopted country. She was glad she had stayed.

Philippe poured the coffee while she sliced bread.

Rrrrrriiing!

Virginia wiped her hands on her apron and followed Philippe to the telephone. "Who on earth could be ringing us this early?"

As he stood with the receiver to his ear, his eyes grew wide. "The wireless," he called making circling motions with his free hand. "Turn it on."

Virginia leaned in close to the radio speaker as Philippe twisted the knob to clear the static. A chill ran up her spine. The news was at once exhilarating yet frightening—the Allies had come ashore on the beaches of Normandy!

She and Philippe had planned to go to the Sherwood camp and hide out with the men in the forest until liberation, but now her mind was in chaos. "What about the six airmen in the studio?" Virginia worried aloud. "The Germans are bound to invoke martial law. Should we go to the apartment? We could be stuck there if the Germans close off the streets."

Philippe peered out between the blinds at the street below. "People seem to be moving about unrestricted. No one is rushing any more than usual." He drew maps from a drawer and traced a route with his finger as Virginia looked on. "We would have to travel back roads to avoid German convoys. It will take three or four days to reach the maquis on foot."

"Do we dare it?" Virginia asked. "Or should we just tell the boys to wait it out."

The phone rang again. When Philippe returned to the table, his face showed additional strain.

"What has happened?"

"Madame is nervous. She is sending another five evaders to the studio."

"My God. There is no way we can hide eleven men in that tiny apartment. But how can we move them? One or two at a time would be risky, but eleven…" Virginia whistled through her teeth.

"Maybe we should see what they think."

They bicycled to the Paris flat where Virginia laid it out for the airmen. "The first options is we make a dash for it. The only train still operating to the south will take us as far as Dourdan. It's another sixty miles from there to the maquis. It will be a four day walk and I don't have to tell you that the Germans will be on the move. We will travel back roads as much as possible to avoid them."

Conversations broke out among the men.

Virginia held up her hand. "The other option is to wait it out. We'll try to find places for you. But once the Allied forces make their way inland, the Germans will close off every road to Paris. Evacuation will be impossible."

Virginia gave them several minutes to discuss it. Then one by one they gave their answers. "I'm for going ... Me too ... Count me in ..." All but one man agreed.

"All right then," Virginia said to the holdout, "I'll bring you what food I can. As for the rest of you, we will need photographs for new identity cards, we'll have to arrange for some guides, we'll need to get train tickets..."

"Wait," the last airman said. "I've changed my mind. I'm going with you."

With so many people fleeing the city for fear that it would become a battleground, it took Virginia three days to get the tickets. Philippe managed to locate only one bicycle which an airman named Sam volunteered to ride. At seven in the morning on June 11, three young women, Michèle, Anne-Marie, and Any, boarded the train, each with a small group of evaders not far behind. Virginia strapped a picnic lunch into her bicycle basket and followed Sam and Philippe out of the city.

They pedaled for three and a half hours before meeting up with the girls and airmen who had already arrived at the woods outside of Dourdan. Despite the cool air and greying sky they picnicked among the trees eating bread, cheese and Virginia's left over chicken.

After lunch, the first girl set off down the road with three airmen. Fifteen minutes later, Philippe sent the next group. Once the third group was on its way, Philippe mounted his bicycle with Virginia and Sam following. As they pedaled on by the hikers, Sam teased the men about their having to walk while he got to ride.

Virginia rode up beside Philippe and nodded to her right. "The sky's looking pretty dismal over there and it's heading our way." But there was nothing but hay fields around—she hadn't even seen a barn. They had no choice but to keep going until they could find shelter.

She buttoned her jacket collar as the first fat drops hit her cheeks. Moments later, the clouds burst open. She bicycled back to encourage the drenched men, apprising them of a village a few miles ahead where they might find shelter. Just north of the hamlet, the group took cover in a large drafty shed while Philippe rode into the town to look for a place to stay.

Virginia wiped the water from her cheeks, ears and nose. The young girls laughed at Virginia shaking her head like a wet dog and at their own dripping chignons and flattened curls.

"It is no good," Philippe said when he returned. "There have been recent arrests and everyone is afraid. The next village is not too far. I'll ride ahead and see if we have better luck there."

Virginia and Sam bicycled to the intersection in town where they were to meet Philippe. Virginia looked nervously back as the groups began to catch up. Bunching up here could be dangerous. She called the girls over. "The German police would have a field day if they stumbled upon this lot. We need to split up and move the groups away from the intersection. I'll wait alone for..."

"Look!" One of the girls pointed toward an approaching rider.

An exhilarated Philippe waved everyone together. He had found a farmer willing to let them stay in his barn by telling him they were five Frenchmen hiding to avoid being sent to work in German factories. Philippe planned to sneak the others in.

They pedaled for an hour down a country road and reached a railroad crossing as the sun came out. From there it was only another mile.

Feeling naked and vulnerable pedaling past open wheat and barley fields, Virginia beseeched the sun to sink a little faster. A faint buzz in the distance crescendoed like bees swarming toward them. She stopped beside Philippe shielding her eyes against the low sun. Black spots in the sky grew into a pack of four small planes prowling like falcons on the hunt.

"They're our boys!" Sam yelled as the planes roared overhead. "American Mustangs!"

The war birds banked and streamed downward, the whine of their engines growling louder as they dove. Virginia spotted the target—a slow-moving freight train less than a half-mile away. Geysers of dirt burst from the ground as the fighters' cannons spit out lead. The tiny planes veered away then swooped back with guns *rat-a-tatting*. A train car exploded, then another. The earth trembled. Car after car blew apart or leaped into the air. Percussive air thumped her chest and showers of red and orange sparks shot skyward like a Fourth of July finale. Virginia stood breathless, captivated by the spectacle. It was terrifying, yet quite thrilling. Dark grey smoke clouds billowed up long after the planes disappeared.

It was hard to drag themselves away, but they had to get the men hidden for the night. Inside the barn, the hikers flopped onto piles of hay like they were feather beds, still celebrating the glorious attack on the train as they peeled off their shoes.

Seeing their blistered, bleeding feet, Virginia said softly to the girls, "They're not going to make it very far like that."

"I have friends near here," Any said. "I can take two men with me."

"I'll take one," Anne-Marie said.

"Thank you." Virginia glanced back at the men stretched out on the straw. "Now we just have to figure out what to do with the rest."

The barn door opened. The farmer, lifting his lantern high, gaped in shock at the sight of the twelve men and four women. The girls broke into French chatter hoping the farmer would not notice that the men were silent. But he didn't seem to be fooled by their charade. He turned and walked out without a word.

"Do you think he will report us?" Virginia whispered.

———

It began with the Russians and Poles and passed from person to person, blowing through Ravensbrück and filling their hopes like wind in a sail. A German newspaper, snuck out of a factory trash bin and smuggled into camp, made its way to the NN block.

One prisoner kept watch out the window for guards while others gathered around the German-speaking translator. "It says that enemy troops have attacked German defenses along the French coast of Normandy. The Germans say they've stopped the enemy advance and reserve units have been mobilized." She smirked as she read on, "It says the French people have nothing to fear. The *Wehrmacht* will protect them from the invaders."

One woman interrupted. "Do you think the Germans have really stopped the invasion?"

"When have the Germans ever told the truth about their battles?" someone said.

"The English would not repeat the mistake of Dunkirk," another reasoned. "And the Americans would not have attacked unless they were prepared to overcome German defenses."

With proud conviction, another woman declared, "Our Résistance groups will create such havoc there won't be a bridge left for the Boche to cross nor tracks for their troop trains to run on. To get to the front, they will have to swim and march all the way there."

The woman at the window waved her hand and the prisoners made the newspaper disappear.

———

An hour after the farmer left the evaders and helpers in the barn, he returned toting a kettle of piping hot soup while his wife carried fresh bread, bowls and utensils. No, the farmer hadn't been fooled by their charade, and he and his wife smiled with pride knowing it was Allied servicemen they were aiding.

In the morning, the two girls left with their three airmen and Philippe provided the remaining three groups hand-drawn maps. "You're on your own today. We will meet here in this woods tomorrow morning around eleven," he said pointing out the spot on the map. "We will try to find some kind of vehicle for the rest of the way. Good luck."

Virginia and Philippe cycled to a market in Châteaudun. After they'd given the password at the side door, a young man with toddler in tow directed them to the city square where he met them fifteen minutes later and led them to a country road outside of town. He left and returned with Henri, a young member of the Comet underground.

"You are American!" Henri said with delight after hearing Virginia speak.

Virginia laughed. "I'm working on my accent."

"Oh no, Madame, you speak very well. I hope you are hungry. My wife is making us supper. Then you will come with me to the place where I hide from the Germans. Is there anything you need?"

"We could use a car or something to transport some of the men," Philippe said. "Their feet are blistered from ill-fitting shoes."

"How many are in your group?"

"There are eight airmen, two women and myself."

"That is a lot of people to move."

"Even if we just transport the worse cases, it would be a help."

"I will see what I can find."

After dinner Henri led Virginia and Philippe to his hideout, a barn where a heavily armed band of Résistance fighters camped. In the morning, Philippe pedaled off for *Sherwood* to arrange for arrival of the others while Virginia and Henri rode to meet the boys at the woods. She had to go herself to make sure the Germans hadn't caught her boys and replaced them with infiltrators.

Yesterday's rain had cleared. The farmer's son hitched a horse to a covered farm cart and set out for the rendezvous. With her spirits refreshed by last night's dinner and a good rest, Virginia and Henri bicycled down quiet back roads and farm lanes, relishing the lazy warm breeze with its scent of sweet spring blossoms. But despite the tranquility, she couldn't relax worrying that it had been a mistake to send the boys on their own.

They reached the woods. There was no one about. A prickly feeling ran up her spine.

"It's Virginia!" Men stepped out from behind the trees—all seven of them and Michèle. They mobbed Virginia like she was the star of their little league baseball team. "Man are we glad to see you!"

"You missed me, huh?" Virginia laughed, relieved to see them as well. "Are you hungry?" she asked as she unbuckled the straps on her bicycle basket and handed out sandwiches, hard boiled eggs and cans of beer. It was such a lovely picnic Virginia had to remind herself that they were fugitives and the road ahead was still filled with danger.

The farmer's son arrived with the cart and three Americans, the two airmen from South Africa, and the Canadian crammed into the tiny wagon. Michèle climbed up front with the driver and Al, an American, volunteered to ride a bicycle that the boy had brought.

Virginia, Henri and Al pedaled off with the horse-drawn cart following a hundred yards back. Progress was slow over the narrow winding roads Henri took to avoid the highways that the German police were more likely to travel. He led them as far as he dared, then wished them, *bonne chance*. Virginia now had to rely on her own map reading skills to navigate the back roads as they made their way south.

Mid-afternoon, she was relieved to come to a road that she had bicycled on the day before. She checked the names of the contacts in Châteaudun while letting the cart catch up a bit.

"Man, it's hot out here," Al said stripping off his suit jacket. "You don't mind if I put this in your basket?"

It was more of a statement than a question as he was already strapping his jacket in while Virginia sipped from her water bottle. "See those hills and buildings in the distance?" she asked. "That's Châteaudun. One more day and we'll be at Sherwood."

Al stretched out his arms cooling himself in the breeze. "To think we were so hesitant about making the trip, and now we're nearly there without a bit of problem."

A hot wind of foreboding breathed down the back of Virginia's neck. She couldn't believe he would say such a thing. "Don't jinx us," she said crossly.

A little farther on, a young Frenchman cycled in from a farm road and fell in behind them. They pedaled along the desolate road for a mile or so. Then their luck ran out.

A big black car appeared in the distance. With gasoline nearly impossible to get, cars were rarely seen these days, especially on a lonely back road—unless you were German. There was nothing she could do but pedal on and hope that the car passed them by.

It didn't.

"Halt!" A German police officer leapt out of the car.

Fright broke over her like a tidal wave. Her worst fear was confirmed when two more officers got out.

"Get off your bicycles. Show me your identification."

Virginia willed her trembling hands to be still as she handed over her papers.

The officer regarded the documents then looked up studying her as she responded to his questions. "You live in Paris. What are you doing in this region?"

"I came looking for fruits and eggs at the local farms."

"Your accent is English." He looked back down at her card. "You are American, I see."

"Yes. But my husband is French and I am a French citizen now. I am permitted to travel about."

"Are these men with you?"

Cold sweat ran down her body. "We are not together. They came from a side road just a little ways back. They were simply riding along." She delivered the explanation with believable sincerity and hoped the German wouldn't notice how she was perspiring.

Then she caught sight of Al's jacket in her basket. It was obviously a man's jacket and it matched Al's pants. It wouldn't take a genius to figure out that she was lying.

The officer snatched her purse away, and while his attention was on her personal things, Virginia's gaze shifted to the cart which had stopped about a hundred yards back. As she watched, the airmen slipped one by one out of the back of the wagon and crawled into the nearby brush.

A smile grew on the German officer's lips as he rifled through her bag. Her stomach churned. The officer looked up grinning at his companions. The air was suffocating. The officer pulled from her bag one after another, the maps, the train tickets, a compass … His stiff officer decorum all but disappeared. His eyes dancing with delight signaled his cohorts that they had hit the jackpot.

Then he lifted out the slip of paper with the names of her contacts. The blood drained from her face. Her stupidity for leaving that list in her purse was going to cost many people their lives—the grocer and his young family, Henri and his gracious wife who had prepared them a delicious dinner, and others whom she had not even met. She couldn't breathe for the thought of the horrors her mistake would bring to those poor people.

The officer looked sternly at Virginia. "You would have been better off if you hadn't lied to me about your purposes here." He handed back her purse and moved to the Frenchman.

After checking his papers and speaking with him, the German released the Frenchman and turned his attention to the airman, Al.

Al's responses of "*oui*" and "*non*" failed to fool the German who laughed at the farce. "You are American. Empty your pockets."

Virginia waited with her purse in hand and her jacket folded over it. While the German was busy with Al, a thought occurred. Under the jacket, she quietly opened her bag and felt inside for the list of names. She kept her arms still as her fingers worked to tear the paper into tiny little scraps which she slipped into the pocket of her jacket.

Clearly pleased with himself, the officer ordered Virginia and Al into the black sedan. They were driven to Gestapo headquarters in Châteaudun. There the lead officer boastfully recounted the story of his glorious catch to his superior, but Virginia was largely ignored. She began to stroll about, taking an interest in the pictures on the wall. Then, glancing to see that no one was paying attention to her, she stole out the bits of paper from her jacket pocket and stuffed them into her mouth.

Nerves made her mouth so dry she couldn't swallow. She pushed the scraps back and forth with her tongue while trying not to move her jaw noticeably. The officer finished his tale and still laughing, turned in her direction. It was now or never. She swallowed hard. Somehow, she powered the paper wad down.

The officer, still beaming, grabbed her purse. The merriment left his face as he rummaged through it. "Where is the paper?"

"What paper?"

"The paper with the addresses!"

"How should I know? You had it last."

Then he spotted a bit of the paper lying on the floor. His eyes bulged. "You ate it!"

She shrugged.

His eyes burned with fury.

She stared defiantly back. A long moment passed. The explosion she expected never came. Then she realized why. As much as he might have wanted to punish her for what she had done, he could say nothing about the paper without exposing himself as the idiot who had given her the opportunity to swallow it. It was little consolation, knowing she might be tortured and ultimately shot, but at least she wouldn't carry the guilt of handing friends over to the Gestapo.

———

At a corner table in a quiet restaurant in San Sebastian, Spain, Tante Go passed an envelope to *Monday* containing information on German troop movements, gun emplacements, and fuel dumps and other intelligence. "You have heard about Virginia?" she asked.

"Yes, I have heard." Monday slipped the envelope into the pocket of his suit jacket. "Philippe must come out."

Tante Go nodded. "Blom told him that it would jeopardize the camp and his wife's chances of survival if he was to be caught. Do you want me to make arrangements for his evacuation?"

They both fell silent as their dinners arrived, but once the waiter moved away, Monday softly replied, "Saturday has arranged to take him out by Lysander."

"Virginia's arrest is very troubling," Tante Go said, pausing with her knife in the air. "But it proves I was right to send Freddy and Janine out."

"We want you and Fernand to come out as well. You have both done more than anyone could ask."

"I'm staying." She brought her knife to bear on a piece of chicken.

"You don't need to take any more risks. We are winning the war now. The line is no longer evacuating men over the frontier."

"Which is why I sent Janine out—she's no longer needed to guide the pilots. But you still need me." She looked him dead in the eye. "And I'm going to see this thing through to the end."

Monday's eyebrows raised a bit, but he conceded with a slight knowing smile as if that was what he'd expected her to say. "I've gotten word that Lily and Monique have made it to England. Sunday will send Janine and Freddy with the next available transport." He cut into his rabbit. "I still wish I could talk you into coming out." Tante Go opened her mouth to speak, but Monday cut her off with a wave of his hand. "I know you won't." He pulled an envelope from his inside pocket and slid it across the table. "Money for Blom. Be careful. The Germans in retreat will be quick to shoot given the slightest excuse."

———

Tante Go hadn't been back in Anglet more than a few days when a messenger brought news as shocking as Dédée's capture. She left Bobonne to clean up the lunch dishes and telephoned her husband to meet her at a plaza near his office.

"It's Florentino," she told Fernand. "He's been shot and taken prisoner."

"Where is he?"

"They've taken him to the central hospital in Bayonne."

"What do you want to do?"

"I don't know yet. But I'll tell you one thing. I'm not going to make the same mistakes I made when Dédée was taken."

CHAPTER FORTY-FIVE

Nadine stared at the girl desperately licking spilled soup from the ground before it soaked into the dirt. The wretched thing had become a *schmuchstück*, a shell of a human with blank bulging eyes, bones protruding through paper skin and body blotched with excrement.

She thought with sadness of the beautiful young girl who had arrived months ago, her belly swollen with new life. Nadine wondered if it would have made a difference if she had butted into the conversation and told the girl what was to come. Could the girl have accepted it any better if she had been forewarned that nurse Gerta would drown her baby immediately after it was born? Or was it better to have said nothing and given the girl a few more months of ignorant peace?

The outcome would have been the same, she knew. The girl wasn't a Résistance fighter or a member of the underground. She was an innocent, an unfortunate soul who had been in the wrong place at the wrong time. Women in the NN block tried to help the innocents; sharing food, carrying more of the work load, comforting them, encouraging them to hang on. But most lacked the rebellious determination that drove underground and resistance fighters to defy the Nazis. Nadine stared down at the girl but felt apathetic. She walked away with her soup. Once they had given up and become *schmuchstücks*, there was nothing left to save.

Each day, Nadine faced her own battle to survive. This morning she'd been assigned to a work *Kommando*. Building roads in the middle of summer was about the most draining job in camp. It was no surprise to Nadine that her name had been called, but she refused to kowtow to the nasty *blockova*, Kate Knoll. Stubborn patriotism might end up killing her, but she would rather die a proud Belgian than live as a German lap dog.

French and Belgian women had the highest mortality rate in the camp. The Germans and Slavs called them weak, but their deaths were due more to pride and defiance. The well-educated French women could have obtained kitchen, administrative, or secretarial jobs, but their refusal to submit resulted in assignment to hard labor and shit jobs.

The guard's whistle sounded. Nadine tucked her bowl into her cloth bag and marched off with the others. Women's bodies were not built for such heavy work, and life in this place wasted away what little strength they did have. Starvation melted the meat off their bones and shrank their muscles until they were nearly gone. The coarse rope chafed Nadine's hands and her fingers throbbed with pain. Pulling a heavy concrete cylinder roller compacting gravel in the sweltering heat sapped her remaining strength. But she kept tugging. If the women couldn't keep the behemoth rolling, the guard would yank out whomever she deemed the weakest and beat her black and blue or shoot her. Then she would be replaced with someone else.

Breathing the heavy, humid air, Nadine slogged on, her prison dress clinging to her, the muscles in her arms, shoulders and neck aching. Sweat dripped off her nose and cheeks. The smell of fresh cut pine did little to mask the odor from their filthy bodies. An inmate once said she wished she could feel like a woman again. *Hell*, Nadine thought, *I'd be happy to feel human again.*

By the end of the day, she was so sore and exhausted she could hardly raise her arms to lift her bowl of soup. She dragged herself to the corner of the barracks where Dédée, was leaning against the wall gazing at the evening sky. Nadine was one of the few who knew who she really was.

"A huge ice cream sundae with chocolate sprinkles," Nadine said.

"Huh?"

Nadine chuckled. "That's what I'm dreaming of. What about you?"

Dédée sighed. "I was just thinking how sad it is that such a beautiful sunset should be wasted on a place like this."

Nadine rotated her shoulders and stretched her neck. "Thank God tomorrow is Saturday. I don't think I could take another day of road crew this week."

"We unloaded a truck today filled with things looted from France," Dédée said, "art work, furniture, medical supplies…"

Nadine frowned. "The Germans are stealing everything."

"Well I've taken a bit back," Dédée said with a wry smile.

Nadine raised an eyebrow.

Dédée opened her pocket and lifted a tiny packet just high enough for Nadine to see. "Penicillin," she whispered.

That evening, a French girl entered the barracks signaling two women to post themselves at the window. When they nodded all clear, she pulled a German newspaper from under her dress. It had been purposely left in a dust bin in an outside factory by a sympathetic Austrian and smuggled into the camp by a Czech worker.

A small group gathered around as Dédée translated. "The city of Cherbourg has been captured by the Americans. The Germans have abandoned the Cotentin Peninsula."

Women hunched over a small silk map that had been found in a German uniform sent to Ravensbrück for reconditioning. Their eyes followed Dédée's finger tracing the army's progress.

"They are moving so slowly," one woman lamented.

"At this rate they won't be here until Christmas," said another.

"It took the Germans only eighteen days to cross Belgium."

Side conversations popped up. Dédée waved her hand and shushed them. "Did you expect the German army to be so easily beaten?" she asked. "They have been building defenses and stockpiling military provisions for three years. Taking Cherbourg is a great victory for the Allies. Control of the port will speed up the delivery of men and supplies."

The woman at the window raised a hand and the map and newspaper were quickly stashed.

———

At the hospital in Bayonne, a nun slid the ledger book across the reception desk. "Please write your name and the patient you are here to see."

Tante Go set her gift basket down and wrote an alias in the book. Her spies in the hospital had given her the name of the patient in the bed next to Florentino.

She walked through the ward paying no attention to the Sisters of

Mercy nurse taking the blood pressure of the man in the first bed or to the mountain guide, Florentino, lying with his leg bandaged a few beds down. She went directly to the bed next to his. "Jean, you poor fellow, how are you feeling? I brought you fruit and some cookies and cakes."

"Thank you." The man smiled like he knew her, but he was probably racking his brain trying to remember who she was.

"You were very lucky that the bomb wasn't just a little closer. Are they taking good care of you? Is there anything you need?"

"The sisters are very caring."

"That is good. I believe it's truly a matter of luck. When it's your time it's your time… " Tante Go jabbered on as though they were old friends and kept up a conversation about nothing for half an hour. "Well, I must be leaving. I still have to stop by the market and get dinner going. Take care of yourself, Jean. It was good to see you."

"I will. Thank you for coming."

As Tante Go got up to leave, her pocketbook slid off her lap onto the floor. She bent down to pick it up and said softly, *"Hoy a las dos."*

She left without once looking at Florentino.

As she rode her bicycle back to Anglet, she thought about Dédée and how the Germans always seemed to move her just before each rescue attempt. Was it luck or had the Germans been tipped off? Would they move Florentino before she had a chance to put her plan in place?

The answer came early that afternoon when three impeccably dressed Gestapo officers barged through the front hospital door. Ignoring calls of *may I help you, please*, the callous leader brushed past the nun at the desk with little more than a sideways glance and a wave of some papers.

"Wait," the nun cried. "Where are you going?"

The lead officer responded with a volley of coarse German words that although foreign to the nun left no doubt that he was in charge.

The second German bumped the nun aside, making way for the third who was wheeling a gurney. They plowed like panzers through the gaggle of fretting nurses. Stunned, curious faces gaped from cots as the Germans stormed straight to Florentino's bed and dragged him onto the gurney.

The big man grimaced but said nothing. Even when the Germans had dragged him off the mountain with five bullets in his shattered leg, Florentino had clenched his teeth to keep from crying out in pain. He'd hated the Germans since they helped put that fascist pig in power in Spain. It would take more than a few pieces of lead to make him submit.

"You cannot move that man," the head nurse pleaded. "His condition is critical. His wounds are very serious."

"He is a criminal," The lead officer said coldly as he and his cohorts shoved the incapacitated Basque around like a sack of potatoes.

Florentino gritted his teeth against the great agony, refusing to let out a sound.

"We have orders to take him to another hospital—one where escape is not possible."

"He is too weak to escape!"

"Get out of the way," the Nazi commanded. The Sisters of Mercy were forced to step aside or be run over by the rolling gurney, though they clamored behind begging the officers to have some charity. The Germans paid them no mind.

"You are not men. You are beasts," the Sisters cried as the officers took their prisoner out the front door and shoved the helpless patient into the back of the ambulance. "You are nothing but thugs! You are monsters! You have no humanity!"

The sisters followed the gurney outside, blessing themselves and sadly watching as the ambulance tore around curves with little concern or compassion for the patient inside.

Three blocks from the hospital, the wagon slowed down and the officers burst into laughter. Fernand de Greef, the *head officer*, pulled a bottle of cognac from the utility box and poured a glass for Florentino and himself. "*Santé*," he toasted. The two friends drained their glasses. Fernand poured another round and lifted his glass. "To Tante Go, and her brilliant plan."

———

Caught with maps, train timetables and an Allied pilot, Virginia knew she wasn't going to talk her way out of Fresnes Prison by acting innocent as Michou had done. By admitting some guilt, she hoped to convince her interrogators that she acted alone in helping the American flier reach the Spanish border. If they bought it, Al would be sent to a prisoner of war camp and she to a concentration camp. But the airmen in the maquis, the underground helpers and most importantly, Philippe would be safe.

That eased her mind a bit—until she met her first torture victim.

Lying in a holding cell, Virginia was awakened in the middle of the night by the clank of the door. A young girl was shoved in by two guards and collapsed in a moaning heap. Virginia couldn't see her face in the darkness as she helped her onto a mattress, but she could feel the poor girl's body trembling and hear the breathless gasps of her sobbing.

"Are you all right?" Virginia asked.

"I-I don't know," the girl snuffled. "It hurts to breathe."

"What happened to you?"

"The Gestapo—they beat me with clubs and when I wouldn't talk they hoisted me up by one arm and one leg. I hung like that all day!"

Light-headedness nearly toppled Virginia. Suddenly, the prospect of torture was very real. With the sobs of the girl in her ears, she imagined every sort of brutality. *Please, God*, she prayed, *don't let me give up any names.*

The guards dragged the girl out in the morning, and Virginia was taken to a six foot by nine foot cell with three other women. Every day in Fresnes was the same: a hot bitter liquid they called coffee in the morning, thick soup at noon, bread at night, nothing to look at all day long but dingy white walls, and total blackness at night until it all began again the next day.

She prepared her mind for the coming torture, telling herself that she could take it, and imploring herself not to weaken. But after several periods of questioning without it, she grew more confident that the Germans believed her account.

She began to look forward to the breaks in the routine—the extra ration of meat or cheese twice a week—the weekly Red Cross parcel with food stuffs like jam, cheese and crackers that the four women divided up—library books once a week—and the walks in the courtyard twice weekly. Though horrible enough, prison wasn't as terrifying as she'd imagined from the Hollywood films back home, but then again the majority of prisoners in Fresnes were not thieves and murderers. Most were basically good people locked up for defying the Nazis.

During her seven week stay at Fresnes, Virginia adapted to the daily routines. She ate all her soup to keep up her strength no matter how it tasted; and despite the heat in the cell, she exercised to keep her muscle tone. She passed the time playing cards and knitting. The women traded books and food by tying packages with yarn and lowering them through the heat shaft to the cell below. They monitored the progress of the war by passing messages through the walls using tin bowls for speaking on one side and listening on the other. But on the first of August, Virginia and others were abruptly herded into a lorry and let out in a great big yard surrounded by high stone walls—Romainville Prison.

Virginia was pleasantly surprised by the decent accommodations. Fifteen women shared two large rooms. There were windows without bars that allowed plenty of light and opened to let in glorious air. There was even a washroom with a shower! The roll calls were short. The soups were pretty good. And the guards were not terribly vicious. After being cramped in a tiny airless cell in Fresnes, Romainville almost felt like a vacation.

The dreadfulness of Romainville, however, was not in its treatment of prisoners. It was the loss of all contact with the outside world and knowing that this was the collection point—the last stop before deportation to Germany.

As the days passed, Virginia's anxiety grew. No one stayed in Romainville for more than a couple of weeks. Hearing name after name being called for deportation tied her neck muscles in knots every time. Would she be among the forty or so leaving, or would she be spared one more day? Admiration trickled from her eyes as the girls whose names were called marched from the formation with heads held high. Despite the horrors that lay ahead, these women accepted their fate with such dignity, it bolstered Virginia's resolve to bravely face her own bleak sentence.

Those leaving collected their belongings while the women left in the yard gathered where they could watch for the departing bus. When it emerged on the road, women waved and shouted, "*Vive la France*" and burst out singing *La Marseillaise*.

One night, awakened by the camp air raid sirens, Virginia climbed down from her upper bunk and joined the others at the window searching the black sky.

"There!" One woman pointed.

The room exploded in cheers.

"Go boys!"

"Give them one for me!"

"Keep it up, boys," another girl called to the sky. "Finish them off before they take us away."

"We will not go to Germany," one said with confidence. "To keep the Boches from reaching the front our résistance groups were assigned bridges and train tracks to destroy. The English and American planes will bomb any that remain. Without tracks, the trains cannot take us to Germany."

"I hope to God you're right," Virginia said.

In the morning, another sign of hope faintly rumbled outside the open window.

A girl waved her hand excitedly. "Listen!"

Nothing compared to the euphoria enveloping Virginia at the thunder of artillery in the distance. Forming up outside for roll call, the women could hardly stand still as muffled booms announced that the Allies were nearly here. They were somewhere on the other side of Paris.

Risking punishment in their room that evening before lights out, one woman waved a tiny blue, white and red flag that she had knitted and kept hidden, while everyone in their room sang the La Marseillaise.

"How long do you think it will take the Allies to take back Paris?" someone asked.

Virginia shrugged. "A week maybe. But it could take a month if they lay siege so as not to destroy the city."

"Two days," another declared with total confidence. "The Americans would not lay siege and let the people starve. That is something only Germans would do."

But even two days would not save them all. Virginia staggered back to her cell stupefied when thirteen of her roommates were called for deportation. They had all arrived on the same day, so she expected they would all be deported together.

The next day, as one of the two remaining, Virginia explained the situation to the newcomers: "Women are deported every afternoon. They are sent back to their rooms to gather their things and are not permitted to talk to anyone. But if we write notes to our loved ones and hide them here in our room, whoever is sent back can take the notes and try to slip them to the bus driver."

"What if the driver won't take them?" a girl asked.

"Then she will drop them out of a bus window, and we will hope that someone will pick them up and deliver them."

"This is crazy," one girl said. "The Germans are losing the war. Yet they guard us women and take us to Germany with soldiers that should be used in battle."

"They will not let us go after spending so many resources trying to catch us," Virginia said.

Janette, an English woman in her late thirties, nodded agreement. "We have shown that we are not afraid to fight back. The Nazis know that if they turn us loose, we will work with the Allies again."

"I would fight again," one declared.

"We are fighting," Janette said. "With so many men needed to guard us and transport us to Germany, we are helping to win the war."

"It seems like little consolation, but I guess it's something." Virginia opened the window wistfully listening to the distant artillery.

"Are you Résistance?" Janette asked.

"Underground."

Janette joined Virginia at the window. "How many men did you help?"

"Sixty-six."

"Then regardless of what they do to us, we know we have already made a difference."

Virginia liked Janette right off. A little older than herself, Janette had more in common with Virginia than the young girls incarcerated with her. *Janette*—Jeanne Marie Boissard—had a kind, attractive face with dark hair and high cheekbones that drew out her gentle motherly smile. An Englishwoman, Janette, like Virginia, loved France. She also delighted in hearing about America.

A few days later, the loudspeakers boomed. "Attention!" "Every woman is to gather her things and prepare to evacuate in the morning."

After all of the speculation about disabled railroads, they had not escaped their fate. Virginia felt as if she had been clinging to a tree branch in a river, and now the branch had broken, sending her helplessly toward the waterfall.

A flicker of hope rose when the evacuation was cancelled as was the one two days later. Although Virginia was happy not to be sent away, she worried over what it might mean. She could still hear the artillery. Had the Germans reinforced their lines?

The camp returned to its normal routine, even arranging for a Catholic priest to hold a mass for the Assumption on the fifteenth of August. Women showered and dressed in clean clothing like they were heading to Sunday church.

"Attention!" the loud speakers boomed. "The camp is to be evacuated immediately! Every prisoner will gather all of their belongings. Bring them to the yard and stand in formation. You have one hour."

Virginia grabbed the messages and slipped them into a jacket pocket. Each girl took her share of the food from the Red Cross parcels. Once they had packed everything up, they carried their luggage to the courtyard. Virginia's was particularly heavy as her friends had the forethought to include a winter coat and gloves despite the August heat.

The three hundred women formed up for a roll call. Two hours in the blistering sun passed while cannons boomed just on the other side of Paris. *If only the Allies would bomb east of Paris*, Virginia thought, *maybe the busses won't come.*

Air raid sirens wailed. For a moment she thought she had gotten her wish.

Drop those bombs on the roads and rails, Virginia prayed. *Keep those busses away.*

Instead of being sent back inside, the women were rushed out the gate into caves that the Germans used as air raid shelters. When they were let out an hour later, a line of busses awaited them. Virginia queued up at the back of the line to be among the last to board, hoping to get a seat near the French driver. Somber disheartened faces stared out from the bus windows as Virginia shuffled toward the door. The explosions nearby punctuated the cruel irony of being taken away when freedom was so near.

She purposely took a little longer standing at the front of the bus pretending to be waiting for the others to move in and settle into place, but she was really waiting for the driver to glance her way. When he did, she lifted her jacket a bit to show the messages. He gave a slight agreeable nod.

Her moment came when the SS officers disappeared outside to check for stragglers. She slipped the notes to the driver along with a handful of francs. Virginia felt a nudge on her arm. More notes were pressed into her hand. She passed them along to the driver too.

"I hate this work," he whispered as he tucked the notes under his seat. "I have been evacuating prisons all day."

"If they are evacuating all of the prisons, the Allies must be close," Virginia whispered back.

"They have reached as far as Rambouillet."

My God, Virginia thought. *That's less than twenty minutes by car!*

But the distance mattered not as the officers climbed aboard and the busses pulled out. Fifteen minutes later they reached the Gare de Patin and were ordered out. Lugging her suitcase in one hand, her bag slung over her shoulder and the coat folded under her arm, she followed the crowd along a line of a hundred freight cars. It was clear now that they were to be shipped to Germany like so much livestock.

But even animals had it better than the sixty women stuffed body against body, with all of their baggage, in a stifling hot box car that would have been crowded with half as many. Virginia and Janette sat on their luggage with their backs against the wall. How appalling it was that pails should serve as their toilet—even more so because one had to weave carefully through a tangle of arms and legs to use them. In short time, the smell in the cramped car went from foul to downright revolting.

The next day the train stopped in a tunnel for three hours. Eventually, it backed out and everyone was made to get off with all their belongings. Counting rail cars, Virginia estimated the number of men and women at three thousand. It must have crossed more than one mind how greatly outnumbered the guards were, but they had machine guns.

After another day and a march of five miles through fields and villages, they were loaded onto another waiting train.

On the third day, the train stopped suddenly. One woman peered out. "They are taking a man out to the field." She didn't need to describe the rest—everyone heard the rifle's report.

Moments later, the bolt to their car clunked and the door rolled open one foot. A guard called in, "If any person from this car escapes, ten of you will be taken out and shot!"

Virginia still held out hope of rescue before the train made it out of France, but this wasn't some Hollywood western where the cavalry arrives just in time. Spirits sank as they crossed into Germany that afternoon.

On the fifth day, they stopped in Weimar, Germany, and the women were permitted to come out and stretch their legs while the men were transferred to another train. One German-speaking woman from Virginia's car asked about their destination.

"They said accommodations are plain, but not bad," she reported back. "The barracks are comfortable. There is hot and cold running water and you may take hot showers whenever you like. They do not shave women's heads and you wear your own clothing."

"What about work?" a girl asked. "Did you ask about the work?"

"He said there are chores, but only to keep the barracks neat and orderly."

Virginia received more great news from an underground acquaintance on the same train: Philippe had made it to England! Now that her love was safe, her gloom lifted and she was ready to face her fate. All she had to do now was to wait out the war until liberation. It was a glorious feeling.

On the seventh day she and the other three hundred women toted their luggage from the Fürstenberg train station along a paradise road of cottages set around a peaceful lake.

Then they reached the gates of hell—*RAVENSBRÜCK*.

CHAPTER FORTY-SIX

The shrill cry of a tortured wild animal tore Virginia from a deep sleep. But it wasn't an animal at all. It was the eardrum-stabbing wail of the camp siren. She sat up, banging her head on the bunk above, and a shower of dust and straw rained down. By the time she finished dressing in the tiny space while dodging the limbs of her two bunk mates, a long line had formed for the toilets. She, Janette and others risked beatings going outside between buildings in the darkness to squat. Ten toilets simply could not accommodate six hundred women in the half hour before roll call.

For the next two hours, she shivered in the chilly September morning until the siren finally blew and everyone dashed for the coffee line. Virginia gulped down her half-pint of bitter coffee while it was still warm. It wasn't much and it wasn't good, but it was all they would get until the midday meal of thin soup and bread. She had loved to garden, but spreading manure in a field for twelve long thirsty hours took its toll.

"Do you think work Kommandos are any better?" she asked Janette.

Janette shrugged. "Some say they are."

They found out a week later on September 11 when she and Janette were part of a three hundred woman Kommando group loaded into box cars at the Fürstenberg station. The train cars were less crowded than the trip to Ravensbrück had been, and perhaps because a woman SS guard was assigned to ride in each boxcar with the prisoners, there was an ample amount of straw for cushioning. But they were still stiff after two and a half days when they climbed out of the cattle cars at the Torgau station. As they marched through the town, Virginia couldn't believe her ears.

"*D'où venez-vous?*" men called down from hotel windows in perfect French.

"*Nous sommes français,*" women called back. "*Nous sommes belges,*" others added.

Moments later, every window in the hotel was filled with men waving and calling to them in French. It was the most wonderful sound Virginia had heard in the twelve long weeks of captivity.

"They must be prisoners of war," Janette said.

For some reason, the SS guards didn't beat the women for breaking silence. From their brief parley with the French men, the women learned that some Allied units had reached Germany. The news so lifted Virginia's spirits that the half-hour hike to the camp felt like a stroll through Central Park.

Inside the gate, the tidy stucco buildings nestled among majestic trees reminded her of a college campus. As she watched a pair of grey squirrels playing chase in the treetops with merry abandon, she imagined how delightful it would be to picnic in these peaceful woods. Maybe, she thought, this Kommando wouldn't be too bad. Then Janette broke her reverie.

"It's a bloody munitions factory!"

Much to Virginia's dismay, Janette was soon proven right. But the thought that they might be forced to make the explosives that the Germans would use to kill their friends and loved ones sickened her.

After a brief orientation, the women were separated into assigned barracks. There the women looked at each other in disbelief. The building was new and clean. There were enough bunks so that each woman got her own! Mattresses were filled with new straw, and there were clean sheets and new pillows. The steam heat radiators actually worked. And there were two washrooms with a long trough sink that had water spouts at intervals so everyone could use them. It all seemed too good to be true. They were brought food—not the tepid water and sawdust bread that passed for food at Ravensbrück, but a thick tasty cabbage soup with fresh bread. There was even a piece of sausage for each person! How incredible it was to be treated like a human being again instead of an animal.

But despite the relative benefits of life in Torgau, many of the women could not accept making munitions to kill their people. The camp commander responded to their protests with indifference. "You do not have to work here if you do not want to. But if you do not work, we will simply send you back to Ravensbrück."

Women were split up between the field and the factory. All seven English and American women, including Virginia and Janette, were pulled from the fields to work in the kitchen. Preparing food for hundreds was mostly peeling and chopping of vegetables until their hands cramped up, but it was warm in the kitchen and the women got to eat all the raw vegetables they wanted. They even managed to sneak some back for their friends. Hearing the coughing at night from the sulfuric acid fumes in the munitions plant, Virginia felt damn lucky to be cutting vegetables.

Unfortunately, it didn't last long. On October 6, Virginia and the other women from Torgau passed back through the purgatorial gates of Ravensbrück.

———

October 16, 1944

In the short time they were gone, a cruel new guard had been unleashed on the NN block. The vicious little German SS officer of maybe twenty-five took great delight in terrorizing the prisoners—stealing from them or dumping their bread and belongings on the floor and then beating them when they bent down to pick it up. When all of the women from the Torgau Kommando were selected for another assignment, Virginia couldn't wait to get away from the nasty cur.

Her stockings, sweater and coat were all taken away and she was given nothing but a light beige skirt and a pink cotton pullover blouse to ward off the autumn chill and the coming winter. Still, the women all agreed that wherever they were headed, it had to be better than Ravensbrück.

They couldn't have been more wrong.

After a day of traveling in a dirty boxcar with no straw to cushion them against the hard floor, and two older male guards who made no attempt to hide their delight at being crowded in with fifty braless women, the train came to a stop. Before the doors even opened, the thunder of mighty engines foretold their fate. It was an aerodrome. And that could mean only one thing—they'd been sent here to build an airplane runway.

They were led along the edge of an airstrip. Off to one side were huge green hangars and in the distance Virginia could see the red roofs of the pretty town of Königsberg. Nestled among the trees as innocently as a university campus, was a cluster of wood frame dormitories surrounding a square courtyard with manicured lawn. She reasoned that if the food and housing were decent, the work could be tolerated.

But once past the courtyard, they filed down a path through the woods to a mud hole inside a high fence topped with barbed wire. Inside the narrow grey buildings they found dirty floors, filthy mattresses and trash left by the Polish men who had occupied the buildings before them. Calling it a pig sty would be an insult to pigs.

This wretched place was to be her new home

———

Elsie Maréchal had endured much in the eleven months since she and her mother had departed St. Gilles prison. She had been made to stand naked in Cologne, had her head shaved in Waldheim, collapsed from her wounds while working at the Siemens factory, been locked in an airless cell in Nuremburg, and spent three days without soup or exercise in Stetten because the inmates had dared to sing and dance in their cells when they heard the news that Paris had been liberated. She had seen the very worst of German cruelty—or so she thought.

Ravensbrück was like nothing she had ever seen. Nausea choked her at the sight of the horrible death that might await. Piled high on an open wagon were dozens of women's bodies—naked, grey, foul-smelling bodies. Their twisted, gaping mouths and skeletal remains revealed how painfully their lives had ended. Hope of surviving slipped away like the white from a cracked egg. If this wasn't hell, it was damn close.

Cruelty lay everywhere, from the maniacal guards with their vicious dogs to the domineering inmates. Anyone who passed out after hours of standing in formation had to be left on the freezing ground until the formation was dismissed. Friends warned Elsie and her mother to avoid eye contact with the sadistic *Oberaufseherin* Dorothea Binz. If the woman got the notion to kick and stomp someone, all anyone could do was watch helplessly and pray that death or unconsciousness would rob Binz of her erotic pleasure. It took determination and a great deal of luck to survive Ravensbrück.

Although the Germans mocked the French and Belgians as being weak, they considered them more dangerous than other groups and split them into different blocks so they couldn't organize. The French and Belgian women prided themselves on their esprit de corps and kept their barracks clean and free of the fleas and lice that plagued other blocks. Working together seemed their best chance of survival.

But the prospect of a slow torturous death pushed many women to give up and end the suffering. Elsie and her mum had survived two years of misery in a number of prisons, but after just a few weeks at Ravensbrück, shoveling coal, unloading trucks, and building roads, Elsie worried that her mum was nearing her breaking point.

After an especially straining morning spent ankle-deep mucking out a swamp for expansion of the camp, the lines on her mother's face said this hard work was taking its toll. Reading the faraway look in her mother's eyes, Elsie knew her mum was contemplating an awful decision.

"You can't quit," Elsie whispered in response to unspoken words. "The Germans are losing the war. Brussels has been liberated."

"You go on." Her mum reached into her cloth bag. "Take my rations and survive. I am too old. I will not make it."

Elsie covered her mum's hand with her own, stopping her from taking anything out of the bag. "It will only be a little longer."

Her mother seemed to lack the strength to respond. Elsie worried that she might simply lay down her shovel and let the Germans shoot her.

"You have seen the flyers dropped by the Allies. They know we are here. It is only a matter of time before they reach us."

"Even if it is only a few months, people in here do not last that long."

The group of guards began to stir. The lunch break was near the end.

When they went back to work, there would be no talking allowed. Elsie tried harder. "I need you to stay with me. Promise me you will not give up."

With a heavy sigh and a resigned tip of the head, her mum agreed.

Elsie bolstered her mum with a gentle squeeze on her hand. "We will walk out of here together."

On Sunday, their day off, Elsie found someone she hoped would lift her mother's spirits. She brought the girl back with her. "Mum, do you remember Nadine from St. Gilles prison? She was arrested a few months before us."

"I'm glad to see you are still with us, Nadine. How long have you been here?"

"One year."

"One year! I didn't think it was possible to last here that long!"

"There are Polish women who have been here much longer than me —many for more than four years."

"Four years?" Elsie panned the ghastly scene like a newsreel camera. "I can't even imagine it."

"Many friends are here," Nadine said softly—"Frantxia ... Elvire Morelle ... Rosa ... Martine ... Lulu and Cyprienne Dassié ... Amanda and Louise Stassart ... and many others—but say nothing. We've heard the Germans will look to silence us before the Allies come."

Madame Maréchal nodded understanding, then asked softly, "Do you know if our colonel is here?"

"Colonel?" Nadine puzzled over that a moment then broke into a smile. She looked around to make sure no one was listening. "Yes. She and her sister are here, but we don't speak of her for fear that the guards may find out who she is."

———

"*Achtung!*" boomed through the loud speakers. "*Der Führer spricht!*"

Shivering, wrapping her arms around herself to preserve body heat, Elsie braced herself for a prolonged stand in the cold. Hitler's speeches were always long-winded. Hawk-eyed guards prowled the formation for anyone not paying attention. Through whispers, German-speaking inmates relayed information. The Germans had launched a counter offensive in Belgium and surrounded the American army at a town called Bastogne. They were advancing toward Antwerp.

Although Hitler's words still had their distinctive punch, his weary voice no longer swooped and soared like the early days. His blaze of fanaticism now seemed more like a dying fire, still glowing red, but without much heat. He claimed this was a great German victory, but the guards weren't cheering every word like they used to.

News of the Germans pushing the Americans back hit Madame Maréchal particularly hard. Elsie wasn't permitted to speak while working, but as she watched her mum numbly unloading boxes from the lorry, she worried over the older woman's distant eyes.

When they broke for lunch, Elsie took her mum aside where they could talk. "It's just a setback. The Allies are going to win."

Her mum sighed. "I know, but stopping the Allied advance means they won't reach us this winter."

The dismal odds of making it through another winter depressed Elsie, but she wouldn't let her own worry show and bring her mum down even further. "The Germans must have thrown everything they had left into this offensive," she reasoned. "That means they will not have the troops necessary to stop the Soviet advance. One army or the other will reach us. Women keep coming in from other camps evacuated ahead of the Russian army. They're coming, Mum. We just have to hold on a bit longer."

Madame Maréchal raised her eyebrows.

"Remember, you promised me you would fight to hold on."

Her mum smiled and patted Elsie's hand. "You're right," she said resolutely. "It's in God's hands."

Elsie didn't care if her Mum's positive attitude was only for her benefit as long as she didn't give up. She changed to a happier topic. "The children are excited about the Christmas party. Even the Jewish kids are looking forward to it."

"I believe the women are more excited than the children," her mum said. "They've been sewing puppet costumes, building the stage, practicing songs, painting sets…"

"Looking after children has given the women something to care about in this awful place."

Madame Maréchal lowered her voice. "I still can't believe Binz allowed the communists to do this for the children."

"It's got nothing to do with kindness," Elsie whispered back. "The Soviet army's getting close. She's only being nice to the Russians to save her own backside."

After lunch, a commotion erupted. Several trucks away, a male guard grabbed a woman's arm and dragged her away from the group. Elsie couldn't make out what the guard was shouting at her, but it appeared the woman had been caught stuffing something into her pocket. The prisoner was ordered to strip. Elsie didn't want to see what she knew was coming, but felt compelled to look. The woman dropped her clothes to the ground and bowed her head. With a cold, blank face, the guard pressed his Lugar to the woman's head. Elsie recoiled at the *burp* of the single shot that echoed off the buildings. The woman fell down dead.

———

"*Aufstehen!*"

Elsie struggled her eyes open.

"*Jeder außerhalb jetzt!*"

Throwing her coat over her shoulders, Elsie trudged behind the others out into the cold dark night. The December wind mercilessly lashed at her ears and face as an angry Dorothea Binz marched back and forth in front of the formation shouting, "One of your women took something from the truck she was unloading and she has paid with her life. Let me remind you that anyone caught stealing German goods will be shot! Anyone taking goods from trains or trucks or food from kitchens will be shot!"

Although she could barely see the *Oberaufseherin* in the darkness, Elsie could picture her distorted expression. Binz had a decent enough face, but it twisted grotesquely when she dealt out her evil punishment.

"Books are not permitted!" Binz barked. "Poetry is not permitted! Diaries are not permitted! Notebooks are not permitted! There shall be no drawings of any kind!"

Behind Binz, flakes of white fluttered like snow in the dim glow of the pole lamps. But it wasn't snow. It was human soot. For the past few months the crematorium had been operating day and night, filling the air with the putrid smell of burning flesh. Corpse crews searched each barracks twice a day now. In the darkness, Elsie couldn't see the grotesque bodies that lay near the ovens, dumped from the corpse cart to make room for more, but she could smell the rotting flesh.

Keeping the women shivering outside was the overseer's way of punishing them for the woman who stole the article from the train. Deprived of sleep and her stomach empty, Elsie fought to keep her eyes open after more than an hour of standing in the cold.

Fflump

It was difficult to see in the darkness, but Elsie recognized the sound. Someone rows ahead of her had collapsed. Nobody moved—it was against the rules to help her. Whoever it was would have to lie there until the formation was over.

Fflump

Somewhere to her left another one went down. Elsie could just make out the shape of her body on the ground. Then a white-haired woman on Elsie's right began swaying. Her labored breathing fogged in the cold air.

Elsie cast her eyes to the side and whispered, "Are you all right?"

The woman looked at Elsie. Her mouth formed words, but they came out as nothing more than wisps of vapor. Her eyelids fluttered.

Elsie wanted to reach out and steady the poor woman, but dared not. She edged closer. Through breathy gasps, the woman tried to make Elsie hear her.

Elsie only made out the word *daughter* before the woman collapsed to the ground, still mouthing inaudibly. Even then she continued to move her lips like she was trying to get her message out with her last breath. Elsie leaned over a bit farther to hear.

Pain ripped through Elsie's back.

"*Steh auf!*" the guard snapped. "Stand up!"

Elsie rose with her hands up to protect her face against the next swing of the truncheon.

"*Lassen sie sie!* Let her be unless you wish to join her." The guard poked the old woman's body with the tip of her boot. The woman's chest had stopped rising and falling. The guard poked once more. Seeing no fog of breath, she strolled on impassively. The death of a human being was of no more concern to the guard than if she had stepped on a spider.

As much as Elsie wanted to feel terrible over the woman's death, she felt nothing. A week ago, she had helped a friend carry the girl's dead mother to the corpse pile. Together they tossed the woman onto the heap. Her friend showed no emotion.

How numb we've all become to death, she thought sadly.

CHAPTER FORTY-SEVEN

The whole camp buzzed with excitement. Block 22 had been emptied and cleaned. Russian women built a stage. A Czech artist created puppet heads, while French and Belgian women sewed the puppet costumes. Polish carpenters and artists built and painted the sets. Women throughout Ravensbrück saved up marmalade and rations of bread to give to the children. And on the floor under a Christmas tree trimmed with colorful paper ornaments, was a pile of little gifts made by women all over the camp.

Saturday, December 23, 1944, after a month of preparation, it was finally time. The children marched in and sat on the floor with the littlest in front. An international chorus filled the room with bright and cheery Christmas songs.

Oberaufseherin Dorothea Binz sashayed to the front of the room like an actress at a movie premiere, escorted by *Schutzhartlagerfuhrer* Edmund Bräuning. Bräuning stood before the closed curtain of the puppet theater wearing something that none of the inmates had ever seen on him—a smile.

"Welcome children. We have a special treat for you today. The ladies have created a wonderful party that I am sure you will enjoy."

The children hesitated, not knowing whether it was permissible to speak or show delight.

Binz smiled and clapped, casting her eyes around to stimulate the children to join in.

"I have another surprise for you," Bräuning continued. "You will each receive an extra ration of bread and fruit."

The children bounced up and down and cheered.

"Now sit quietly and enjoy the show."

The children didn't understand a word of what the Russian-voiced puppets were saying, but the silly and slapstick antics of puppets chasing each other around the stage made the children laugh just the same.

Women crowded the windows and open doors enjoying watching the children as much as the children enjoyed the show. Sadness was all these poor kids had known of late. Many had been orphaned during the Warsaw Ghetto uprising when German troops and tanks crushed the Jewish revolt.

The squeals of the little ones brought Elsie memories of Christmas with her brother Bobby and how they would beg their parents to let them stay up just a little longer to play with their new toys. Seeing their tiny faces light up with glee awakened a happiness that Elsie had thought was long dead. Such joyful memories had Elsie dabbing away trickles of water from the corners of her eyes.

A beaming Russian woman reached up on tip toes and topped the tree with a silvery paper star. "It is time for presents," she cooed.

The music director swung her arms, leading the chorus into the beautiful refrain of the German Christmas standard *O Tannenbaum*.

The children grew very quiet. Smiles dropped from their little faces. The glee of just moments ago vanished as the old tune stirred emotions. Most of these girls and boys were all that was left of their families. Soft sniffles and sobs began in different parts of the room.

The singing died as women in the chorus wiped their own eyes. Elsie choked back the lump in her throat.

Flustered, Binz and Bräuning made a hasty exit. The international children's committee formed to coordinate activities for the Children's Christmas party had had an unanticipated consequence— cooperation among the ethnic groups.

———

The six women in Virginia's detail stopped digging while two of them pushed and pulled on the tree stump. It didn't budge. Virginia had hoped the melting snow would help loosen the soil, but all it did was leave a muddy mess. They took up their picks and shovels and went back to prying the earth from around the stubborn root.

"It is April and the cherry trees are filled with glorious pink blossoms,"

Janette said dreamily. It was actually two days before Christmas, but since it was Janette's turn to host an imaginary dinner party, she could choose the season. "We will have a fresh garden salad with a creamy Roquefort dressing that I make myself. I'm preparing Cornish hens—one for each of us. I have stuffed them with a bread and sausage dressing with chunks of apple to give it a bit of sweetness." She thrust her spade into the earth and kicked it forward with the heel of her wooden shoe. "I've made a green bean casserole topped with toasted onion strings and selected a nice chardonnay to go with dinner. Then we will have peach cobbler with a sweet sherry." She dragged her spadeful of dirt to the rim of the hole and tipped it over the pile.

Virginia closed her eyes and inhaled. "It smells delicious."

"You must tell me your recipe for Roquefort dressing," one of the girls said.

"Certainly." Janette jabbed her shovel back into the dirt. "It is very easy to make."

Virginia thought it wonderful to see her friend cheerily sharing her recipe. Janette had battled fatigue and dysentery of late. Despite stuffing mattress straw under their sweaters every morning, Janette still suffered terribly from the cold. She couldn't take the frigid wind on the open airfield where they had been laying sod. Thankfully, when the ground surface froze the sod work had stopped and they were moved into the woods where the trees helped block some of the wind.

After another half hour of poking and shoveling, the women had exposed enough of the bigger lateral roots to cut them. Two girls went back to tugging on the stump. "My grandfather uses a horse to pull stumps out," Tita grunted. "The Germans expect skinny women to do what a well fed horse struggles with."

"Maybe we can throw a harness on Olga," Virginia said as she and Yvonne pushed the stump from the other side.

"Hah! You French *vimen* are *veak* like *babushka*," Yvonne said in a mock Russian accent.

With four women pulling and pushing and two prying up the lateral roots, the stump slowly began to move. Once they got it leaning over, two girls dug away at the soil holding the tap root. After more tugging, digging, and sawing the lateral roots, the women finally made the beast lose its grip on the earth and wrestled it to the ground.

The women collapsed against the dirt walls.

"As easy as sticking fingers in your nose!" Tita quipped between heaving breaths.

Together they dragged the gnarly thing out of the hole.

Virginia shook the tightness from her arm muscles. From the triumphant faces you'd think they'd won an Olympic medal.

Women perked up at the faint whine of a truck engine. They brushed the dirt from their clothing and milled about the tree stump pretending to work, while making ready to run. The engine grew louder. Virginia's mouth began to salivate. They shuffled a bit toward the road.

The truck stopped. The guard's whistle blew and everyone made a mad dash to line up. Pushing and shoving, the bigger, stronger Poles and Russians elbowed the French women aside. The guards watched in amusement as each woman fought for her sustenance. Those whose soup bowls were filled first would get in the back of the line for a chance at seconds. Despite the knocking about, the line formed quickly as no one would be served until all had gotten into formation.

The French women took their soup into the hut where a warm stove gave them respite. There was no use sticking around the truck. They considered it beneath their dignity to fight for what was left at the bottom of the pots. Besides, the big wolfhounds would beat out the poodles anyway.

When the break ended it took threats of beatings to make the women leave the warm shed and go back out into the cold. Surprisingly, at the end of the day, the guards let one of the women take a small Christmas tree back to their block.

Then on Sunday, the camp commander announced that they would all have tomorrow off for the Christmas holiday. Virginia and Janette celebrated by mixing saved up bread with a bit of margarine and sugar to make a pudding. Artistic women hung paper angels and stars on the tree. It was a wonderful day.

Then came the dreadful news. A week ago, the Germans had surrounded the American army in Bastogne. The Allies were in retreat.

The news had cast a pall over Ravensbrück too. Madame Maréchal took it particularly hard. Elsie encouraged her, but it was difficult to be positive when she herself felt defeated. The war dragging on until spring now seemed a certainty.

Two days after Christmas, hope returned—the Americans had retaken Bastogne. But at Ravensbrück selections for the *transport noir* increased. A second crematorium was built. Bodies were burned around the clock and they still couldn't keep up with the number of women dying. The prospects of making it to liberation dimmed.

By February, the guards had become visibly anxious over Germany's impending defeat. More prisoners arrived almost daily, evacuated from camps that had closed in the face of the advancing armies. As overcrowding increased, so did deaths from starvation. The SS, however, didn't concern themselves with matters of prisoner hunger. They were busy burning camp records—the evidence of their atrocities. Then they turned their attention to the rabbits—the Polish girls who were the guinea pigs for the heinous experiments.

In early February, a breathless Belgian girl rushed into the NN barracks. "The Poles have been tipped off! The rabbits are going to be locked in their barracks tomorrow!" Elsie jumped to her feet.

"Rabbits?" a confused new inmate asked.

"They are not real rabbits," a woman explained. "They are girls that the Germans experimented on like they were lab rabbits. And locking them in their barracks could only mean one thing." The woman drew a finger across her neck with a *gickkk* sound.

The new inmate's eyes popped wide.

"Yes," the Belgian girl said. "It will be bad for them." She spoke to the new inmate, but her eyes signaled the others to meet her in the washroom.

"What are the Poles going to do?" a woman asked when the trusted friends met in secret.

"They want us to hide some of the rabbits."

"If the Germans catch us, it will be our necks instead of theirs," one cautioned.

"We can't just let the Germans kill them," Madame Maréchal said.

"How many are there?" someone asked.

"Eighty-four were experimented on," the Belgian girl said. "Only two dozen are still alive."

Elsie drew her hand contemplatively down the back of her head. "The rabbits are proof of what the Boches have done to us," she said. "We must keep them alive until one army or the other reaches us."

"But how?" the cautious one asked. "Binz will have every barracks searched."

"There are so many women in camp now there is no room to hide anybody," another warned.

"We have to help," Elsie said. "There has to be something we can do."

————

The huge guy on the little motorbike and the little guy on the big bicycle would have made a comical pair if not for the specter of death that rode with them. The arrival of Doctor Adolf Winkelmann, whose butt hung off both sides of his little motorbike, and his short consort, Doctor Trommer, who traveled on a very large bicycle, meant that there was to be a selection.

The doctors watched with tired, bored expressions, as the women marched around in a circle, lifting up their dresses to show their legs. Elsie, Nadine, Diane and the other young healthier girls marched around the outside of the circle to obscure the doctors' view of the older women like *Diane's* mother, Louise Stassart, and Madame Maréchal. With the mere wag of a finger and a letter scribbled next to their name in a ledger, they could end the lives of women whose legs were too swollen, cheeks too pale, or walk too labored.

"Women who are selected will be transferred to the camp *Mittwerda*," Overseer Binz announced. "They will rest until they are strong enough to work again."

But no one ever returned from *Mittwerda*. Rumors of a gas chamber had been confirmed by a note found in the hem of a dress that had been sent back in a pile of prison uniforms to be reconstituted: *If you find this note, it means I was killed in the gas chamber.*

———

Friday, January 26, 1945

Nothing stirred in the bleak white woods. The snow was too deep and the air too cold for forest animals to venture from their burrows. Only the prisoners of Königsberg would be sent out in such conditions—whether they died through starvation or freezing made no difference to the Germans. Virginia could barely talk, her face paralyzed by the icy wind. Snow packed around the unsecured tops of her wood-soled galoshes until she could no longer feel her toes. Every breath of frigid air burned her nostrils. Where she had grown up in Florida, freezing to death was just an expression. Here, it was all too real. She had to keep moving or she would surely succumb to the elements.

She thrust her spade into the lower levels of the dirt walls where the ground wasn't frozen solid. It came away only half full, but in her weakened condition, that was all she could swing up into the steel dump container.

With picks and shovels women tore out the earth walls on both sides of the trench. Once the container was full, they pushed it up the tracks and dumped the dirt where other women shoveled it into place. When the ground was leveled wooden railroad ties were laid.

In this remote region of the Reich, there were no cranes to lift the heavy steel rails, so the Germans used malnourished women as slaves. Women lined up along the rail and lifted together on command. Virginia's legs wobbled as they carried the rail to its place. Pain seared her arms and back. Her knees threatened to buckle under the enormous weight, but she dared not let go, knowing that if they let it slip, someone would be severely injured. Once it was down others hammered in the spikes.

A detail of French male POWs marched by. The groups waved to each other, and although they were not permitted to speak, their presence nearby gave the women comfort. As soldiers, the men were allowed to receive Red Cross packages and with permission of the camp commander, generously shared food parcels with the women. But the women received nothing as the guards divvied the contents up among themselves.

More traffic than usual passed by on the road and as the day wore on it grew to a steady stream of trucks, cars, and oxcarts heaped high with boxes, blankets, trunks and suitcases. Virginia kept shoveling to keep up the appearance of working, but inside she was near ready to burst. She and her friends shared bright-eyed glances of hope as they worked. The horde of people fleeing Königsberg could only mean one thing—the Soviet Army was getting close!

Bolstered by what they had seen, women on the brink fought to postpone death one more day. But after eleven hours of straining in the bitter cold, some lost that fight on the march back to the camp. Virginia wished she could help carry those who had fallen face-down in the snow, but she was too weak, and with her dilapidated shoes falling off every few steps, she could hardly keep up herself.

"You there!" a guard called.

Virginia turned and the guard pointed to her feet. "Take those off!"

Virginia reluctantly obeyed. She marched on in snow-caked socks over the freezing gravel, blocking out the pain by thinking about liberation, and imagining a great party when the Russian army entered the camp.

Doctor Perity, a fellow inmate, examined Virginia's feet when she returned to the block. "You are lucky. Your feet are red, but I see no frostbite."

The women talked long into the night, excited by the nearness of their would-be rescuers. But on Monday, word came that the French POWs had been evacuated. Virginia worried the women would be evacuated as well and sent back to Ravensbrück.

The next day was bitterly cold. Virginia felt guilty staying with the other shoeless women back at the block, but she was thankful she didn't have to go out to work. Now she could conserve what little strength she had left for liberation.

Cold air rushed into the barracks shortly after lunch as the work crew came streaming in. Returning to the block this early on a weekday was unheard of.

"The guards made us drop our tools where we stood and line up," said an excited prisoner. "We came back nearly at a run."

Earlier, Virginia had heard that the German civilian employees had fled.

Late afternoon, two women from another barracks burst in. "The *Oberaufseherin* just drove off with her airman boyfriend! The back seat of her car was loaded with suit cases and clothing!"

Virginia's pulse raced at the thought that their misery might finally be over. It seemed too much to hope for. Yet when darkness fell, screams of excitement erupted outside. The courtyard filled with women—Russian, Czechs, French, Belgian, Poles, Danes, Italians—everyone shouted and cheered as fifty foot flames lit up the night. The airfield had been bombed!

"Look!" someone shouted.

The prison gate was wide open. The guards were gone! A mob of Slavic women began streaming through.

Virginia took several steps.

Someone grabbed her arm. "Wait! You will be shot by the Germans."

Virginia stopped then looked back at the Russians shouting and running wildly on the outside of the compound.

She shook her arm free.

"The Germans will return and those women will be mowed down by machine guns," another warned.

The warning gave her pause. But the allure of the open gates was too great for Virginia to resist. She had to go through them if only to feel a moment's freedom.

Macabre shadows danced across the flames of the conflagration as hundreds of women descended on the buildings like locusts on a wheat field. In the lights of the open windows and doors, Virginia could see the women ransacking and looting.

Deciding not to venture into that frenzy, she walked on. No one had touched the wood and coal pile. She filled two buckets and waddled them back to the French block, astonishing the others as she dumped out the life-warming fuel. "I'm going back for more," she said.

Tita accompanied her, but had to stop and rest. Virginia went on alone and followed some women down a ramp into a cellar and there before her eyes were rows and rows of food stores. She stared in disgust and disbelief, overwhelmed by so much food while women starved. This time, when she returned with a gallon of jam and as many cans of food as she could carry, her friends in the block cried.

She went back and found Tita by the kitchen. A German patrol came and started shouting at the looters. While their attention was focused on others, Virginia and Tita each grabbed a handle of a full dairy can of milk and hurried off.

Meanwhile, the Polish guard had distributed all of the remaining bread and margarine. Sweet jam, bread, margarine and vegetables washed down with delicious milk felt like a banquet. They feasted until their bellies bulged.

Then the door swung open. Two girls rushed in. "Georgette's been shot by a German patrol!" Marcelle said.

"It is nothing," Georgette said. "Just my shoulder. I will be all right."

Doctor Perity pulled off Georgette's bloody blouse. "Get me a pan of water and some salt," she said as she examined Georgette front and back, "and a clean cloth."

The others hid their plunder while the salt brine boiled on the stove. "You are a lucky girl," Doctor Perity said as she cleaned and dressed the wound. "The bullet went straight through."

"The Germans are coming!" a girl at the window called.

Georgette slipped her blouse back on and covered herself with a coat. She hid in the shadows of her bunk.

The door burst open.

"You are still prisoners," a stern German officer said. "Anyone caught plundering will be shot!"

Virginia sat on her bunk listening attentively while holding her breath to still her panic.

"Clean this place up. I will return in one hour. If this room is not clean, you will be punished."

The women did as ordered and when the officer returned several hours later, all of the women pretended to be asleep.

The next morning, the patrols were nowhere to be found. Women ventured out in small groups. While the Slavs carted more food off from the cellar, Virginia and Yvonne ventured into the mess hall where the plates were still full of food. The Germans had run away so fast, they hadn't even eaten their lunch.

They returned to the block with a haul of meat and vegetables and a big pot of boiled potatoes. Once the door was closed behind them, two Frenchmen came out of hiding.

"They escaped when the prisoners were evacuated," Tita explained.

"We are going to fight with the Russians when they get here," the men said. "They are only ten miles away."

"We should go too," one woman said.

"Where?"

"To the Russians, of course."

"We do not know where to go," another said. "We have food and shelter here. If we go wandering about without direction, we will freeze to death."

"She's right," Yvonne said. "We have waited these many months— what is a few more days? Virginia and I will go get more food."

They were in the square when they spotted a German patrol near the prison gate. A German pointed.

They'd been seen!

Yvonne and Virginia bolted before the soldiers could raise their weapons. They darted around the building corner on feet energized by the fear of being shot like Georgette, and flew between the buildings searching for a place to hide.

Virginia pointed. "In there!"

It was a food preparation building. By the time they dashed down a ramp that led to a basement, they could hear the clump of boots in the kitchen above them. They snuck through a dark pantry to a smaller room filled with beer kegs. They had no time to find a better hiding place. Virginia squeezed behind the barrels and scrunched down.

Moments later, a German soldier entered shining a tiny flashlight.

The beam swept across the walls, the floor and the barrels right beside her. Another sweep of the light, then it went out. She listened to the soldier's footfalls disappear from the adjoining room. She breathed once again.

The footsteps returned.

Again, the light passed in front above and behind.

Virginia prayed.

The soldier's feet shuffled along the floor, the light moving along with him.

Virginia risked shallow breaths.

Bap Bap

Two muffled gun shots sounded outside.

The flashlight went out. Again, the soldier left.

Virginia remained still as a possum. After a few minutes, she cautiously peeked out to find Yvonne doing the same. Neither girl moved from her hiding place; each ready to duck down at the slightest sound. Outside, an engine rumbled to life. Virginia rose slightly, listening as the truck cranked through its gears until finally disappearing in the distance.

Back at the block, they learned that the two Frenchmen had been shot while eating in the cafeteria.

The next morning, Janette and Tita were suffering from severe dysentery from their stomachs' inability to adjust to their big meal. The Soviets were reported to be less than four kilometers away. And Virginia, despite her close call, ventured out once more.

The square was littered with food scraps, cans and wrappers dropped in the snow. The SS dorm looked like it had been hit by an Oklahoma twister. The downstairs had been cleaned out of anything of value, so Virginia and Yvonne ventured up a stairway to an attic.

Hastening back to the block with the spoils—two light blue SS blouses, a grey skirt, a double-breasted gabardine and a pair of black shoes—Virginia couldn't wait to take her new-found treasures to the washroom so that when the Russians came, she would be wearing clean lice-free clothing. She'd barely gotten her prison uniform off when the courtyard erupted in shouts, screams and gun fire.

Virginia threw her old clothes on and hurried out to the main room.

A French girl rushed in, pale as a corpse. "It's the Germans! The SS from Ravensbrück have come to take us back!"

CHAPTER FORTY-EIGHT

The evacuation of Königsberg drove many women to the brink of death—there seemed no rational explanation for it. After the Germans' offensive in the Ardennes failed there was no longer any delusion that they could win or even hold out to negotiate an armistice. They were beaten and they knew it.

The first day's march broke down the reserves of many of the women as the Ravensbrück SS pushed hard to put distance between them and the Russians. It was especially difficult for those with severe dysentery like Tita and Janette, and even worse the next day when the group slogged through a blizzard. Virginia virtually dragged Janette along, despite her crying and pleading to just let her die.

Finally, after midnight, they reached a rail yard and were loaded into boxcars. Janette had to be lifted in as she no longer had the strength to climb. By the time they reached Fürstenberg in the middle of the next night, the women were so weak they had to be dragged out of the boxcars by the SS. They fell in a heap of bodies on the cold ground. With whips and clubs, the SS prodded them to their feet and herded them forward. By dawn on February 4, 1945 they were once again inside the purgatory of Ravensbrück.

———

Elsie leaned forward, closer to her mother's ear. "Don't you give them any." She glared at the pack of kids. Even women who had tried to look after them had had enough of their begging and stealing. The hungry little hyenas congregated at the end of the soup line, their beady eyes ever scanning, searching for a sympathetic woman who might give them some soup or bread; or a weak, frail one whom they could steal from.

"And hold onto your bag," Elsie told her mum. She didn't want to be like that. It wasn't in her nature. But some of the children had become quite brazen and stealing food was stealing life. They were robbing the older and weaker women of their chance to survive until liberation.

The moment she and her mother got their soup, the pack encircled them, begging and pleading. Elsie gave her mum a gentle shove to remind her to keep moving. Just ahead, four skinny twelve-year-olds blocked the path of one poor old lady. When their begging failed to produce results, one brazen boy grabbed the woman's bread ration and ran off. The remaining three then turned their attention to Madame Maréchal.

One boy rushed in for the snatch, but Elsie was quicker, yanking him backwards before he'd gotten his hands on her mum's bread. "Get away from her you little bastards!"

Elsie felt a hard tug on her cloth bag. She whirled around and elbowed the would-be thief hard in the ribs and followed it up with a knee to the stomach. She charged at the two others who were still pack-hunting her mum. They gave up and turned their attention back to the food line where they might find easier prey.

When the boys were gone, Elsie looked at her soup bowl. Half of the liquid had sloshed out. She wanted to cry. It meant there would be none for her. With a heavy sigh, she took what was left of her dinner back into the barracks where she climbed to a top bunk and tapped on the ceiling boards. "It's me," she whispered.

Two white eyes appeared in the dim light. Elsie handed up her bowl and spoon.

"*Dziękuję*", the young girl said in Polish then switched to English. "Is enough, what you have?"

"Yes. I've eaten half. The rest is for you." Nothing would show the atrocities committed by the Germans better than seeing how the Nazi butchers mutilated this poor girl. Elsie truly admired her courage for still wanting to live despite the debilitating damage. Besides that, she had become a good friend.

Elsie repeated the process with the morning meal.

"You no go to work?"

"It's Sunday."

"Oh. I forget."

"Here," Elsie said. "My mum sent some bread."

"*Tank* you. How is your *mudder*?"

"She is all right. But I worry about the selections. Her legs are swollen and she is not walking well..." Elsie covered her mouth. "I'm sorry."

"You have not to be sorry. You did not do *dis* to me."

"I know, but..." Elsie couldn't imagine what it must be like to have your sciatic nerve cut and live the rest of your life with one useless leg.

"When war is over, you go to school to be nurse, yes?"

"I don't know. I haven't given it much thought lately."

"I *tink* you very good to be nurse."

"Look at this," a woman called.

"What is happening?" the Polish girl asked as women crowded the windows and spilled through the door to have a look.

"I don't know." Elsie climbed down and followed the others outside.

Hundreds of half-dead blank-eyed women limped through the gate, their legs reflexively responding to the prodding clubs and whips of the SS.

"The Germans must have closed another camp," someone said.

"They look like withered corn stalks."

"Oh my God," a woman exclaimed as the light of dawn began lifting the shadows from the women's wretched faces. "I know them! They are the ones who were sent to Königsberg!"

———

The six hundred women from Königsberg were crammed into a tent that only held two hundred. Virginia and her friends searched for a spot to lay down and rest, but the floor was such a tangle of arms and legs that even going outside to do one's business took the agility of a high wire artist and drew a great deal of leg punches and shoves when someone was inadvertently stepped on.

The day after arriving back at Ravensbrück, Janette would eat no more. Her eyes were dull and unfocussed. Virginia and a friend carried her on a stretcher to the infirmary only to find the room full of women on the verge of death. It was obvious their friend would receive no attention. Janette had slipped past the point of knowing where she was and dwelled in that realm between life and death where there was no pain, no cold, and no more hunger.

Virginia leaned in and said softly, "Go to sleep now, dear friend. Soon, you will be home in France. The cherry trees will be in bloom."

The fog momentarily lifted from her friend's eyes. Janette smiled up at Virginia. She looked finally at peace.

"Good night." Virginia kissed Janette's forehead, staggered outside into the darkness and wept.

The conditions at Ravensbrück were even worse than when Virginia had left in October. She was so weak from the march back that three days later, when called for an *appel*, she suffered the guard's beating because she couldn't move quickly enough and the transport left without her.

A week later, she was assigned to a barracks where she shared a bunk with two of her friends. But the young guard from last fall had become even more sadistic. Unlike the others who spent no more time than necessary in the flea-infested barracks, this guard was always about, torturing the weak with evil games for her amusement and stealing whatever she pleased. Virginia underestimated just how far the woman would go and unwittingly became her victim.

"Give me your ring!" the guard demanded one day.

Her wedding ring was all she had left of her sweet Philippe. It had carried her through many dark days by reminding her that she would one day be reunited with him. She had never thought it would be taken from her finger while she was still alive.

"Give it to me!"

"I can't." Virginia held up her hand. "My knuckles are swollen. It won't come off."

"Get up! Go soap your finger. Get it off!"

The tiny bar of ersatz soap produced very little lather. As Virginia worked it around her fingers anyway, the hopelessness overwhelmed her and broke down what remained of her defensive shell. She had taken the freezing temperatures, the hard work, the agonizing march, the humiliations and all of their beatings without allowing her pain to show, but now she could no longer hold back the tears. As she twisted the ring around her knuckle she sobbed to the woman at the sink next to her, "She steals from Americans, too?"

The woman stopped washing. "You are American?"

Virginia nodded through her tears.

The guard had entered the washroom, and now her callous expression turned to surprise. Her tone changed. "You may keep your ring," she said and walked out.

On February 25, Amanda Stassart, *Diane*, who had guided airmen from Belgium to Paris in Lily's network, held her mother, Louise, in her arms, stroking the woman's hair as she breathed her last.

Rosa, the little lady in black who had sheltered men in Paris was also dead—she had voluntarily taken the place of a woman with a young family who had been selected for the gas chamber.

Next, the Grim Reaper set his sights on Madame Maréchal.

They both suspected it, but Elsie's fears were confirmed when a French girl who worked in the infirmary warned them that Madame Maréchal's name had been checked off.

Elsie grabbed up her mother's bag. "We need to hide you."

"Where would I hide?" her mum said as if she thought the idea absurd. "There is no more room behind the coal bins or in the loft."

"Women are hiding in the typhus barracks. The SS won't go in there."

"I'd rather die quickly in the gas chamber than slowly of typhus."

"The Polish block," Elsie said. "They will help us. I'll go talk to them."

Madame Maréchal grabbed her daughter's arm. "If they don't find me, the whole NN block will be punished. They will pick others to go in my place. They could pick you. No, if I have been selected, then I will go."

Elsie couldn't believe how calm her mother sounded, like she was politely leaving the last chicken wing on the platter. The end of the war was near. Her mother was still healthy enough to make it. Elsie couldn't let her die because a man on a motorbike had checked off her name.

Not one of the women whose names were called begged. No one cried. No one showed any emotion. It was their final act of defiance. Elsie tried to prepare herself as the block senior read the names, but a thought nearly paralyzed her: she hadn't given her mum a hug goodbye before they formed up. If she tried now, they'd both be shot.

The block senior stopped reading and dismissed the formation without calling her mum's name. Elsie didn't learn until the next day that the selection doctor had indeed put a mark by Madame Maréchal's name, but a Jewish prisoner doctor who had come to know her mother in St. Gilles prison had secretly erased it.

CHAPTER FORTY-NINE

For Virginia and the others at Ravensbrück, the closing days of the war brought a mixture of hope and despair. Each night the prisoners gathered around their hidden map following the progress of the Allied forces. The British, French and American armies had crossed the Rhine into Germany, and the Russian forces were only fifty miles from Berlin.

But Virginia couldn't summon much optimism. She read the hopelessness in the eyes of her friends, and knew that they could see the same in hers. They had melted away to little more than skeletons. She could feel her life essence fading with each passing day. She wouldn't discourage the others by saying it out loud, but she could admit to herself that none of them were going to live to see liberation. Corpse crews were no longer keeping up with taking the bodies away. On the other side of the room, lay a woman who had been dead since yesterday. Virginia and her friends didn't even have the strength to drag the body outside.

With the mounting German losses, most of the guards had taken to drinking the day away. Food rations had been reduced even further. But not all of the guards had relaxed their hardened ways. The nasty young SS guard still prowled about. Virginia could feel her circling like a vulture waiting to cut the ring from her dead finger.

On Sunday, February 25 the *blockova* marched to the center of the room and demanded, "Where is the American who was at Königsberg?

Virginia followed the blockova to the washroom where another woman awaited her. "Take off your clothes, Virginia. All of them."

Virginia apprehensively did as told and was handed a can of anti-vermin powder to rub all over her body. Then she was given clean clothing, including a coat and without explanation was sent back into the barracks.

Three days later, the *blockova* informed Virginia that she was wanted at once. An SS guard was waiting for her at the door. Virginia's heart sputtered. Her shaky legs struggled to keep up with the guard. By the time they reached the administrative office on the other side of the compound, Virginia was breathing like she'd carried timber over on her shoulders. She must have appeared on the verge of collapse when she stood before the desk because the secretary brought her a chair. Virginia was shocked. No one had ever shown concern for a prisoner before.

After only a short wait, the secretary ushered Virginia into an inner office. Virginia wished she could understand what the woman behind the desk was saying because her tone was pleasant and she seemed to be explaining something. Mostly, Virginia hoped that the woman did not expect a response. The SS were always quick to punish those who didn't comprehend German. Instead, the officer issued instructions to her secretary. Moments later a male guard appeared and Virginia gathered that she was to go with him.

She struggled to keep up as he led her out the camp gate, past the kitchens, and into an office with a female SS officer and her secretary.

"You are Madame d'Albert?" the officer asked in good English.

"Yes."

"You are American?"

"Yes."

"Where are you from?"

"I was born in Florida, but I live with my husband in Paris now."

After a few more questions, she was sent with the young secretary out into the hall. "I speak English a little," the secretary said in a heavy accent. "Tonight, you *vill* be happy. You go away." She brought Virginia to a cell, but assured her as she locked it, "You stay here only five minutes."

Excitement coursed through Virginia, but at the same time, she worried it could be another Nazi lie—a charade for their amusement. Were they just toying with the American, she wondered, or were they being nice because the U. S. Army was getting closer?

The door unlocked and she was let out by the same man who had brought her there. Her hopes fell as he took her back down the path and into the camp. He marched her to the infirmary where she was ordered to strip in front of a doctor. Next she was taken to a block where about sixty German internees were dressing in civilian clothes. Clothing was piled into Virginia's hands. She put everything on, a dress, sweater, jacket, coat, two scarves, two pair of underpants and two slips. She couldn't fathom why she would be leaving with German women, but she followed them dutifully back out the gate and up the path to the office building where they were lined up in the hall.

One by one the women's names were called and Virginia found herself standing alone in the hallway. She feared she had misunderstood the directions. Being caught out of the compound without German escort could be perilous. After much hesitation, she risked knocking on the door of the English-speaking SS woman.

"Ah, there you are," the woman greeted. "Here, sit by the stove. Your train won't be here for another hour."

"But where am I going?"

The woman looked to see that no one was nearby then leaned in and spoke just above a whisper, "I don't know for sure, but I heard two officers talking about taking Genevieve de Gaulle and an American to a Red Cross camp near the Swiss border."

Virginia felt ready to burst. She didn't know de Gaulle, but had heard of her brave work in the Résistance and of her kindness as a nurse in the infirmary. As the niece of General Charles de Gaulle, the voice of the Free French who inspired hope from London throughout the war, Genevieve was something of a celebrity to the French prisoners. But she had suffered the hardships of Ravensbrück just like everyone else. Only after the liberation of Paris, when her uncle had been installed as the interim leader of France, did they move her into solitary confinement and begin feeding her better.

Accompanied by three guards, two male and one woman, they set out for Berlin, about fifty miles south of Ravensbrück. As excited as she was to be leaving, Virginia's body simply had no energy to keep up. She tugged herself up and down stairways clutching the bannister like an old woman. The men said nothing as she fell behind on the walk, but the female guard impatiently grabbed Virginia's arm and dragged her along.

After being slowed further by an air raid, they finally reached their station. She'd almost forgotten what it felt like to ride in a passenger coach instead of a cramped foul-smelling boxcar. The seat was comfortable, the train car warm. Virginia fell asleep.

In the morning it was like she had entered a different world. Farm after peaceful farm passed by, stretched out on gently rolling hills. Spring had tipped the maple branches with red buds. She was thankful to be traveling with Genevieve whose easy charm and knowledge of German had softened the temperament of the officers. They spoke neither English nor French.

They reached the station outside Munich after midnight and crowded into a tram. Entire blocks of the once picturesque city had been reduced to rubble. Downcast defeated faces stared out from makeshift shelters fashioned from blankets and wood scraps. When the tram stopped, the guards found a restaurant still operating, but it was so crowded that there were no seats available and all they managed was a round of beers for the group.

With no prospects of finding rooms for the night, they searched for the Gestapo headquarters where Virginia and Genevieve were locked in a cell to share a narrow cot. Early the next morning another train took them south, but on the outskirts of Ulm, it stopped while a massive formation of American bombers roared overhead. Seconds later, huge explosions rumbled through the city. They undertook the long hike to the station, but were turned back and had to spend the night in a small town inn.

Virginia struggled all the next day. Despite verbal prodding from the female officer anxious to get out of the cold, Virginia couldn't get her drained body to move any faster. They walked several exhausting miles only to find that the station in Ulm had been reduced to rubble and they had to walk yet another five miles to the next station.

That night, they found Stuttgart in ruins as well. At Gestapo headquarters, they were instructed to go back to Ulm and walk five miles to a station to the south of the city. Virginia had nothing left.

"Genevieve," she called.

Genevieve stopped and allowed her to catch up. "What is wrong?"

"I cannot go on."

"I'll tell them."

They took refuge from the cold in a crowded inn. But before they could even find a place to sit, the air raid sirens wailed. An immense explosion rocked the building. The guards urged them outside. "We have to get to a shelter."

The building that had been across the street when they arrived was now a smoking hole in the ground. The guard detail headed in the direction of the running crowd. Virginia followed, but at her own slow pace, walking down the middle of the street unconcerned about the possibility that at any moment a bomb could end her life. It didn't matter to her.

A friendly truck driver gave them a lift to the next town. While waiting at an inn for the four o'clock train, Virginia confronted an appalling sight in the large wall mirror: a haggard bony-faced old woman with lusterless eyes, grey complexion and clumps of unruly hair staring back at her. She had to look away from the revolting creature.

By the time they reached the Liebenau station in late afternoon, a wet spring snowstorm had moved in. The SS decided to press on. Darkness fell. Melting snow dripped off her scarf and ran down her face. Trudging through the heavy slush, Virginia had to keep reminding herself that the end of her long journey was only three miles away. She closed her eyes a moment, touching her wedding ring to give her strength, and numbly put one foot in front of the other.

More than an hour later, there was still no sign of the camp.

"I cannot go any farther," the female guard said. The Germans knocked on a door and asked the inhabitants to let her stay the night.

How ironic, Virginia thought, that a healthy young woman like that could simply give up while Virginia had no choice but to go on.

Wind whipped their faces. There seemed nothing on this desolate road but woods. They had been in the cold for more than an hour and a half with no sign of the camp, when the SS officers finally admitted they were lost. They had no choice but to go back to the shelter of the train station.

Virginia had been evacuated from Romainville just as the Allied army reached Paris; spirited away from Königsberg within breath of the

Soviet army; and now, her remaining energy ebbing, she could die in the cold less than three miles from survival. Could the Fates be any crueler?

The men seemed sympathetic to the hardship their getting lost had put her through and were patient with her slow shuffle. She tried to command her legs to move a little faster, but her body wouldn't have it.

The haggard group finally made it back to the train station at half past two in the morning. It was the sixth difficult day of their journey. Virginia wiggled out of her snow-drenched coat, and laid her exhausted body down on a bench by the fire.

She felt a slight shake on her arm and opened her eyes. The sun was up. The station clock said seven-thirty.

Genevieve nodded toward a well-dressed, grey-haired fellow chatting with the SS officers. "That is the commandant of Leibenau. He has come to lead us to the camp."

As they hiked in the bright sunshine, Virginia recognized the route from the previous night. They had been on the right road after all. If they had walked just another half-mile, they would have made it.

An incredible feeling of hope covered her like a warm blanket.

She was going to live.

———

Friday, March 2, 1945

Nadine woke up with pain in her ear and a fever. She dragged herself outside, but after only a short time in formation, the blockova sent them back inside to collect their belongings, warning that anyone not outside in five minutes would be shot.

She grabbed her cloth bag. Inside was a toothbrush, a spoon, a bowl, a small bag of salt and a chunk of stale bread. These, and the clothes on her back *were* her "belongings", and the Germans could take them from her at any time. She hurried back out where the women and a number of children were formed up into rows of five and marched out of the camp.

A long line of cattle trucks awaited them guarded by machine guns mounted on jeeps. Engines rumbled to life. Where they were going, nobody knew; but German orders had leaked out—all *Nacht und Nebel* prisoners were to be eliminated so the French and Belgian political prisoners could not bear witness to the German atrocities. Ravensbrück only had a small gas chamber and its second crematorium had been so overworked with the SS burning records and bodies that it had blown up in February, so most were sure their destination was Auschwitz.

They were driven to a railroad siding and crammed body against body inside locked cattle cars. After four hours of steadying themselves against the rocking train, and bearing the nauseating stench from the bucket in the corner, the train came to a stop. The whine of planes and the rumble like thunder left no doubt that somewhere not too far away Allied planes were wreaking destruction. When the bombing stopped, the train began to move, but they didn't make it too far when it stopped again. Yet the women were not allowed out to stretch their legs.

By evening, the temperature had dropped another ten degrees. Women succumbed to exhaustion, nodding off in a tangle of bodies bouncing with the rhythm of the train. Nadine tried to sleep, but she was far too cold.

The train crept on through the night. Short runs, long delays, planes overhead and bombings of the tracks hampered progress all the next day. There seemed to be no end to the cold, the muscle ache and fatigue.

By the end of the third night, Nadine no longer cared if she lived or died. The pain was constant. The cold was too much to bear. When she woke the next morning, she felt a trickle of something warm on her cheek. She wiped it away and brought her fingers up before her eyes. Even in the dim light, she recognized that it was blood. It was oozing from her ear. A wave of fear broke over her. She hadn't gone to nursing school like her mother and sister, but she knew this was bad. Her body was telling her that it had taken enough. As she lay back looking at the mass of women in their contorted positions, she knew they were all waiting for the same thing—death to end their misery.

The train squealed to a stop. The *thrunk* of door bolts broke the silence. Nadine picked her head up. Their door opened.

"*Raus!*"

They uncurled like bent wires from their cramped positions. After three idle days and the fever, Nadine's muscles had lost nearly all their strength and she descended the ramp on wobbly old lady legs. Cold air smacked her in the face. By the time they had formed into rows of five, she was chilled to the bone. Guards with machine guns and side arms ordered them forward. Through dark villages they walked with the shimmering moon the only light, and the clack of wooden shoes and the thump of jackboots the only sounds. Then, from somewhere in the front, a shot rang out. Another echoed from the rear. A few minutes later, Nadine saw the corpse of the first victim lying on the side of the road.

The grade rose and the hike grew more laborious. Her joints aching, feet blistered, she struggled to keep up. Her eyes stung from the wind and cold. Her empty stomach felt like raw meat being tugged apart by wild dogs.

Several rows ahead of Nadine, a young woman carried a baby in one arm, holding the hand of a young child with the other. She tried to shift the weight of the child in her arm, but her muscles and lungs were so strained, she staggered with every step. Another shot rang out from somewhere in the back.

The pace was unrelenting, the breathing heavy and hard. The girl with the children faltered even more. She bounced the child back up and struggled forward, but she could only bear it a moment before she slowed again. A guard marched up the side passing row after row. All at once he grabbed the girl with the children, yanked her out of line and shot her. Without a word and without breaking stride a woman picked up the baby and another took the child's hand and marched on.

The grade rose mercilessly. Nadine's chest heaved. Her lungs burned. Farther up the hill off to their right, the moon cast its light on parapet walls and towers that stood on the high ground like an ancient castle lording over the villages below.

More shots came from behind. In front, another woman began to falter, fading back, catching up, and then fading again. She slowed more and more, getting in the way of those behind. A Moment later she was yanked out of the formation and shot.

As Nadine passed the body lying in the weeds on the side of the road, her only thoughts were of how little time it had taken—mere seconds and the woman was at peace, no more cold, no more pain. The dream filled her mind. The spring weeds sprouting like asparagus along the side of the road called to her. Her feet kept moving, but she pictured herself slowing down and letting women pass her by. All she had to do was walk to the side of the road and lie down. The Germans would do the rest.

The piquant taste of asparagus found its way into her mind. She could see the tender stalks roasting in the pan, smell the deliciously bitter aroma as her mother stirred them about with a spatula. The thought of her mother shook her out of her dark thoughts. How cruel it would be if her mother learned that her daughter had survived three years only to give up just as the war was ending. She picked up her pace. She had vowed she would fight the Germans to her last breath. Now she raised her head and hiked on.

After a grueling five mile hike uphill, they arrived on the heights above the Danube at Mauthausen concentration camp—a fortress with impenetrable granite walls topped with barbed wire. Dawn was breaking and prisoners were already lining up outside their barracks. Soup was brought out of the kitchens for the inmates, but the new arrivals weren't given so much as a crust of bread or a drink of water.

They were herded into a large room where doctors performed quick superficial medical exams. On her stomach and back, the doctor marked a large red K and sent her to follow the others into the shower room.

"Gas chamber," women whispered as they nodded toward the overhead pipes and shower nozzles.

Could anyone be that cruel? Nadine asked herself as she stared at the shower heads above her. *Did I survive four days in a suffocating train and fight the pain all the way up the hill only to be gassed?* A friend linked her arm in Nadine's. Nadine took her hand and together they waited.

With a startling *gggiickk*, the shower heads burst to life. Squeals erupted throughout the room. It was water! Nadine closed her eyes letting it splash her face, then gulped the glorious liquid as it washed over her dry tongue.

When she stepped out of the shower, a male French prisoner handed her a small towel and said softly, "We have to remove that K. It means you are ill and will be sent to the gas chamber." He scrubbed her back hard while she scrubbed the front. Although the area was still somewhat red, it worked to keep the guards from spotting it before she dressed.

Eighteen of the five hundred eighty-five women had died on the hike up the hill, but Nadine had survived. So had Elsie, Madame Maréchal, Diane and Elvire Morelle—for now.

After only a day's rest, Nadine was sent down into the pit to load quarry rock into hoppers that rolled on steel tracks. Mauthausen was a work camp with a reputation for having the cruelest guards and its own brand of brutal death. Alongside the camp one hundred eighty-six steps carved out of the mountain led down into a rock quarry that had once supplied the granite used to build Hitler's ostentatious buildings in Berlin. The grand spectacle of the Third Reich was no more, but the prisoners labored on.

The SS carried on their death-by-work program as if the German army wasn't collapsing. Down in the crater, Nadine took care to never look directly at her oppressors so as not to become their entertainment. Killing was an amusement to the Mauthausen officers. Expressionless, she lugged heavy rocks from the rubble pile and wrestled them over the rim of a steel trolley. Skeletal prisoners who could no longer lift the weight were sent to the gas chamber. Men who stumbled while struggling up the *steps of death* with twenty-five kilogram blocks on their backs were beaten. And when boredom overcame the SS officers, they amused themselves with quarry races, killing the slowest men to make it to the top of the steps with their heavy load; or by pushing men off the *parachute wall* to their death.

After the work day, despite being sick herself, Elvire Morelle helped Nadine back to the barracks. Nadine's fever had increased and her cough rattled in her chest. "Come on," Elvire said. "We'll go to the infirmary."

Nadine shook her head emphatically. "They will kill us if we go there."

Despite the bleak odds, Nadine clung to the belief that some would survive until liberation. Sympathetic Austrians living in the area, secretly kept the camp underground informed of the progress of Allied forces. Nadine dared not think about it too much, but with each bit of good news, her hope of surviving grew.

Neither went to the infirmary.

———

Elsie adjusted her kerchief to better cover her ears. Despite the approach of springtime, it was another cold and nasty morning in the hills above the Danube. Most of the young new French and Belgian arrivals to Mauthausen had been selected for a work *Kommando*.

The moon was still out when the lorries left the compound. In the darkness in the back of the truck, a shaky young voice asked, "Where do you think we are going?"

"Do not worry," someone answered, "if they wanted to kill us they would have done it back at camp."

Another woman warned the young girl to be careful. "The guards here are as vicious as they come. A man was caught with contraband in his pocket. The guards made him take off all of his clothes, doused him with water, and watched him freeze to death."

"You do not need contraband," another added. "They kill us for sport."

"Just do as you are told," the first woman said to the girl. "Do not give them cause to single you out. And maybe you will live to see liberation."

The trucks drove to Amstetten, about nineteen miles from Mauthausen, where the prisoners were ordered to clear away the rubble from an American bombing raid. All that remained in this part of the city were bomb craters and partial walls.

Elsie felt no compassion for those who might have been inside. She felt no sense of victory that the American planes had done all this damage. All she felt was the cold damp weather, the fatigue of digging out concrete and twisted metal with undernourished muscles, and the sting of her cracked dry hands and feet.

The guards warned that if anyone got the notion to slip away, the remainder of her crew would be shot. Down the street, Austrians worked separately from the women in the striped prison clothing.

Through the cold and the strain, Elsie struggled on with nothing but her bare hands, not even a pry bar to help shift the heavy chunks of concrete out of the way. She was tugging on a long piece of lumber, trying to break it free when a whistle blew.

"*Komm her*," the head guard called to everyone. "*Höhr auf zu arbeiten und komm her.*"

Two guards had a girl by the arms. The woman overseer reached into the prisoner's pocket and held up an object too small for Elsie to make out. "This girl has taken something she has found. You all know the penalty for this!"

The guard turned to the girl. "Take off your clothes!"

Elsie expected the overseer to put a bullet in the back of the girl's head. Instead, the guard commanded all of the prisoners to march around the girl in a circle while singing a German song.

"LOUDER!" the guard commanded.

When the women's voices grew loud enough to overshadow all other sounds, the guard took out her truncheon and savagely swung it at the naked prisoner. The other guards joined in, clubbing the woman over and over.

The singing drowning out the woman's screams brought back terrible memories. Elsie could still see the Gestapo agent calmly walking over to the radio and turning up the volume before viciously beating her.

The girl fell to the ground. Guards kicked her hard in the ribs, face, and back. The fragile body recoiled with each strike until her breathing stopped and she went limp.

"Back to work!" the overseer commanded.

Elsie closed off her mind to what had happened. Women shot dead along the road to the camp; women dying from disease; waking up to find the girl on the floor next to you still and lifeless … one had to put those things out of one's mind and carry on.

Half-rations and thin soup provided such little sustenance, the guards had to keep yelling at the prisoners to keep them moving. Elsie pushed on, carrying off debris one piece at a time with no more thought than a worker ant. Under the concrete rubble and mangled metal she found a cloth rag and wiped her runny nose. She stuffed it into her pocket and bent back down to wiggle out a wooden beam to drag to the pile.

Elsie felt a nudge on her arm. The girl beside her nodded toward the clouds. The sky was filled with planes—big planes—bombers. Then the whistle of bombs broke the air and the ground shook. Women screamed and ran for cover. The percussion from a blast knocked Elsie off her feet. She lay face down covering her head with her arms as dirt rained down around her.

It was over in minutes, but the heartache had only just begun. Women staggered back to the rubble to the sounds of their fellow prisoners crying in pain. Working harder than they had worked all morning, the women dug to find their friends. They carried out body after body hoping to find some still alive. One hundred were dead, and many injured. Those still able, like Elsie, were put back to work.

In late afternoon the prisoners were lined up for the return to the camp. Before moving out, the guards inspected each row of women. One stopped at Elsie and looked over her clothing. "Out!"

Elsie couldn't imagine what was wrong. She followed the guard's eyes to her bulging pocket. She'd forgotten about the rag! "But it's…"

"Out!" the guard repeated. She drew her side arm and waved for Elsie to move. "Go up on that pile. Remove your clothes!"

"But…"

"Now!"

Elsie climbed to the top of the pile of rubble. She dropped her dress to the ground beside her and removed her scarf. The cold air stung mercilessly. She cursed her stupidity in stuffing that rag in her pocket. How cruel it was to live so long with such misery only to die over something so trivial. As she waited for the guard to put a bullet in her, she thought of her mother who would be devastated. She would surely give up. The entire Maréchal family would be dead except for Robert.

Shivering, Elsie hugged her arms around herself trying to ease the agony of the icy air. Her tightened muscles ached. *Get it over with!* her mind screamed. But down on the street the guards paid no attention as they methodically continued with their preparations for departure. Suddenly, she understood. The guard wasn't going to shoot her. Death would not come quick and easy. She would stand naked in the vicious cold until she died of hypothermia.

CHAPTER FIFTY

Teeth chattering, her thin arms hugging her naked body, Elsie could find no relief. Atop her mountain of rubble, nothing blocked the relentless cold. Down below, cozy warm in her long grey gabardine overcoat, hat, gloves and scarf, the woman SS guard strolled about as if making someone slowly freeze to death was no more troubling than swatting a fly.

The prisoners stood in formation while a detail loaded the bodies into lorries. Elsie knew that if she wasn't dead soon enough to suit them, she would likely be stomped to death. Her only hope was if the guards were in a hurry to get back to the camp. Then they might opt for a quick bullet to the back of the head. She pictured her body being tossed into the lorry and prayed that her mother wasn't put on the detail to unload it.

Closing her eyes, she asked God for a quick end. Her toes were becoming numb. She marched in place to keep up the circulation, leaving footprints of blood on the freezing concrete.

Suddenly, a girl began screaming hysterically. The guards rushed over, knocking women aside to get at the frenzied girl.

Elsie teetered back and forth on tip toes trying to see what was happening. Had the girl gone mad? Had she just learned that a loved one was among the dead? As Elsie looked on, she realized that all the guards, including the one who was keeping an eye on her, were preoccupied with the hysteria that commanded everyone's attention.

She had to take the gamble while the guards were distracted. The worse they could do was to kill her quicker. She picked her dress off the ground and slipped it over her head. While the guards were busy shaking the screaming girl to make her stop and shoving others back into formation, Elsie wiggled her toes into her shoes, threw on her jacket, tied her scarf on her head and climbed down the pile. She sneaked into the middle of the formation and tried to look innocent.

With the French women being relative newcomers to Mauthausen, the guards hadn't had time or the inclination to learn their names or distinguish one from another. As long as they didn't demand that she be turned over, she had a chance.

The girl got control of herself and the guards hustled everyone into the lorries before there were more delays. Not a word was mentioned about the prisoner with the bulging pocket. Elsie didn't speak on the ride back to the camp. Many of the women didn't know her and the fewer people who could identify her the better. All through the night, she worried that the guards would remember and come for her.

It seemed absurd to be happy to be sent back to the quarry, but Elsie was relieved when the immediate danger had passed. Through luck or providence, she had managed to hide from death. But day after day of backbreaking work with no sign of rescue made her think that maybe dying on the pile would have been more merciful. Their meager rations had been cut even more. By the beginning of April, hundreds were dying daily. Elsie grew so weak she no longer cared whether the guards beat her. She felt like one of the last leaves on the tree, watching the others fall and waiting for the wind to blow.

———

The *maître d'hôtel* poured glasses of red wine for the three English officers seated at a table in the Belgian hotel lounge. Brigadier Norman Crockatt opened his wallet and held out several francs.

The waiter shook his hand vigorously and set the bottle on the table. "No no. It is my pleasures to buy you a drinks, *Messieurs*. God bless England. God bless America. I *sank* you very very much."

"*Merci*," Crockatt said raising glass. "*Vers la Belgique! Viva la Belgique!*"

Airey Neave and Jimmy Langley raised their glasses and repeated, "*Vers la Belgique!*"

When the beaming waiter left the table, Crockatt got down to business. "Airey, I want you to take the reins on our Awards Bureau. We will have to categorize the helpers according to the role they played—those who provided one-time aid, hosts, guides, sub-chiefs, chiefs ...

Those who took the greatest risks should receive the highest decoration."

"We will need to verify each candidate," Jimmy put in. "Some people will claim to have participated in aiding airmen in order to cover up their collaborating with the Germans. And others may not come forward for fear of Nazi reprisals."

Airey, his brows furrowed in thought, crushed out his cigarette. "The only way we can verify them is through pilots and other members of the underground. We'll have to go back through our evader reports."

"We can start by interviewing the chiefs and sub-chiefs," Jimmy said.

Crockatt set his glass down and leaned forward. "Speaking of chiefs, any word yet on Franco or our post mistress?"

Airey shook his head sadly. "I've received a dispatch from the officer I sent to Ravensbrück. The records there report that she didn't make it. Frantxia is dead as well."

"Suzanne?" Crockatt asked.

"No word as yet. A number of the women were evacuated by the Swedish Red Cross. I've sent an officer there to interview them. I sent another detail to Dachau to look for Franco. But many from Ravensbrück were sent to camps that remain to be liberated."

"Terrible tragedy, this war," Crockatt said sadly. "All the more reason for us to honor those who sacrificed so much." He poured more wine for Jimmy and as he refilled Airey's glass said, "I want you to give this project some stick, Airey. Use whatever resources you need. Note any of those helpers in the armed forces. They should receive service awards."

"Yes sir. I'll get started straight away."

―――――

Elsie didn't want to freeze to death naked on a rubble pile, but starving to death wasn't much better. The influx of prisoners from other camps was so great that by the third week in April, rations were down to one moldy slice of bread a day. Hearing the thundering explosions of cannon maybe three miles away, the prisoners were like balloons of anxiety ready to burst. Day after day, they waited, but the Russians didn't come. The prisoners grew weaker.

The guards half-heartedly prodded the inmates to keep them busy, but Elsie was almost beyond caring what they did to her. Dozens starved to death each day. What did it matter, she thought, if the guards shot her and brought the relief of death a little quicker? But there was her mother to think about.

As soon as they were dismissed from Saturday's formation, Elsie hurried back to where she had spotted a yellow flower, which was miraculously still there. She dug around the root with her bare fingers and showed her handful of dandelion greens to her mum. "Look what I found."

Madame Maréchal coughed her way to a sitting position.

Elsie pressed some of the leaves into her mum's hand. "The Russians are getting closer," she said as she bit into a bitter leaf. "It won't be long now. Soon we'll be free and have plenty of food."

Her mom accepted the lie with a nod and smile. "Dandelions are good for you, you know."

"Yes, but they could use a little oil and vinegar. Tomorrow I will look for more."

But she never got the chance to look for them. In the middle of the night, lights switched on in the barracks. The *blockova* tramped through the building shouting, *"Beeilen sie sich! Schnell! Schnell!"*

The entire block of French and Belgian Night and Fog prisoners emptied out into the yard. Women exchanged worried looks as they formed up. They'd only called the political prisoners out and everyone knew that the SS had orders to kill all Night and Fog prisoners before liberation so they wouldn't talk. Their fears increased when they were taken to the building that contained the gas chamber/shower room and ordered in at gunpoint. There seemed no doubt of the Germans' intentions.

Standing at the precipice of death, Elsie realized that she really *did* care what they did to her. She wanted to live.

"The Red Cross is coming to take you away," the German overseer said. "You are going to wait here until they come for you."

The women still had their clothes on, so there was no pretense that they were to have a shower. Then came the sound of the door's deadbolt. Women screamed. Elsie held onto her mother. All eyes looked up toward the pipes and shower heads. Would they see the gas spewing through the nozzles? Elsie wondered. Would they smell it? Her skin prickled. Her nerves were tight as a bear trap spring.

Anxious minutes passed. The only sounds were the nervous whimpers of the women. Standing and waiting with nothing happening was almost worse than the gas they feared. But after ten minutes the knots in Elsie's neck began to relax. Slowly she loosened her grip on her mother.

An hour passed. Women gave up on standing and some drifted off to sleep. Elsie awoke to the sound of the door unlocking.

They were marched out through the open gate past rows of Mauser rifles held at the ready. Once they were out of the compound, the SS officer halted them and pointed to an open area on the edge of a huge excavation. "Go wait there for the Red Cross trucks."

The women shuffled apprehensively to the field. Pits such as these were typically used as mass graves for murdered prisoners. There was no sign of any Red Cross trucks. The women were totally exposed and could be surrounded by Nazis jeeps with machine guns. There would be no escape. Elsie dragged herself toward certain death—her heart a beating drum.

She clung to her mother's arm as together they watched the woods in one direction and the compound in the other, not knowing from which direction their executioners would come.

Her ears pricked up at the whine of a truck engine ascending the hill. A white lorry with a big red cross painted on the sides and roof appeared on the road below. She couldn't believe it. A second lorry appeared, then a third, a fourth … they just kept coming! Elsie felt tears running down her face uncontrolled. Such a lump was in her throat, she couldn't speak.

A man with a Swiss Red Cross armband walked down the line as the women climbed up into the back of the trucks. His face was a mixture of anger and disgust. He asked one of the women if she had eaten and his face flamed red at the half-slice of moldy bread she showed him. He called to two of his drivers, "Come with me."

As the three walked toward the camp, Elsie prayed for them to just forget about it and turn around. She knew how dangerous the SS could become if challenged. The Germans could change their minds instantly and order everyone back into the camp. But after twenty long minutes, the men returned and went from truck to truck passing out loaves of fresh bread.

The three hundred mile journey was plagued with detours: long indirect routes to find bridges that had not been blown up, slow going through throngs of refugees, and back-tracking to bypass cratered roads and bombed cities. Finally, on the third day, the driver passed the word back that they were less than an hour from the Swiss frontier.

Hearts lightened. The women sang French songs for the next forty-five minutes. Then the convoy came to a stop. They hushed to listen.

German voices shouted warnings. The women looked to each other in horror as guttural voices barked out commands. The unmistakable sound of jackboots tramping on pavement grew nearer. Suddenly the canvas flap to the lorry flew open. German soldiers waving machine guns ordered the women out.

The Red Cross leader spoke rapidly in German, hands waving, beseeching the soldiers to hold their fire. He turned to the ranking guard, who looked to be not much more than a boy, and pleaded with him.

The starched boy-soldier brushed passed the Red Cross leader, proclaiming he had orders to shoot all prisoners.

"Those orders have been countermanded by German high command," the Red Cross leader insisted. "This evacuation has been ordered by Himmler himself. If you kill these women you will be shot for disobeying orders."

Elsie could see the demarcation markers for the Swiss frontier just down the hill. It was just a short walk away, yet this could be as close as she might ever get.

The argument went on and on. Eventually, the Red Cross leader convinced the German to call his superiors. Women anxiously stood beside the lorries, their eyes fixed on the soldiers with machine guns awaiting orders to shoot.

An eternity passed. Negotiations continued.

Elsie felt a tap on her shoulder and turned to find their driver passing through the crowd with a finger to his lips. He signal the women to get back into the truck. When the last woman had snuck aboard, the driver climbed into the cab.

The brake was released and the truck silently began to roll. Wide-eyed, breathless, the women willed the truck to move faster.

Machine guns barked.

Women screamed and threw themselves down on the floor keeping as low as so many bodies would allow.

The lorry was still rolling down hill, gaining speed. Elsie's heart raced.

The engine roared to life and the truck accelerated. The grade changed—they were now climbing uphill.

Then the truck braked to a stop.

"Welcome to Switzerland!" the driver called back.

The compartment erupted in cheers and sobs.

After only a brief stop at the border the truck drove on arriving at Lake Constance on the border of Austria and Switzerland. The last truck in the caravan passed them by, riddled with bullets, and pulled to the curb in front of the door of the hospital. Stretcher bearers and nurses with wheel chairs were already hurrying toward it.

Elsie had thought she would never be affected by death again. But watching the bloody bodies and seeing stretchers with sheets covering the dead, her heart was overcome with sadness. Her eyes stung at the senselessness of these poor souls being robbed of their freedom when they had come so close.

Applause burst from the hospital staff and crowds as the women climbed down from the trucks. The wards overflowed with foul-smelling former prisoners covered in lice and fleas. Many were taken to a nearby school where they were fed waffles and fruit while they waited their turn for medical attention. The sheer number of women to tend to must have overwhelmed the nurses, but they worked undaunted, showing no revulsion. They treated each fragile thin woman with kindness, gentleness and patience. They had probably never encountered a group of more grateful and cooperative patients.

When it was her turn, Elsie was taken to a private area for a bath. There were no men wandering in and out—no wretched inmates with scissors poised to cut her hair—no doctors scrutinizing her body to decide if she should live. It was just her and the nurse who bathed her. The clean water buoyed Elsie like floating in a soft warm cloud. She surrendered her head to kitten-soft fingers that gently massaged their way over her scalp. With comb and tweezers, the nurse worked through the tufts of hair ridding Elsie's head of lice. For the first time in a long time, Elsie didn't have to be the tough strong woman.

As she and her mum had suspected, her mother's lungs were infected with tuberculosis. They could have stayed in the Swiss hospital, but soon after they arrived, they telephoned Robert to tell him they were alive. Once her mother heard her son's voice, she had to go home.

All they had to wear were their striped prison coats, but they left Switzerland on the next available train. They changed trains at the first station in France. The moment they appeared on the platform in their prisoner clothing, the crowds in the streets cheered them and began singing La Marseillaise. An older gentleman kissed Elsie's cheeks and handed her a glass of wine and a baguette. At each stop, people gave them food. By the time they arrived in Brussels days later, Elsie's stomach felt sick from overeating.

Being among the first to arrive in Brussels from the camps, they were easy to spot. Robert nearly smothered them with his hugs. Her grandmother smiled and kissed them, but there was no hiding the concern in her eyes, especially, when Madame Maréchal could not suppress a cough.

As Robert led his mother and sister away, Elsie felt a tug on the baguette that she'd been carrying for three days. "No! That's mine!" All of the animal rage of survival coursed through her. She ripped the bread from the hands of her attacker, her wild eyes flared in fury. "Get away!" She clutched the bread hard in the crook of her arm. Her free hand clenched in a fist.

"But it is old and stale, dear" her grandmother said, her eyes concerned and confused. "We'll get you some more."

"Just let her be," Madame Maréchal said gently. "It's all right, Elsie."

Elsie's eyes filled with tears as her mother held her and stroked her head. Her mum was the only one who could understand.

The war had taken everything from them. They had no money. Their home was gone. Even the clothes on their backs were not theirs, not that they wanted to keep their striped prison outfits. Robert got them new clothes and a dear friend put them up in an expensive apartment. Elsie bathed for an hour in bath salts, but the smell of the camp lingered on her skin—or at least that's what her mind told her.

After her bath, she slipped into her new nightgown and strolled the quiet bedroom, running her fingers along the surface of the wooden dresser, smelling the perfume on the tray. She took the towel from her head and brushed her hair. She almost felt like a girl again. By the time her hair dried she had become quite sleepy. The luxurious bed welcomed her like she was a princess. The sheets smelled fresh as spring, and the blankets were soft and warm. She closed her eyes and fell into the bed's embrace. As tired as she was, sleep would not come. She tried lying on her side with her head cradled by the pillow. She turned onto her back and stared at the ceiling. Finally after hours of tossing and turning, she realized the problem. She got up, dragging the blanket from the bed, and lay down on the hard wooden floor. There she fell right to sleep.

CHAPTER FIFTY-ONE

The task was Herculean. Thousands of people had aided the Allies in occupied Europe. Claims were coming in from all over— Holland, Belgium, France, Italy—and each one had to be written up and reviewed. Those who had been verified were stacked in one pile while the others required more investigating.

The phone rang. Airey cursed the interruption, but after a brief shocking report, he hung up the phone and called in his secretary. "Ring up Bee Johnson. Tell him I have an assignment and I need to see him at once."

———

Lily poised the small photo over the scrapbook page. This one, she recalled, was a twenty-two-year-old American gunner. Now that the war was over, she could finally put together the photos of the men she had helped. She wanted to remember each brave boy who had risked his life to defeat the Germans.

The Allies had arrived too late to save her father. He had been among those locked in a prison train which was set afire as the Germans fled in the face of the approaching Allied armies. Thankfully, the Red Cross had been in time to rescue her sister. Nadine wouldn't have survived much longer.

Lily tucked the photo into the corner holders. As she wrote the name Hank Johnson beneath it, she tried to remember a little bit about him. She and Bob Grimes had collected Hank at a restaurant in Brussels and taken him for his photo. She'd made up a new identity card for him with the name Jean-Marie Dupré. "Ahh, I remember. He was called Tennessee."

Rrrrinng.

Lily set the pen down and picked up the telephone. "Hello."

"Hello, Michou? It's Harold Cherniss."

"Yes, Hello Harold."

"Michou, are you free? You must come to my office right away."

"Is something wrong?"

"I just need to show you something."

The war was over. Michou couldn't imagine what the American Intelligence officer had to show her, but it was clearly urgent.

"Thank you for coming so quickly," Lieutenant Cherniss said when she arrived. One by one, he laid out twelve small identity card sized photos on his desk facing Michou. "Do you know this boy?"

"Yes, of course. It is Pierre Boulain—Jean Masson."

"Please look carefully, Michou. It is important."

"I am sure. It is Pierre Boulain and Jean Masson. They are the same person. He is the boy who betrayed the Comet line twice. He was shot and killed by the Résistance. Why are you showing me this?"

Harold shook his head and snickered.

"What is it? What has happened?"

"He is very much alive! His real name is Jacques Desoubrie. He claims to have worked for the Comet underground during the war and now he is working for us in Nuremburg. But his career as a double agent is about to end. I've got to call Airey. He's going to love this."

Michou picked up one of the photos and shook her head sadly. "So many of our friends suffered and died because of this boy."

"Yes, but we've got him now. And we've got Prosper Dezitter, the man with the missing little finger and his girlfriend, Flore. And we're going to get 'em all and put 'em on trial. We will need you as a witness."

Michou thought of Frédéric de Jongh, Georges Maréchal and the others shot at Tir National Rifle Range. She thought of Franco and Madame Maréchal struggling with tuberculosis. She thought of the horrors poor Virginia, Martine, Diane and so many others must have gone through and of those who didn't survive the death camps. And she thought of Nadine...

"Will you testify?"

"No problem."

Bee Johnson tucked his cap in the crook of his arm and followed the young nurse down the corridor of the Swiss hospital. Though he had seen newsreels of the atrocities, the sight of so many young men and women so abused by the Nazis that they lacked the strength to get out of their beds still shocked and appalled him. Looking into the hollow eyes of people who were nearly skeletons, he vowed to never forget who did this to them.

"Well, this is her ward," the nurse said leading him through the door, "but of course she's not in her bed."

"Where is she?" Bee asked.

"Off helping someone I suppose. Who can keep track of that girl? Why don't you go have a seat, Mr. Johnson, and I'll go see about a vase for those flowers."

"Thank you."

The nurse returned after a few minutes. "Look who I found."

"Bee, how nice of you to come. Are those for me?"

Bee stood up and handed Dédée the flowers, kissing her cheeks. "How are you?" Her hands in his felt exceedingly bony. Her face was thin and drawn. She sat down on the bed with her emaciated legs dangling over the side. She looked so much older than her twenty-eight years. He wondered what those monsters had done to the beautiful young girl with the fiery blue eyes he had met in the south of France only four years ago.

"We'd been told you died in Ravensbrück."

"I did. Or at least that is what the SS thought when they came for me. There was a girl who looked a lot like me. When she died, I switched clothing and identities."

"Of course." Bee laughed. "I should have known the Nazis could never outsmart you."

"Who else have you seen?" Dédée slipped over to help adjust the pillow for the woman in the next bed. "How is Tante Go?"

"That woman's got bollocks." Bee shook his head chuckling. "We were going to have a look around for a new inland route over the mountains. Seeing my *handsome* British face, the Germans tossing the train took me for an evader and Tante Go and Yvonne Lapeyre as my guides. When we were arrested, she threatened that if they didn't let us go she would report them to the Kommandant ... You know she worked like crazy to try and get you out. We all did."

"I know. I am very grateful to have such good friends."

"She and Fernand did manage to save Florentino in a most daring raid after he'd been shot and captured, but I'll let her tell you about that one."

"Florentino was shot? Is he all right?"

"They put five bullets in him. He'll always have a limp, but he is getting on well. Do you remember Albert Day?"

"Yes, an American pilot."

"That's right. He has kept his promise to come back to see Janine. I don't know if there is a romance budding, but Tante Go is keeping her eye on him. I think she's afraid one of those pilots will steal her away to America."

"What about the others?"

"Franco is very ill with tuberculosis."

"I wish I could go see him, the poor fellow."

"He's in a good hospital. I'm sure he will pull through."

"Well, it is in God's hands."

Bee raised an eyebrow. Dédée was never much for religion. "*God?*"

She laughed at his reaction. "Yes, God. He and I have become quite close over these past few years. What about Charlie—Charlie Morelle?"

Bee could see she was already reading the answer in his eyes. "I'm afraid Charlie Morelle died in Dachau. He was visited by General Leclerc a few days after liberation. Once Charlie learned that the war had been won, he went to sleep."

Dédée fell quiet. She turned away and rearranged the flowers in the vase. He couldn't see her face, but she reached a finger up and wiped by her eye. She leaned into the bouquet and inhaled. "These flowers are lovely." She wiped her eye again then turned to him with a smile.

"I understand his sister, Elvire, is here and is recovering."

Dédée nodded, adding that Nadine and Suzanne were there as well.

Bee continued in a more cheery tone. "It seems Cupid has been busy of late. Peggy Van Lier is now Mrs. Jimmy Langley, and Michou is engaged to a daring young paratrooper, Pierre Ugeux."

"Little Michou. How about that!" For a moment, the sweet smile and those lively blue eyes of the adventurous young girl he'd met on the Spanish border so long ago were back. Then they disappeared again. "Madame Maréchal left here quite ill…"

"She and Elsie are home and recovering," he said.

"Frantxia?"

Bee shook his head.

"Oh, that's so sad."

"Come along," Bee said. "I'll tell you about the others on the way."

"On the way? Where are we going?"

"I'm taking you home."

AFTERWORD

Night and Fog is the story of the World War II underground line *Comète*, which helped about eight hundred Allied airmen evade capture by guiding them through more than seven hundred fifty miles of German controlled territory to get them safely back to England. While this account is based on actual events, I have presented their story as I have imagined the partisans living through the difficulties they faced.

I wasn't able to cover everyone in the book's closing scenes, so you may be wondering what became of Jeanne Macintosh and Anne Brusselmans when the war ended.

Jeanne Macintosh had been sentenced to death for aiding airmen. Deported to Germany, she suffered like so many others in the camps. She was liberated by Russian troops before the Germans could carry out the sentence. Sergeant Frank Andrews, the RAF airman smitten with Jeanne, was freed from Stalag IVB by Allied troops. He returned to England and found Jeanne. They married in September, 1945.

Anne Brusselmans remained faithful to the cause, working with Comet and aiding airmen until Brussels was liberated September 2, 1944. Years later, Anne's daughter Yvonne was widowed and decided to move to the United States to give her children a better life. Anne wanted to go with her, but despite aiding scores of American airmen her application was denied. After a long time trying to get in, she was finally permitted to stay in the U.S. To find out how she did it, read Belgian Rendez-Vous 127 Revisited, by Yvonne Daley-Brusselmans. You'll appreciate the irony of her plight and who stepped in to help.

Eyewitness accounts, recollections of partisans, and evasion reports vary. I tried to present each historical event as I imagined it after reading the different versions. For example, Lily had stated that Diane dropped her off at Fresnes Prison, but Diane's report indicates that she had been arrested a month earlier. In my story I have Virginia dropping Lily off at the prison instead of Diane because I know Lily was working with Virginia at the time and I wanted to bring her into the story (Virginia didn't actually see Fresnes Prison until her own arrest). Some accounts have Lily calling to Martine from outside the prison walls while others have her calling from inside (Both versions say she was held for two days as I have described). Some scenes such as the luncheon between the Dumon sisters have been completely fictionalized by me as were some of the close calls with German agents. Michou and Nadine each had 50 or more close calls which went undocumented, so I fictionalized some of those encounters as I imagined what might have happened.

Before researching my previous novel, Torben's Fountain, I had a number of preconceived notions about the "French" Underground which probably came from watching old movies when I was growing up (It's been dubbed the *French* Underground, not because they were all from France, but because of the language they spoke). But the more I learned, the more awed I was by the courage and sacrifice it took to rescue airmen and smuggle them through German occupied countries, over the Pyrenees Mountains and past Spanish border guards.

British Military Intelligence puts the number of successful evaders helped by the underground at 2,373 British and Commonwealth men and 2,700 Americans (ref. Home Run, by John Nichol and Tony Rennell). Comet endured longer than any other underground line, saving about 800 Allied military personnel. They also assisted scores of others fleeing the Gestapo and those wishing to fight with the Allies. But the partisans payed dearly for their efforts. About 1,300 Comet members were arrested. Over 150 paid with their lives. Many of those who survived camps like Ravensbrück and Mauthausen were so ill with malnutrition, typhus, tuberculosis and other infirmities they teetered at death's door a long time before slowly rebounding. Some never fully recovered.

It's impossible to know for sure how many people fought in the resistance and underground in occupied countries. Decorations and awards were presented to those known to have participated, but their greatest reward was in knowing that when their nation needed them, they answered the call. They do not see themselves as heroes and will modestly tell you that saving young foreign men who were risking their lives fighting for the liberation of their countries was all that mattered to them.

They were everyday people from different backgrounds working together for a common cause. It was important for me to show how each person carried on in secret while worrying about what might happen to their families if they were caught. They may have been ordinary, but the courage it took to do what they did made them extraordinary.

Some lines of dialogue of the underground participants have been herein incorporated verbatim, as recorded in sources which informed this telling; more specifically:

An exchange between Dédée and her mother (chapter 1) was based on Sherri Greene Ottis, *Silent Heroes*, The University Press of Kentucky, 2001, p 120.

The recounting of Polish airmen interaction with the Brusselmans family (chapter 9) was based on Yvonne Daley-Brusselmans, *Belgium Rendez-Vous 127 Revisited*, Sunflower University Press, Manhattan, Kansas, 2001, pp 39 & 40.

An exchange between Dédée and Nemo (chapter 10) was based on Airey Neave, *Little Cyclone*, Coronet books 1980 (reprint of 1954 edition), p 68.

Anne Brusselmans diary entry regarding her intuition of Nadine's arrest (chapter 12) was based on Denis Hornsey, D.F.C. (transcribed by), *Rendez-Vous 127* p 70.

A telephone exchange between Anne Brusselmans and an unknown German agent (chapter 12) was based on Yvonne Daley-Brusselmans, *Belgium Rendez-Vous 127 Revisited*, Sunflower University Press, Manhattan, Kansas, 2001, p 45.

A telephone exchange between Anne Brusselmans and Baroness H. (chapter 12) was based on Yvonne Daley-Brusselmans, *Belgium Rendez-Vous 127 Revisited*, Sunflower University Press, Manhattan, Kansas, 2001, pp 43 & 44.

An exchange between a German agent and Nadine's betrayer (chapter 12) was based on John Nichol and Tony Rennell, *Home Run Escape from Nazi Europe*, Penguin Books, New York, 2008, p 140.

A telephone exchange between Anne Brusselmans and Monsieur P. (chapter 13) was based on Yvonne Daley-Brusselmans, *Belgium Rendez-Vous 127 Revisited*, Sunflower University Press, Manhattan, Kansas, 2001, p 46.

Exchanges in the Maréchal Affair (chapters 14 & 15) were based on Airey Neave, *Saturday at M.I.9*, Pen and Sword Military, 2010, pp 148 & 155; Denis Hornsey, D.F.C. (transcribed by) *Rendez-Vous 127*, pp 55, 56 & 58; and John Nichol and Tony Rennell, *Home Run Escape from Nazi Europe*, Penguin Books, New York, p 173.

The cable received by Airey Neave reporting Dédée's arrest (chapter 21) was based on Airey Neave, *Saturday at M.I.9*, Pen and Sword Military, 2010, p 157.

Exchanges between Dédée and various interrogators (chapters 22, 23, 24 & 25) was based on, Derek Shuff, *Evader*, The History Press, Gloucestershire, 2010 (reprint of 2003 edition), pp 106, 107 & 108.

I would encourage anyone who is interested in learning more about the underground to read RAF and USAF evader reports. You can also log on to Comète Kinship Belgium or Ligne Comete Line – Remembrance, which is an organization dedicated to keeping the heroic memories alive through education, reenactments and various other programs. Check them out at www.cometeline.org.

OTHER BOOKS BY SEBASTIAN RIZZO

Torben's Fountain

https://sebastianrizzobooks.com/

AUTHOR'S NOTE

Within My Writes

I grew up in a generation where we were told to eat what was on our plates because kids were starving in China. Of course our smart aleck comeback was: *so send my spinach over to China,* or *how does me eating spinach help them?* We had food to eat and a roof over our heads so the suffering of children on the other side of the planet meant little to us.

We've all been affected by books we've read or movies we've seen, but I never knew how much writing a book could change my way of looking at things. Now, when I find myself grumbling about carrying a garbage can out to the road on a hot day, I think about the thirsty women in Ravensbrück pulling a heavy roller under a blazing summer sun. In the cold weather when I'm shivering through that twenty foot stretch of frosty air between my warm car and my warm house, I think about the harsh mountain crossings in the dead of winter and the guides and evaders who had to plunge into the icy waters of the frigid Bidassoa River and wade across to Spain. When I'm stuck in a long line, I remember how the people in Europe had to cope with the rationing that went on for years. And when I'm bored because I've nothing to do, I imagine what it was like for the airmen who had to sit tight, sometimes for weeks in small rooms, while waiting for the underground to evacuate them. Like it or not, from now on whenever I can't sleep because my pillow is too hard, I'm going to think of the narrow wooden planks where the prisoners slept three to a bed.

I'm sure telling our children's children that women in Ravensbrück had nothing to eat but stale bread and thin soup isn't going to make them eat their vegetables, but I know that when I'm hungry because it's two hours past meal time, my mind will harken back to those who struggled to survive in concentration camps for years with little food and days with none at all.

The fact is I've been forever affected by reading and writing about the hardships the women and men in occupied countries went through. But I'll be forever grateful that I got the chance to tell their story.

ACKNOWLEDGEMENTS

First and foremost I'd like to thank my wife, not only for being my first reader, but for being my best friend and my biggest supporter. Writing can be a very frustrating business and her encouragement keeps me going during those difficult times when the story seems like it just isn't coming together.

There is so much more to publishing a novel than learning to craft a story. I'd like to thank all of my family members who jump in and provide assistance whenever it's needed, especially with the internet which to me is a maze of frustrating twists and turns.

Writing a novel is a long process with no guarantee of success. Sometimes you want to just stick your manuscript in a drawer and go do something easier. To my friends in my local historical societies, I thank you for all of your kind words about the column pieces I write for the local newspaper. Your encouragement picks me up and gets me through those times when I begin to doubt myself and my abilities.

I'd like to thank my friends in the Historical Novel Society, Historical Writers of America and New Jersey Authors Network for all the support and help they provide. I'd also like to thank my friends in the Facebook groups: Historical Fiction Book Lovers, and Beta Readers, for all their tips, insight and reviews, especially Mike Harding and David Refeh for their assistance.

Writing a story with so many characters and events was challenging beyond anything I had written before. I'm so grateful to my line editor, Christina Frey, for understanding the difficulties and helping me make sure my story was told in the strongest way possible. She's simply the best. I would also like to thank Caitlin O'Brien not only for being so thorough and helpful, but for being delightful to work with.

The world war in Europe ended more than 75 years ago, but it is through organizations like Comète Kinship that the spirit of the participants is kept alive. I would especially like to thank Brigitte d'Oultremont and Geoff Cooper for clearing up some questions I had while writing this book.

Made in the USA
Middletown, DE
06 September 2022